Rites
&
Wrongs

by

Sandra Levi

Published by

MELROSE BOOKS

An Imprint of Melrose Press Limited
St Thomas Place, Ely
Cambridgeshire
CB7 4GG, UK
www.melrosebooks.com

FIRST EDITION

Cover designed by Sean Gladwell

ISBN 978 1 906050 47 4

Printed and bound in Great Britain by
William Clowes Ltd, Beccles, Suffolk

For my family, especially Brian.

This is a work of fiction. Names, characters, places and incidents are the product of the author's imagination, and are used fictitiously. Any resemblance to persons living or dead is entirely coincidental.

WE COME INTO THIS WORLD HEAD FIRST
AND GO OUT FEET FIRST;
IN BETWEEN IT IS ALL A MATTER OF BALANCE.

Paul Boese.

CHAPTER 1

1948

The rabbi drove carefully that day. He didn't always when his family was in the car, but on this occasion he didn't want to shake up the pregnant girl in the passenger seat any more than was necessary. He glanced across at her and noticed that she was peeping at him from the corner of her eye. He pulled himself up to his full height and thought, she must be scared stiff.

'Everything all right?'

'Smashing.'

Wilfred Steinberg was a handsome man. A woman in his congregation once told him that he looked like a younger version of Douglas Fairbanks Junior, and that had pleased him enormously. Without thinking, he took one hand off the wheel of the Humber and meticulously stroked his black moustache firmly into place. Then he turned off the main road in the direction of Broom Lane.

The two of them looked an incongruous pair as the car drove into Hanover Gardens. He, dressed in his working attire of pinstriped trousers and black jacket, with his Homburg hat tilted at the merest hint of an angle. And seventeen year old Peggy Purnell from Liverpool, wearing a borrowed tweed coat to hide the bulge resting on her lap underneath the thick, scratchy cloth.

'This is it.'

He pulled up outside number seven, then got out of the car and went to open the passenger door for her. She eased herself out, feeling acutely uncomfortable. Nobody had ever extended such a courtesy to her before, and in her confusion, she knocked her head against the door being held open. Her frizzy brown hair, which had been tucked neatly inside a knitted beret, now looked as if it was all going to tumble out. She took a quick look about her at the other houses in the road.

'Is everyone round here Jewish?'

Wilfred went to open the car boot, and took out her small, cardboard suitcase.

'More or less.'

'I've never met Jews before.' She pulled her coat tighter to her body.

'Don't worry, we haven't got horns.'

He indicated that she should follow him up the crazy-paved path towards the front door. A few straggly rose bushes lined the pathway, obvious to any observer that this was not a lovingly tended garden. Wilfred took out his key and opened the front door.

'We're here!' he shouted.

Frances appeared in the kitchen doorway, carrying a dark haired baby on her hip. She looked startled, as if she'd been caught in the glare of headlights, and blinked repeatedly. Nervous though she was, the newcomer noticed that Frances Steinberg's dark eyes were deeply lined, her pale face looked weary, but it was obvious that she had once been a pretty woman.

'Hello,' she said, extending her spare hand. Peggy shook it weakly then smiled at the baby. 'This is Jake, our youngest.' The girl took hold of his little hand, and his fingers curled around hers.

'Why don't I show Peggy to her room?'

'I'll do that,' Frances said firmly, then thrust the baby into her husband's arms. 'Did you have a long journey?' she asked disinterestedly as Peggy followed her towards the staircase.

'Yes, I …'

'She's here, she's here!'

Peggy looked up to see seven-year-old Michael charging down the stairs. Deborah, his younger sister and the more timid of the two, preferred to stay at the top, inspecting the newcomer.

'Children, this is Peggy,' Wilfred shouted up, 'she's come to help your mother. Why don't you show Peggy to her room, then mum and I can have a chat?'

2

*

Peggy climbed the stairs tentatively, carrying her suitcase. Michael was nudging her from behind, and with every step she took, he looked up cheekily towards his sister. When she drew level with Deborah, the little girl formally shook her hand then took it upon herself to escort her solemnly along the narrow corridor.

'This is your room, it's next to mine. Michael sleeps in that one with Jake, and Mummy and Daddy are in the big room over there.'

Peggy nodded and walked into the unfamiliar bedroom. It was a small room, containing a single bed with a faded satin eiderdown, a wardrobe and an old fashioned dressing table and chair.

'Do you like it?'

'It's very nice.'

She looked around and at that moment secretly wished she were back home in the even smaller room she'd shared with her sister, brother and a rabbit, on the Liverpool council estate she'd grown up in.

Michael watched from the doorway, scrutinising her every movement suspiciously. When she took off her coat, he stared at her swollen stomach for a long time. Turning her back on him self-consciously, she put her suitcase on the bed and opened it. First she took out a small crucifix that had been lying on top of her clothes, and put it down gently on the dressing table. The boy seemed fascinated by it, and his eyes kept straying from the crucifix to the mezuzah on the door lintel, then back again to the cross. Deborah hung her head shyly as Peggy then took out a tiny blue bottle from the suitcase and placed it next to the crucifix.

'What's that?'

'Evening in Paris.'

The little girl picked up the small bottle very carefully and sniffed it. It smelled of heady tuberoses, and she placed it reverently back down.

'When I'm grown up, I'd like a bottle like that.' Peggy smiled, then took a hairbrush and comb out of the suitcase. 'Can I arrange them nicely for you?' Deborah asked.

'But don't touch that thing,' Michael warned, striding into the room and pointing at the crucifix.

3

'Why not?'

'Just … because, that's all.'

Deborah and Peggy seemed nonplussed, but he fixed his gaze steadily on Peggy's stomach, and stared until she was beginning to feel really uncomfortable under his scrutiny.

'You talk differently to us,' he said, then turned sharply from the bedroom and made his way downstairs.

*

That first evening, the whole family sat together at the kitchen table. Frances had made meatballs and mashed potatoes. While the family ate enthusiastically, Peggy picked at her food, moving it from side to side on her plate. Frances looked across anxiously at the barely touched food.

'Don't you like it?'

Peggy blushed a deep crimson.

'I've never eaten Jewish before.'

'It's only meatballs.' Michael smirked, and his father shot him a warning look.

'But it's the first time I've ever 'ad anyone's balls.' Now she looked to be on the verge of tears.

'Just eat the potatoes then,' Deborah said helpfully, 'Michael will eat the rest.'

Later that night, when the rest of the family was asleep, Michael crept into his sister's bedroom and padded silently across the floor to her bed. She was sleeping soundly, but he lifted the covers and snuggled in beside her. When she realised her bed had been invaded, she hit out at him irritably, but he caught her small arms, and held them down by her sides.

'I don't like her, she's fat like mum was before Jake came.'

'Who cares? Leave me alone.'

'I'm going to tell on her.'

'What for?' Deborah was more alert now because this was getting interesting.

'That cross, it's a sign of the devil and she shouldn't have it in our house.'

'Are you going to tell Daddy?'

4

'I'll burn it first.'

The following morning, when Frances came into the bedroom to wake her daughter, she found both children asleep next to each other. She screeched to her husband, who was getting ready in the bathroom. He had just finished shaving, and was splashing Old Spice liberally over his cheeks, wincing as the cologne hit the newly shaved skin.

'Wilfred, he's done it again! You're going to have to speak to him, it's not natural.'

*

Peggy's tasks were detailed on a long list that Frances had stuck on the back of the pantry door. Although it was now used as a pantry, the tiny room had originally been constructed as a homemade air raid shelter. It was so cold inside that throughout the year Frances could make cream cheese out of curds, and hang them in a muslin bag to drip into a bowl. She also pickled her own cucumbers there, which were stacked in muslin covered jars on the shelves, and sometimes she even made chutney. Frances was an excellent cook on the days when she was feeling well.

On that first morning, and still wearing her dressing gown, Frances stood over Peggy while she went down the list of chores.

'First thing in the morning, you have to prepare breakfast for the family, and if I'm not good, you have to get Jake out of his cot, change his nappy, then give him his bottle.' She declined to mention that this would happen quite a lot, because she regularly felt unwell.

'The children can get themselves ready, but then you have to dress Jake and prepare him for his morning nap in the pram.' After that, Frances said, Peggy had to walk him in his pram with the children to school, before returning home to complete the housework. 'And if we need any groceries, you can buy them as soon as you've seen the children safely inside school.'

Both children went to the Cheetham Hill Methodist School, which was odd considering they were Jewish. But neither Wilfred, Frances nor any of the other local Jewish parents who sent their children there, found it strange at all because it was one of the best schools in the area. Eventually it was forced to impose a Jewish quota, otherwise the Jewish children would have overrun the place completely.

'And when you get home, there's the cleaning, washing and ironing to do.' By the middle of the afternoon, Peggy had to collect the children from school again, then it was home for tea and, for her, more washing up.

When Deborah reached the age of six, her parents decided that both children were old enough to walk the two-mile journey to school and back on their own.

'Tonight we'll be eating in the dining room, which is where we normally eat,' Frances continued. 'You'll help me serve, then you can take your meal in the kitchen.' After supper Peggy was expected to help bathe the children, then return to the kitchen to finish the washing up.

During this time, more often than not, Frances lay down in the lounge with her feet propped up on a stool. Within the family it was generally understood that she had an illness, but that illness was never given a name. On one occasion Deborah decided it was time she knew the nature of the illness, so she asked her aunt Ruby, Frances's sister.

'What exactly is wrong with my Mummy?' Her aunt stared at her, open mouthed, horrified that the child had dared stray into grown up territory.

'Women's troubles,' she answered finally, then busied herself with some pressing chore. 'Nothing for you to worry about.' Her tone of voice left the little girl in no doubt that she wasn't to ask any more awkward questions on the subject.

At the end of her first working day in the house, Peggy fell onto her bed in complete exhaustion. It was eight thirty in the evening, and when she awoke the next morning, she realised to her horror that she was still dressed in the previous day's clothing. Her bedside light was still on, and she hadn't moved from the original position where she had first lain down on the bed.

*

Two months after her arrival at the Steinbergs', Peggy was trying her best to get the elder two children ready for school, and as usual Michael was doing his level best to frustrate her efforts. Wilfred had already left home for work and Frances was still asleep, but Peggy was feeling out of sorts that day and she shouted at Michael.

'Hurry up or you'll be late.'

'I don't want to go to school today.'

He had just taken a look out of his bedroom window and couldn't even see the houses on the opposite side of the street. A thick fog was swirling, a commonplace sight in the days before the Clean Air Acts.

'It's a real pea souper out there, I think we'd better stay at home.'

'You've got to go, your ma says so.'

'Then why doesn't she take us?'

'Because she's not feeling well.'

Deborah shuffled downstairs disconsolately, and started putting on her coat and scarf.

'She never feels well,' she muttered, then looked up and saw the trace of a sympathetic nod on the maid's face.

'Be that as it may, you're both going.'

'What about Jake?'

'He's better off here, the fog's no good for a little 'un's chest.'

Then, muffled up against the damp with their scarves over their mouths, and woolly hats pulled down over their ears, the three of them left the safety of the house. Deborah held tightly to Peggy's hand, but walking along beside her, she sensed Peggy wince in pain several times.

Suddenly, out of the mist, Michael spotted a horse-drawn cart coming down the road in the opposite direction. It was followed by an old woman dressed in layers of shabby rags, which had once been a coat. She dragged her legs behind the cart, carrying a bucket and shovel, and Michael jumped up and down excitedly.

'Look, it's Mabel Manure!' He pulled an ugly face, jeering at her. 'Here comes Mabel, here comes Mabel Manure!' Peggy stared at him in astonishment.

'Is that her real name?'

'It's what we call her,' he explained, 'cos she collects horse poo for the gardens, *and* she smells as well,' he added cryptically, looking straight at Peggy.

Her eyes opened wide, her nostrils flared, and it looked as if she was about to hit him hard. He steeled himself, already preparing his defence for when his father questioned him about his rudeness, but instead of touching him as he expected, she doubled over and clutched her stomach. Her face went deathly pale, and although it was cold, beads of perspiration gathered on her forehead.

'Come on, you'll be late,' she managed to gasp.

That afternoon, after school was over, Wilfred was waiting for them at the school gates. This was quite unexpected, and his children were so pleased, they completely forgot to ask where Peggy was. On the journey home, he went by a sweet shop and bought them a bag of mixed sweets, which he shared out. Michael ate his at once, but Deborah stuffed hers into her pockets. She'd already decided to share them with her best friend Barbara, the daughter of the Orthodox rabbi who lived in the street. Barbara wasn't allowed to eat sweets unless they were strictly kosher, and Deborah was shrewdly preparing to use her supply of goodies to trade favours with her friend.

The fog had now lifted, and a weak sun shone on the cobbled streets of Salford. Walking home, the three of them passed people on the streets whom Wilfred recognised, and each time he doffed his hat to whomever he greeted.

'Mrs Abelson, how are you?'

'Thank God, I'm well rabbi, it's kind of you to ask.'

'Don't mention it, my dear.' He doffed his Homburg again, and they continued on their way.

Deborah snuggled into her father's side. She always felt protected when he was nearby. Unlike Michael, who skipped along independently, she walked close enough to smell his distinctive aroma of cigarette smoke mixed with the Old Spice he always wore. To her, in those days, that was one of the headiest scents in the world.

When they arrived home, Frances was preparing supper with Jake propped up in his highchair, watching. On this occasion, she had once again laid out the plates in the kitchen, so the three of them sat down at the table and waited. Nobody asked or offered any explanation as to why Peggy wasn't there. Her presence was taken for granted and equally so her absence.

That night Frances served succulent veal chops with fried onions, mashed potatoes and cabbage. In spite of her infirmities, Frances was never slow to harangue the elderly German butcher, Mister Halberstam, when her meat order wasn't up to her exacting standards. She always insisted on buying the best she could afford, and her cooking did justice to the ingredients.

But when she put Wilfred's plate down in front of him, her husband stared at the meat suspiciously, then sniffed it like a wild boar looking for truffles. His family watched as his eyebrows knitted darkly, and a distinct chill had entered the room.

'Is there garlic in this?' Michael and Deborah looked across at their father anxiously. 'You know I can't stand it.'

'Funny,' Frances answered witheringly, 'you always manage to eat it at Evelyn Fraser's house.'

'She doesn't cook with it.'

Frances raised her eyebrows, and gave her children a conspiratorial look. Deborah hated it when her mother did that. It was as if she wanted her children to be on her side, with her husband frozen out as the opposition.

'It's very nice, mum.' Michael glared at his father, but Frances had already busied herself with Jake's bottle, and nodded by way of thanks. When she raised her eyebrows again, Wilfred pretended not to notice. He realised he was beaten and was anxious to change the subject.

'I'll be driving you two to school tomorrow,' he said.

'Why can't Peggy take us?'

'She's not here,' Frances snapped, as if the maid's absence had been done deliberately to frustrate her. 'She'll be back soon.'

That was the only explanation for Peggy's confinement that the children ever got, and just to make sure this train of conversation was not followed up, Wilfred then pulled out the evening paper and spread it on the table beside his plate. Michael and Deborah watched him eating only the potatoes and cabbage, and both of them raised their eyebrows in unison. In the Steinberg family, all its members were expert at eyebrow raising.

*

At that precise moment of eyebrow aerobics, Peggy was screaming loud enough to wake the devil, or so the midwife stated. The maid was lying on a sweat-stained bed with her legs akimbo, in the green-painted delivery room of a Catholic nursing home for unmarried mothers. Meanwhile, another nun with her sleeves rolled up, stood ready to catch the new baby when it made its appearance. She whispered words of encouragement, and begged Peggy not to shout so loud.

'You're not the first woman to give birth, you know,' the midwife admonished, but Peggy felt as if her insides were being ripped out of her body, and she let out another howl.

'How would you know?' she screamed. 'It bloody well hurts!' The nun winced.

'And mind your language too,' the midwife added. The nun who was stationed at the foot of the bed urged her to push harder.

'I'm pushing as hard as I bloody can.'

'That's it,' the midwife announced triumphantly, 'I can see the head.'

Peggy thought that her body was being torn down the middle into two halves. She tossed crazily from side to side in the room that resembled a prison cell. And just when she thought she could bear it no longer, there was a squelching sound and she felt something force itself out painfully from between her thighs.

'It's like shitting a ruddy football.'

Both women looked very cross, but encouraged her to give another final push. Then she felt the body wriggling out in an excruciatingly painful movement, and her head fell back against the damp pillows. She was exhausted.

'It's a boy.'

The midwife held the wrinkled child aloft, while Peggy stared at her son.

'Give me a minute to cut the cord, then you can have a proper look at him.' But the nun wagged her finger at the midwife, who muttered, 'Sorry, I forgot.' Then she put clamps on the umbilical cord and snipped it quickly, but Peggy no longer cared what they did to her.

Shortly after, the midwife handed the baby to the nun, who wrapped it in a green sheet and hurried out of the room. Then she turned to Peggy with a trace of sympathy on her face.

'Now my dear, one final push for the afterbirth, and you can have a well earned rest.'

'Is she bringing him back?'

'Best not, eh?'

*

Peggy stayed in the home for a week. Every night she found herself weeping and tried to stifle the noisy sobs into her pillow, while around her other mothers nursed their babies. As soon as her son had been taken from her, the nuns had forbidden her to look for him. They insisted it was for her own good, and she was too intimidated by them to try to argue.

Most of the other women there had regular visitors – mothers, siblings, even boyfriends. But Peggy had no one to relieve the boredom or cheer her up. Her own mother had virtually disowned her and thrown her out of the house when she became pregnant.

'Oh the shame you've brought on us!' she'd wailed. 'And what sort of an example is that to set for your brother and sister?'

Her mother had taken herself to confession, and the parish priest had assured her that her daughter's fall from grace was not her fault, and that she'd done all she could to bring up her children respectably.

'The problem belongs with your wayward daughter,' he insisted, 'but just to be on the safe side, say three Hail Mary's and an Our Father, and get that girl of yours to come in and see me.'

'And don't you go thinking you can come back to my house until you've got rid of it,' her mother insisted. 'Father Docherty says he'll give you all the help you need.'

Afterwards, the priest took it upon himself to find employment for Peggy. He decided that it had to be far enough away from his parish to avoid further embarrassment, so consulted his bishop for advice.

'In my opinion she'd be better off working for a non-Catholic family, maybe a Jewish one?' the senior cleric suggested. 'Nobody will know her amongst their lot. I'll have a word with an acquaintance of mine, a young rabbi in Manchester. He does a lot of good ecumenical work, and I'll ask him if he knows any of his brethren needing domestic help.'

Every night in the nursing home, whenever Peggy went into the bathroom, she could see the damp patches on the front of her night dress where the milk had seeped through. Her nipples ached and felt like hot boils crying out to be lanced. While cleaning her teeth at one of the sinks, her tears of pain and anguish fell onto the chipped enamel basin.

'Don't worry, the milk will soon stop when there's no takers,' another girl assured her.

This piece of well-intentioned advice only added to Peggy's overall distress, and she begged the nuns,

'Please, can I see my baby, just the once?'

'We don't think so,' they replied. 'Besides, his new parents will be coming soon to collect him.'

Shortly after she'd given birth, the nuns told her that she'd been assigned a moral welfare worker. Peggy had no idea what to expect, but when a powerfully built woman, with wiry grey hair and wearing a severe tweed suit, walked purposefully towards her bed, she feared the worst. The woman introduced herself curtly as Miss Stebbings, and didn't even bother asking Peggy her name.

'To my mind,' she explained in a dry, matter of fact tone, 'as you've agreed to give the baby up for adoption, you no longer have any legal rights to him, and we have to do whatever is in the best interests of the child.' Then she added brusquely, 'And as you have no obvious means of supporting that child, I believe you've made the best decision. No snivelling.' The social worker wrinkled her nose in distaste. 'Put this experience behind you, and my advice, for what it's worth, is keep away from men, they're nothing but trouble.

*

Deborah missed Peggy while she was away. Before she'd left, the two of them had become good friends. Peggy was always kind and attentive towards her – behaviour that was quite different to what the child experienced from her own mother.

Frances had always been careless with her daughter, and bath times were a particular source of anguish. Her mother would drag a flannel steeped in hot water across her child's back.

'Ouch, that hurts!'

'Don't be such a fuss pot.'

Frances never bothered testing the water before plunging her child in, and even at such a tender age, Deborah thought it a miracle that her mother hadn't boiled her alive. But when Peggy took over the task, her movements were caressing and gentle, and she always put her elbow into the bath water first. Afterwards she would brush Deborah's long hair carefully, paying special attention to any knots. Frances's method was to pull the brush roughly through her locks, and when she came to any knots she'd battle her way through them until the child's eyes watered.

'Sometimes,' Deborah confided to Peggy, ' I don't think my Mummy really likes me.'

'Of course she does, love,' Peggy replied unconvincingly.

But the one member of the family who wasn't too keen on Deborah's burgeoning friendship with the maid, was Michael. He was having a hard time adjusting to Peggy so soon after having accepted the presence of a new baby in the house.

'Why d'you spend so much time in her room?' he demanded of his sister.

'Because we talk about things, and laugh.'

'You used to talk to me, and we laughed as well.'

'She lets me try on her clothes.'

'OK then, you can try on mine if you want.'

'Don't be silly. And she lets me play with her make up.'

'I'll give you first go with my cricket bat.'

'And she promised I could have her perfume bottle when she's finished with it.' Then she saw the downcast expression that had crept over her brother's face. 'Oh all right, I'll play with you.'

Wilfred, a very tactile man, was the complete opposite of his wife, which made life pleasanter for his little daughter. Frances chose to overlook this aspect of her husband's personality, so Deborah was the one who got to sit on his knee in the evenings, and was amply rewarded with cuddles. Michael had to wait his turn and try to grab his father's attention whenever he could.

'It's so sissy the way he strokes you,' he'd scoff behind his father's back, but secretly he craved the attention every bit as much as his sister did.

In spite of the petting, Wilfred always managed to avoid real conversation with any of his children. At home he would invariably be working on the text of a new sermon, or buried in a newspaper or book, and his automatic 'ums' and 'ahs' in reply to their questions, convinced them that he wasn't actually listening to what they had to say.

However, neither child felt free to go to their mother with their problems. She remained closeted in her own world, and they instinctively knew not to make demands on her. As a result, most feelings and emotions at number seven Hanover Gardens were kept tightly locked in private compartments, and each individual owner was careful never to lose the key to their own compartment.

*

One day, after Deborah heard a knock on the front door, she went to open it. Peggy was standing there with her small suitcase. She looked thinner and more forlorn than the last time she'd seen her, but the child felt a huge surge of joy to see her again.

'Peggy's back, Peggy's back!' she shouted hysterically to no-one in particular. Michael came bounding down the stairs when he heard the noise.

'Old smelly's back,' he joined in cheerfully, but neither child noticed Frances in her dressing gown, supporting herself against the banister rail.

'What did you say? Apologise immediately.'

'He didn't mean anything,' Deborah tried to intercede on his behalf, and when that didn't alter the look on her mother's face, she took hold of Peggy's hand and dragged her into the hallway. Frances came down the stairs, glaring stonily at her son.

'Just you wait till I tell your father when he comes home.'

Michael turned to Peggy with a resentful look on his face.

'Sorry.'

Peggy gave him a weak smile in response, but he didn't linger long enough to see it. He ran back upstairs, and Deborah followed him to make sure he was all right.

When she opened his bedroom door, she couldn't see him, so got down on her hands and knees and looked under the bed, which was his usual hiding place. His shoes were sticking out, so she decided to join him in there. She could feel the heat coming off his body.

'I'll get her.'

'But it wasn't her fault.'

'She came back, of course it was.'

'So what are you going to do?'

'I'll teach her a lesson, just you wait and see.'

In spite of his sister continually pestering him, he refused to say how he intended to punish Peggy, and by the time the maid had settled back into the routine of the family, Deborah took it for granted that her brother had forgotten all about his ill feelings towards her.

*

Peggy had changed. She wasn't the same cheerful person after she returned, and Deborah could have sworn she often saw traces of tears in Peggy's eyes. But whenever the child asked her why she looked sad, Peggy invariably gave the same evasive answer.

'You're too young to understand.'

Eventually this started to annoy the child, and she began to have more sympathy with her brother. Added to which, Peggy didn't welcome her into her room as often these days, and it was obvious that baby Jake had definitely taken over as the main object of Peggy's affections. She cooed and fussed over him as if he were her own child. Because Deborah couldn't understand the change in her, she gradually returned to spending most of her free time with her elder brother.

One spring bank holiday after a long and dreary winter, Frances asked Peggy to hang out the washing in the back garden. Normally their damp clothes were hung on a pulley which was suspended from the larder ceiling, and could be raised and lowered by pulling on its thick ropes. However, on that day, although there had been intermittent rain showers, the sun was now shining brightly and there was a light breeze, ideal weather for drying clothes.

Deborah was playing with her favourite doll when Michael beckoned her furtively into his room. He had his fingers over his lips in a warning gesture so as not give the game away. Frances was taking an afternoon nap in her own room, and the two of them tip-toed into his bedroom, which had a fine view over the back garden.

'OK, I'm ready.'

'What for?'

'To teach her a lesson.'

'You're always saying things like that, I bet you're not going to do anything.'

'You just watch me.'

With that he clambered over his bed then hoisted himself onto the windowsill. Once he had positioned himself squarely in the open window frame, Deborah's hands flew to her mouth in horror.

'No Michael, don't jump!' she screamed.

But before she could do anything to stop him, he opened the fly buttons of his trousers, and took his penis out. Edging even closer to the sill, he carefully pointed his little member out of the window, and released a full arc of urine which streamed into the garden, landing on top of Peggy's unsuspecting head. She had been so engrossed in pinning the damp clothes onto the line, that she barely had time to move out of the way, and looked up to see if it was raining again.

'Crikey, I think she saw me.'

Deborah's immature heart was thundering in her chest, and she knew for certain that all hell would shortly break loose. By the time Michael had got down from the windowsill and finished doing up his trousers, both children could hear their father's footsteps pounding up the stairs. Deborah started whimpering.

'Don't know why you're crying, it'll be me who gets it.'

Then the bedroom door flew open, and Wilfred made a grab for him. He was holding a large clothes brush in his hand, and his face was mottled with rage. Before he opened his mouth, his daughter started howling in terror.

'Bend over.'

Michael stood his ground, so Wilfred grabbed him by the scruff of his neck, then forced him down over his knee. Deborah was wailing like a banshee, but Wilfred didn't even look at her. He had pulled Michael's trousers and underpants down to his ankles, and aimed several painful whacks at his naked bottom. His son bit on his lip to try to stop himself from crying.

'My children, of all people,' he panted, 'should know how to behave themselves.'

When it was over, Michael lay in a crumpled heap on the floor. Wilfred stood up; he was still shaking, and looked as hurt as Michael.

'And next time, you'll get it as well,' he snarled at Deborah, then walked slowly out of the bedroom. When the door had slammed behind him, she bent down to comfort her brother, but he pushed her aside.

'Go away,' he cried, sobbing into the carpet.

*

Not long after this incident, Frances was admitted to the Jewish hospital for tests, and in her naivety, her daughter thought they were probably the same as the tests she did at school, such as spelling, arithmetic and dictation.

'I'm not going to ask her how she got on,' she confided to Peggy, 'just in case she didn't do well.'

Nobody in the family ever thought to explain the real nature of the tests to the children, so whenever Deborah's friends asked why her mother wasn't at home, she would usually reply:

'Because she's studying.'

In Frances's absence, Peggy was becoming more involved in the day to day running of the house, and whenever she took Jake out in his pram, he always returned with something new. Sometimes it was a teddy bear, or a bobble hat with matching mittens. If his brother and sister remarked on these gifts, she would insist that his old ones had worn out, so she had to buy him new ones.

'Besides, those others didn't even suit him.'

When Frances eventually returned home, she too noticed the changes to her youngest son and enquired as to the whereabouts of Jake's old things. Peggy always pretended she had no idea what Frances was referring to.

'I'm not happy about it, I'm sure she spends all her wages on Jake,' Frances confided to Wilfred when they were alone.

'You can't penalise her just because she loves the child.'

'Just so long as she doesn't forget whose baby it is.'

*

Wilfred was one of the luminaries of the progressive movement of Anglo Jewry, and as such was at the epicentre of that world. Because of this, he confidently expected his family to enjoy his achievements and bask in his illustrious shadow.

Their lives revolved around his job, and as a result the Steinbergs were one of the most visible families in the town. Wilfred was therefore determined that his family members should reflect his considerable achievements. He was a hard taskmaster, but they understood the rules.

'You can't come to synagogue wearing those dirty gloves.'

His eagle eyes had spotted that his daughter's white cotton gloves were filthy because she'd been trailing them across privet hedges on the first part of their journey to the synagogue.

'Go home and make sure Peggy washes them. Your nose is running, haven't you got a hankie?' he barked at Michael, who'd been sniffing for most of the journey. When the boy did his final *coup de grâce* of wiping the offending nose across the sleeve of his best jacket, his father lost his patience altogether.

'Back home immediately till you learn some manners.'

For Michael that was no punishment because he knew that now he had the next few hours free to kick his football against the garden wall without fear of interruption, unless Frances was at home. Even Peggy soon picked up the Sabbath rules and mores of the household.

'Brush your teeth properly!' she'd shout. 'It's Shabbat.' She'd learnt the correct terminology, but it sounded strange with her strong Liverpudlian accent.

When Wilfred began his Saturday morning journey to the synagogue, he was the picture of elegance. There was not a stray piece of lint or fluff to be found on his clothing, because he had brushed everything thoroughly the night before. His Homburg was matt, and there were never any grease marks on either the inside or outside of it. His hair was neatly trimmed, and there was never even the merest hint of dandruff on his black jacket collar.

He'd been going to the same barber for several years. Gino, the Italian, also trimmed his moustache and kept him up to date with the town's gossip. Wilfred's fingernails had been buffed by the same manicurist in Kendal Milnes, the finest department store in town that he'd also been going to for years.

'I don't know where he gets the money from, I wear the same coat for years, and he can afford to take himself off to Kendal's every week.'

Frances complained about her husband's spending so often that Deborah often lay awake at night worrying about the state of her parents' finances. But all this fastidiousness on Wilfred's part, built up the image that he wanted to project of a modern, progressive rabbi.

In spite of wanting to look his best at all times, Wilfred had a genuine love for the members of his congregation, and a deep commitment to serving them. People regularly remarked to his children about their father's charisma, but as neither of the elder two knew what the word meant, they just nodded in acknowledgement.

'Must be something to do with Christmas,' Michael decided eventually.

Every Sabbath afternoon, after the family had finished lunch, Wilfred went to Strangeways prison to visit the Jewish prisoners who were serving sentences there. It didn't matter what the weather was like, be it blizzards, rain or brilliant sunshine, he left the house at three o'clock in the afternoon, and didn't return until the early evening. However, these pastoral visits were a real thorn in Frances's side.

'There can't be that many Jewish prisoners in there, but he always manages to come home after it's too late to do anything else,' was one of her frequent moans, or: 'If only he thought as much about his family as he does about those *ganovim*[1], we'd all be better off,' was another.

What she failed to notice at the time, but was to find out within a couple of years, was that after her husband finished his prison visiting at about five, he invariably went out for afternoon tea. But it was always to the home of his favourite at the time, the doe-eyed Mrs Evelyn Fraser.

On days when he wasn't ministering to the criminal fraternity, he made it his business to visit any of his congregants who were sick.

---

[1]*wrongdoers*

Indeed, at the festival of Passover he insisted his family join him in the Jewish hospital, where he always conducted a traditional 'Seder' for the patients.

Doctors, nurses and patients would sit together at a long table and Wilfred always gave them an evening to remember. Some of the patients were in wheelchairs, several with drips and plastic bags attached to them. Those who were too ill to sit on chairs had their beds wheeled into the room, which at other times served as the hospital's main waiting area.

There was a distinct aura of decay lingering over many of the patients, added to which there was the ever-present smell from the hospital corridors, a mixture of disinfectant and stale cabbage. It made Deborah want to gag every time she was taken there, and she would have used any excuse she could conjure up if she thought she could have avoided going. It was the one night of the year that the child dreaded the most.

Sick and elderly patients always tried to pet her or stroke her long hair. Invariably they wanted to hold her little hands inside their own wasted, gnarled hands. If she tried to edge away from them, a well-meaning nurse would push her even closer, as if her childish presence could speed their recovery. She felt trapped with their sour breath on her face, but Wilfred insisted they were doing a *mitzvah* or good deed by being there. On these evenings Deborah wanted nothing more than to run from the hospital to the safety of her own home, and Peggy's welcoming smile.

CHAPTER 2

Both Frances and her husband hailed from large and generally dysfunctional families. The children's maternal grandmother was a formidable woman, whom they called Booba. During her childbearing years the woman had given birth to five living children and several more dead ones.

Frances was the eldest of the girls, then came a brother Itzhak, who called himself Issy. The next to be born was Ruby, who was given the name Rochele, and Booba's youngest daughter Edie was named Esther. Her other son was Henry, whom she had named Hanoch, and evidently, none of her children appreciated their given names.

Frances had actually been named Frumeleh, and as none of her siblings had ever come across another poor soul saddled with that unfortunate name, they were quite pleased with the new name she gave herself on the day she started school.

It was a well-publicised family myth that Booba owned a doll factory, at least that's what Deborah told her friends at school. In reality, the factory consisted of two rooms in Willesden High Road in North London, where boxes of identical pottery dolls were stacked from floor to ceiling. In the front room, two women, a Jamaican and an Irish machinist, sewed the same style of dolls' dresses in several gaudy colours of satin. The colours and styles only changed if Booba bought a job lot of fabric that was going cheap.

Booba's real name was Hannah Katz, and she lived alone, having thrown out her husband, Peretz Katz, when she realised he couldn't make enough of a living to keep her and her children.

She herself was a formidable businesswoman, who sat in the back room of the so-called factory at a desk she shared with her son Itzhak, while she negotiated sales of her dolls to department stores. Itzhak spent most of his working life on the road, but when he was delivering to stores in Manchester, he always stayed overnight with his sister Frances.

Booba worked until her mid nineties. She traded ferociously with hapless buyers in her own bastardised mixture of Yiddish and English, a dialect she perfected to the degree that even the seamstresses in the next room spoke in the same jargon.

'And next time I vant you bring mit you fur mihr an order for finnef und tswantzig tousand fund!' she would shout down the phone. Roughly translated that meant, next time I want an order to the value of twenty five thousand pounds. If a deal was not going the way she wanted, she wasn't averse to using none-too subtle blackmail. She would grab her left breast, and wail as if in pain, 'Mine hertz, mine hertz,' to indicate she might be having a heart attack. She used that trick virtually till the day she died, not from a heart attack but from choking on a lump of fried liver.

She and Peretz had come to Britain as refugees from Poland. Her husband, whom the grandchildren called 'Zaida', was a scholarly man, who spent most of his day studying and praying. When his wife told him to leave their home, Frances and her sister Ruby hated their mother from that day onwards.

Hannah Katz had very definite ideas as to what she expected from her daughters.

'But I want to go to college and make something of myself.' Ruby wailed, trying to persuade her mother to reconsider the future she had already mapped out for her.

'Better you should do something to help me mit mein dolls.'

'I hate your dolls, I can't even set foot in my bedroom because it's stuffed full of them.'

'Mein dolls is vot gives you food in your big *pisk*[2]!' her mother screamed back, and Ruby knew the argument was lost.

Her sister Frances hated their mother even more, for forcing her to keep house for the family while she was out working. But more than anything else, she hated her mother for pushing her into

[2] *mouth*

marrying Wilfred, even though she'd fallen crazily in love with him the first time they met.

The courtship of Frances Katz and Wilfred Steinberg had gone according to the customs of the time. Introductions were made through a third party, after rigorous checks had been completed on both sides. Wilfred's side wanted to know if there would be a financial gain for him out of the marriage, and his formidable future mother-in-law wanted assurances that any future son-in-law of hers would be a strict adherent to the faith.

To further help facilitate the union, she decided to stretch the truth, and told the middle man that Frances was only twenty years old when in fact she was twenty four. To further complicate matters, Wilfred's side claimed he was twenty-four years old when in fact he was only nineteen. However, the main reason Wilfred agreed to a marriage was that he too believed the myth of the doll factory.

He was the second youngest of four brothers and three sisters. His late father had been an impoverished cabinetmaker, and both his brothers had gone into the furniture business with varying degrees of success. Wilfred was close to his siblings, but particularly close to his youngest sister Gwen. She was pretty, with natural blonde hair, a smiling face and a sunny personality. It was to her that he always turned when he needed friendship and reassurance.

After Wilfred and Frances met for the first time, his eldest brother Ron asked him what he thought.

'She was OK, quite pretty in fact, but I'm not sure because she looked much older than her age.'

'*Schmok*[3], you're not sure! She's got *gelt*[4] and you haven't got a pot to piss in. Make yourself sure.'

Frances, on the other hand, was really excited after meeting Wilfred.

'So, *nu*[5]?' Ruby asked.

Frances blushed.

'He's not bad.'

'Just that, not bad?'

'No, he's gorgeous.'

The two girls danced round the room crazily. At last one of them had found an escape route from their mother, who at that moment

---

[3]*idiot* – [4]*money* – [5]*what gives*

was lurking unseen with her ear to the keyhole. Hannah too was feeling quite excited and relieved. She would finally be getting rid of one of them, the one she'd already began to think was destined to be left on the shelf. Now she could breathe easier and concentrate on her other two.

To make matters worse, nobody thought to mention to the Katz family that Wilfred was only a poverty-stricken student, who couldn't even afford to buy a new suit for the engagement party. And neither did anyone think to mention to his family that the doll business already supported two families, theirs and Itzhak's, and there was barely enough money from it for either of them.

*

The early years of Wilfred and Frances's marriage took place during the war, and had it not been for the surreptitious help that Peretz gave his daughter, the newlyweds would have struggled to survive financially. When their first child Michael was born nine months to the day after the wedding ceremony, Frances was thrilled to become a mother, but then the bombs started falling over the East End of London where they were living.

Wilfred was still studying at a rabbinical college, which his mother-in-law approved of, thinking that when he graduated he would take on a congregation nearby, and maybe help her out during the week with deliveries. Realising this, Wilfred accepted a job offered by a small, progressive community in Manchester, about as far away from his bossy mother-in-law as he could get.

'Mum, I've got some news.' Her daughter Frances telephoned her one-day. 'I'm expecting again.'

'Are you mad?' her mother screeched down the phone, so loudly that the two machinists in the next room tutted knowingly. 'What sort of a man would get his wife pregnant at a time like this?'

As a result, Wilfred could never get close to his mother-in-law, nor did Hannah Katz think much of her son-in-law either. She rarely visited them in Manchester because she feared Frances's new home wasn't kosher enough for her to eat in, and Wilfred's modern brand of Judaism was an anathema to her also.

On the evening that Frances went into labour for the second time, Wilfred was taking the Friday night service at his new synagogue. She knew she couldn't telephone him, so she called her sister Ruby instead.

'My waters have broken, I don't know what to do.' Ruby by now was newly married to Sam, a man who believed he was an expert on every situation known to man, so she consulted her husband.

'Sam says what water?'

'The baby's for God's sake.'

'Tell her to get to a hospital immediately!' Sam shouted out. 'They'll know what to do with her.'

'Did you hear that?' Ruby demanded. 'Just do as he says.'

Gathering herself together, Frances ran to her neighbour's house, and asked the woman if she would look after Michael till Wilfred got home. Then, realising that the only means of transport was the regular bus service, she grabbed her packed suitcase and stood in the local bus shelter waiting for the next bus. She felt terrified and alone, and when an air raid siren started with its shrill moan, she doubled up in pain.

'Are you all right?'

An elderly man prodded her arm. He was the only other person in the shelter, and although he was concerned about the deathly pale woman, who was trembling and holding herself around her middle, he also wanted to leave her and go to the nearest air raid shelter.

'I'll be okay.'

Just then the bus arrived, and he helped her aboard as quickly as he could, before hurrying off in the opposite direction towards the air raid shelter. When the all clear sounded, the man looked at the departing bus in the distance, and kicked himself.

After the service that evening, Wilfred left the synagogue and went home, by which time Frances was well into her labour.

'You just get yourself to the hospital, Rabbi, and I'll stay with the little 'un till you get back,' the neighbour offered.

Wilfred then rushed to the delivery suite of the local hospital, but baby Deborah had already been born. He picked up the small bundle that was his daughter and cradled her tenderly in his arms.

'Sorry I wasn't able to bring you in.'

'I should be used to that by now.'

'I'll get you some flowers tomorrow.'

'Don't bother. Look Wilfred, I'm tired. Put her back in the crib, I want to get some sleep.'

By the end of her second day in the maternity ward, Wilfred received a telephone call from the hospital matron.

'Rabbi, this is Matron Fisher speaking, I don't wish to alarm you, but your wife is acting very oddly.'

'In what way, Matron?'

'She refuses to feed her baby, and I do think you should have a word with her.'

'Refuses?'

'I've said to her, mother you must feed this child, but every time we put the baby on her breast, she keeps pushing the child away. I really need you to come in immediately and see what you can do. The poor little mite's hungry, and we don't want to start her on a bottle when her mother's got plenty of good milk.'

In those days, postnatal depression hadn't been given a name or even recognised as a serious problem. It was dismissed simple as baby blues, and the mother was expected to pull herself together and carry on as normal. But Frances was a complicated woman, full of contradictions, and at the time she just couldn't.

*

After the war ended, and just when she was beginning to enjoy life with her small family, Frances fell pregnant again for the third time. On this occasion she didn't even bother phoning her mother to give her the news, but sent her a short note instead. Wilfred was now earning a better salary, and they no longer had to rely on handouts from Peretz; although after paying all the bills, they had very little money left over.

This pregnancy had come as somewhat of a surprise, because since the birth of Deborah, marital relations with her husband were not high on Frances's list of priorities. So after a while, he had stopped bothering to ask her, until one evening when they had returned from a dinner party at the home of his special friend and her husband, Evelyn and Harry Fraser. Frances was getting ready for bed and about to take off her dress, when he came up behind her.

'You looked very pretty tonight. Here, let me help you.' He unzipped the dress and she flinched.

'How much have you had to drink?' He ignored the question then started to open her brassiere. 'Wilfred!' She struggled but he persisted.

'Very pretty.'

'I'm tired.'

'You're always tired.'

'Don't do that.'

'I'm your husband, damn it.'

He pushed her roughly onto the bed, and started pulling at her panties. She realised that struggling was futile because he was much stronger than she was, so she lay there as passively as she could until he had done what he wanted to do.

Afterwards, while he was lying panting on the bed, she disengaged herself from underneath him and went into the bathroom to wash herself down. But in her heart of heart she feared the worst – that he might have impregnated her again.

Jake was born nine months later, and Hannah Katz made a rare visit to Manchester to see her daughter and grandchildren. She only stayed long enough to take a quick look at the baby, then criticised her daughter about the state of the sheets on her bed.

'You call diss a sheet, more like a rag to me.'

'We can't afford new ones.'

'For diss your husband moved you to Manchester?'

Hannah did however make time to talk to Deborah, her favourite grandchild, and explained that she couldn't see the child as often as she wanted to.

'So because I don't see you so much, I'll send you mein dolls instead.'

'Oh, thank you, Booba.'

'But what about me?' Michael demanded.

'Boys don't haf dolls, vot are you, a sissy?'

He ran to his room, and wouldn't come out until his grandmother was in the taxi taking her to London Road Station to catch her train back.

'Now, I vill send you von for each festival,' she told Deborah before her departure, 'and you know, *kindele*[6], ve Jews haf plenty of festivals.'

*

'Can I hold your baby?'

'You'll dirty her.'

'I won't, promise, cross me heart and hope to die.'

Eileen Kelly made the sign of the cross over her chest, but Deborah was still reluctant to hand over her brand new doll, the one she'd taken to school that day. It had already attracted lavish attention from all the girls in her class. Like all its predecessors, it was made of porcelain china, and its blue eyes and spiky black eyelashes were wide open because they couldn't blink. Even her grandmother hadn't yet perfected the art of closing dolls' eyes.

Eileen, who was dressed in ragged clothing and wearing her elder brother's shabby boots, two sizes too large for her, was the classmate who lusted after Deborah's doll the most. She kept spitting on her grubby hands then trying to wipe them down her skirt in an effort to be worthy of it.

'She's so beautiful, what do you call her?'

'Rosemary. Tell you what, I'll let you hold her, but only as far as the school gates.'

'If you like, I could look after her for you,' Eileen said hopefully. 'I could be her nurse and do all the jobs for her.'

Deborah stopped in her tracks, giving the idea some thought.

'Maybe, I'll ask my Mummy if you can come for tea tomorrow, and we'll decide then.'

With that she took her precious bundle out of the girl's hands. Eileen gazed longingly at the doll until Deborah had skipped out of sight, but as soon as she got home, she forgot all about Eileen until the next day.

When Deborah and Eileen arrived at the back door of number seven Hanover Gardens the next day, Frances was busy pouring hot water from the kettle into a teapot. Michael was tucking into jam sandwiches, which had been laid out on plates, and Peggy was

---

[6]*child*

28

washing up at the sink. It was she who first spotted the two girls and gasped in horror.

Untroubled, Deborah blithely opened the back door while Eileen stood next to her, lovingly holding Rosemary. She was wearing the same stained and bedraggled clothing as the previous day, and even though she'd tried to comb her matted hair on the way to the house, it didn't look any different.

'Mummy, this is my friend Eileen, and she's going to be Rosemary's maid, just like Peggy.'

Later that night, Frances's mouth contorted into a grimace as she inspected every inch of her daughter's scalp for nits. She yanked the nit comb roughly through her long hair, and the child cried every time her mother combed it through. A large chunk of hair would be left inside the comb, which Frances threw into the toilet bowl, then started her search again. Even Peggy winced as the comb was dragged roughly from top to bottom.

'I'll pop her into the bath and do it if you like?' Peggy suggested when she saw Deborah's blotched, tearful face.

'And next time don't you dare bring that disgusting girl here!' Frances shouted, ignoring Peggy.

'But she's my friend.'

'Maybe you should find another friend, love,' Peggy suggested gently.

'And did you see the state of her shoes?' Frances stopped yanking briefly to address Peggy.

'Our teacher's having a collection to buy her some of her own,' Deborah said, relieved that her mother was temporarily distracted from the hair pulling.

'Here, you take over.'

To her daughter's relief she handed her over to Peggy, then reached for her handbag, which she kept by her side at all times. She rooted inside for her purse, then pulled out a ten-shilling note.

'Give this to the teacher tomorrow, but don't ever go near that girl again.'

That evening, Frances would have dearly loved to discuss her daughter's unfortunate choice of friends with her husband, but to her dismay he came in late, well after she'd gone to bed.

'Why are you so late?' she demanded when he crept into their bedroom. 'I kept your supper warm for you.'

'I ate something in the office ... a sandwich ... at my meeting.'

'What sort of meeting?'

He turned his back to her, taking off his jacket while he quickly gathered his thoughts.

'Council of Christians and Jews. Go back to sleep – I'll be as quiet as possible.'

But Frances didn't want to sleep, she wanted to talk to him.

'Deborah brought home the most awful—'

'Frances I'm tired, can't it wait till tomorrow?'

She lay down again irritably, but when he turned off his bedside light, she began pondering that these days he seemed to go to a lot of late meetings without telling her about them beforehand.

'Next time, tell me if you're going to be late, so I can throw your food in the bin.'

*

Michael had crowned himself the undisputed leader of the medley of children who lived in Hanover Gardens. It was usually his decision as to whether they played cricket or football across the street, using opposite neighbours' gates as either goal posts or the boundaries of the cricket pitch.

Deborah wanted to be in his team, particularly when Tony Kushner was playing. She had developed a massive crush on him, and if they were playing cowboys and Indians, she was more than happy to be the Indian to his cowboy; or if they were playing cops and robbers, she was equally happy to be the robber to his cop.

Once, with a supreme effort, she plucked up the courage to ask him why she always had to be the underdog.

'Tony, could I be the cop today?'

'No Deborah, you can't.'

'Oh all right then.'

With any other boy she would have fought doggedly for her rights, but gazing into his handsome face, she knew that she would have to be content to remain his worse half for as long as he needed her to be.

One day the gang was playing cricket, using the street outside the Kushner house as their pitch. Michael had told his sister she had to play inside leg. She wasn't sure what that meant, but as long as Tony was fielding nearby, she did as she was told. She knew her aim was to catch the ball, but Tony invariably got to it first, and when he did she looked at him with undisguised adoration.

At that moment, Michael was bowling to Lionel Canterovicz, the eleven-year-old brother of Deborah's friend Barbara, and both were the offspring of Rabbi Nahum Canterovicz who lived further down the road. The Steinbergs and the Canterovicz seniors never acknowledged each other. Although they passed each other several times on the street, they barely even nodded. Wilfred explained to his children that he and Canterovicz were ideologically on opposite sides of the religious fence, and if the other rabbi could have broken the friendship between their two sets of offspring, he certainly would have.

Lionel hit the ball that Michael had just bowled, then started his run across the street. But a passing cyclist got in his way, and Michael hit the stumps.

'You're out, you're out!'

Lionel stared angrily at the departing cyclist.

'That's not fair, it was his fault.'

'Give me the bat.'

'No, it's still my go!' Lionel protested.

'That's cheating.' Michael ran over to get possession of the bat. Tony Kushner was also losing patience.

'I've not had a turn yet.'

Then he too plunged into the mêlée of children trying to wrest the bat from Lionel. Michael managed to get a hold of it, but Lionel twisted round and the bat inadvertently made contact with his nose – at least that's what Michael later insisted. Blood spurted from the prominent Canterovicz proboscis, spilling onto his shirt and onto the ground. Tony and Deborah looked mesmerised at the stains, but Lionel was whimpering and clutching his nose.

'I'm going to tell my dad.'

Tony took this as his cue.

'I've had enough of this game, I'm going home.'

Deborah was deeply disappointed that he had given up so easily. She expected more of her knight in shining armour.

'If that's the case, you can't play with my bat any more,' Michael snarled.

'Then you can't play with my ball, so there.'

With that, Lionel grabbed the cricket ball from Michael's hand, and still holding his nose, ran down the street towards his house.

Later that afternoon, when Rabbi Canterovicz thundered up the driveway of number seven, Peggy was in the kitchen holding Jake on her lap. She was trying to coax him to eat some scrambled egg, and cooing at him over every mouthful that he took.

'You know you're my own little treasure, and I'll never let anyone take you away from me.'

Deborah had grown used to her talking to her little brother like that, so she hardly looked up, and continued on the crayon drawing she was making. They both heard the doorbell ring, but Peggy was holding Jake, and Deborah was too engrossed in what she was doing.

'Is nobody going to answer that?' Frances shouted from upstairs. Peggy sighed and reluctantly put Jake into his highchair.

'She's been in that bloody bed half the day.' She left the kitchen and hurried to the front door. The doorbell rang again and Peggy shouted, 'Keep your hair on, I'm coming!'

As soon as she opened the front door, the tall, bearded Canterovicz pushed his way into the hall. Lionel was hovering behind him, still holding a handkerchief to his nose. Even from the kitchen table, Deborah could see that the blood on it was brown and dry.

'Where is he, that hooligan of yours?'

'Who is it, Peggy?' Frances called out, and Peggy shouted back: 'I think you'd better come down, Missus!'

From her vantage point in the kitchen, it looked to Deborah like the rabbi was exhaling steam from his nostrils, like a dragon. But he kept his round velvet fedora firmly on his head all the while.

Frances came down the stairs slowly. She was still wearing her pink candlewick dressing gown even though it was the middle of the afternoon. She held on to the banister rail, and moved with difficulty. Her face was pale, but she looked defiantly at the intruder. She motioned to him to move into the lounge, then she followed him and Lionel in there, closing the door behind them.

Deborah got off her chair and tiptoed into the hallway. When she looked up the stairs, she saw her brother rushing from his bedroom into the toilet. Peggy held Jake in her arms and motioned to Deborah to kneel down with her ears to the lounge keyhole. The child could hear the rabbi's rasping voice.

'And if I so much as catch hold of that son of yours ...'

'You've had your say, now I think it's time you left.' Frances sounded very angry but dignified. Then Canterovicz raised his whiney voice even higher, and the two eavesdroppers could clearly hear him without the need for snooping.

'Your family has been nothing but trouble since you arrived in this street. You can even smell the bacon frying from this house.'

'How dare you! You have no right to come round here insulting my family!'

'Did he say bacon?' Peggy looked at Deborah incredulously, and she nodded. Then the maid sat Jake down on the carpet, marched purposefully towards the lounge door, and flung it open.

'Shall I phone Rabbi Steinberg, Missus?'

Peggy was shaking her head with righteous indignation, and the cross she wore around her neck swung from side to side as she did so. Canterovicz spotted it and shuddered.

'Rabbi? You call that apostate a rabbi? He's a disgrace to Judaism!'

With that he grabbed hold of Lionel's hand, and marched his son out of the lounge, but just before he reached the front door, Lionel turned towards Deborah and whispered,

'Is Michael playing tomorrow?'

None of them could persuade Michael to come out of the toilet. His mother leaned wearily against the toilet door, looking so white that Peggy thought she might faint.

'It might be better if you went back to bed,' she suggested.

'Maybe you're right.'

She seemed relieved that Peggy was taking charge of the situation, but as she made her way back to her bedroom, she clutched at her stomach as if she were in severe pain. Peggy raised her eyebrows, then asked Deborah to take Jake to his room and wait for her there.

'Michael, love, it's me, Peggy.' She used her most cajoling voice outside the bathroom door. 'Why don't you come out now?'

'Because he might come back.' Michael's muffled voice sounded terrified.

'I don't think so, love.'

'Where's dad?'

'He's at a Masonic meeting. Come on, love, it'll be all right. Hurry up.'

'And mum?'

That was when she lost her patience.

'Michael, for heavens sake! I need to bloody wee!'

*

Because of his position in the Progressive Jewish movement, Wilfred and his family suffered taunts from the Orthodox section of the community, as well as from non-Jews. Michael often came home from school with a bloodied nose from trying to defend his faith; however Deborah seemed to have escaped that particular problem relatively unscathed.

But one day, just as she was leaving the school playground, two shabbily dressed boys pointed their fingers and pulled leering faces at her. At first she tried to ignore them, but that only increased their belligerence, and soon she began to feel anxious. Most of her schoolmates had already left the playground, and sensing blood, the boys swaggered over to her.

'You killed Christ, didn't ya?'

'No, I didn't.'

'Says so in the bible, says you Jews killed him.'

The other boy now joined in triumphantly. She was really scared because it was the first time she'd ever heard of this Christ person, and she was sure she'd never met him, let alone killed him.

'It wasn't me, honestly,' she insisted in a tiny voice, but the two of them were closing in, and there were no teachers to be seen. Tears pricked the backs of her eyes, and she was becoming quietly desperate. 'I don't even know him.'

'Me dad says it was your lot.'

Then one of the boys picked up a stone and threw it at her. It narrowly missed her head but the shock caused her to run away from them as fast as her legs would carry her. They gave chase, but she quickened her speed till she thought her lungs would burst. Eventually, in the distance she saw some others from her class and caught up with them, making sure to position herself firmly in the centre of the group.

Her breath was coming out of her chest in short, rasping gasps, but as they got closer to their homes, the group began to disperse, and Deborah decided to run again just in case the two boys had followed them. Her immature heart was still thumping when to her immense relief, she almost collided with Peggy, who was out wheeling Jake in his pram. Deborah fell against the pram in relief.

'Now then, what's all this about?'

She lay panting across her brother's legs but managed to splutter out:

'They said ... I ... killed ... Christ.'

'Who did?'

'Boys ... chased me ... but it wasn't me ... it must have been ... someone else.'

'We'd better speak to your father about this.' The maid's face was sombre; she'd heard something similar before from Michael, and now even she was tiring of it.

Wilfred came home early that night, so it wasn't long before he'd heard the whole story. Deborah had taken up her usual position on his knee, and she nuzzled dramatically into his jacket when she got to the bit about being hit by a huge boulder, having decided that a stone sounded too feeble.

'Tell me again, who said that?'

'Two boys at school, but it wasn't me, Daddy, honestly.' But instead of getting angry as she was expecting, her father merely grinned.

'Then what did they do?'

'They chased me.'

'Well my sweet, if anyone says anything to you like that again ...' she waited for the pearls of wisdom to drop from the mouth of the cleverest man she knew '... tell them from me that it wasn't us who killed him, it was the Leeds boys.'

Surprisingly, he was still grinning, and she heard no shouts for vengeance. And with that, he gave his daughter a tight, enveloping hug and ruffled her hair. When she emerged from his embrace, she looked up and saw that Frances had been watching them from the doorway. Her mother's lips were tightly pursed, and the look on her face was one of pure envy.

CHAPTER 3

It was generally acknowledged within the family that Peggy spoilt Jake. Whenever he couldn't get his own way or yelled or stamped his feet, it was Peggy who was the first to pick him up and give him whatever he wanted. If Frances noticed, she said nothing, because she was spending more and more time these days in her bed. Once, when her two elder children came home from school, they saw her sister Ruby's car outside the house, and heard their mother shouting shrilly at her sister.

'Stop interfering, you know I don't want another operation. If I take it easier, it'll all settle down in time.'

Deborah and Michael were puzzled. They never knew exactly what 'it' was, but whenever they looked at their mother's face it always looked pale, with dark circles under both her eyes. More often than not, she clutched a hot water bottle to her stomach when she was like this, and it seemed to them that their father stayed out of the house more than usual when these episodes occurred. When this happened they often heard her challenging him.

'How come you have so many meetings to go to these days?'

'It's the new synagogue executive,' he'd reply a fraction too quickly, 'you know what they're like, each one of them trying to outdo the other.'

However, on the days when he did come home at a reasonable time, it was to Peggy that he'd go and chat over the day's events rather than to his wife.

'So how's your day been today, Peggy?'

'Very good thank you, Rabbi. Can I make you a nice cup of tea?'

'That would be most kind.'

'And I baked that apple cake you like, I'll bring you a piece.'

'I'm most obliged to you.'

He spoke to everyone in those old fashioned, courteous phrases, and whenever he talked directly to her, Peggy would blush and hang her head to one side. When she brought him his tea and cake, she waited until he signalled that it was every bit as good as the last one she'd made. But if Michael dared ask if he too could have a piece, she would invariably snap at him.

'No, that's for your father.'

'Do you know, Peggy, sometimes I think you're the glue that holds this family together?' Wilfred gathered up the last crumbs on his plate. 'I don't know where we'd be without you.' At that she blushed an even deeper crimson, and hurried out of the room perspiring.

Most days Peggy wheeled Jake to the park, and if Deborah was at home and had nothing better to do, she sometimes let her tag along with them. On reaching Jake's favourite spot, which was the duck pond, she would sit him on her knee and take out a large bag of chocolates hidden beneath the pram blankets. She would then encourage him to eat them, and his little face and hands would end up covered in chocolate stains.

'Do you think he should have so many?' Deborah was perturbed by the amounts her brother was consuming.

'It's all right, he likes them,' Peggy replied, matching him chocolate for chocolate. 'But don't go telling your Mam, will you? She'd kill me if she found out.' Then she spat onto her handkerchief, and tried to wipe some of the mess off Jake's face. 'A little bit of chocolate won't do any harm.' Quite often they concluded their park visits with cornets of ice cream bought from the park cafe.

When they got back to the house, Frances had prepared tea. Peggy took Jake's coat off and lifted him into his high chair, then Frances brought him a dish of mashed bananas, and tried to feed him. But every time she got near his mouth with the spoon, he pushed her hand away.

'No, no 'nana.'

Eventually his mother lost her patience, and forced a large spoonful into his mouth. Jake's eyes widened like saucers, he started to heave, then vomited the entire contents of his stomach over the kitchen floor.

'He must be sickening for something,' Peggy said quickly.

Frances was concerned and held the back of her hand over his forehead, while the maid stared in embarrassment at the mess on the floor before quickly mopping it up.

'Strange, he doesn't feel that hot.'

Deborah looked towards Peggy, but nothing more was forthcoming on the subject.

That was the day when Deborah realised that Peggy wasn't always the truthful soul she had trusted her to be. She decided not to tell her mother the truth, but neither did she forget Peggy's lies.

*

Increasingly the maid was taking over more and more of the family responsibilities, and to Frances's chagrin, she realised that Peggy was becoming indispensable to the family. The only time Peggy took time off was when she went to the local Catholic church on Sunday mornings. Apart from those weekly visits, she spent most of her free time at home with the Steinbergs.

'You never go out,' Frances scolded her, 'a girl of your age should have a boyfriend, isn't that right Wilfred?' He nodded disinterestedly. 'You should be out enjoying yourself at dances and things.'

'But you haven't been well enough for me to go out.'

'I can manage. I did before you came, and I'm quite capable of doing it again thank you. Go into town and make some friends.'

'Don't you want Peggy in the house?'

Michael decided to question his mother one Sunday afternoon, while he was watching all-in wrestling on the television with his father. Wilfred loved the wrestling, and his mouth twitched and grimaced in time with the falls and punches. Frances was sitting on the couch besides her husband at the time, and occasionally tried to move closer to him, but he was far too interested in the television to notice her proximity.

'I don't mind.'

'Didn't seem like it to me.'

Deborah was bored by the wrestling, so stood up and went looking for Peggy. After finding the maid in her room, she made herself comfortable on Peggy's bed.

'Are you going to go out?'

'I suppose I'll have to.'

'Where will you go?'

'Pictures, I suppose.'

'Can I come with you?'

'No, not on my day off.'

'Can I try your perfume?'

Peggy picked up the bottle and dabbed a bit on Deborah's forehead. When the child went back downstairs to rejoin her family, with a quick manoeuvre worthy of the best all-in wrestler, she managed to wedge herself in between her two parents on the settee.

'What's that smell?'

'It's Peggy's, she says it's very fashionable.'

'It stinks.' Frances wrinkled her nose in distaste.

'I quite like it,' Wilfred said, then returned to the screen.

*

Frances's sister Ruby was a frequent visitor to the house, but only when Wilfred was out. She liked to flounce in and order everyone about, much to Peggy's annoyance. She was always well dressed, and often came with a parcel of her discarded clothes to give to her sister. Frances took them with good grace because she could never have afforded such expensive models, but occasionally it irked her to have to rely on her sister's cast offs. However, she had her own way of retaining her self-esteem.

'Another new *schmatter*[7]?' she'd remark as Ruby paraded in her latest outfit, and this invariably wiped the smirk off her sister's face. Frances hated her sister's boastfulness, but Ruby too had her own ways of getting even.

'Everyone's wearing this colour this season, it might even suit you.'

---

[7] *rag*

She allowed the words to dangle in the air while her mink tails, which were draped around her neck, dropped onto an armchair. Then she sat down opposite Frances with a concerned look on her face. Her sister clutched her hot water bottle even tighter.

'So how are you feeling today?'

'A bit better.'

'Is the *shickser*[8] helping?'

'She's not bad.'

'And Wilfred?'

'You know my husband, always busy working on some new project or other.'

'He'd do a lot better if he spent more time with you and the kids.'

This phrase, although often repeated by Frances, was too much to hear from her sister's lips, so in spite of herself, she immediately sprang to her husband's defence.

'My Wilfred's a professional man, not like your Sam. He can't just leave the warehouse like Sam does whenever he feels like it. Professional men have to act ... well, professionally.'

Then Ruby tried another tack and looked patronisingly around the room.

'Sam's bought a new car, a Rover.'

She waited for the impact to sink in, and was pleased to notice an almost imperceptible look of envy in her sister's eyes.

'That's nice,' Frances replied a fraction too quickly.

On this particular day Deborah had been privy to this exchange, but she soon got bored with their one-upmanship, and went outside to see if her friend Barbara was playing. An hour later, while the two of them were busy with their dolls, Deborah looked up to see her aunt leaving the house. She waved goodbye as Ruby clip-clopped on her high heels down the garden path. But no sooner had Ruby left, than Deborah heard her mother calling out.

'Deborah?'

'What?'

'Come inside, I need you.' Deborah lifted her eyebrows to heaven and Barbara gave her friend a conspiratorial look of sympathetic understanding. 'Now, please!' Frances shouted again.

---

[8]*maid*

With a long-suffering sigh, Deborah got up off the ground as slowly as she could.

'Will you look after my baby till I see what she wants?'

'OK, I'll sit her here next to my baby.'

When Deborah reached her mother's room, Frances was curled up on her bed, and Deborah had to admit that her mother didn't look well.

There were two single beds in her parents' room, both covered in pastel green coverlets, and at that moment Frances's complexion appeared to blend in easily with the colour of her bed covering.

'I need you to go to the chemist …'

'But I'm playing.'

'… and get me a packet of sanitary towels.'

'What's that?'

'It doesn't matter, just do it. There's two shillings in my purse – and bring me the change.'

'Can't Peggy go?'

'Why do you always have to argue?'

'Oh very well, if I must.'

Her daughter didn't think there was any need to hurry on her errand. There were lots of interesting paving stones in Broom Lane, and they afforded a good opportunity to practise hopscotch. By the time Deborah reached the shops on Cheetham Hill Road, she was the self styled county champion and had achieved her own personal best. Each paving stone became a challenge to overcome to promote her to this elevated position, and by now she was feeling particularly pleased with herself.

The chemist shop was past the butcher's, the wine merchant's, and the paper shop. It was also past Woolworth's, and Deborah spent a considerable amount of time gazing in their windows, planning what to buy with her next batch of pocket money.

Finally, when she stepped inside the chemist's, she had completely forgotten what she'd been sent for, so she walked around the shop trying to spot something that would jog her memory.

'Can I help you?'

A man in a pristine white overall approached her. She was totally stumped, but managed to remember there was an S in the word.

'Can I have a packet of … stationery or something?'

'I think you've got the wrong shop, young lady.'

'No, she definitely said the chemist's.'

'Well, can you describe it, then?'

'It's in a packet I think.'

'Most things are nowadays. Why don't you go back home and find out more?'

'She'll kill me if I don't get it.'

'We're open till six.'

She completed the route home a lot faster than the one going, and as she feared, her mother was furious when she entered her bedroom empty handed.

'Can't you do anything right?' Deborah was welling up with aggrieved tears when her mother scribbled a note on a piece of paper and thrust it at her. 'And hurry this time.' Then she winced and bit her lip.

This time she ran all the way there and back. But when she was nearing her own home, the little girl was amazed to see an ambulance waiting outside their house with its back doors open. She couldn't resist the opportunity of peeking inside it, but it was empty except for medical equipment and some blankets. When she looked up, she noticed several of the neighbours outside their own houses, watching.

Intrigued, she ran up the garden path and almost collided with two ambulance men carrying Frances out of the door on a stretcher. Anxiety was etched over Peggy's face as she watched from the front doorway, holding Jake on her hip. Michael was by her side, blinking a lot and trying to look manly. Deborah racked her brain, wanting to say something reassuring to her mother, but the men just carried the stretcher straight past her to the waiting ambulance.

'I got your thingies,' she called after her mother, but there was no response. She took a quick look round for her father, but there was no sign of him.

'Where's Daddy?'

'I don't know,' Peggy replied grimly, 'his secretary said he left the office ages ago.'

'I expect he's in a meeting.'

'I expect so.'

A few days later, Michael and Deborah were allowed to visit their mother in the hospital. In preparation, her daughter picked some spring flowers from the grass verges outside their house.

'You mustn't do that.' A neighbour spotted her uprooting them, but it was too late and she clutched a bunch in her hand.

'My Mummy's in hospital, she likes flowers.'

'Well, it'll be all right this time, but this is public property, so don't do it again.' As she made her way gingerly towards her front door, he called out: 'And give my best wishes to Mrs Steinberg.'

'Do you know her?'

'Of course, everybody knows your family.'

The two children had to catch a bus to the hospital, and Michael had been entrusted to look after his sister. But she was so nervous at the prospect of travelling alone with her brother, that as soon as they boarded the bus, she needed to go to the toilet. To stop herself from having an accident, she jiggled from side to side on the seat besides him.

'Stop doing that.'

'I need the toilet.'

'Why didn't you go before we left?'

'I didn't need it then.' Her bunch of daffodils, which was sitting on her lap, was already looking wilted.

'You can go when we get there.'

'On my own, what if I get locked in?'

'Oh for heaven's sake.'

The bus stopped directly outside the hospital, and when Deborah stood up, she was mortified to find that she'd left a telltale wet patch on the seat. Michael noticed it and almost pushed her off the bus. Luckily, the conductor, if he'd spotted it at all, never said anything.

Their mother was in the Chaim Weitzman ward of the Jewish hospital, which was a long room containing at least thirty beds. Most of the patients there had one solitary vase of flowers on their bedside tables, but Frances had several on hers, and even more on the floor surrounding the bed. There were also boxes of chocolates, paperback books and piles of magazines. When her children reached her bed, she was propped up on several pillows and she seemed pleased to see them.

'What's the matter with you, Mum?' Michael asked immediately.

In the past, whenever they'd asked the same question of other adults, they'd always been given an evasive answer. Their aunt Ruby referred to it as 'women's troubles' but the two children had no idea what sort of trouble women got into.

'It's nothing, Mick. Don't worry, I'll be home soon.'

'I brought you some flowers.' Deborah handed over her pathetic bunch. 'They got a bit squashed.' Her mother nodded, then asked them to tell her all the news. When Deborah blurted out, ' That Mrs Fraser's been round a lot,' Frances stiffened.

'Yes, she keeps bringing us food, all Dad's favourites,' Michael enthused, 'and she's a good cook.'

Then, as if overcome by sudden, overwhelming weariness, their mother lay back on her pillows looking drained. The children exchanged anxious glances, realising they'd said something wrong, but couldn't understand why.

'Guess what, Mum, Jake's started to read!'

'And he can do the whole ABC book on his own, and he's really good at it.'

'That's nice.' Frances's eyes seemed to have lost the lustre they'd had when her children first arrived, so the two of them sat quietly, and stared around at the other patients.

'I'm tired, children, perhaps you could come back another day?'

'I'd like to come in the car next time.'

'Yes, you'll never guess what she did on the bus, mum? Michael's eyes were shining at the prospect of relating the story.

'Shut up, she's not interested.'

'Tell me next time, Mick.'

As soon as they left the hospital and were again standing at the bus stop waiting for the bus, Michael remarked:

'It's miserable in there.'

'I don't like it either.'

At that time, neither of them were to know that throughout their childhood, they would have to visit their mother there on many more occasions.

*

Each member of the family was increasingly turning to Peggy for the love and comfort that Frances was unable to supply. While she was still in hospital, whenever Michael and Deborah accompanied their father to the synagogue, well-meaning friends and busybodies were prepared to give them advice on her condition, and seemed to know more about it than they did themselves.

'Your mother used to be a fit young woman,' an elderly woman in the congregation told the two children luridly, 'but she lived through the war years, and by the time she had you,' she said, pointing to Deborah, 'her body was turning against itself.' Deborah shuddered and wondered if she'd told her that so she could take some share of the blame?

Listening to these well meaning diagnoses scared them stiff, and it was to Peggy that they turned for reassurance. Michael found it particularly soothing when Peggy clasped him to her bosom and stroked his hair, a position he was reluctant to relinquish whenever it happened.

One night, when Michael and Peggy were watching the television together, Deborah came into the lounge and found her brother lying with his head snugly positioned against the maid's chest, and she overhead him saying,

'I wish I was your baby.'

'Why d'you say that, love?'

'Then you'd cuddle me as much as you do Jake.'

Both of them were startled when Deborah entered the room, but the little girl sniffed in derision at what she'd just overheard. She didn't need that sort of thing from Peggy, because whenever her father was home, his knee had become her undisputed comfort zone.

*

Wilfred's life outside his home had remained a closely guarded secret for many years. But his two elder children were intelligent and resourceful, and as time went by, they got to know more about him than he ever imagined possible.

'Our school are putting on "The servant of two masters",' Michael announced one evening, 'and I've got a part in it.'

'What's it about?'

'You wouldn't like it, but Mum and Dad will.'

The performance of the play was scheduled to take place at the Free Trade Hall situated in the centre of the city, but Frances already had an excuse as to why she couldn't attend.

'I'm sorry, Mick, it's far too soon for me to go out after being in hospital.'

He was bitterly disappointed when Wilfred also said he couldn't attend because he had to speak at an important meeting in the town hall that same evening.

'Well, I can go instead of you two.' Deborah suggested, seeing her brother's downcast face.

The parents conferred, and decided that as long as Wilfred dropped his daughter off at the Free Trade Hall before the play started, then it would be all right for Michael to bring her home on the bus afterwards.

On the night of the performance, as her brother had predicted, Deborah didn't like the play at all, in fact couldn't understand it from the moment it started. What she did know, however, was that her father was speaking at the town hall, which was just around the corner to where she was now sitting.

So after struggling with the play throughout the first act, she decided to slip out and go and listen to her father's speech instead. The programme stated that the play was in three acts, so she figured that she had plenty of time to get back in time for the end of it.

Nobody paid particular attention to her when she left, and shortly afterwards she climbed the steps of the town hall. But this time a uniformed official regarded her suspiciously.

'And where do you think you're going, young lady?'

'To hear my father, Rabbi Steinberg.'

He shrugged, wondering what sort of a parent left his child to find her own way at this time of the night.

'Follow me, I'll show you the way.'

The large hall was already crowded, and the only available seats were at the back. She sat down in a seat he indicated, and all she could see were the backs of people's heads.

'Don't worry, I know where you'll get a better view.'

He then took her up a flight of steep stone stairs and showed her onto the balcony, where she was able to take a seat on the front row. Remembering her manners, Deborah thanked him very politely.

'Would you mind if I kneel on the seat to get a better view?'

'That won't be a problem. Now are you sure you'll be all right on your own?'

'I'm fine thank you, and my Daddy will look after me afterwards.'

The Mayoral party had started to arrive on the dais, and when she spotted her father, Deborah waved to him excitedly, but he never looked up in her direction. Even if he had, all he would have seen of her would have been her small waving hand.

However, from her vantage point on the front row of the balcony, she could clearly see that her father's attention was being drawn elsewhere, to an attractive, well dressed woman who was sitting on the front row downstairs. His daughter watched them exchanging frequent smiles and glances, as if they knew each other very well.

'And so my Lord Mayor, I'd like to sum up thus. This great city of ours must always act like a beacon, both for our indigenous citizens, and those members of the community who have newly arrived from the third world. Thank you.'

The person who had just finished speaking was a local Member of Parliament, and Deborah thought that his speech was as boring as Michael's play. She was tempted to leave and try the play again, but when he sat down, the Mayor then went to the microphone.

'I'd like to thank the Right Honourable Basil Leveridge, Member of Parliament for Gatley South, for his succinct address. And now, Rabbi Steinberg, can we have your views?' When her father took the microphone from him, Deborah beamed with pride.

'Thank you, my Lord Mayor, and I must say at the outset that it's always a pleasure to address such a prestigious gathering. Firstly, may I take this opportunity of thanking you for yet again hosting ...'

That was when Deborah dozed off, and to her consternation and shame, she awoke to the noise of everyone's footsteps leaving the hall. Summoning up her wits, she quickly decided to look for her father, and chased down the stairs towards the hall. She was just in time to see him leaving with his arm protectively steering the attractive woman out. Then the doors shut firmly behind them.

She panicked, it was late, and Michael would be searching for her. But when she ran down the town hall steps, she spotted her father's car parked in front of the building. He was about to get in it, but so was the woman. Deborah yelled out:

'Daddy, wait!'

But they never heard her and the car drove off. In mounting terror, she ran all the way back to the Free Trade Hall as fast as her legs would carry her, and luckily for her, the audience there were only just starting to leave.

'Michael, you were great, the best.' She tried rehearsing a convincing speech in her head, but she was so puffed out she could hardly mouth the words to herself.

Eventually her brother found her waiting in the hallway, and although she was bursting to tell him what she'd seen at the town hall, she realised she couldn't say a word about Wilfred and the woman, because that would have meant admitting that she hadn't watched his play.

She decided instead to wait till she got home, then whisper to Wilfred that she'd chosen to tell him instead of Michael. It would be their special secret, and throughout the bus journey, she grinned in anticipation of the pleasure that both her father and she would have from this little deception. As soon as she reached their house, she ran into the lounge looking for him.

'Where's Daddy?'

'He's at the town hall,' Peggy said, looking up from the television, 'and your mother's in bed.'

'But I saw ...' Peggy looked at her and Deborah reddened, 'Michael's play.'

'Yes, I know, love. Now hurry and get ready for bed or you'll be too tired for school tomorrow.'

Wilfred's daughter never got to talk about that little secret and it became yet another piece of information to be filed away in the deepest recesses of her mind, waiting until such time as she needed to make sense of it.

*

Deborah's seventh birthday was looming, and she'd already stored in her brain more adult information than a young child needed to have. But anticipation of her forthcoming party, and the presents she would receive, were fully occupying her spare time.

She'd invited all her friends to her party, including Eileen Kelly, who'd scrubbed up as best she could. Eileen was wearing the one pair of shoes that truly belonged to her, the ones the whole class had clubbed together to fund, and although they were already quite scuffed and now on the small side, the girl looked an improvement on the last time she'd been for tea. Even Frances spoke to her like she did to the other children.

Frances had baked fairy cakes for the occasion, which Peggy decorated with different coloured icing sugars, and there were also sandwiches and jelly on the table. Eileen ate as if it was her last meal on earth, and five minutes after she'd finished scraping the crumbs off her plate, she ran into the toilet and vomited the whole lot back into the toilet bowl.

Deborah was having a wonderful day, basking in everyone's attention, and by the time her guests had gone home, she felt as if she owned the whole world, and behaved accordingly.

'Deborah, time for your bath,' Peggy called out.

'No, I'm busy.'

'Come on, I haven't got all night.'

'I had a bath.'

'When?'

'Last week.'

'You dirty little devil, get in here right now.'

'Don't you call me names.' She glared defiantly at Peggy.

'Get undressed.'

'Shan't.'

'Do as I tell you.'

'You're not my mother, you can't tell me what to do.'

'I'm in charge when your parents are out, now get undressed.'

Deborah narrowed her eyes to try and outstare the maid, but Peggy stared back even more determinedly. So Deborah tried another tack and said peevishly:

'I know a secret about you.'

Peggy stopped and looked at her, trying to figure out what the girl was referring to. But Deborah had spotted the uneasy look in her eyes and decided to press on with her advantage.

'I know more about you than you think.' Peggy scanned the child's face. 'So you can get in the bath if you want, but I'm not going to.'

She knew she was being very cheeky, and part of her wanted to stop, but the look on Peggy's face told her that she'd accidentally stumbled on a weak spot.

'I'll tell your parents when they get home,' Peggy said, looking strangely sad, and Deborah realised she'd be in trouble if the maid carried out her threat.

'Oh, very well then.'

That night, after Peggy had gone downstairs, Deborah crept into Michael's room, and encouraged him to hide under his bed, which was the safest place they knew for exchanging confidences.

'So then I said, I know more about you than you think, and she went bright red and it really frightened her.'

'What do you know?'

'Nothing really, but she seemed ever so scared.'

'Perhaps she killed somebody?'

'I don't think so, but I've seen her reading the *News of the World*, and Mummy says it's full of filth, so if she's horrible again, I'll tell them that.'

By the time she crept back into her own bed, the combination of too much excitement and too many cakes had taken its toll on her. She couldn't sleep, so summoning up her most dramatic whimper, took herself to her parents bedroom door.

'I've got a tummy ache,' she whined, then pushed the bedroom door open.

Her mother was lying on her bed wearing a pretty satin nightgown that Deborah hadn't seen before. There was only one small side light on in the room, and her father was sitting on the side of France's bed smiling down at her. When the two of them saw their daughter in the doorway, they both looked as if they'd been caught doing something wrong.

'I feel sick.'

'Go back to bed, it'll go away.'

'No, it's getting worse.' She clutched herself like she'd seen her mother do. 'Can I sleep in your bed, Daddy?'

'Tell you what, I'll come and tuck you in, then you can sleep in your own room.' Wilfred tried valiantly, but Deborah continued whimpering and even managed a few tears.

'I always feel better in your bed.' Then, without further discussion, she pulled his bed covers open and climbed into his bed.

'She shouldn't, Wilfred,' Frances said angrily.

'You can come in now,' she encouraged her father, 'I've left you plenty of room.'

When she turned towards her mother to say goodnight, there was such a bitter look on her mother's face, that she thought better of it. Wilfred sighed resignedly, then turned off the bedside light and got into bed beside his daughter.

CHAPTER 4

The next birthday in the family would be Michael's, and it occurred on November the Fourth. That year he asked his parents if he could celebrate with a bonfire party, and they agreed on the proviso that only the adults could light the fireworks.

For several weeks prior to the big day, Michael spent every penny of his pocket money on fireworks, which he bought from the local newsagents. Peggy also bought him two large boxes, and Wilfred promised he too would buy another box before the party.

The fireworks were stored out of harm's way, on top of the sideboard in the dining room. Every day, all three children went into the dining room to check that they were still there, and every day Michael and his sister discussed the merits of the various ones, anticipating how long each would last, or how much noise they would make. Michael enjoyed relating lurid anecdotes he'd heard at school about who had been terrified by fireworks, and which of his friends had even been injured by them, and as each day passed, the stories became more exaggerated.

By November the Third, they had worked each other up into a lather of anticipation, and were in their usual spot in the dining room, marvelling at the size of the final collection. Their mother was sitting in the lounge, knitting in front of the fire, and listening to the radio at the same time. Peggy was in the kitchen, feeding Jake, and they were still waiting for Wilfred to come home for the evening.

'Do you think I should try one just to see if it works?'

'Good idea, but you'd better hurry because Dad will be home soon.'

The two of them waited quietly until they heard Frances leave the lounge and go into the kitchen to start preparing the evening meal, then Michael rolled up a few sheets of old newspaper.

'I'll get a light from the lounge fire, then we can run into the garden. If they see it going off, we'll say it came from another house.'

It seemed a foolproof idea, so to make herself useful Deborah climbed up on a chair and brought down all the boxes of fireworks, then put them on the floor for Michael to make his choice. He selected a Roman candle, which she held onto whilst he hurried next door with the newspaper.

Within seconds he was back in the dining room with the burning newspaper, but even Deborah could tell that the flame wasn't going to last very long, and her heart started to thump.

'It's burning too fast.'

There was fear in her voice, then Michael let out a howl because his shirtsleeve was singeing. In mounting panic he dropped the burning embers of the newspaper onto the floor, trying to stamp them out. But some sparks had already fallen into the boxes.

It hardly took a minute for the firework display of the year to begin. Unfortunately Michael and his sister missed most of it because they were too busy trying to extinguish the flames from his shirt, the carpet and nearby curtains. Rockets, bangers, Catherine wheels and Roman candles all exploded in the dining room, and the entire Steinberg family was forced to flee for their lives.

The children had never seen a working fire engine before; and neither it seemed had most of the other residents of Hanover Gardens, who came out onto the street to watch. But by the time the firemen had completed their job and started to pack away their hoses, the dining room of number seven looked like a scene from the Blitz.

The furniture that had survived was completely sodden with foam and water, and the carpet was now a mass of cinders. What till recently had been Frances's prized flock velvet covered walls, now resembled charred and peeling newspaper.

And if the adult members of the family hadn't been so concerned about Michael's burnt arm, they might have noticed the large bald patch that Deborah had acquired in her once lustrous hair. Luckily for her, there was so much soot surrounding it that only Peggy noticed the gap after she bathed the child. Deborah begged her to say nothing, and between them they devised a way of brushing the remaining hair so that the bald patch hardly showed, except in a strong wind.

Only after Wilfred had spoken to the insurance company, and contacted all the necessary agencies to put their house back in order, did their children receive the full brunt of their parents' collective anger.

'Of all the dangerous, idiotic things to do,' their father began, and that was when, true to form, Deborah started wailing. But Michael began to cough, a deep, hacking sound, which was something new in his repertoire. 'For heavens sake, Deborah, stop caterwauling! Make no mistake you two, this is going to cost you every penny of your pocket money for at least the next twelve years, do you hear me?'

Actually they didn't hear him as well as he intended because Michael was now convulsed in a fit of coughing. His eyes were bulging, and he couldn't seem to catch his breath, but Wilfred carried on regardless, hardly noticing that his son's face was beetroot red. It was taking him all his willpower not to lash out and hit both of them as hard as he could, but God works in mysterious ways, because it was then that Frances intervened.

'If you hadn't encouraged them to buy fireworks in the first place ...' This was music to her children's ears, but he then turned his fury on her.

'Isn't that just typical of you, always blaming me?'

'Well, if you spent more time looking after your own family, and less with ...'

Michael and Deborah watched in horror because it looked as though he was going to lunge at his wife instead of them. Then, in spite of his cough and heavily bandaged arm, Michael threw himself across the room, positioning himself between his warring parents. Wilfred's arm was raised and his fists were shaking in paroxysms of anger, and Deborah began screaming even louder.

'No Daddy, it wasn't her fault!'

Then Peggy appeared in the doorway looking askance, and Wilfred caught sight of her. That was when he dropped his fists and ran out of the room. Then they all heard the sound of the front door crashing shut, his car revving up, and finally driving away. Each one of them, including Peggy, was in tears.

'Don't worry, I'll pray for you all next Sunday.'

All she got in response was a hostile silence. It was as if each individual didn't dare speak in case they disturbed the fragile balance between the warring parties. Finally, Michael ran upstairs to his bedroom, and the only thing they could hear was his hacking cough.

'Michael, love, should I make you a cup of hot milk and honey?' Peggy called after him solicitously.

'Leave me alone.'

'But that cough sounds really bad, let me see if you've got a temperature.'

'I'm OK, there's nothing wrong.'

*

From that day onwards, the family dynamics subtly changed. Jake mysteriously gave up crying; instead he rocked the upper half of his body back and forth in his cot for hours. Sometimes he banged his head against the cot sides as well, in a slow, rhythmic banging, and if anyone tried to stop him, he continued doing it, but even faster.

What with Michael's hacking cough and Jake's persistent head banging, Frances decided she needed to ask the doctor to visit. But after a thorough examination of both of them, the doctor couldn't find anything physically wrong with either boy. He took Frances aside.

'Tell me, are they worried about anything?'

'Of course not!' she snapped.

'No stresses at school, bullying?' he probed, but she insisted that everything was just fine. When he finally alluded to their home life, she shut the door firmly on that line of enquiry.

'Everyone's very happy in this house, Doctor, after all I'd know if they weren't.'

This was the line she adopted throughout their childhood, because to admit otherwise would have been to admit to failure.

'Then the only thing I can suggest for Michael is some good country air. It could be a case of asthma developing, but fresh air might be just the thing for the lad. As to the little one, I'm sure he'll grow out of it in time.'

When Wilfred and Frances resumed talking civilly to each other, the subject of Michael's cough was high on the agenda. They decided that if it got no better, they would have to send him to a boarding school in the heart of the countryside for a few terms, as the doctor suggested. However, when they mooted the subject to their son, he became quite distressed.

'You're only doing this to punish me because of the fireworks, aren't you?'

'Of course not, it's because of that cough.' But Michael started coughing louder than ever and his face got redder and more flushed. Even Peggy tried to reassure him that going away was for his own good.

'It's only for a few terms, love.'

'I don't believe you, you're on their side.'

At suppertime he said he wasn't hungry, and stayed in his room till he went to bed. This sort of behaviour only convinced his parents further that a boarding school would be just the right course of action for a wayward son such as theirs.

'It will get rid of that damn cough, and make a man of him,' his father asserted.

'And just how do you propose to deal with your problem?' Frances muttered to herself.

'When I grow up, I'm never going to get married,' Deborah confided in her friend Barbara.

'Why not?'

'It's too much trouble.'

'Then you can't have babies.'

Deborah considered this for a bit.

'I'll look after my dolls instead. Anyway, how do you get babies?'

'Don't ask me, I don't know.'

'Our Peggy will know.'

'Ask her and then tell me what she says.'

However, as this was not one of Deborah's most immediate priorities at the time, she forgot to ask Peggy the question until some time later.

*

As she was growing up, it never ceased to amaze Deborah that in spite of the constant tensions of their home life, or maybe because of it, her father's empathy with others was legendary. She could never understand why people he knew (and even some he didn't know) all came to him with their problems. It was a well known fact in the community that anyone who approached him would get a sympathetic hearing, and he would always do his best to help sort their problems out.

Some of them even asked for help in areas Wilfred knew absolutely nothing about – for example their failing businesses. But if the problems were outside his field of knowledge, he wouldn't hesitate to involve others who could lend their expertise.

'You must give him the money, not lend it, he can't afford to pay you back.'

His children often heard this shouted into the telephone when a man was struggling in business and those around him refused to help out.

'So sell the shares if you have to, it's your duty to pay for your mother in the old age home,' was another of his many stock solutions.

As a result, Wilfred was consulted on every sort of problem, whether it was financial or marital, or even fertility problems if a couple couldn't conceive and wanted his help to adopt a child. He knew doctors, lawyers, hospital matrons, bankers, and all types of people who could help him solve the myriad of problems that were laid on his doorstep.

Wilfred's secretary Mavis had been with him since before Deborah was born. She was a loyal and devoted Christian, who knew more about Judaism than most members of his congregation. She had bleached blonde hair that fell loosely on her shoulders, and a fulsome figure, and she fretted over him like a mother hen. In her office, which was next to his, she kept a cupboard full of sweets and biscuits because he had a sweet tooth, and whenever his children visited his office, she would ceremoniously open the cupboard for them to take their pick.

'They don't give you much peace do they, Rabbi?' she would invariably say after each supplicant had poured out his heart.

'Poor devil's lost everything, but I'll never understand why they come to me and not their bank manager.'

'Because they know you'll listen.' He'd give a resigned shrug, then light up one of the thirty or more cigarettes he smoked every day.

'Do me a favour, Mavis, ring my wife and tell her I'll be late tonight, I've got a Masonic meeting.' That was his usual excuse, and the one to which she would nod loyally and ask no further questions.

Occasionally, as a treat, he took his children to a city centre hotel for tea. This usually happened when Frances was in hospital; but whichever hotel they went to, the desk staff always seemed to know him. Sometimes they even addressed him as Doctor Steinberg.

'You're not a doctor. Why did they call you doctor?'

'It's just a figure of speech.'

One day, before they collected Frances from yet another round of hospital tests, he took them to the smartest hotel in Manchester.

'And make sure you're on your best behaviour,' he instructed his children before they went in.

When they had finished their tea and were passing the reception desk on their way out, Wilfred doffed his hat to the receptionist, and she smiled back warmly.

'Will you be requiring your usual room this evening, Doctor Steinberg?' He ignored her and pushed his family out hurriedly. Deborah turned round in surprise.

'Daddy, what did she mean?'

'She must have got me mixed up with someone else.'

'But she knew your name.'

'Hurry up, your mother doesn't like to be kept waiting.'

Ever since the night of the firework fiasco, Frances had needed more regular stays in hospital, and Peggy took it upon herself to explain their mother's frequent absences to the children.

'You see, when your kidneys are under stress, they can't work properly.'

'What's a kidney?'

'Little things inside you, and they make other parts of your body work better.'

'Like steak and kidney?'

'Something like that.'

They came to accept her absences as a simple fact of life. As long as they had Peggy to rely on, their lives carried on as normal in spite of Frances not being there.

Increasingly, however, whenever major decisions had to be made, Wilfred would consult with Peggy first, then told his wife afterwards what had been decided. Being stuck in a hospital bed, Frances appeared to accept this at the time, and had little option but to agree. But as soon as she was on her way home, the bickering invariably started again.

'What do you mean, you're going out tonight?'

'It's my job, if someone needs me at night, I've got to go.'

'What if we need you?'

'You've got Peggy.'

At that she exploded.

'The *shickser*?'

'Stop it, both of you.' Deborah tried to intervene from the back seat, but Michael pulled her back and he started coughing again. When they continued carping at each other, Deborah suddenly yelled out: 'I'm going to be sick!'

The car tyres screeched to a halt, and other cars hooted angrily behind. Wilfred quickly jumped out of his side of the car, and Michael pushed his sister out of the rear door. Once on the pavement, her father held her as she put her head between her knees. She surreptitiously inserted a finger into the back of her mouth. It always worked, and she threw up on the pavement. She figured it was a small price to pay to stop them arguing.

*

That year a mellow Spring turned into a scorching Summer, and Peggy would lay out the family meals on a wooden table in the back garden. Frances was feeling a lot better, and had even started to make her own cream cheese again. When it was ready, she would bake mouth-watering cheesecakes with it.

A temporary truce had descended between the warring parties, and Frances's sister came to visit. Frances had baked her a cake to take home to her husband Sam, and Ruby was so pleased that she blurted out:

'Sam and I are taking a house in Torquay next month. It's got five bedrooms, why don't you come down with the children?'

'What a wonderful idea, and it will do Michael the world of good before he goes to boarding school. Do you want me to bring Peggy as well?'

The thought of having a maid on hand appealed to her sister, and before she left the house that afternoon, all the plans for their visit had been drawn up.

For the children, used to the grime of the industrial north, Torquay was paradise. Apart from the occasional day visits to Blackpool or St Annes, this was the first real holiday they'd ever been on. The property that their aunt and uncle had rented was a large Victorian villa set within the spacious lawns of a tree lined garden.

'I've never seen such a beautiful garden,' Frances enthused.

Well-tended flowerbeds, containing roses, dahlias, primulas and hibiscus were dotted everywhere, and several striped deckchairs were strategically placed under the trees. There was even a canvas hammock strung between two trees, which the children fought to sit on.

'It's my go now.'

'You were on it yesterday.'

'You are so mean.'

'Quiet, both of you,' Peggy intervened, 'me and Jake are going on it.' Then both Deborah and Michael would glare at her in annoyance.

Every day, they all trooped down to the beach, where striped wooden beach huts dotted the shoreline. Although Ruby and Sam had no children of their own yet, they had hired a beach hut for the month, and were quite happy to let the children make full use of it. Wilfred joined them after the first week, and the day after he arrived, the whole extended family made the trek down to the sea front.

Sam led the way, followed by Frances and Ruby, who was pushing Jake's pram. Peggy, as usual, had been left behind to tidy the house while they were out. Ruby loved having her there, because normally she only had the services of a cleaning lady once a week, and this daily slave was a luxury she was beginning to get used to.

The road to the sea front was lined with tall poplar trees, some of which overhung to create a tunnel effect over the road. The sun dappled through their leaves, making an almost surreal atmosphere while walking in and out of the light and shade.

There was a railway bridge up ahead, and the adults in the party had already crossed it, but on this day Michael and Deborah were trailing behind the rest of them. Suddenly Michael darted ahead to catch up with the adults, leaving his sister alone. She hadn't noticed his disappearance because she was too engrossed in the patterns of the shadows created by the leaves from the overhanging trees.

Before she knew what was happening, she was forcefully jolted out of her reverie by the hooting of a steam train about to pass underneath the bridge. Then she was completely enveloped in a thick fog of steam from its engine. The sickly smell of carbon filled her nostrils, and she couldn't see anything through the cloud. The less she saw, the more panicked she became. She tried to inch her way forward, but all the while she was screaming in terror, alone on the bridge.

Finally, once the steam had dissipated, she ran ahead to join the others, with sooty tear marks down her cheeks. For the rest of that day, her heart thumped in her chest like a ticking clock.

That night it rained for the first time since they'd arrived in Torquay. Jake and Deborah were in the big attic bedroom they shared with Peggy, who was downstairs in the kitchen, washing up. Deborah had been fast asleep for a few hours and in the middle of a disturbing dream, when there was a gust of wind, and a branch from a tree banged against the windowsill. She sat bolt upright, somewhere between sleep and wakefulness.

'I can't find you, Mummy, I can't see you in the fog.'

Eventually, when she plucked up the courage to look, she could see that the curtain was blowing out through the open window. She heard Jake stirring, so got out of her bed and gingerly tiptoed to the window to shut it.

By the following morning the rain had cleared, and the sky was once again cloudless. Wilfred was downstairs in the kitchen having breakfast with his children, and the rest of the family was still asleep.

'Anyone fancy a donkey ride this morning?'

'Yes, us.'

They were finishing off their breakfast, and couldn't believe their father's offer. He seemed so relaxed and in such good humour on this holiday that they wished it could last forever.

The donkeys that had worked on the beach since they were big enough to carry children on their backs, were pitiful, mangy creatures. They would no doubt continue to do so until the day they were sent to the knacker's yard, but they were docile enough never to disturb their riders. Once his children had been put in the saddles, Wilfred walked alongside Jake's donkey and remarked to Michael,

'I'm glad your cough has cleared up, the sea air has obviously done you the world of good.'

'So I won't need to go to boarding school after all?'

'I'll have a word with Mum about it.'

Michael grinned from ear to ear, and kicked his donkey's sides to make it go faster. Wilfred then had to quicken his pace to keep up, but while they were moving across the sand, a strident voice rang out.

'I say, Steinberg, thought it was you!'

They looked up and saw a middle-aged man wearing plus fours and a waistcoat, puffing his way down the beach towards them. Wilfred waited until Basil Leveridge, Manchester's most prominent Jewish Member of Parliament, had caught up with them.

'Enid's back there in the hut, she said she was sure it was you.'

'Nice to see you, old boy.'

'We're at the Imperial, where are you staying?'

'My brother-in-law's taken a house five minutes walk from here; the whole family should be down shortly.' The MP nodded quickly, as if he had more urgent things on his mind than Wilfred's relatives, then tried to draw him away from his children's prying ears.

'Er, perhaps we could get them all together with Enid, then you and I can go for a quiet drink somewhere?'

He put his arm around Wilfred's shoulder, and attempted to steer him further up the beach, but Wilfred hesitated because he wanted to keep an eye on his children, so the newcomer was forced to speak in front of them.

'Glad I've bumped into you, need a small favour, one Freemason to another so to speak.' Wilfred nodded, and Basil continued in a whisper: 'Young woman in the office,' he turned round to check if he was being overheard, 'foolish girl, you know how they are ...'

He paused for a reaction, and was gratified that the rabbi's head bobbed up and down sympathetically, as if he also knew for sure that girls were foolish; or that was how it appeared to Deborah atop her donkey.

'And when I saw you, I thought to myself, Steinberg's just the man to sort this out.'

When they shook hands later, having promised to meet again before the week was out, Michael spotted that their handshake was somewhat different to how he had been taught to do it. But as he also needed his father's goodwill at the moment, he decided not to challenge him on it. He reckoned if he could just stay in Wilfred's good books till the thorny issue of boarding school had been settled, then his future would look decidedly brighter.

All the Steinbergs were trying to make the most of every moment they had left of their holiday, and even Frances seemed happier and more relaxed than she'd been for a long time. It was now their penultimate day in Torquay, and the children were playing in the garden, while Frances and Ruby sat on the hammock, rocking back and forth with Jake. Sam was sprawled out on a deckchair with a handkerchief knotted on his head at all four corners, covering his bald patch. He was smoking a fat cigar and making sporadic notes on the *Racing Pink* newspaper.

It was a balmy evening, and they sat there for as long as they could. Finally, Ruby went into the kitchen to make the adults a cup of tea.

'Where's the *shickser*?' she called out from the kitchen window. Michael shouted back:

'If you mean Peggy, she went to the beach.'

'Who told her she could?'

'She's entitled to a day off.' Frances defended her, but Michael was already on his feet.

'We can find her if you like?' Sensing an adventure, Deborah stood up too. Their mother thought for a bit, then said:

'OK, but straight there and straight back.'

'Promise!' they shouted in unison, then ran down the garden path before she could change her mind. As they were running off, Deborah heard Ruby call out:

'Where's Wilfred, does he want a cup?'

'I think he went upstairs for a *shluff*[9].'

The two children ran along their usual route to the beach, all the while telling each other dirty jokes. (That is, as dirty as jokes get

---

[9]*sleep*

when you are that age.) When they reached the promenade, they made their way immediately to their beach hut. However, there was no sign of Peggy or indeed anybody, either in front of the huts or on the beach.

'We should separate, you go left and I'll go right, and see if we can find her,' Michael suggested. After five minutes he yelled out in his loudest bellow:

'I can't see her!'

'Maybe she's had an accident?'

Then, to their astonishment, the door to their beach hut opened, and their father emerged from it looking embarrassed and adjusting his trousers.'Daddy, they sent us to look for Peggy, but she must have been in an accident!' Deborah shouted as she ran up to him.

Then through the hut door, which was now ajar, she spotted Peggy. The maid's hair was all messy, and she appeared to be trying to fasten her skirt. Michael bounded over, and at that moment it was hard to decide which one of the four was the most confused.

'I was looking for my glasses,' Wilfred started, his face flushed.

'You're wearing them.'

It was at that moment that Michael started coughing again. Peggy stood up, her eyes darting from one to another, and she seemed very frightened.

'They were in the hut,' she added in a tiny voice.

'That's right.' Wilfred looked so unhappy that Deborah instinctively reached out and took hold of his hand.

'Well that's all right then, you've found them.' But her father didn't hear because Michael's cough was now so bad that all anyone could hear was the hacking and wheezing of him trying to catch his breath.

*

In September Michael started at Brinsdown House, a boarding school in the heart of Devon. When he returned home at the end of his first term there, his cough had almost completely disappeared and he spoke with a clipped, home counties accent. He referred to his parents as mater and pater, and he wasn't interested in playing with his younger sister any more. Nobody ever spoke of that evening on the beach. It was as if an unspoken pact had been reached, and the four people concerned carried on as if it had never happened. Their aunt Ruby was the only one to remark cryptically:

'What the eye doesn't see, the heart doesn't feel.' Then she snorted derisively.

CHAPTER 5

Two years later

Wilfred was again spending more time out of the house, and Frances was having increasingly frequent bouts of illness. One evening Deborah took her mother a cup of tea to her bedroom.

'Is he home yet?'

'If you mean Daddy, no.'

'If he's not careful he'll get caught, then where will we all be?'

She made constant references to these episodes in front of her daughter, and it always made Deborah anxious when she spoke like this. But young though she was, she knew better than to get involved in this type of conversation.

'I must finish my homework.'

When she was back in the sanctuary of the kitchen, she confided in Peggy.

'Why is my mother always so miserable?'

'I expect her kidneys are playing up, love, and it's not only her kidneys these days. She also needs an operation on her other bits.'

Deborah didn't want to know what bits Peggy was referring to this time, however of late she couldn't help but notice that her mother's once brown hair was speckled with grey, and the bags under Frances's eyes had become deeper and darker. While she was contemplating this, her mother reappeared in the kitchen and frenetically started pulling ingredients out of the pantry.

The two of them stared at her, astonished, particularly when she started taking out mixing bowls and frying pans as well.

'What are you doing?'

'Cooking.'

'Why? It's late.'

'I must make the children's meals for when I go back into hospital.'

'But I can do that for you,' Peggy insisted.

'I do it better,' Frances snapped, then opened the fridge and took out a packet of minced steak, which she proceeded to pummel into a bowl. Jake appeared in the kitchen doorway.

'Peggy, will you play with me?'

'Leave Peggy alone, she's busy, we all are.'

Deborah watched her mother from the table where she was going through her schoolbooks.

'Then will you play with me, Debs?'

'No, I've got homework.'

He then went back to Peggy, who by now had her hands in soapy water at the sink.

'Will you play with me later, then?'

'I can't, love, I've got to do these dishes.'

Frances looked up crossly from the bowl, and threw more ingredients into it.

'Peggy's got too much to do, go and play on your own.'

'If you like I can finish that for you,' Peggy suggested, 'then you can take it easy.'

'There's far too much to do, I might be in for weeks. Here, take this.'

She handed Peggy a dirty dish she had finished with, but somehow it slipped out of Peggy's wet hands and she dropped it. It fell to the floor, smashing into tiny shards.

'You stupid girl, now look what you've done!' Everyone looked down at the bits littering the kitchen floor.

'It wasn't my fault.'

'You're useless.'

'No, I'm not, it's you, you're incompetent.'

Frances's mouth fell open in shock, and she seemed to be rooted to the spot. Her nostrils quivered, and her breathing became laboured. The children hardly dared breathe.

'What did you say?'

But Peggy held her ground, although her voice came out a bit quieter.

'Everyone knows you are.'

That was when Frances started screaming.

'Get out! Get out of this house! Pack your bags and go!'

However, Peggy wasn't going to go without a fight, and stared back contemptuously.

'I'll tell your husband.'

At that, Frances sat down heavily on the nearest chair, her face ashen, and her daughter thought she was going to cry.

'Get out,' was all she could manage to say, then Peggy tore off her rubber gloves and stormed out of the kitchen, banging the door behind her. Frances looked stricken.

Throughout the evening, the children could hear their parents shouting in their bedroom. First Wilfred would hurl an insult, then Frances would respond with another, equally cutting remark. Michael had come into Deborah's bedroom, something he hadn't done since he got back from Devon, and they huddled together whispering.

'If we stand outside their room, we'll hear more clearly.'

'What if Peggy sees? Oops, I forgot, she's gone.'

However, Michael decided to take his chances outside the door, even getting down on his hands and knees to peer through the keyhole. Later he reported that their father had paced up and down while he shouted, and their mother had lain on the bed with her head buried in her pillow.

'And how do you expect us to manage while you're in hospital?'

'But it will only be for a few weeks.'

'Have you already forgotten, you've been told to take it easy after the operation?'

'She was insolent to me and I won't have it.'

'She runs the house perfectly well, what more do you want?'

'How could you take her side after what she said to me?'

'Because she was right, that's why.'

'You bastard,' she spluttered.

Jake called out and Michael got to his feet as fast as he could. He reached his sister's room just before their mother left her bedroom to attend to their brother.

'I don't care what you say, I'm going to bring her back!' Wilfred shouted after her.

Then Michael stepped out into the corridor.

'She was rude to Mummy.'

Deborah held her breath, envying her brother's bravery.

'Mummy's not herself.'

'But—'

'No buts, we rely on Peggy, so I don't want to hear another word about it.'

With that their father went down the stairs, grabbed his coat and hat off the stand, then ran out, slamming the front door behind him.

After he'd gone, Deborah sidled into her parents' bedroom. Frances was back on her bed, and the rims of her eyes were red and swollen. Deborah half expected a rebuff, but instead her mother beckoned her over, and took hold of her daughter's hand, caressing it. This was such a rare thing for her to do that Deborah felt overwhelmed.

'Don't worry, Mummy, we can look after you.'

'I only kept her on because of you kids.'

'Michael and I can do the housework …'

Her mother gripped her arm tightly and her nails dug into the child's skin. She pulled her closer and hissed:

'Listen to me, one day they'll catch him out, then he'll be out of a job. But I've got nothing, and we can't live on nothing.'

'Who'll catch him?'

'You're too young to understand,' she said, lying back on her pillow but facing away from her daughter. Then, on an impulse, Deborah did something she rarely got the chance to do – she kissed her mother's only exposed cheek. Frances gave her the briefest of nods in acknowledgement.

On her way back to her own bedroom, Deborah mused that most of the caresses she'd received as a child had either come from Peggy or her father. But the sad look on her mother's face when she left her alone, haunted her daughter for many weeks to come.

When Wilfred found Peggy at the station, she was sitting on a bench with her suitcase by her side, waiting for the last train to Liverpool. Nobody ever found out what he said to persuade her to go back with him, but by the time they returned to the house, the rest of the family was asleep. Two days later as scheduled, Frances went into hospital for her operation, and their lives returned to normal.

But their normal was different to other people's normal, although they didn't actually realise it at the time.

*

Michael passed a scholarship to go to Manchester Grammar school, the best boys' school in the city, which was situated on the South side of town. Wilfred and Frances, in one of the few joint decisions they ever made, decided to move house so that Michael could be nearer the school instead of having to take two long bus journeys to and from the other side of the city every day.

The new house they acquired was much larger than the last one, and was situated in a road full of more secular people. They now had several Christian neighbours, a few Moslem students who were lodging in the road, and a sprinkling of Sephardic Jews. In the main, the local residents were professional people, and makeshift cricket and football pitches across the street were not tolerated for the children who lived there.

Their new house had a large lounge and separate television room, which Peggy called the snug. Unlike in their old house, Peggy made it her business to come and go as she pleased in all the rooms, except when they had guests. Before, she'd only come in to watch the television when Wilfred and Frances were out, but now she behaved like any other member of the family, and Frances had no option but to concur meekly.

One evening Deborah was lying on the floor in the snug, drawing and designing dresses, which she hoped she would one day wear. Michael and Peggy were sitting next to each other on the sofa, watching a quiz game on the television. In it the quiz master was telling the contestants to either take the money or open the box.

'Open the box!' Peggy kept shouting at the set.

When Deborah looked up from her drawings, she saw her brother doing something that shocked her to the core. Every time the maid shouted 'Open the box!' he would squeeze one of her breasts, but she didn't seem to mind because she continued smiling. He kept on doing it until Peggy spotted Deborah staring at them.

'He's a real chip off the old block,' she laughed self consciously, 'just like someone else I could mention.'

'Do you mean your boyfriend?' Michael said cheekily.

'Mind you own business.'

Then she winked at him, and that annoyed Deborah even more. She started to pack her coloured pencils back into their box then stood up abruptly.

'It's time for my hair wash.'

'OK, run your bath, and I'll be up shortly,' Peggy said.

'No, you must come now.'

'I promise I'll be up shortly, off you go.'

Deborah stomped out of the room and climbed the stairs as noisily as she could. She was angry but not sure why. She kept thinking about what she had just seen, and it occurred to her that she no longer trusted Peggy as much as she used to.

*

Amongst the members of his congregation, Wilfred was known for his charm and charisma, and everyone he came into contact with got his full attention. But if they were female and pretty, they merited a more than special dose of the Steinberg charm.

Whenever his relationship with Frances was at a bad low, he made contact with his sister Gwen, with whom he shared a special bond. She still lived at his old family home in Newcastle, and was the youngest of his siblings. She was the one with the most effervescent personality, and she was also very pretty, with natural blonde hair that tumbled from her head in curls. Wilfred had always been her favourite within their family.

'Gwennie love, how's things?'

'Oh, I'm fed up, Wilf,' she answered in her sing-song Geordie accent, 'it's so boring here, and our Mam keeps going on at me to find a nice boyfriend, but there's just nobody I fancy round here.'

'Your troubles are over, my love, because I've got just the thing for my little sister. I've got to go to a conference in London soon, and there'll be several young rabbis there from Australia and America. I'm sure there'll be at least one of them who'll take a fancy to you.'

'Oh Wilf, I can always rely on you to cheer me up. I'll take a sickie off work, Mam won't mind.'

'Good, that's settled then. It will be nice to spend some time together, so I'll get my secretary to send you all the details. I'll book you a room in the same hotel, my treat, then I'll meet you off the train, and we can go together.'

Wilfred thought it prudent not to mention to Frances that he preferred to take his sister rather than his wife, so as arranged, he met Gwen at Euston station on the morning of the conference. When she stepped off the train, he enveloped her in a bear hug. Then he took her case, and they walked hand in hand towards the taxi rank.

Unfortunately, and unseen by them, one of Wilfred's most influential synagogue members had also just alighted at Euston station from the Manchester train. He was horrified to spot his rabbi enveloped in an embrace with a pretty woman who was clearly not his wife.

'Henry, could I have a word with you, in private?' Leonard Isaacs, the man who had seen the pair at the station, beckoned over the synagogue president the following Sabbath morning. 'This is a rather delicate matter, but I feel obliged to let you know what I witnessed with my own eyes last week.'

He related his story, and the shocked president in turn relayed the information to all the executive members of the synagogue council.

'But the rabbi's a very sociable man, he hugs lots of people,' one of them said in Wilfred's defence.

'There's hugging and there's hugging, if you get my meaning?' the president replied cryptically.

'Come on, Henry, you can't presume the man is guilty on the strength of tittle tattle.'

'There's only one way to settle this, we'll have to call a special executive meeting, and demand to know from the rabbi himself if there's anything untoward going on in his private life.'

Wilfred received a telephone call from the synagogue president later that same night. He took it from the phone on his bedside table, and was as nonplussed as the caller on the other end of the line.

'Who was that?' Frances looked up from the book she was reading.

'Henry Lister, says they want me to attend a special meeting. Can't think why he needed to ring me so late.'

'What's it about?'

'No idea, but he says it's of the utmost importance.' In spite of being tucked warmly inside her blankets, a shiver ran down Frances's spine. It felt as if all her worst fears were about to materialise. 'Can't be much, otherwise I would have known about it.' He turned off his own bedside light. 'Goodnight.'

At the extraordinary meeting called by Henry Lister, the entire synagogue executive was present, and the president addressed them in his gravest voice.

'It is my duty as president of this synagogue to tell you of some grave allegations that have been levelled against the rabbi.' Wilfred sat bolt upright as if he had just suffered an electric shock. 'And I cannot stress to you how serious these allegations are.'

'Henry,' Wilfred spluttered, 'I haven't the foggiest idea what you're referring to.'

'Rabbi, did you or did you not meet another woman, who was patently not Mrs Steinberg, off a train at Euston station in London, embrace, then walk hand in hand with her in full view of the public?'

In spite of himself, Wilfred found he was sweating as he racked his brains to recall the incident they were referring to. Finally, after what seemed like an eternity to all those gathered round the table, he burst out laughing.

'That's not another woman.' He smiled round the table, but not one person was smiling back. 'That was my sister Gwen.'

'Rabbi, it would be a very serious matter if you are not telling us the truth; after all, we expect nothing less of our religious leader than to uphold the highest moral standards possible ...'

'Henry, have I ever lied to you?' But he was surprised how uncomfortable he was feeling at the moment.

'I think, rabbi, you owe it to us to prove that this woman is indeed your sister as you say.'

Wilfred quickly looked around the room for signs of dissent from the president's point of view, but although some of them looked acutely uncomfortable, he was unable to detect any significant protest from them.

'Don't worry, I'll make sure you have your proof.'

That evening, his sister listened with growing incredulity. She had just come in from her job at the library, and before she'd even taken off her coat, Wilfred was demanding to speak to her.

'So you've got nothing to say to your old Mam then?' his mother asked sarcastically.

'Sorry Mam, but it's important I speak to our Gwennie.'

'So you want me to come to Manchester with my birth certificate, or you could lose your job?' Gwen said in an incredulous voice after he'd related the whole story.

'I'm afraid so, darling.'

'What sort of people are they?'

'Small town bigots unfortunately, but they control the purse strings.'

'Well, at least I'll get to see the children … and Frances of course.'

'We'll all be delighted to see you again.'

The children were indeed happy to see their favourite aunt, but Frances was less so. She envied any woman who was close to her husband, and Gwen was no exception. This whole episode irked her, rekindling all her worst fears, and although she never said it openly, she blamed her sister-in-law for being the cause of the problem.

'Gentlemen, may I present my lovely sister Gwen, and just to prove to you that she is who I say she is, this is her birth certificate.' He tossed the paper contemptuously over to Lister, who duly passed it round the table. 'And as you will no doubt see, gentlemen, we share the same surname.' Most of the members looked down at their feet in embarrassment, but one finally spoke up.

'I think we owe the rabbi and his sister an apology, don't you, Mister President?' Lister's face had turned to a mottled red colour, and he was breathing heavily.

'Well, yes …'

'Don't bother, Henry,' Wilfred cut him short, 'and now, gentlemen, as you've had your proof, my sister and I are going out for lunch. If by chance someone should see us in the Kardomah café, I'd be grateful not to be woken at another ungodly hour to call me to an urgent meeting.'

With that he picked up the birth certificate, put his arm round his sister's shoulder, and ushered her out of the room, leaving the members of the executive sitting in confused silence.

The next day, sitting round the breakfast table after Wilfred had left for work, Frances spoke to her sister-in-law alone.

'How long do you intend staying with us?'

Gwen looked up in surprise, because her brother had asked her to stay for at least a week and she'd booked the time off work.

'I thought …'

'It's just that I'm very busy at the moment, what with Jake starting school, and …'

'Don't worry, Frances, I understand. I'll be on the train home tomorrow.'

*

According to his teachers, Jake was a very bright child. While others in his class were only able to read simple storybooks, Jake was already tackling some of his sister's books. Peggy had taught him the alphabet before he could even walk, and now he found the class books he was given far too easy.

He insisted that for his bedtime story, Peggy read him *Kidnapped* by Robert Louis Stevenson. When Deborah listened in, she could tell that Peggy found the language difficult, and she often heard her little brother correcting the maid's pronunciation in his childish voice.

Their next door neighbour was a German professor. He was tall and blond, and nobody in the family, except Jake, took much notice of him. He usually left for work early in the morning, and the family would hear him return while they were eating their evening meal. At weekends the professor had a succession of young men visit the house, most of whom the Steinbergs presumed were his students.

Most days Jake rode his tricycle up and down their own driveway and sometimes he strayed into the neighbour's. The professor, who Jake informed them was called Cosmo, never objected to his intrusions, in fact he seemed to enjoy the little boy's visits. Sometimes he even invited Jake into his house, and gave him sweets or an apple, and each time he ruffled Jake's hair affectionately and told him he was always welcome to come and visit.

Occasionally Deborah heard them talking together, and Cosmo would always enquire whereabouts Jake had got to in *Kidnapped*.

'Oh we've finished that one. Now we're reading *The Old Curiosity Shop*.'

'Dickens eh? Not bad for a four year old.' He seemed fascinated with Jake's progress, and Jake was the only one of the family he appeared to have any interest in.

One warm summer's day, Peggy and Deborah were in the kitchen making iced lollipops together.

'What's that noise?'

'I can't hear anything.'

'Listen, it's like a tapping coming from next door's garden.' Peggy went to the back door to listen.

'You'd better put those in the freezer because Michael will want one when he gets home from school,' Deborah suggested.

'There it goes again.' This time it was Deborah who went out into the back garden to investigate the noise. 'What's he doing?'

'Sounds like he's banging away at a typewriter.'

As she said this, Jake appeared from around the corner. He had just ridden out of Cosmo's driveway, and both his pockets were stuffed full with sweets.

'Where did you get those from?' Peggy demanded.

'Cosmo.'

'Who the heck's Cosmo?'

'Herr Steifel, the man who lives next door.' Peggy sniggered, 'Herr means mister in German.'

'How do you know that?'

'He told me, and I know lots of other German words. He let me read some of the book he's writing.'

'What's it about?'

'I'm not sure, but he does his typing in the back garden when it's nice.'

Jake left them staring suspiciously at each other while he went into the kitchen and poured himself a glass of water. When he'd finished his drink, he went back outside to retrieve his bike.

Peggy and Deborah were having the same thought. This needed investigating, because as far as they knew, no other member of the family had ever been inside Herr Steifel's house.

'Tell you what,' Peggy whispered, 'I can just about see into his garden from my bedroom, how about we take a look?'

As soon as Jake was safely out of sight, they hurried upstairs to Peggy's room. They could still hear the keys of his typewriter and the carriage return going back and forth when they went to peer out of the window. To their intense disappointment, neither of them could see any of the action that was taking place behind the rose covered trellis fence that separated the two gardens.

'How about if you climb up on top of my dressing table and I hold on to your legs, you might be able to see something from there.'

'But it's too far away from the window.'

'We'll have to pull it nearer.'

The two of them pushed the piece of furniture over to the window. The dressing table was narrow and it rocked precariously when Deborah clambered up on top of it, but Peggy held firmly on to her legs.

'Well, what can you see?'

'I can see his willy.' Deborah sucked in her breath and tutted.

'Don't be daft.'

'Honestly, it's pink and brown colour and covered with hairs.'

'Get down, let me have a look.'

'He's still typing,' Deborah added, as Peggy forced her down from the dressing table then eased herself up shakily instead.

'Well, if that's not the rudest thing I've ever seen. Him a university professor, without so much as his knickers on!'

Peggy's weight proved to be too much for the piece of furniture, and Deborah screamed as it threatened to topple over. When she realised she was going to have to forego the pleasure of looking at Cosmo's private parts any longer, she muttered darkly:

'I'm going to tell your father.'

'No, I will, I was the one who saw it first.'

All hell broke loose when she imparted her knowledge to her father that evening. However, it wasn't the fact that the neighbour was typing in the nude that fascinated Deborah the most, it was the knowledge that he had a patch of hair above his penis that she found most unbelievable. She'd never seen an adult man or woman naked before, even though she'd seen Michael and her younger brother in the bath when they were young. Up till that day, Deborah had no idea that pubic hair actually existed, and privately she came to the conclusion that their neighbour must be a freak of nature.

But what she couldn't have anticipated when she told her father what she'd seen, was his reaction. Before he did anything further, he decided it was of the utmost urgency to discuss the situation with Frances, something he rarely did these days when problems occurred, and when he told his wife the story, she was horrified.

'You must warn both the boys, then go and see him. Types like that target young boys, and Jake must never play anywhere near his house again.'

'You're right. I'll tell him straight, I'll say I never want to have this sort of conversation with you again, or I'll be forced to inform the university authorities.'

'And the police.'

'Well, we've no proof he's done anything wrong yet.'

But that didn't console Frances.

'As if I haven't got enough to worry about, without having a German homo living next door.'

The following evening the entire family watched from the doorway as Wilfred walked determinedly down his own garden path, then up the neighbour's path. They heard him knock on Cosmo's front door, and as if to emphasise the severity of the situation, he rang the doorbell as well. Then they heard the front door opening, and the German professor welcome him effusively. After that, the door closed behind the two of them.

When he finally returned home, they were all waiting for him and demanded to know what had happened, but he merely shrugged.

'Nice chap, fully understands.'

Deborah stood there with her mouth open waiting to hear her father throw some light on the crucial issue of the curly hair on Cosmo's nether regions.

'But what about him wearing nothing to cover his thingy?'

'Don't worry, he says it won't happen again. He said he didn't realise he could be overlooked.'

That was the moment when his daughter realised there were far too many gaps in her education, and she was going to have to find someone else to fill them in. It was obvious that neither of her parents had any intention of giving her a rudimentary biology lesson; and furthermore, it dawned on her that within their household, her education was not considered to be a great priority.

Over subsequent years, it became crystal clear that in line with her parents' way of thinking, her brothers were the ones who had to be properly educated. That meant they were expected to go from school to university, and fulfil their full potential. But she was not going to be given that option.

Since she'd been a small child, all she'd ever heard concerning their plans for her was the phrase, 'She'll have to do a good *shidduch*[10].' Not being conversant with Yiddish, she presumed it referred to some sort of job, and not her potential marriage prospects, which it turned out to be.

*

After the Cosmo incident, or maybe because of it, Deborah started to pay more attention to boys. That is, boys other than her brothers, and one of them in particular. His family sat in the front row of the synagogue, on seats reserved and paid for by the wealthiest members of the congregation. This particular family only attended the synagogue on the high holy days, the most important festivals of the Jewish calendar.

From her vantage point sitting alongside her mother, Deborah found she could gaze across at the boy uninterrupted.

'Deborah, what do you keep staring at?'

'Nothing.'

'Then read your prayer book.'

One day, to Deborah's utter joy, the boy returned her stare, and after the service was over, he hung around, ostensibly looking for Michael, but Deborah soon figured out that it was her he really wanted to talk to.

His name was Marcus Lubin, and Deborah was completely taken by his bluest of blue eyes, his cleanest of clean shirts, and his most well pressed of pressed trousers. In fact, she was bewitched by everything about him, and eagerly looked forward to the next Jewish festival, when he would once again be home from his boarding school.

As well as his other attributes, Marcus also had a beautiful singing voice. This fascinated Wilfred, who himself could barely sing a note

---

[10]*marriage*

in tune. Occasionally, to his sister's unbound joy, Michael would invite Marcus to play. Both of them were keen stamp collectors, and Marcus would duly arrive in his parents' chauffeur-driven Bentley, with his impressive stamp collection neatly assembled in leather bound albums.

'First we can look through each other's collection, then maybe do some swaps? Michael suggested.

'Sure,' Marcus replied, all the while looking round for Deborah. The two boys then started comparing and swapping their less important stamps.

'I wish I had as many as you.'

'You can look through them, I need to go to the toilet.'

Marcus intended using the opportunity to go and look for Deborah, and he found her waiting shyly in her bedroom doorway.

'Are you coming to Mick's room?'

'Do you want me to?'

'Sure, see you in a min.'

'Yeah, see you.'

Then she sidled into her brother's bedroom, and as soon as she slipped through the door, she immediately caught sight of Michael doing something very suspicious. It was obvious that he was trying to secrete a penny black – taken from Marcus's album – in his trouser pocket.

'Put that back!' Her brother spun round guiltily.

'He won't notice.'

'If you don't, I'll tell him.'

'Whose side are you on?'

He seemed very aggrieved, but she continued looking at her brother through narrowed eyes until they heard the sound of the toilet flushing. He quickly took the stamp out of his pocket and slid it back into the album.

After tea, Wilfred embarrassed both his elder children by asking Marcus to sing something. The boy himself had no such misgivings, and with their father's encouragement, he stood up on a chair and gave the Steinberg family a clear rendition of 'Oh My Papa'. It moved Wilfred deeply, but his progeny were forced to wait impatiently until the impromptu concert was over. Deborah and Michael were interested in Marcus for reasons other than his voice.

Two weeks after he'd returned to boarding school, a letter arrived for Deborah. In it Marcus wrote about all the mundane things he'd been doing at school, and even she had to admit that the letter was not only badly spelt but also rather tedious. But when he signed off, he did it in what she believed was the most romantic way possible.

'Yours till walking sticks walk.'

Oh the joy she felt! Within minutes she'd written him a long letter back and couldn't wait for his next letter. But when he returned to Manchester for the Christmas holidays, to Deborah's abject dismay, he'd found a new love whose name was Susan.

Susan was two years older than Deborah, and had already started to develop impressively in her chest area. She also had a mop of blond hair and it was to her house that Marcus now took his stamp collection. For a week Deborah thought her heart would break, but life moved on and so did she.

*

Frances was in hospital having more tests, and was due to be released a week later. Whilst she'd been away, Jake had been regularly complaining that he had a toothache. One morning Wilfred decided to take a look in his mouth, which made the child complain even more.

'It still hurts.'

'Perhaps you should take him to the dentist?' he suggested to Peggy.

'I've had a toothache too,' Deborah said, fancying the chance to miss an afternoon off school.

'Maybe you should take them all, it's time they had a check up?'

Sefton Seymour was the family dentist. Although his surgery needed a fresh coat of paint, and the equipment in it had been inherited from his father, another dentist, he was nevertheless a jolly man. The children liked him because he always gave them either a new toothbrush or some sugar-free gum after their appointments.

Michael was first to sit in his chair, then Deborah. After giving their teeth a good clean, the dentist pronounced them to be tip top condition. However, when Jake sat down, it was a very different story.

'What a mess, this will never do. You'd better tell Mrs Steinberg to phone me tomorrow.'

Jake went pale, filled with foreboding.

'She can't, she's in hospital.'

'She's had a hysterical tummy,' Deborah added gravely, but for some strange reason that she didn't understand, Sefton Seymour guffawed with laughter.

'Don't you mean a hysterectomy?'

'That's what I said.' He was still smiling when he told Peggy she had to bring Jake back later that week.

'I'll leave an hour free.'

'Surely you won't need all that time for his little teeth?'

'There's a lot of work to do here, I'm afraid.'

'But he's so young.'

'Do you like sweets, young man?'

'Yes, me and Peggy love them.' Peggy turned away in embarrassment.

The night after their visit to the dentist, Wilfred took them to see their mother. The three of them perched on her hospital bed, trying to give her all their news in one go.

'Jake's got to have at least four fillings, and we don't need any,' Michael told her.

'It's not my fault, Mummy,' Jake protested, and she looked at her husband.

'I've said all along she buys him too many sweets.'

'You can't stop her spending her own money, she loves him.'

'Just because she gave hers away ...' Wilfred put up a warning finger, but Deborah and Michael sensed that something significant had just been said, or in this case, left unsaid.

'It's time we were going.'

'But you've only just got here!'

'I've got a synagogue meeting.'

'You should think up another excuse, you've been using that one too often.' Then she turned her face into the pillow.

A week later their mother returned home, and the children noticed that Wilfred didn't have as many meetings to attend as he'd had whilst she'd been away. This caused a collective family sigh of relief.

*

Although she was back at home, Frances was not yet strong enough to accompany the family on their weekly visits to the synagogue, and Wilfred considered Jake too young to come without his mother there to oversee his behaviour. After arriving at the synagogue, he allowed his elder two children to sample the contents of Mavis's sweets cupboard, then went on to conduct the service in his own distinctive manner. Dressed in his rabbinical vestments, his voice reached to the furthest corners of the room, and each member felt as if the rabbi was communicating with them personally.

The decorum during Wilfred's services was always exemplary. When he gave his sermon nobody stirred or fidgeted, and even the smallest children seemed to sense that they had to behave. When the congregation were supposed to join in they did, and listened respectfully when they were not.

He was proud that his synagogue boasted one of the finest choirs in Manchester. He had encouraged its formation, but the one asset he lacked himself, was a tuneful singing voice. Yet he loved to join in enthusiastically whenever the choir were singing. His tuneless voice was an affectionate joke, but because the choristers respected him so much, they put up with it as long as he never attempted to sing solo.

'Good morning, children,'

Henry Lister murmured as the two Steinberg children took their places near him in the synagogue.

'Good morning,' Deborah replied, but he continued to stare at her, waiting.

'Good morning, sir.' Michael nudged his sister, as he quickly supplied the missing title, and the man nodded formally.

Lister was a man who, if not commanding respect, certainly commanded fear from those he came into contact with. Before returning to civilian life, he'd been a high-ranking officer in the army, and on the back of his synagogue seat was a small bronze plaque that read *Henry Lister OBE*.

During the services he wore a formal black top hat and a tailcoat. One of his presidential jobs was to carry the Torah, the covered scrolls of the law, around the congregation during the services, followed closely by Wilfred. The purpose of this was to allow the men in the congregation to touch the scrolls with their prayer shawls, then put the fringes of the shawl to their lips and kiss them reverently.

'It's not fair.'

'What isn't?'

'That I'm not allowed to do that,' Deborah whispered to her brother, when the procession passed by them and Michael performed this small ritual.

'Well you can't, it's men only.'

Ever since she'd been small, Deborah had been in awe of this procession – in fact throughout her childhood, processions per se had always intrigued her. Wilfred too had a penchant for them, and regularly took his children to see the Christian Walks, as they were called. Had Deborah been given the chance, she would have happily changed religions so that she could join in the Whit Walks, the Protestant ones held on a Friday or the Catholic ones on the following Monday.

Most of all, she fantasised about wearing one of the identical pink, green or yellow satin dresses with wide petticoats that the Christian girls wore as they held their banners aloft. One week, sitting in synagogue and bored with not being able to participate, she devised a plan to stage her own version of their processions.

The sun was shining through the stained glass synagogue windows when she plucked up the courage to put her plan into action. She waited until Henry Lister passed by carrying the Torah scroll, and let all those who wanted to kiss it do so. She continued waiting until her father followed behind him, grinning at his children when he spotted them. Then she did what she'd been mentally rehearsing for weeks.

'I need a wee.'

'You can't go now.'

'But it's urgent.'

'Go then.'

Michael shrugged, unsure as to why she was announcing her bodily functions to him. Then she nipped out of the row, and solemnly followed the procession as it made its way to the back of the synagogue.

She looked up from under her lashes, smiling shyly at people sitting near the aisles, and feeling quite secure that Lister and her father were unaware of her presence. She even swished her skirt from side to side like the girls in the Walks did, and as soon as the procession reached the back of the synagogue, she headed out through the nearest exit.

Because she had at least fifteen minutes to while away before the second Torah procession, she went into the ladies toilets, restyled her hair, occasionally did a wee although invariably she had to force herself, then waited behind the closed glass paned doors for her re-entry. There she waited for her cue, and sure enough the procession would be on the turn when she again nipped in behind them. With a proud look, she was once again in her own private processional world leading her back to her seat.

It was after her third week of Christian fantasies that her processions came to an abrupt halt. Her father was in the middle of his sermon when Henry Lister slunk in beside her on their row.

'The Hebrew term *mussar klayot* means regret or contrition,' Wilfred was explaining to the congregation. 'God alone knows our deepest thoughts …'

'And so do I,' Henry Lister's voice hissed in her ear, 'I'll see you after the service, young lady,' he snarled, and then was gone.

She trembled during the remainder of the service, and positively quaked when the president beckoned her over. The congregation was filing out past her father, and as was his custom, he shook hands with all the adults and picked up and kissed the young children, who clearly adored him.

'I'm just going to have a quick word with my friend,' Michael said, sensing trouble.

'Stay with me, please.'

But he had abandoned her, and as she slowly approached her nemesis, she wondered whether or not to start crying. But a quick look at his face told her he would be immune to any such artifice.

'I take it you do know you're not supposed to follow the Torah round?' he barked. 'It's a solemn, holy moment, not a mannequin parade!' Fear prevented her from speaking, then his voice rose an octave: 'So in future, go to the toilet before the service starts, do you hear me?' Her eyes were wide with terror. 'Well?' he screeched, and several people turned round to stare at them.

'Yes, Mister Listerobe.'

'What did you say?'

'I said yes Mister Listerobe … sir.'

'Are you being funny with me?' By now Deborah had to cross her legs to save herself from the complete ignominy of wetting herself.

'No, Mister Listerobe, sir.' Then she started crying, but he continued glaring at her.

'I'm going to have words with your father.'

He stomped away, and by the time she made it to the toilets, to her dismay there was a suspicious damp patch in her best knickers. Because of this, she felt uncomfortable on the journey home, particularly when Wilfred stopped to doff his hat at several of his congregants.

'Deborah, you haven't said "good shabbos" to Mrs Finkelberg.'

'Don't worry, Rabbi, the child's probably hungry and wants to get home quickly.'

'Good manners are still good manners, my dear.' Then he doffed his hat again. Just before they reached their street, Wilfred turned to both of his children.

'What did you think of my sermon today?'

'Yeah, it was OK,' Michael started, 'but after the service do you know what happened to Deborah?'

She glared at her brother, who was bursting to tell their father before they arrived home. Wilfred looked towards his daughter enquiringly.

'Well, tell me what happened.'

Michael couldn't contain himself, so instead of waiting for his sister to speak, blurted out the story in graphic detail. To her shame, he related everything she'd been doing for the past three synagogue visits, and how it had all ended.

'So he was quite right to tell you off.'

'But when I said sorry Mister Listerobe, he got even madder at me.'

'What did you call him?'

'Mister Listerobe.' To her amazement, instead of shouting at her, her father burst out laughing.

'She's telling the truth, Dad.'

'I know she is, Mick, but his name is Henry Lister.'

'But it says Lister OBE on his seat.' Deborah insisted.

'Darling, OBE is an honour.'

'What's an honour, what does it mean?'

'Other bugger's efforts,' he murmured, then chuckled to himself all the way home.

*

Not only had Henry Lister become the bane of Deborah's life, but he was also a problem for Wilfred, although her father was reluctant to confide in anyone else. However, Frances feared the man greatly. In her mind, it was only a matter of time before her husband was finally caught out for his womanising.

'He watches your father like a hawk,' she'd say nervously to any of her children who'd listen to her, 'and we all know what would happen if he ever caught him out.' Her other mantra started with these words: 'There are rights and there are wrongs, and it's only your father who doesn't know the difference.'

She always left the words dangling ominously in the air, but until they were teenagers, her offspring were unwilling to probe further into their father's supposed misdemeanours.

However, they were old enough to realise that their family's future prosperity lay very much in Lister's hands. They could see how popular their father was, but the synagogue had become Henry Lister's fiefdom, and after the debacle over Wilfred's sister, Lister had no intention of allowing his rabbi any latitude.

The man was an old fashioned puritan, who saw himself as the guardian of everyone's morals, and he was determined not to bring the good name of the synagogue into disrepute. Or that was how Frances saw it during her most fearful moments.

Not only did she fear that Wilfred's attraction to and from other women would one day see her family destitute, but she also feared almost everything that was outside her sphere of influence, and because so much of it was, her life was lived in a constant state of panic.

But her continual nagging was having an effect, and now even Michael had started to resent his father, but this time it was because of his affection for other people's children, not to mention their mothers.

'Why do you let every snotty nosed kid hug you after the service, but we're not even allowed to stand near you till they've had their turn?'

'What's the problem?' Wilfred looked up at his son in surprise. 'They see me once a week and you have me every day.'

'But you're always busy, so we never get a look in.' That took all Michael's reserves of courage to say, and Deborah waited apprehensively for the fall out.

'Nonsense.'

That was all he ever said on the subject – then he buried himself in the evening paper instead.

Some time later, after his attempt to confront his father, to add insult to injury, Michael overheard Wilfred praising a boy for passing a scholarship to the Grammar school.

'And when I passed,' he told his sister in exasperation, 'he just took it for granted and hardly noticed.'

'That's not fair.'

'But if I'd failed to get into the bloody school, he'd never have spoken to me again.'

'Sometimes I don't think he knows anything about his own kids?' Deborah added sadly.

Both of them had long since given up on expecting normal reactions from Frances, but they still cherished the hope that one day Wilfred would take pleasure in their accomplishments. It was again brought sharply into relief when Deborah too passed the exam to go to the best girls' school in the town. Because nobody in the family except Michael thought it was a special achievement, she too was forced to accept it as just another unimportant event in her life.

CHAPTER 6

The occasion of Cardinal Dominic Heering's first ecumenical visit to a Jewish place of worship was considered to be one of the greatest days in the community's history.

Preparations for the visit had been going on for several months, and negotiations had taken place between the synagogue and the diocese, and between the diocese and the Vatican. Wilfred had been the prime mover in arranging this, the first joint service ever to take place between the two faiths within the city.

Frances was as excited as her husband, and fully entered into the spirit of things. When Wilfred announced that the cardinal himself would be coming to dinner prior to the planned visit, she was overjoyed at having the opportunity of boasting to her sister.

Wilfred was the happiest he'd been for a long time. He knew this would be one of the greatest achievements of his career so far, and he told his family that it would do a lot of good for the Jewish community.

'So it's important you all behave well and make a good impression.' Then he turned to his wife, and suggested with a certain lack of diplomacy: 'Why don't you make a hair appointment beforehand? It needs doing.'

But the person who was bursting with the most excitement was Peggy. She'd never before had the opportunity to meet such a scion of her church, and she wanted the dinner party they were throwing on his behalf to be the best it was possible to serve.

'They're good eaters,' she advised her employer, 'and they know a thing or two about food and the horses.'

'I'm not going to serve them horse meat!' Frances exclaimed.

'No, what I meant was they all like a bit of gambling on the gee gees.'

So with the maid's active encouragement, Frances pored through her dog-eared copy of the Florence Greenberg cookery book, and together they planned the meal they would serve to the cardinal. Frances duly compiled lists of ingredients whilst Peggy searched the larder to check if they had them all in.

Once the menu had been decided, she sent Peggy and Deborah off to the butcher's. Frances thought that it was time her daughter started her training in the art of running a household, and insisted she and Peggy should oversee the meat order.

At the butcher's, the two of them watched Mister Halberstam lift out half a cow that was hanging in his freezer, and lay it on his bench in front of them. But Peggy was not satisfied with the beast.

'Too fatty.'

Then Halberstam spotted the cross hanging from her neck.

'I take it you're something of an expert on kosher meat?'

'Fat's fat.'

Deborah nudged her in encouragement, while he patiently replaced the carcass back in the freezer. He was about to bring out the next one, when Deborah decided to express an opinion.

'That one's too thin.'

The butcher sighed wearily, and eventually, after pointing at two more carcasses before he lugged them onto the table, the two of them found the perfect cow. But Peggy wasn't finished with him yet.

'And make sure you cut off all the gristle or we're not paying you.'

Once all the ingredients for the perfect meal were in place, Frances and Peggy, with the occasional bit of help from Deborah, worked day and night on the planned menu. Finally, on the evening of the dinner party, she and Peggy stood back, newly coifed, and admired the fruits of their labour.

'We make a good team you and I,' Peggy said, but Frances chose not to respond. 'And don't forget to kiss his ring,' she added as an afterthought.

'Why?'

'Because that's what you do.'

'Well, we don't.'

'But he's a cardinal, and one day he could be the pope.'

In spite of Deborah's input with the menu, the children were not invited to the dinner party. They were expected merely to greet the guests at the door, then disappear. But as soon as the front doorbell rang, Michael and Peggy sprinted to the door together, then tussled over which one of them should open it. He managed to prise her aside, and she glared ominously while Henry Lister and his wife entered. When she saw who it was, Deborah stayed well hidden, only too pleased to let Peggy deal with their coats.

Wilfred ushered them into the lounge, then shortly afterwards the doorbell rang again. This time it was Peggy who got there first, having hovered nearby in the intervening time. When she opened the door, she almost fainted with joy. The cardinal entered majestically, followed by two other clerics.

Both Wilfred and Frances came to greet them, and from her vantage point halfway up the stairs, Deborah noticed her mother dither when the cardinal proffered his hand. In the event she didn't so much kiss his ring; more like licked his index finger after they clasped hands. Wilfred looked bewildered and quickly ushered them into the lounge to meet his other guests.

That night Peggy was responsible for serving the food, and the first time she passed a plate of canapés around the room, she hovered near the cardinal longer than anybody else. When she came into the kitchen to refill the dish, she was clearly in a state of trance.

'Save some of those for us.'

But either she didn't hear Michael or simply chose to ignore him, before taking the plate straight back into the lounge. Jake was thoroughly bored with the event, so took himself off to his room, but his sister and brother peeped through the lounge door, and saw that Peggy had once again positioned herself firmly on the Catholic side of the room. Wilfred was forced to cough to attract her attention, but she was so awe-struck, she didn't notice him either.

'Peggy, over here please,' he hissed.

'Yes, your Eminence.' The cardinal stifled a giggle, and one of the priests spluttered into his whiskey.

'Thank you, that will be all.'

From the sound of the conversation emanating from the dining room, the evening was going well. Michael and Deborah munched on the remains of the canapés sitting on the upstairs landing. Two hours later when they realised that some of the guests were about to leave, they watched quietly over the banisters.

The Catholic party was the first to leave, and both Steinbergs showed them to the front door. This time Frances just offered her hand, but hearing a commotion coming from the hallway, Peggy rushed out of the kitchen still wearing her plastic washing up gloves. As the cardinal was about to exit, she grabbed his hand in her own wet one, sank to her knees, and kissed his ring passionately.

Wilfred looked horrified and tried to move her, then the cardinal also tried to extricate his hand in as kindly a way as possible.

'Forgive me father for I have sinned.'

'Haven't we all, my child, haven't we all?' he replied, then with a resounding tug, managed to detach himself from her plastic gloves.

At the end of the evening, after all the guests had left and Wilfred and Frances were about to go upstairs to their bedroom, Peggy waylaid them and begged her employers to let her attend the ecumenical service that was to be held in the synagogue. They agreed but with a few misgivings.

However, on the day of the service, Peggy, not wishing to do anything wrong, asked Deborah about the synagogue service.

'And what do I do when I'm in there?'

'Same as you do in your church, I suppose.'

'Are you sure?'

'Yes, you sit where you can find a seat, and the rest is straight forward.'

By the time the maid arrived at the synagogue, most of the congregation was already seated. She saw the family sitting in their usual seats at the front, then found herself one of the few spare seats towards the back of the room.

At the beginning of the service, Wilfred came out of his vestry with the cardinal resplendent in his scarlet robes, by his side. He led him onto the pulpit, and the choir began the first rousing hymn.

'Ma tovu, ma tovu ...' their voices rose majestically and Peggy crossed herself instinctively. The people on either side of her seemed a little surprised, but she was so taken with what was going on that she didn't notice.

Halfway through the service the cardinal was invited to address the congregation, and after he'd finished speaking, Wilfred announced that there would now be a period of silent prayer and contemplation. It was at this point that Peggy sank to her knees on the floor in front.

'Our father, which art in ...'

'Are you all right?' The man by her side thought she'd fallen off her seat, and hoisted her back up onto her feet. 'Here, let me help you up.'

She flushed with embarrassment, and people nearby craned their necks to see what had happened. Her eyes darted from one side to another, and anxious faces stared at her. Feeling utterly confused, she made the sign of the cross, then rushed out of the row towards the nearest exit.

However, from that day onwards, the family was convinced that Peggy had developed delusions of grandeur, especially when answering the telephone. She would speak in a newly acquired accent, a cross between Liverpool Scouse and BBC English, and now when answering the phone, she would say.

'Steinberg residence, the housekeeper speaking.'

'Who's that?'

'Miss Peggy Purnell,' she would reply with all the hauteur she could muster.

This was particularly embarrassing if any of the children's friends called, but there was nothing they could do about it. They laughed about it behind her back, but maybe it was simply because they were growing up, and their embarrassment level was rising to keep pace with their development.

*

It seemed that almost overnight, Michael had developed a precocious interest in girls. He was smitten with one in particular, the willowy Renee Mintoff, but more of her later. Also about this time, Jake's teachers told Wilfred and Frances that their youngest son was more advanced than any other children in his year, and there was even talk of letting him sit the eleven plus exam when he was only nine. But his teachers eventually decided against it in case he might be the victim of bullying by older children if he passed it.

'Deborah, how did you get that dreadful bruise on your forehead?'

Frances had taken to scrutinising her daughter's face more regularly now, and as usual found it wanting.

'I bumped into a lamppost.'

'If you looked where you were going rather than staring down at the pavement, you wouldn't hurt yourself so often.'

Her daughter had become very self-conscious, and rather than let the world see what she thought was her enormous Cyrano de Bergerac-type nose, she kept her head firmly down when she was walking, and as a result frequently bumped into lampposts and other stationery objects. The girl was convinced her nose was growing daily, and nothing would persuade her otherwise.

'Barbara, have you got a bra yet?'

'Mum says I don't need one.'

'I do, but I'm too embarrassed to ask.'

'But if you need one, you must ask your mother.'

'She's just not interested, even if I looked like a freak.'

Suddenly her friend spotted the latest crop of bruises that Deborah had tried unsuccessfully to cover with her hair, and she let out a gasp.

'What happened to your face?'

'I don't know, one day I looked like me, and the day after my nose was enormous and I'd got pimples on it. And what's even worse, my school blouses are too tight because my thingies are growing. What should I do?'

'Don't worry, I expect it will be back to normal by Sunday.'

Deborah spent hours locked in the bathroom, trying to do her hair in ways that would cover her face so that no one could see her deformities. Then one day, just when she thought things couldn't get any worse, another catastrophe happened, only this time she was convinced it was fatal.

Standing outside the bathroom door, Jake could hear her sobbing. He'd been waiting to get in for ages, but she kept shooing him away. Then Michael walked by and casually enquired if she wanted to play cricket. By way of reply, she screamed like a mad woman, and the ferocity of her voice surprised all of them. Finally Peggy called out anxiously.

'Is everything all right, love?'

'She's gone mad, I only asked her a simple question.'

'And she's been stuck in there for hours.'

'Deborah, can I come in?'

The girl badly needed a friend at that moment, so unlocked the door and opened it a fraction. Peggy went in, and the two boys tried to come in after her.

'Only Peggy, and I'm sick of you two pestering me all the time.'

When Peggy shut the bathroom door behind her, Deborah instantly dissolved into tears. Peggy went over to her and put her arm round her, but Deborah couldn't be pacified.

'Now tell me all about it.'

'I'm very ill, Peggy, and I don't know what to do.'

'You look all right to me.'

'But I'm bleeding.'

'Where?'

'Down there ...'

'That's only your monthly, love, it's nothing to worry about.'

'My what?'

'Hasn't anybody told you about it?'

'I've been cursed, haven't I?'

'Cursed?'

'I've heard girls at school say they've got the curse, but I never knew what it was.'

'That's the one,' Peggy said in a matter of fact way. 'I'm surprised your mother hasn't said anything.'

'How could she? She's always away in hospital.'

'Then I suppose old Pegs will have to help you out. Come on, let's go to my room.'

The boys were still hovering on the landing when Peggy took Deborah into her room. When she closed her bedroom door firmly behind them, they shrugged, nonplussed.

'Weird.'

'They're different to us. Fancy some cricket?'

In her bedroom, Peggy opened a wardrobe drawer, then handed the anxious girl a packet of sanitary towels. Deborah looked at them blankly, so Peggy demonstrated how to use them. She realised it was now up to her to explain about the process of menstruation, although she'd never actually used that word before because she considered it too vulgar.

After listening to her biology lecture, and once she'd been reassured that there was nothing seriously wrong with her, Deborah wanted to prolong their conversation with further complaints against her mother.

'Nobody else has a mother like mine, and she's never listens to a word I say.'

'But you've got to feel sorry for her, love. It's her kidneys that don't work properly, so every time they play up, she has to go to hospital to get them sorted out.'

'But will she be all right eventually?'

Peggy looked at her grimly.

'She won't make old bones, that's for sure.'

*

As time went by, each one of them found their own individual way of ignoring what they couldn't change, and every few months Frances went back into hospital with some variant of the same problem. When she came home again, the family too returned to the previous status quo as much as was possible.

However, her sister Ruby did not play by the same rules, and one day she swept in with her foxtails flying and snorting with indignation.

'Frances, I know it's none of my business,' she started ominously, 'but when I stopped by your house last week, the *shickser* said Wilfred was out, but I could clearly see his car was still in the drive. Now I'm not suggesting anything untoward was going on, but if you want my advice, the sooner you pull yourself together and take charge of this household, the better.'

'You're right, it is none of your business.'

'I don't understand you, I'm only trying to help.'

'We don't need your help, thank you very much, we're fine just as we are.' But the implications of her sister's words were not lost on Frances.

Because each member of the family had learnt to cope largely on their own, nobody paid much attention when Jake started acting strangely. He would come home from school, then run straight to his bedroom, where he would stay barricaded inside until suppertime. They presumed he was doing his homework, when in fact most of the time he lay on his bed weeping.

'Jake, it's suppertime.'

'I'm not hungry.'

'I'll eat his if he wants.'

'Don't you dare, I'll call him again.' Peggy went to the foot of the stairs and called out again, but he shouted back from behind his closed bedroom door.

'I told you I'm not hungry!'

'Tell him he must come down immediately,' Frances snapped.

'Did you hear that? Your mother wants you down here now!'

When he eventually shuffled downstairs, Peggy tried cajoling her favourite into eating his supper.

'You must, Jake, growing boys need their strength.'

'He didn't eat yesterday either,' Deborah added.

'It's none of your business.'

'Don't talk to her like that,' Peggy interjected, and Frances looked shocked that the maid had remonstrated with him and not left it to her. But she found herself at a loss for words, because Peggy had instinctively taken the authoritarian role and hadn't thought to include her.

Peggy now ate all her meals at the family table. This change in status had occurred while Frances had been away on one of her hospital sojourns, and the maid had no intention of ever reverting back to the old ways.

'Why didn't you eat yesterday, Jake?' Frances asked, looking at Peggy as if appealing for permission to speak.

'Oh, leave me alone, all of you.'

Then he ran out of the kitchen, and Michael and Deborah exchanged puzzled glances, but as soon as they'd finished, they went upstairs looking for him. He was lying face down on his bed, and they looked at each other, trying to decide whether or not to get involved.

'Tell him to stop this nonsense and come down immediately.'

They could hear their mother shouting from the kitchen, but Deborah sensed that a touch of kindness was what her brother needed most at the moment.

'Jakie, you've got to tell us if something's the matter.'

'Go away.'

'Maybe we can help?'

They sat down on either side of him on the bed, but although he tried to wriggle out of their way, he was now firmly wedged between them. Eventually he muttered into his pillow:

'Roberts is a bully.'

'Peter Roberts?'

'Always picking on me just because he's bigger.'

'Are you sure? He seemed very nice to me.'

'He says you're spotty.' Ouch, that really hurt, and she inadvertently touched a newly sprouting pimple on her chin.

'You've got to fight bullies,' Michael decided, 'show them you're not scared.'

'He doesn't like you either, called you speccy four eyes.'

Michael pulled off the new National Health spectacles that he'd been advised to wear because of his short-sightedness, and now both he and Deborah felt incandescent with rage.

'We'll show him, I'll teach you to box.'

'And if you can box, you can hurt him back.' Deborah too was determined not to

let those insults go unpunished.

'You've got to show bullies they can't get away with it,' Michael insisted with grim determination on his face, and already shadow boxing in the air. 'Challenge him to a fight.' At that his brother shot up on the bed, looking even more terrified.

'We'll do it properly. Deborah and me will be your seconds, and we can have it at the rec.' He was referring to the recreation ground at the back of Jake's school. 'Then we'll see how clever he is.'

'Yeah,' Deborah added, determined that Roberts was going to pay for that insult to her skin eruptions.

During the weeks that followed, Michael coached his brother every night, even finding him some old boxing gloves. He told Deborah to write out the challenge in her best handwriting, and he also told Jake's best friend Nigel to deliver it to Roberts's house. In the letter they specified the time and date of the match, although secretly they'd been telling everyone else about it beforehand.

They decided not to let anyone at home in on the secret, although by now Jake was so scared that he ruined a pair of underpants the day before the fixture. Deborah concocted a story that she'd seen a bird take them off the washing line, flying away with them in his beak, and Michael swore blind that they'd both seen it happen.

When the day of the match came, excitement was palpable amongst the local school children. One boy got his mother to cut up oranges for the contestants at half time, and in a moment of weakness, Michael decided to let Peggy in on the secret.

'But what if Jake gets hurt?'

'He knows all the moves now, so he'll be all right.'

'Then I'm going to come, just to check.'

'You can't do that.'

'Why not?'

'It's kids only, just a playground match.'

'How about if you say a few encouraging words to him before he leaves the house?' Deborah suggested, but Peggy was so choked up that she couldn't say anything at all.

At the appointed time, they had to drag Jake to the recreation ground, all the while telling him what to look out for when the fight started. He barely heard a word they were saying, and if they hadn't been holding on to him so tightly, he would have run away, never to return. Jake's best friend watched in consternation, biting his lips.

'Can I do anything to help, Deborah?'

'No, Nigel, just wish him luck.'

He went across to his friend looking as frightened as Jake did.

'Best of luck, Jakie.'

'Thanks, Nige.' Jake could hardly speak the words for trembling. Nigel abruptly turned away, and went to stand as far away from the action as possible.

'Was he crying?' Michael whispered to his sister, who raised her eyebrows in the finest Steinberg tradition.

Eventually, the motley crowd of youngsters who had gathered at the ground, parted to let the contestants into the makeshift ring. Michael and Deborah gave Roberts the most menacing looks they could muster, then someone called out 'round one', and Roberts was let loose on their younger brother. At first the two boys circled each other warily, until Michael screamed out:

'Cover your face!'

Then Roberts ran at Jake and punched him hard on that very area – and to his brother and sister's horror, they saw Jake's eye swell up to twice its usual size and half close. But then Roberts made his fatal error, and shouted triumphantly at Jake:

'Hit me if you dare, Jew boy.'

At that Michael darted forward, but Deborah pulled him back.

'This is Jake's fight, not yours.'

'Get him, Jake, do it for us!'

Neither of them could believe what they saw next. In a blind rage, Jake flew at the bigger boy, punching, scratching, doing anything he could to inflict pain. He was like a boy possessed, and Roberts retreated in shock when blood started to flow from his nose and a deep scratch on his neck. They were even more astounded when Roberts lifted his hand to signal he needed time, but Jake was having none of it. He dived onto the other boy, who stumbled, then Jake pinioned him to the ground in a frenzy of kicking and grinding. His bitterness knew no limits.

Blood was flying everywhere, and it looked so nasty that several of the other children tried to drag Jake off him. But the honour of the Steinbergs had finally been avenged, and Michael and Deborah pulled their hero away from the crowd that was now trying to save Roberts.

Even though Jake's face looked like pulp, they hoisted him onto Michael and Nigel's shoulders, then did a triumphant procession home, followed by a group of cheering Jewish boys.

'He did it, he did it!'

The group screamed in unison when they thronged through the back door of the Steinberg house. Then they lowered Jake onto the floor, but before letting go of him, Nigel clutched his friend's hand.

'I'm so proud of you, Jakie.' Then he grabbed his shoulders and planted a wet kiss on his cheek.

'Better watch him, that one,' Michael whispered to Deborah.

Hearing the commotion, Peggy rushed into the kitchen and after a sharp intake of breath at the way he looked, cuddled Jake to her bosom. The elder two wondered if their newly found respect for him was in danger of turning to embarrassment, so they quickly ushered Jake's new fans out, and their brother's supporters retreated down the garden path, chanting:

'Jakie, Jakie, turned Roberts into a cakie!'

That was the first and last time the youngest Steinberg ever fought with his fists. From that day onwards he would only ever fight with his mouth, using well-turned phrases that rendered his opponents speechless. In time he honed that skill to perfection, and when he was a grown man, his words became as lethal a weapon as any physical violence could ever be.

*

Having withstood the potential fallout of being found with Wilfred in the beach hut, over the subsequent years Peggy became as confident as any other of his women friends. Although they were unaware of it at the time, the children had in effect colluded with their behaviour by not telling anyone else about it. Instinct must have warned them not to, and after a while they forgot about the incident, rather than live with the discomfort of remembering it.

Peggy had now gained enough confidence to resent the competition from other women, and she seemed to sense there was only one person who would understand how she felt, and that was Frances. So she was trying to be more solicitous of her employer than ever, and pander to her every whim.

'Let me make you a nice cup of tea. Why don't you go and lie down, and I'll bring it up to the bedroom?'

Frances enjoyed this level of attention, and concurred meekly. When Peggy came up to her room with the tea daintily set out on a tray, and with some home-made biscuits arranged in a circle on a plate, she put it down carefully in front of Frances, then waited.

'Thank you, Peggy, those look delicious.'

'You know that Fraser woman, the one with black hair with bits of grey in it?'

'What about her?'

'I didn't think it was my place to say anything before, but she was always round here when you were in hospital.'

'Don't be silly, she's a friend.'

'Call her a friend huh?'

'I'll thank you not to meddle in my affairs.'

Peggy sniffed and edged towards the door.

'As you wish.'

But the seed had been sown, and Frances, never slow to react when it came to other women, started making plans to put a stop to that friendship once and for all. Meanwhile, Peggy sat down in the kitchen to enjoy her own tea, with the self-satisfied smile of the victor upon her face.

*

Michael's barmitzvah was scheduled to take place in the autumn, and it was going to be a very grand affair. Wilfred thought they should invite every member of the congregation, because to choose between them would be invidious. So now the guest list was in danger of running away with itself, which was not the sort of occasion Frances had in mind.

However, the biggest problem the mother of the barmitzvah boy agonised over for months beforehand, was the choice of her outfit for the party. This was going to be held in the Masonic hall, and the venue had been chosen because it could seat several hundred people. These guests would be served afternoon tea and cakes at what was euphemistically termed a 'tea dance'.

'Don't worry if you can't find a dress, I can always lend you one of mine,'

Ruby offered, but Frances was determined to shine in her own dress for her son's big day. She did however take up the offer of Ruby's foxtails, which she wore around her neck during the synagogue service. In the event, the fur reacted badly against her skin, and sitting next to her, Deborah watched her mother scratching her arms and sneezing frequently during Michael's rendition of his biblical portion.

The service was followed by a family lunch in the synagogue hall, to which distant relatives – including aunts, uncles and cousins from both sides – were invited.

'On this magnificent occasion, I'd like to say a few words on behalf of the guests.'

Ruby's husband Sam scraped his chair back, and tapped a spoon against his wineglass for silence. He decided to give what he insisted was an impromptu speech, but one for which he had prepared copious notes.

'And why is he the only one who can say a few words?' an elderly uncle of Wilfred's demanded to know when Sam had sat down. The uncle was eighty years old, and wouldn't be silenced. So the assembled gathering were forced to grit their teeth for the next half an hour while he droned on about *gematria*, the biblical theory of numerology.

'And to prove my point that this is indeed an auspicious day for Michael, if you add up the numbers of today's date, and divide them by the number thirteen which is his age, you will see that his barmitzvah had indeed been foretold in the bible.'

Finally he sat down then looked around the room, waiting for some applause or at least enlightenment to dawn on his audience. But all he could see before him were half-closed eyes and the occasional soft snoring.

After that, everyone shouted for Wilfred to add some light relief. He got to his feet reluctantly, because he had prepared his main speech for the tea dance the next day, and didn't want to be repeating himself.

'Do you know, you look just like a young Sophia Loren?' one of Wilfred's cousins said to Deborah when her father had finished speaking.

'Who?'

'The actress.'

If he'd said Audrey Hepburn then she would have thrown herself round his neck with joy, because in her mind Audrey was the gold standard for women, not an Italian starlet with thick eyebrows and a large bosom. Every day, Deborah did all she could to hide her burgeoning one, but Hepburn didn't have to resort to such measures because she didn't have anything to disguise.

'*Mazeltov, mazeltov*[11],' uncles and aunts trilled at Michael, who had performed with all the expertise drilled into him over the past several years. He hadn't let his father down, and that was a great relief for all of them.

---

[11]*congratulations*

At the tea dance the following day, Frances literally shone. One of the choir ladies had given her the name of a dressmaker, who traded under the name of Madame Pauline. Although of dubious French origin, Madame Pauline subsequently became Frances's style guru, and the faux French woman had designed and made a truly awful outfit for the occasion.

It was in shiny gold lamé, and Madame had embroidered it with a profusion of gold sequins. When Frances took delivery of the dress the week before, she nearly cried with disappointment. But she had neither the time nor the money to purchase a replacement. Even the bolero that the dressmaker had constructed to go over the dress was scattered with another mass of sequins.

'It looks like Christmas decorations,' Michael told his sister after he'd had the first viewing of the outfit.

'Don't tell her.'

'But how can I dance with her in that? All my friends will laugh!'

'You'll have to tell her she looks lovely,' his sister counselled him. 'Or she might not come.'

Madame had also made a dress for Deborah, but true to form, she had over-gilded the lily. The bodice that enclosed Deborah's 'petites poitrines' as the dressmaker referred to them, was covered with a layer of ruffles, thus making the girl's chest look double its size. Deborah immediately threw a tantrum, and subsequently hated every moment of that celebration, especially when her Uncle Sam invited her to dance with him.

'Will you do me the honour, young lady?'

'No thanks.'

'I won't take no for an answer,' and with that he proceeded to drag her onto the dance floor, manoeuvring her round to the music by using his enormous belly to guide her.

She knew her aunt had told him to ask her, because she'd spent the previous hour sulking at the top table. Once on the floor, she was too embarrassed to look at the other dancers, but by the end of the dance, which seemed to last an eternity, she knew the time to the second on the gold fob watch that hung from his waistcoat pocket over his belly.

*

Within a year of his barmitzvah, Michael and Renee Mintoff were an item, and everyone in the synagogue youth club knew it. They were practically inseparable, and spent all their spare time holding hands and staring blissfully into each other's eyes. When he was with her, Michael hid his glasses, so many of the enamoured looks that passed from him to her were in fact due to bad myopia.

Jake was still too young to join the youth club, but amongst his own friends he was developing a sharp wit and sardonic personality, and whenever he caught sight of the star-crossed lovers, he vowed never to become as pathetic as he thought his brother was now. Renee was very pretty. She had long, silky hair, which she wore piled up on her head in a style called the beehive. Whenever Deborah tried to copy her and style her own hair in the same way, it would inevitably have to be held together by a dozen strategically placed hairgrips. Renee's hair seemed to have no trouble staying in place without a grip in sight.

But the main thing Deborah found hard to forgive in Renee were her delicate, high cheekbones, just like those of her heroine Audrey Hepburn. At the time she didn't know any other girl who could match up to Michael's girlfriend, and her jealousy was compounded even more by the fact that Michael no longer sought his sister out to confide in.

One evening Wilfred spotted his son and Renee smooching together at a youth club dance, and decided that Michael was too young for that sort of thing.

'You'd do better concentrating on your school work, that's what's important at your age.'

'I think it's more important to have friends.'

'What do you know? You're still wet behind the ears.'

'I know she's the one for me, and I wouldn't mess around with other ...'

Michael quickly realised he'd gone too far when his father's look darkened.

'And If you fail your exams because of all this messing around, you'll be kicked out of school. And I for one can't afford to educate you privately, do you hear me?'

That night, for the first time in ages, Michael came into his sister's room and sat down disconsolately on her bed. He needed to find an ally, someone who'd see things from his point of view.

'He just doesn't get it. We're going to get married, no matter what he says.'

'That's a big decision, don't you think you should discuss it with them?'

'They'll only tell us we're too young.'

'Have you bought her a ring?'

'Yes, at Woolworth's, but I'll get her a real one when I've saved up.'

At that moment, Deborah realised that there was no advice he would have taken from her or anyone else, because he was so totally smitten with Renee. But she did worry what would happen when their parents found out the extent of their feelings for one another.

She didn't have to wait long to find out. It was a Sunday afternoon, about a week later, when someone rang persistently on the front door bell and wouldn't take their hand off it. That day was one of her father's rare weekend afternoons off, and he'd installed himself in front of the television to watch his beloved all-in wrestling. Most other weekends, he had to attend barmitzvahs, weddings, funerals or tombstone consecrations, so he was really looking forward to this opportunity of relaxing at home.

'You could wake the dead with that noise,' he remarked without moving off the sofa.

Nobody else thought to answer the door because it was Peggy's day off and she was out. Frances was in bed, and the children were all in their rooms doing homework.

Eventually, when the bell ringing became too much, Wilfred stood up from the sofa in a foul mood. One of the burly wrestlers had just been thrown out of the ring, and it looked like he intended to do serious retaliation to the one who had just jettisoned him out.

'Don't worry, I'll get it!' Michael called out, running down the stairs. 'Keep your hair on, I'm coming!'

When he reached the front door and opened it, a short, red faced man pushed his way inside, edging him out of the way. Hugo Mintoff, his future father-in-law, strode in angrily, and Michael shrank back in fear.

'Where's your parents?'

'Please Mister Mintoff ...'

Wilfred heard the commotion, and finally went to investigate.

'Hugo, old chap.'

The other man stared at him with bulging eyes.

'Steinberg, this nonsense has got to stop immediately.'

'My dear fellow, I've really no idea ...'

Then Mintoff pointed at Michael, who was by now cowering against the wall.

'Ask him, he's been filling her head with nonsense, and they're only fourteen for God's sake.'

Hearing more than the usual weekend level of commotion, Frances had left her bed and was now half way down the stairs.

'Michael, what's he talking about?' she asked quietly.

Jake and Deborah had also come onto the landing, trying to make sense of the conversation taking place in the hallway. It soon became obvious that the adults were suddenly all agreeing with each other, and Michael was now on the receiving end of their collective anger.

It sounded almost too painful to continue eavesdropping, so the younger two went back into their rooms and waited. Shortly afterwards, their father led the other man towards the front door. He had his arm round Mintoff's shoulder, and both of them were smirking.

'No harm done, eh?'

'Just so.'

Wilfred opened the front door, and Mintoff left. They went back onto the landing and caught sight of Frances watching Michael sadly. Their brother was crying, and she was doing her best to comfort him, but he shook her away.

Some weeks afterwards, Michael told Deborah that whenever he waited for Renee outside her school, her friends always surrounded her protectively, and if he called out to her, she would turn her back on him and walk off with the other girls.

CHAPTER 7

Wilfred's spending habits were getting out of hand, or so their mother asserted to the only member of the family who would listen to her. Of her three children, she had chosen her daughter as her confidante, a role Deborah disliked very much when it was bestowed on her.

'It's only because she wants me to know what a difficult man my dad is.'

'All dads are difficult,' her best friend at school nodded sagely.

'But it feels like she's training me to fight her battles, and I don't want to.'

Deborah's problems were further exacerbated when she also started to notice the failings that her mother pointed out about him, and she too began to resent them. She was now thirteen years old, and Frances had finally begun to have a stronger influence over her daughter.

'What did I do to deserve a man like this?'

Deborah felt sorry for her mother, and without realising it, she was slowly inheriting Frances's mantle of victimhood. One day when Wilfred returned from his weekly visit to the barber's, which was located in the smartest department store in town, he came into the house carrying several of the shop's carrier bags.

'What's in those bags?'

Deborah's tone of voice was so accusatory, and so similar to his wife's, that he was shaken when he heard it.

'You sounded just like your mother then.'

Hearing the noise, Frances came down the stairs, as usual clutching a hot water bottle to her stomach. Wilfred took off his coat, then left the bags casually beside the coat stand.

'What's in those?'

'Was it both of you or an echo?' he grinned, but she and Deborah continued staring at the bags disapprovingly. 'It's only bits and pieces. Is dinner ready?'

But Frances couldn't take her eyes off the big carrier bags, which obviously contained big 'bits and pieces'.

'Since when could you afford to shop at Kendal Milne's?'

It didn't take him long to pick up where this line of questioning was leading, but he endeavoured to keep his daughter out of it.

'Deborah, love, make me a cup of tea.'

Even though by now she too had misgivings about the bags, she went into the kitchen, but her mother's voice boomed out in a tone that was designed for her to hear.

'I scrimp and save, a few bob here, a few bob there ...'

'Not now Frances, I'm tired.'

'When did I last get a new coat? Even Peggy wears better clothes than me, but it's all right for you to shop at Kendal's, only the best for Wilfred Steinberg.' That was the point when he snapped.

'Nag, nag, always nagging. I come home from work, and what do I hear but your constant nagging. Do you know, sometimes I look at your miserable face and it makes me feel sick?'

Frances's face was white, and she turned round and ran back up the stairs, still clutching her bottle. Deborah watched from the kitchen doorway, her heart pounding.

'How many sugars?' she snarled. It wasn't much but she felt she had to add some sort of protest on her mother's behalf.

They continued their fight long into the night, and while they argued, Deborah could have sworn she heard rhythmic banging noises coming from Jake's bedroom, just like he used to do when he was a baby. She never found out what Michael made of it; since losing Renee Mintoff, he was so permanently mired in his own misery that Deborah didn't think he even noticed other people's pain any longer.

'I hate him, I hate him,'

Deborah chanted to herself over and over again in the safety of her own bedroom. It never occurred to her in those tension-filled days that maybe her father was as much a victim of his marriage as her mother was.

*

When the situation in the house had reached near breaking point, something happened that diverted everyone from their daily level of angst. On this occasion, it was the forthcoming visit of the venerated Holocaust survivor and theologian, Leo Weitz.

The Steinberg children first got to know about it when they overheard their father telling Evelyn and Harry Fraser. They were standing in the synagogue hallway one Sabbath, and the Frasers were the last people to leave the building that day. Deborah couldn't help but notice that whenever Evelyn Fraser was hovering around her father, her mother made sure she was near enough to keep her eye on them.

Evelyn's husband Hershel, who called himself Harry, was as docile as his wife was predatory, but he held Wilfred in awe, and had an overwhelming respect for him. Considering how close the rabbi and his wife appeared to be, that was rather short sighted of him, but if he knew about it at all, he certainly never let on. Deborah and her brothers sometimes wondered if, in a strange way, Hershel took pride in the fact that his wife was one of Wilfred's favourites, a sort of Jewish *droit de seigneur*.

On this occasion, Evelyn appeared to know what his children didn't, which was that one of the most learned and saintly Jews of his generation was coming to visit their synagogue. Weitz, a German scholar and philosopher, had been incarcerated in a concentration camp during the war, and went on to become a leading figure in world Jewry.

Wilfred had invited him to visit his synagogue and preach there. Not only was this a spiritual coup, but it was also a great public relations one, and Wilfred intended to milk it for all it was worth.

'You've done so well to get a man like him,' Evelyn cooed.

'Absolutely, the man's practically a saint,' her husband concurred.

'He is indeed, and do you know, Hershel, the German government have even minted a special stamp in his honour, and they haven't done that for too many Jews, I can assure you.'

'Those bastards, who'd have thought it?'

'He sent me one, it's a first edition and very rare. I'll treasure that for the rest of my life.'

'It should be worth a bob or two one day.' Hershel pursed his lips, nodding sagely as if he were actually a philatelist.

'And he's staying at our house overnight,' Frances interjected, looking straight at Evelyn in order to emphasise her role as the rabbi's number one wife.

'I'd love to meet him.'

Wilfred patted her arm reassuringly, then turned to his wife.

'Remind me to put Evelyn and Hershel on the list, dear.'

Even though Deborah couldn't see her mother's face, she sensed her stiffen, and later that day, whilst the family was sitting around the lunch table, Frances and Wilfred discussed the arrangements for Weitz's visit.

'We'll have to give him our room, it's the most comfortable, then we can sleep in Deborah's room.'

'Why mine?'

'Don't make a fuss, it's only for one night. You can sleep with Peggy.' Deborah's eyebrows shot up in indignation.

'Don't worry, you won't catch anything off her.'

Michael sniggered at his father's remark, then thought better of it when he saw the look on his face. Instead, he concentrated on his plate, and gobbled a mouthful of chicken.

Two days later, during a Latin lesson at school, Deborah decided to make some capital of her own on the back of the proposed visit. She and the other girls were supposed to be doing a paragraph of translation in their exercise books, and the teacher was preoccupied with writing a passage on the blackboard. So Deborah turned to another Jewish friend in the class, Laura Rabinowitz, who was sitting at the adjacent desk, and carefully slid a note across to her. When the other girl opened it, her eyebrows rose in admiration, and she leaned towards Deborah.

'A saint, and he's sleeping in your bed?'

'Practically a saint, so I volunteered to let him have it.'

The teacher turned round sharply.

'You two, stop talking.'

Deborah lowered her head towards her book, but keeping her eye on Laura, saw her friend pass another note back. It read, 'I thought saints were supposed to be dead.'

'This one isn't,' she whispered indignantly, 'and my dad's got a stamp with his face on it.'

'Can I see it?'

'Are you two deaf?'

As neither girl wanted a detention, they indicated that they'd discuss the subject after the lesson, but when they met up in the break time, Laura was still sceptical.

'I'll prove it to you then.'

Deborah decided to bring the rare, first edition stamp into school the next day, and she had made up her mind that she wouldn't just limit the viewing to Laura, she would also show it to all the other Jewish girls who wanted to see it.

It wasn't easy taking it from its temporary dwelling place in Wilfred's desk. She'd overheard him say that when he could get round to it, he intended to have the stamp properly mounted, then he'd put it in a display cabinet in the synagogue hall, where he kept other Jewish memorabilia.

So the next morning, as soon as he'd left the house and before she left for school, she took the stamp from his desk, and quickly put it into an envelope for safekeeping. It stayed firmly inside her satchel during the first lessons of the morning.

Word of the treasure soon spread amongst the Jewish pupils, and when break time came, most of them gathered around Deborah in the playground for the official unveiling of the saint's likeness.

'One at a time, one at a time,' she instructed patronisingly.

'I haven't seen it, let me see it.'

They pushed and jostled each other to get a better viewing, and she handed it round with as much largesse as she could muster. They sighed collectively in envy that Deborah Steinberg was going to have the subject of an official stamp minted by the German Democratic Republic, sleeping in her bed. On that day, she basked in new glory and respect.

Finally it was Laura's turn to hold the delicate object in the palm of her hand, when the whistle blew for the end of break time. This was the signal for the girls to get into class lines, and Deborah was anxious not to lose sight of the stamp. So she put out her hand to take it from Laura, but the other girl kept a tight hold on it in case it blew away. Deborah gave a little tug, and before either of them could do anything about it, the stamp started to tear down the middle.

Both girls stared in horror at the tiny piece of damaged paper. Leo Weitz's face had been split into two halves divided by his spectacles, one lens and one nostril in each half.

Deborah died a thousand deaths that November day. Never before or since have two girls from Withington High School turned the same shade of green, at exactly the same moment. While the lines of pupils marched back into their classrooms, Laura and Deborah ducked into the nearby toilets to panic in sisterly unison. It would cost them a detention, but they were beyond caring at that moment.

'If we're very careful, maybe we can glue both halves back together?'

'That won't be any good!' Deborah screamed at her, and tears welled in the other girl's eyes.

'But he might not notice if you put it back?'

'He's going to kill me.'

'Then pretend it's been stolen.'

At that moment Deborah was wracking her brains as to how to save her own life, then something occurred to her.

'No, I've got a better idea.'

That afternoon, after their detention, both girls crept through the house and into the lounge. Laura stood guard in case anybody came, and Deborah put the damaged halves of the stamp back into the desk drawer it had come out of. She wedged one half inside the drawer, then closed it, leaving the other half just visible. Mission accomplished, they both ran for their lives.

Luckily for them, the planned visit was due to take place the following weekend, and Wilfred was far too preoccupied with the arrangements to spend much time at home or more particularly at his desk.

'When Mister Weitz comes, instead of sleeping with Peggy, can I stay the night at Laura's?'

'That might be better,' Wilfred concurred. 'Less of a queue for the bathroom in the morning.'

Deborah had very little recall of the actual visit, or even what the man himself looked liked in the flesh. Michael told her he was inspirational, but his sister was still too paralysed with fear to take in any of the finer details of the visit.

In the synagogue she sat mutely beside her mother, and heard not one single word of what the great man said. If he was as marvellous an orator as everybody else attested, then she never noticed. She was just waiting for the denouement to be over, and to know she still had a future to look forward to.

But events took a surprising turn when Wilfred accused Peggy of destroying his valuable stamp. After the saintly visit was over, he basked in the glory of persuading the great man to come to Manchester, and even Frances now looked at her husband with genuine respect, which was a rare thing these days. Afterwards he was so busy with interviews from the national and local Jewish press, that he was barely able to spend time at home at his desk.

Finally, the furore died down, and on the day that he found what was left of his precious stamp, his daughter had lost nearly half a stone in weight from inability to get more than a mouthful of food down at each meal. As she had predicted, her father was incandescent with rage, but at the actual moment of discovery, Peggy was innocently dusting and vacuuming in the lounge, while singing along to Alma Cogan on the radio.

'Why do fools fa-ll in love. Why-ye do fo-ols fall in love?' She flicked the duster in time to the music. 'In lo-ove.' She stopped when she saw the thunderous look on Wilfred's face. 'Sorry, was I disturbing you?' He marched over to the radio, banged on it to turn it off, then started shouting.

'Of all the stupid, idiotic things you've ever done, this is the worst!' He threw the torn pieces of the stamp at her. She looked bewildered as the tiny pieces of paper landed on the floor.

'I don't know what you're talking about.'

'This.'

'I never touched it!' she protested, but he continued ranting about her stupidity, heavy handedness and carelessness. When he finally stopped for breath, she ran upstairs to her bedroom, slamming the door behind her.

She didn't reappear until the next day, and studiously avoided looking at him. She banged the breakfast plates down on the table, then slammed a jar of jam down, and finally the butter dish.

'I reckon if that butter hadn't been stuck hard, it might have jumped out onto the floor,' Michael grinned.

But Peggy ignored him completely. She picked up the bread knife with a vicious look in her eyes, and now it was Wilfred's turn to quake. When she hacked into the loaf, each member of the family winced.

Deborah felt guilt-ridden, and decided she must talk to Peggy after school. When she returned home that afternoon, she went straight up to the maid's room, and found Peggy scanning the back pages of the evening paper.

'What are you reading?'

'None of your business.'

'It's not my fault he's been horrible to you.'

Little by little, Peggy calmed down and let Deborah sit on her bed like she used to in the past. But she noticed that Peggy had drawn pencil rings round some of the advertisements in the situations vacant columns.

'Please don't leave us, I don't know what we'd do without you.'

'It's not your fault love, it's his.'

'I'm sure he didn't mean what he said, it must have just torn in the drawer. Please don't go, Pegs.'

'Well, just for you I'll give him one more chance. But if he ever accuses me again of doing something I didn't do, then I'll leave – and you can tell him so.'

Deborah didn't tell her father directly what Peggy had said; she decided to tell her mother instead. She knew it would cause a row, but she reckoned her parents had so many rows anyway that one more wouldn't make much difference.

Frances was on her bed with a damp flannel over her eyes when her daughter imparted the information.

'Are you asleep?'

'No.'

'Can I get you anything?'

'No thanks, I've just taken some Aspirin.'

Deborah then related the whole saga to her mother, but felt sick with guilt whilst she was doing so.

'He's mad, what can I do?'

'Mad, like crazy?'

'Only a madman would carry on the way he does.'

But at that moment mother and daughter were thinking about two separate issues, and when her father came home that evening, Frances decided not to speak to him at all.

'I've sent him to Coventry,' she confided to Deborah, rather liking the impact it seemed to have on him. From then onwards she addressed all her remarks to him via her daughter.

'Ask your father if he wants any supper.'

'She says, do you want any supper?'

'No thanks.'

'He says no thanks.'

'Ask him why not, has he eaten at somebody else's house?'

'Tell her if she can't be bothered to make a man feel welcome in his own home …'

'He says … oh this is silly, did you hear that?'

'Then tell him he should go where he feels welcome.'

'You can tell your mother …' but Deborah had already heard enough and was at the door.

'I've got homework to do.'

Unfortunately for her, one particular word from this debacle had stuck in her mind, and it worried her throughout that night. Although she knew she deserved to feel bad because of what she'd recently done, she desperately needed some reassurance.

'If someone's mad, does that mean their children will grow up to be mad too?'

She and Laura were lying on the grass verges of the hockey field during their lunch hour. It was a fine sunny day, and the girls were allowed to take their packed lunches there, but Deborah couldn't manage more then a few bites of her sandwich.

'You mean like, if they have dark eyes will their kids inherit dark eyes too?'

'Yes, something like that.'

'I suppose so, I mean it's in the genes, isn't it?'

But that was not the answer Deborah wanted to hear, and there was no one else she could discuss it with. If her brothers had also inherited the madness gene, there was no point in discussing it with them, so she tried to put it to the back of her mind, but that uncertainty as to her own sanity always lingered.

It took her many years to understand that her father was not mad, just very unhappy. It also took many more years to realise that her mother's frequent bouts of ill health were exacerbated, or maybe even due to her own unhappiness.

Unfortunately for all members of the family, divorce was frowned on in those days, and divorce by a rabbi would have been likened to a criminal offence. So there was little any of them could do about the situation they were living through.

*

One day, Deborah was alone in the house when she heard the front doorbell ringing. She leaned out of her bedroom window, trying to see who was standing there.

'It's me, dear.'

Evelyn Fraser was standing on the doorstep, and hearing the noise of the window opening, she looked up expectantly. But on a crazy impulse, Deborah decided to prevent her from coming into the house. She opened her window fully and called down:

'My mum's out.'

'But your father asked me to …'

'He's not here either.' She knew that her behaviour was inexcusable, but a strange compulsion made her do it.

'Can't you just let me in for a minute and I'll explain?'

'No.' Then she said something she would come to regret. 'Why don't you just leave our family alone?'

'I beg your pardon?'

Evelyn Fraser was now totally affronted, but it gave Deborah the chance to slam the window shut. Afterwards she leaned back against her curtains and thought, what have I just done?

She figured out correctly that Evelyn must have rung her father as soon as she could, and when he came home that evening, he glowered menacingly at his daughter. But he was biding his time till he could get her alone. Sensing a problem, Michael glanced from one of them to the other, as if he was watching a tense tennis final, and when Frances left the room, Wilfred started.

'How dare you speak to one of my congregants like that?'

She was trembling, but the thought occurred to Deborah that no other members of the congregation came round to the house uninvited.

'What's so special about her?'

'She's a friend of the family.'

'No she's not, she's your friend, just another of your ...'

Then Wilfred did something he'd never done before. He stood up and was about to lunge at his daughter with his hand raised, but Michael, who had been watching this exchange with ghoulish interest, quickly inserted himself between his father and his sister.

'Get out of the way, this has nothing to do with you!'

'If you touch her, I'll kill you.' This was something new, and Wilfred stopped dead in his tracks. 'I mean it.' And to Michael's immense surprise, Wilfred backed away.

'Don't you dare talk to me like that.'

But Wilfred's voice had lost its stridency, and he looked bewildered. Also, to her immense surprise, Deborah felt pity a surge of pity for her father, even though her mind was in such confusion at the same time.

'I'm too young for all this!' she screamed, then rushed past both of them and up the stairs to her bedroom. Behind the closed bedroom door, she felt very alone and deeply saddened.

*

Wilfred's power within his household was on the wane, and he was only too aware of it. At one time he only had Frances to contend with. Now he had all of them, and that included Peggy.

But it soon became apparent that the less attention he was paid at home, the more he stayed away, and paradoxically the more care he took with his appearance. He'd always been a fastidious man, but these days he was vain to the point of it being obsessional.

One morning he was rummaging through his wardrobe, trying to select the perfect shirt to wear. Deborah was passing his bedroom door on her way down to breakfast, when she saw him pick up one shirt after another, then discard them on the bed as unsatisfactory. Finally, he pulled out another shirt, studied it carefully, and then with a sigh of complete exasperation, threw that also on the bed.

'Peggy!'

'I'm coming.'

She knocked and entered the bedroom, glancing down at the pile of clean shirts that had been strewn carelessly about. She started to gather them up and straighten them, but he pulled at her arm and thrust another in front of her face.

'This collar's not properly ironed.'

'Give it here, I'll do it again.'

'And this one's just as bad.' Then he scooped up all the remaining shirts in the wardrobe, and threw them at her

'Keep your hair on, I said I'd do them again.'

'They might wear them like that where you come from, but we don't here.'

Peggy stopped and considered, nodding her head at the same time. Then with the utmost deliberation she dropped the pile of shirts she had just scooped up, back onto the floor in front of him.

'If that's the case, give them to someone else to iron, and that goes for the rest of your dirty work.' With that she marched out of the bedroom, and Wilfred was left staring at his shirts, with his mouth gaping open.

When he located his wife, she was in the bathroom cleaning her teeth. He barged in and shouted at her.

'That woman's become too big for her boots, she'll have to go!'

Frances turned round in surprise, and inadvertently spat the toothpaste water on the floor in front of him.

'Are you mad? You know I'm having my operation next week. I can't possibly come back to some stranger in the house.'

'She's too insolent.'

'And whose fault is that?'

He was seething, and trying to clean the toothpaste water off his slippers at the same time.

'Then don't complain later that I didn't warn you.'

Like so many other times, the situation was temporarily smoothed over, but Peggy had started to buy the evening paper again. Whenever she had any free time, she pored over the back pages where the jobs were advertised.

But as was the usual custom in the Steinberg house, an even greater crisis than the badly ironed shirts cropped up, putting that one firmly into perspective.

Frances went back into hospital, this time for her gall bladder to be removed. Deborah, who was now studying biology at school, knew where all the parts of her mother's body that she no longer possessed, should have been. Peggy was once again in charge, but Wilfred stayed away from home more than ever, and appeared to be deeply embarrassed whenever he was alone with her.

Jake's best friend Nigel was a pale, red headed boy. It was obvious to everyone who came into contact with the pair that Jake was by far the cleverer of the two, and Nigel followed him slavishly, doing whatever Jake told him to do.

'If our Jake told you to put your head in a gas oven, you'd ask him what number to turn the gas to,' Michael teased him, but Nigel was still Jake's most ardent admirer, and more loyal to him even than Peggy.

During her mother's absence, Deborah had been at school one day feeling unwell. It was the monthly 'curse', and she was suffering badly from period pains and stomach cramps.

'Miss, can I be excused to see matron?'

'First finish your essay, Steinberg, then you can go afterwards.'

By the time Deborah went to see the school nurse she was almost doubled up with pain, so the woman suggested she should go home. She duly caught the number 42 bus outside her school, which stopped in the small town of Withington. Looking out of the window when the bus picked up more passengers, she thought she spotted Jake and Nigel outside a betting shop, and they both appeared to be reading the *Racing Pink* newspaper. But when the bus pulled out into the traffic, she decided she must have been mistaken, because her brother would definitely have been in school at the time.

After getting home, she put herself to bed with a hot drink and some aspirins, then slept for a few hours. When she awoke she heard the sounds of voices coming from her parents' bedroom. Thinking Frances might have been discharged early from the hospital, she got out of bed and without bothering to put any shoes on, went towards her room. She was about to open the door, when she heard Nigel Foulks speaking in a disguised voice on the bedside telephone.

'This is Rabbi Wilfred Steinberg, and I'd like to put ten pounds on Sporting Challenge,' Deborah was rooted to the spot. 'All right, I'll open an account with you if you insist.' Then she heard Jake encouraging him quietly.

'Make it fifteen and each way.'

Before she could open the door to investigate further, she had another spasm and had to rush to the toilet, and by the time she got back to the room, both boys had disappeared.

Still feeling bad, she went back to bed and slept solidly through till the next morning. Seeing her like that, Peggy decided not to wake her till the others had left the house, and by the next morning she had almost forgotten what she'd overheard the day before.

After school that evening, Michael and Deborah were at the kitchen table when Jake came in looking pale and very anxious.

'Why are you twitching?'

'Shut up.'

'Look – he's twitching, Debs.'

Jake's face kept going into a spasm, and his body seemed to shudder at the same time. Peggy looked across at him.

'Don't mind them, love, you've probably been sitting in a draught.'

'Why weren't you on the school bus today? I looked for you.'

'I stayed on late.'

'Not like you,' Michael grinned, 'and one of your pals said he hadn't seen you in class today.' Peggy looked up from the oven.

'Get off my back, will you.'

'I was only asking.' But Jake was already on his way out of the kitchen.

'Perhaps I'd better have a word with him.'

But when Peggy tried to enter his bedroom, he shouted at her to leave.

'You're as bad as they are, why can't everybody just leave me alone?'

'All right, but first tell me, Jake, why you're biting your fingernails down to the quick?'

'Before you start, I'm not ill.'

'Jakie, what's the matter?'

She said it so gently, that he immediately dissolved into tears and fell against her chest. She rocked him back and forth as he sobbed against her.

'I'm in big trouble, Peggy.'

'There, there.'

'I've lost two hundred pounds.'

'What?' She released him, and shot bolt upright.

'On the horses.'

'Bloody hell!'

'And another fifty on the dogs.'

'But that's more than I earn in a year.'

'I just don't know what to do about it, Pegs.'

The following day, Peggy took the unusual step of going to visit Frances in the hospital. She related the whole sorry story to her employer, and when Frances was discharged two days later, Deborah came home from school and found her mother rooting through her jewellery case in her bedroom.

'Are you feeling better, Mum?'

'I'm fine, but leave me alone, I'm busy.'

'Doing what?'

'Mind your own business. Oh, and on your way out, please ask Peggy to come up.'

She then dismissed her daughter with an impatient wave of her hand, and as soon as Peggy went to join her in the bedroom, the two women shut the bedroom door firmly behind them.

The following day Peggy went to a pawnbroker's shop with Frances's jewellery. The shop manager opened the case containing a double row of cultured pearls that had been a gift from Booba, and scrutinised them carefully.

'You haven't looked after these very well.'

'I know, but she says they're very good ones.'

'Clasp needs a good clean, I'll give her ninety, best I can do.'

'Don't be daft, they were her mother's.'

'Ninety five then, can't say fairer than that.'

'I'll take them to Beaverbrooks.'

'Hundred and ten, and that's my final offer.'

Jake was so terrified that his father would find out about his gambling habit and the missing money, that he was studying harder than he'd ever studied in his life, and never once dared leave his bedroom. His brother and sister had both been sworn to secrecy, and warned not to breathe a word of what had happened to Wilfred. But in spite of that, every day their mother made it her business to reduce Jake to tears.

'Who can vouch that he stayed in school today?'

'I can,' Michael assured her. 'He was there all day.'

'And where did he spend his lunch hour, in the bookies?'

'No, school canteen like normal,' Jake muttered.

'I no longer know what he thinks normal is these days.'

She was determined to punish him, and her methods were like the slow drip of torture. After a week of this treatment, Michael and Deborah felt really sorry for him, and they would sneak into his room to try to cheer him up.

'Hang on in there, Jakie boy, she'll stop eventually.'

'If she doesn't, I'll bloody kill her.'

Although Frances was furious at the amount she'd been offered by the pawnbroker, she had no option but to take it, and when the money was safely in her purse, she sent Deborah to the post office to empty her savings account as well. The postmaster counted out one hundred and twenty pounds in ten-pound notes in front of the girl. She pushed the money inside her school satchel, but when he called her back, she feared he was going to ask for it back. Instead he passed her the savings book that she'd forgotten to pick up in her haste to get away.

In spite of Frances's efforts to pay off Jake's debts, unbeknown to her Peggy was also determined to rescue her favourite. Everyone in the house knew that she saved her wages in an old tea caddy, which she hid in the back of her wardrobe. Frances had regularly tried to persuade her that the money would be better off in a savings account, but Peggy liked to have cash readily available, usually to treat Jake.

On the afternoon that Deborah came back from the post office, Frances was agitated because it still wasn't enough to fully clear Jake's debt to the bookmaker. Her other two children hadn't dared mention the fact that it was actually Wilfred's debt, as the account had been opened fraudulently in his name.

'That boy will be the death of me,' she muttered as she counted the notes in her hand.

Finally, after counting them one more time, she left her bedroom and came down the stairs. The lounge door was ajar, and she caught sight of Peggy emptying the contents of her tea caddy and pressing them into Jake's hands.

'What do you think you're doing?'

Jake and Peggy looked as guilty as each other.

'It's not much, only twenty six pounds.'

Frances marched into the room as stridently as her recently removed stitches would allow.

'This is not your problem.'

'But it's his birthday soon.'

'He's my son, not yours, and I'll sort this out on my own, thank you very much.' She snatched the money out of Jake's hand, and pushed it back to Peggy.

'I was only trying to help.'

'And usurp me even further. I'm his mother, not you.'

Jake sidled out of the room, not knowing whether to defend his real mother or his surrogate one. But once he was out of earshot, Peggy raised her voice.

'He's a growing boy, he needs more attention.'

'I know what my children need. Now if you don't mind, I'd like to be by myself.'

With that she waved Peggy away. Once Peggy had slammed the door behind her, Frances sank down into a chair and ran her fingers through her hair.

'Oh God, what will it be next?'

They didn't need to go into Peggy's room to know that she would once again be scanning the situations vacant column of the evening paper. And as they feared, a few days later, on her day off, she left the house, smartly dressed in a periwinkle-blue suit with a small matching hat sitting on top of her curly hair. What she didn't know was that Michael and Deborah had decided to follow her.

Luckily for them, she didn't need to take a bus; instead she walked along several streets, with them dodging in an out of driveways behind her. Eventually she arrived at an avenue of large Victorian mansions, the type built for wealthy cotton merchants at the turn of the century. She finally stopped outside one of them to check the address, then walked briskly up the garden path and rang the doorbell.

They quickly hid behind a thick privet hedge. From their vantage point, they could hear the sound of a dog barking fiercely. When the front door opened, the owner was holding a huge bulldog on a leash, and it greeted Peggy by jumping up onto her suit. Both Michael and his sister clearly heard Peggy's gasps of fear, then the sound of her high heels retreating back down the path towards them.

'Sorry … some mistake … don't like dogs.' They couldn't hear the rest of her excuse because they were now crouching down behind the next door neighbour's parked car, so as not to be discovered.

'I've got cramp in my legs.'

'Stay where you are or she'll see us.'

'She's so frightened, she won't notice anything.'

They watched as Peggy ran back down the road, then when she had safely reached the main road, saw her extract the newspaper from her handbag, and scan the back page again. After a few minutes, she started off down the road again with them following closely behind, and again she walked towards another leafy avenue.

'Lucky for us there's plenty of families looking for help round here,' Michael said, as yet again they dodged behind privet hedges. 'At least we don't have to take a bus to follow her.'

'But if she finds another family we'll all be up the creek.'

By now, they'd crossed two busy main roads, then re-crossed them again after Peggy asked someone for directions. They continued behind her for another fifteen minutes, and eventually found themselves in a dismal looking road, which backed onto a row of shops. It was harder to hide here, but fortunately she didn't turn round and wasn't aware that they were following her.

Before going to the front door of a semi detached house, she hesitated then knocked because there was no doorbell on it. At first nothing happened, so she knocked again even louder. The door opened, and a large black man opened it. Standing behind him was a group of several dark skinned children. The man more or less dragged Peggy inside, and they decided to wait at the rear entrance of a car lot till she came out.

Even they were surprised how little time the interview took, and she was once again scurrying down the garden path as fast as her heels could carry her. She didn't even give the house a backward glance, but by the look of consternation on her face, both Deborah and her brother knew that the Steinberg family was safe at least until the next blow-up.

*

Sparse hairs had started sprouting on Michael's upper lip and chin, and his Adam's apple protruded from his neck almost overnight. At about the same time he outgrew all his trousers, which now reached only to his ankles, and he spent hours in front of his mirror trying out new ways of presenting himself. But in spite of his best efforts, he only managed to look like a gawky teenager.

'God, I'm good-looking,' he told the bathroom mirror after layering Brylcreem on his hair then styling it for ten minutes.

'Who says?'

'How long have you been there?'

'Long enough, Mister Teasy Weasy.'

Jake mimicked his brother by running his fingers through his own thick hair then turning it into a quiff in the middle of his forehead. Even though he was the younger, Jake was turning into a good-looking boy, and Michael, for all his efforts, was not. But when Jake looked into the same mirror all he saw was ordinariness as opposed to his brother who only saw a handsome young adult.

'Sometimes he gets on my nerves, telling me how special he is, and how I'm nothing in comparison,' Jake confided in his sister.

'I'll take him down a peg or two.'

She knocked on Michael's bedroom door, and went inside. He was still posing in front of his mirror.

'What are you doing?'

'Admiring myself.'

'Then you're the only one who does.'

'You're just jealous.'

'If you think you're so special, you need new glasses.'

'It's all right for you to talk, you just have to say *I've got a pain*, and everybody runs to help you.'

'That's not true.'

'And if Jake does something wrong, Mum and Peggy fall over each other to sort it out, but nobody gives a damn about me.' In spite of his self-pity, Deborah had to admit that her elder brother was more and more overlooked these days. 'But don't you worry, one of these days I'm going to do something that will have you all sitting up and taking notice of me.'

The following evening, Deborah took a cup of tea up to her mother's room, and Frances encouraged her to sit on the edge of her bed.

'We haven't talked for ages.'

She was reluctant to stay in case she had to listen to more disparaging remarks about her father, but couldn't think of a good enough excuse to avoid it. So she sat down and waited.

'So how did you get on whilst I was in hospital?' Deborah looked towards the door in the forlorn hope that something would happen outside that could legitimately beckon her away. 'Was she here all the time? On second thoughts, don't answer that.' Her daughter diplomatically decided to try to divert her attention.

'Guess what, I got an A for French, and Mrs. Hopkins says ...' Deep down she knew she couldn't keep this momentum up, and eventually the words she had kept buried for so long, tumbled out of her mouth as if they had a life force of their own. 'Mum, why did you have three kids if you were so unhappy with him?'

'Not for want of trying, I can assure you. I did everything Ruby told me to, drank a bottle of gin, sat in a hot bath, and even tried a knitting needle.' Her answer left her daughter reeling, and she stood up abruptly. 'I mean, eventually I was glad it hadn't worked.'

'You tried to get rid of us?'

'He wasn't always like this.'

Then Deborah turned on her with all the contempt she was feeling.

'You're as bad as he is.'

'But it was the war and ...'

She stomped out of her mother's room, slamming the door behind her.

*

Peggy finally found a boyfriend. It had taken her a long time, but all of a sudden she was cheerful and smiling around the house, and couldn't wait to get dressed up on her days off. Most reassuring of all, she stopped buying the evening paper.

'Where are you going, all dressed up like that?'

'Like what?'

'You look so pretty, Pegs, I haven't seen you look as nice for ages.'

'Can you keep a secret, Deborah?'

'Of course I can.'

'I've met this chap, he's called Eric and he's a policeman, and he's taking me to the pictures tonight.'

'What's he like? Where did you meet him?' Deborah was almost as excited about Eric as Peggy was.

'At the Rialto. Honestly Debs, it took me ages to pluck up the courage to go there. Anyway, I saw him standing at the bar with his mates, and he sort of smiled at me then came across and offered me a drink. So we started to talk, and … well, that was it.'

'Promise you'll tell me all about it when you get home?'

'All right, but not a word to anyone.'

An hour after Peggy had left the house to go on her date, Jake asked his sister if she knew where Peggy was.

'I can't find my football boots, and she's the only one who'll know where they are.'

'She's out.'

'Where?'

'With her boyfriend.'

'She hasn't got a boyfriend.' But when he looked at his sister and saw that her face had gone beetroot red, he knew it was true.

'Why didn't she tell me? What's his name?'

'Eric, he's a policeman, but you mustn't tell anyone.'

'I don't believe it – PC Plod!'

But instead of being pleased for Peggy, he looked distinctly irritated. Deborah presumed it was because he now had to look for his own boots, so reasoned that no harm had been done by imparting that little bit of information. Within ten minutes, however, Michael rushed into her room.

'Is it true about a boyfriend?'

'Oh God, I promised I wouldn't tell anyone.'

'And his name's PC Plod?'

'Don't be silly, it's Eric.'

'Lucky bugger.'

That evening over the supper table, even Wilfred asked her the same question. Deborah was furious with her brothers for telling him, but expected her father to be pleased for Peggy. As it turned out, the only one who did look pleased was Frances.

'It's about time she found someone of her own.'

A few weeks later, Frances suggested that Peggy might like to bring her boyfriend home for tea. Each of them, for their own reasons, was desperately eager to see him. Frances baked a cheesecake for the occasion, and laid out the tea service on the kitchen table. Deborah noted that she didn't use the dining room as she did when her friends came for tea, but at least she'd issued the invitation.

Peggy and Eric arrived on the dot of three, not a minute before and not a minute after, and everybody except Wilfred was at home. Eric was a tall, ruddy-faced man, with a thick mane of ginger hair. He was wearing a suit that seemed too tight for his large frame, and he sat nervously at the kitchen table while Peggy kept giving him reassuring glances. After he'd finished his first cup of tea, and eaten two large slices of cheesecake, Michael started questioning him.

'So Eric, what d'you think of the new Lord Chancellor's ruling on open prisons?' Eric looked up, startled, and some crumbs of cake stuck to his lips.

'Another piece, Eric?' Frances asked.

'No thanks, that were lovely.' Frances compressed her lips at his misuse of grammar.

'So Eric, you were saying about the prison system?' Michael started again, but this time Peggy gave him a dirty look.

'He's off duty now,' she said crossly.

'They say the law is an ass,' Jake chirruped in cheekily, 'but personally I believe our legal system is better than most.'

'I'm not right well up on that sort of thing.'

'Then what are you up on?'

Michael took one look at his brother and the two of them stifled giggles with their hands over their mouths.

'Sorry, got to go, Eric – homework and all that.'

'Me too, Eric.' The two boys rushed out of the kitchen, and collapsed in helpless laughter in the hallway.

'Don't mind them, love.' Peggy reassured him, 'they're just kids.'

'They're not stupid, I'll give 'em that.'

'Will you excuse me too, Eric?' Deborah asked in her politest voice. 'It's been very nice to meet you.'

She extended her hand to him, and when he shook it, his grip was so strong she thought he might have dislocated some of her fingers. Then she too left the kitchen, intending to find her brothers and give them both a piece of her mind. When she caught up with them, they were still sniggering in the garden.

'You're just a couple of stupid show-offs.'

'She could do better than him.'

'He's not even good-looking,' Michael sniffed, then picked up an old tennis ball and started hurling it against the garage wall.

CHAPTER 8

Two years later

Deborah's social life was not going according to plan. At least, not the sort of plan her mother had envisaged and mapped out for her. She regularly made a point of telling Deborah about girls as young as sixteen, the daughters of people she knew, who were getting engaged. This, according to her calculations, didn't leave much time for Deborah.

She always stressed to her daughter what good matches these adolescent brides had made, leaving Deborah in no doubt as to what her mother expected of her. But unfortunately for Frances, Deborah was essentially a shy girl, and not one who could flaunt herself easily in front of others.

'And the wealthy ones know she's not going to come into any inheritance, so they're not likely to throw their sons at her,' her aunt Ruby added to the debate.

'So don't hang about too long, and don't be too picky,' was her mother's summation of the situation.

In spite of their foreboding, Deborah was developing into an attractive young woman, and because there was no dowry on offer, her mother reckoned that her daughter's face and overall appearance would have to be her fortune when the time came.

There was a youth club attached to the synagogue, which attracted a lot of youngsters, and along with others of her age, Deborah joined in with the activities organised for them. These included rambling in the Derbyshire hills, after which all the participants invariably came back soaking wet because none of them possessed the rudimentary equipment of hiking boots or even plastic mackintoshes.

They also had a dramatic society, and the man in charge of their productions was called Eddie Flax. He was an enthusiastic drama teacher, who encouraged the participants to make their own costumes, paint scenery, and generally put as much effort into each production as possible.

'Listen, boys and girls,' he addressed his would-be thespians, 'I'm going to enter our next production in the Dorothy Henshaw Gold Cup competition, so from now on it's shoulders to the wheel and all hands to the plough, so to speak.'

'Sir, what play are we going to do?' his usual male lead asked.

'It's called "Jeptha's Daughter", Martin.'

'What's it about?'

'It's about a man who made a pledge to God.' At that all his company let out a collective sigh of boredom. 'No, honestly, it's a first class story.'

'Can't we do something more modern, sir?'

'But it's a very appropriate play for a synagogue group to do. The point is that if the king—'

'What king?'

'Jeptha, that's his name.' He tried to stay patient. 'If he won a certain battle, he vowed he would sacrifice the first living thing he saw after his victory, and that turned out to be his own daughter, giving the play its dramatic edge.'

'Who is going to play him?' Martin asked, knowing full well it would be himself.

"We'll have auditions,' Eddie assured him, giving him a sly wink at the same time.

Deborah was given the part of the hapless king's daughter, and she was determined to shine in the role. With Peggy's help, she made her own costume, using an old nylon nightdress, and Michael offered his help with scenery painting. In time the fledgling company created what was supposed to be old Babylon, on a black backdrop with blue paint for the sky, a yellow sun, and palm trees for authenticity.

Martin's mother aged her son's black hair with lots of talcum powder. She also knitted a false beard for him using wool she unravelled from a grey jumper of her husband's. Both he and Deborah wore crimson capes made from crepe paper to indicate their royal lineage, and gold cardboard crowns.

The competition was scheduled to take place in a local church hall, and along with other competing youth clubs, Eddie's group duly turned up with their costumes and props. Their play was chosen to go on first, and the cast fought for space with other would-be thespians in the vicar's vestry, the room that had been set aside as a dressing room.

About an hour before they were due to perform, a harassed looking vicar demanded to know if their costumes were fire proof. Nobody knew, so the vicar insisted that all the costumes had to be treated, which involved dipping them in a pail of noxious smelling liquid that was supposed to render them fireproof.

In the event, the only thing this actually achieved was to make all the costumes wet and uncomfortable, and it took Eddie's cast a supreme effort of will to act their hearts out with smelly liquid dripping off them and landing in small puddles all over the stage.

That performance turned out to be the only competition their youth club ever won, so maybe the vicar did them a favour after all.

The other highlight – or in Deborah's case lowlight – of her social life, was the youth club dance. This took place every six months, and was supposed to help the teenagers make new friends. But the reality was that the boys lined the walls, trying to look nonchalant, and the girls facing them desperately waited to be asked to dance.

'What are you going to wear?' Peggy tried to help Deborah dress for the occasion.

'I've only got the dress that aunt Ruby gave me.'

It was a hand-me-down and far too big on the bosom. But it never occurred to Frances that if she was trying to get her daughter to meet the marriageable sort of boys, she should get her clothes that showed her off to the best advantage.

'If you wear that, we'll need to stuff a few handkerchiefs down your bra,' Peggy suggested.

'Do I have to?'

'Of course – boys like a bit of cleavage.'

But even with the addition of several handkerchiefs and a wad of cotton wool, the girl still couldn't fill the dress out. Peggy styled her hair and lent her some of her make-up, but because of the ill-fitting dress, Deborah was unhappy with her appearance, and as soon as she entered the hall, tried to blend into the background as inconspicuously as she could.

On these occasions, the enthusiastic Eddie would wear his other hat – that of dance co-ordinator and chief barker. Before every new number, he would announce into his microphone what the next dance was going to be. So determined was he to make even the shyest teenager get up on the dance floor, that he bullied them mercilessly until he achieved his aim.

It was now midway through the evening, nobody had yet asked Deborah to dance, but what was even worse for the girl, was that her father had just arrived in the room. As soon as he entered, a large group of youngsters gathered round him as usual, and he appeared to be regaling them with a story that made them laugh and giggle. It was obvious to his daughter that they were really happy to see him, and when he shooed them back to their friends, she watched and envied them.

'Isn't that your dad over there?'

'Yes.'

'Why don't you go over like the others do?'

'I will later.'

Deep down she envied the other youngsters, and wondered why she couldn't feel the same way as they did about her own father. When they looked at him, they saw a man full of fun and understanding, but when she looked at him, she saw only problems.

After chatting with another group, he went across to Eddie Flax, and they greeted each other warmly. Then, with Wilfred by his side, he made his next announcement.

'The next dance, boys and girls, will be a ladies' excuse me.' Tucked away in her corner of the room, Deborah froze as he continued: 'So, girls, here's your big chance to ask the boy of your dreams to dance.'

At that moment, she wanted the floor to open up and swallow her, because she didn't have the courage to ask any boy who was remotely good-looking, convinced that they would turn her down. Unfortunately, out of the corner of her eye she could see her father willing her on, and the more his eyes bored into her, the more anxious she became.

Most of the girls worked quickly and soon all the best boys had been taken. In a cold sweat, Deborah plucked up the courage to approach the plainest boy in the room, one of the few who was left. He wore pebble-thick reading glasses and had a bad crop of acne. She didn't choose him because she actually wanted to dance with him, only because she thought he wouldn't refuse. Also she could still see her father's face, and it seemed to be getting darker and darker by the second.

'Excuse me ...'

'Yeah?'

'Would you like to dance?'

'Nah.'

This was humiliation in its purest form, and she had never before experienced it to such a degree. Close to tears, she ran out of the room, her cheeks burning with shame. When she reached the ladies toilets, she rushed into a cubicle where she stayed for the rest of the evening, shredding pieces of toilet paper to pass the time.

But there was still worse to come for her. Sitting nervously beside him in the car, her father never uttered a word until he collected Michael from a nearby coffee bar where his son had been meeting school friends. Then they set off on the journey home.

'I wouldn't have thought it possible,' he began in a tone that sent shivers down her spine and made her brother's ears prick up. 'My daughter spent the whole night without even one dance. You're as pretty as all the other girls, so how come you were completely ignored?'

'Leave her alone, Dad,' Michael tried to intervene, but Wilfred carried on as if he hadn't heard.

'How do you think I felt, seeing my daughter, a complete wallflower?'

'All right, she's heard you now.'

'My own daughter.' His voice rose as he rammed home his point.

'It's always about you, isn't it?' Michael said suddenly, but Wilfred chose to ignore him.

'And you can tell your mother to buy you a new dress, I give her enough money.'

'For God's sake, leave her alone. She couldn't help it.'

Wilfred swerved dangerously into the kerb and put his foot down hard on the brake.

'This has nothing to do with you, so shut up.'

'Then stop bullying her.'

'How dare you speak to me like that!'

Deborah could feel the tension in the car like icy water being thrown at her, but breathing hard and with his face a purple colour, Wilfred eventually started the engine again. As soon as he pulled out into the traffic, Michael continued recklessly:

'We can't all be perfect like you.'

She knew the matter wouldn't end there, and tried to put her hand out to stop him. But as soon as they reached home, she ran out of the car and went to the only person who would understand.

'He made those kids feel so great, and me feel so awful, I hate him, Peggy.'

'What a waste.'

'It's because I'm ugly. Helen Green wears mascara and tight skirts and boys ask her to dance all the time, and they do things to her. What am I going to do?'

'Now you listen to me. First of all, you're very pretty, so don't let anyone tell you different.'

Then Peggy told Deborah to close her eyes and she liberally applied mascara onto the girl's long, thick eyelashes, and when she opened her eyes again, they had been transformed into giant, black panda circles.

'Peggy, I look so common, it's wonderful.'

'There now, you look gorgeous.'

Deborah stared into Peggy's mirror, and a vamp in a badly fitting dress was staring back at her.

'But how do you get them to dance with you?'

'Look deep into their eyes, then laugh at all their jokes.'

'Most of them aren't even funny.'

'That's not the point, and never let them know how clever you are. Men don't like women who are cleverer than them, and that's all you need to know.'

'Is that how you got Eric?'

'More or less.'

*

The vexed question as to what type of a man her father really was had been troubling Deborah more and more. Try as she might, she couldn't reconcile the two sides of her father's personality, the public one that people loved so much, and the private man who was the source of so much pain to his family.

His pastoral care of the elderly was so exemplary that one old lady even thought he was the messiah, and as a result his children benefited immensely from her misconception. She bought them all wonderful gifts, which were far more generous than anything they'd ever received from their parents. It was obvious that Wilfred Steinberg loved his fellow men, and they always responded in kind, but his daughter always came back to the same nagging question.

'Is our dad really religious?'

'He's a rabbi, isn't he?'

'I know he does all the things rabbis are supposed to do, but is he holy – like Leo Weitz, for example?'

Michael pondered the question but couldn't come up with an answer either. They were only too aware of his faults, but to listen to their mother, they would have come away thinking that he was a dangerous, unprincipled lunatic, living life on a precipice.

But as she got older, it dawned on Deborah that her mother's problems were largely of her own making, and Frances's attitude to anything that she didn't understand was to see it only in the starkest shades of black and white. There were no shades of grey in Frances's thinking.

'I reckon he's like the curate's egg,' Michael said finally, 'good in parts. Perhaps they both are?'

*

One Friday night, when Wilfred was waiting to be served his dinner, he turned to his youngest son.

'How did you get on in your maths test?'

Frances was in the kitchen, preparing to serve the chicken soup. It was a peaceful Sabbath evening around the dining room table until Wilfred asked Jake the question.

'He failed,' Michael said nonchalantly, then Jake grinned nervously.

'No big deal.'

Both of them saw their father's eyes widening ominously.

'You won't get into university without maths.'

'University isn't the be all and end all'.

'Then what sort of a career do you envisage for yourself – road sweeper, refuse collector perhaps?'

'Oh, shut up.'

That was the moment Wilfred exploded, smashing his fist onto the table. Peggy, who had just entered the dining room holding a plate of soup, froze in the doorway.

'Don't you dare speak to me like that.'

'Then get off my back.'

Peggy took one fearful step into the room, and although Wilfred saw her, he had no intention of stopping now.

'Now, you listen to me. If it hadn't have been for my influence, you'd never have got into that school in the first place.'

'That's not true …'

Deborah started to say, then thought better of it. Jake was clever enough to have got there on his own merit, so she had a lot of sympathy when he shouted back at his father:

'And if it wasn't for you, we'd all be in the gutter, and if it wasn't for you …' Peggy lifted her hand as if to stop him, but he continued recklessly, 'we might be a normal family!'

His youngest son was sweating, and his face was puce with anger. Frances was now also at the door, and she stared in horror as Jake pushed his chair back from the table, then ran towards the glass partition doors separating the lounge from the dining room.

'Sit down this instant!'

But Jake was in such a blind rage that he smashed his fist into a pane of glass. It shattered into dozens of tiny shards which dropped onto the floor, then he ran out of the room with blood gushing from his hand. Peggy shoved the plate of soup into her startled employer's hands, then ran after him.

'Finish your supper,' was all Wilfred could say.

It took Peggy a long time to calm the boy down, and as soon as she could, Deborah excused herself from the table and went to her own room, still shaking from the outburst. She could hear Peggy soothing Jake, and she also heard his tortured sobs.

'He doesn't mean it, love, he just wants what's best for you.'

'He thinks I'm a nancy boy just because I can't do maths.'

'No he doesn't.'

'And sometimes I wonder if I am.'

That made his sister sit bolt upright on her own bed.

'Now you're talking daft.'

'But it's obvious – look, I've never had a girlfriend, and even Nigel Foulks has taken a girl to the pictures, and he's nothing to look at.'

'Maybe the right one has never come along?'

'Maybe they think I'm odd too.'

'If I were your age, I'd go out with you.'

'Don't ever leave, Pegs, I don't know what I'd do without you.'

At about three o'clock the following morning, Wilfred woke up with severe pains in his chest. He was crying out, clutching his chest, and sweating profusely. Frances was alarmed, and called the doctor. Michael and Deborah went to see if there was anything they could do to help, but she shook her head.

'Go back to bed, he'll be all right.'

As soon as the doctor arrived, Michael rushed him upstairs. Deborah was waiting outside her bedroom door, but Jake, if he heard any commotion at all, decided to stay firmly in his room, as did Peggy. Deborah caught a glimpse of her mother looking very drawn when the doctor went into her room, and after a few minutes she heard him say:

'We must get him into hospital.'

An ambulance arrived shortly afterwards, and now all the family watched anxiously as the crew carried him out on a stretcher, followed closely behind by Frances and the doctor. They had never seen their father ill before. He never caught anything, neither influenza nor stomach upsets, and always seemed strong and invulnerable.

Deborah watched with mounting trepidation. Frances was the sick one, not him. This was some terrible mistake she reasoned, but after the ambulance had driven out of their road, she spotted Jake leaning over the banister. His face was a picture of unadulterated guilt.

Nobody slept much during the remainder of that night, and they just toyed with their breakfasts the next morning. Peggy insisted they went to school even though they argued vociferously with her; but just when the three of them were about to leave the house, a taxi drew up outside and Frances got out of it with deep lines etched on her face. They waited for her at the front door.

'Probably just a warning,' she said, looking from one to another. 'But they're keeping him in just to be on the safe side.'

'What caused it?' Michael asked, then she shot a cruel look in Jake's direction.

'Worrying about him, I expect.' Michael and Deborah winced, but Peggy added loyally:

'And all that fatty food he eats doesn't help.'

'Can we see him?'

'You can take him some clean pyjamas after school.'

'Why don't you go up to bed now?' Peggy suggested, 'and I'll bring you a nice cup of tea.'

'Thank you, that's very kind.'

And for the time being another temporary peace descended on the household, but Jake steadfastly refused to go with the other two to the hospital, and they in turn felt a degree of sympathy for him.

After school that day, Deborah collected her father's pyjamas and some basic toiletries, then on an afterthought, slipped his favourite after-shave lotion into the package. He had been taken into the Royal Infirmary, and it took her and Michael quite a while to locate the ward he was in. Eventually, when they found the cardiac unit, they approached the nurses' station.

'Can you tell us where we can find Rabbi Steinberg?'

'Oh, he's already got a visitor.'

His son and daughter exchanged puzzled glances.

'Mum said it was only the family who were allowed.'

'I know that, but the lady said she was his cousin.'

'Well, can we go in too?'

'I'm afraid only one of you can go in at the moment. Two visitors maximum, that's the rules, but when the lady leaves, the other one can go in as well.'

Michael indicated Deborah should go first, so she picked up the bag of toiletries and walked down the ward in the direction the nurse had indicated. Every time she passed a bed, she peered at the occupant, but couldn't see her father in any of them.

She was about to go back and enquire again, when she spotted curtains drawn round a bed at the far end of the ward. She approached it cautiously, then heard the sound of a woman's laughter.

'You know I don't mind bringing it, Wilfred, but do you really think you ought to be eating this sort of thing?'

'I can't eat the muck they serve in here Evelyn, so you're doing me a *mitzvah*[12].' Deborah froze outside the curtains.

'But you told me you've got a family history of heart disease.'

'This was nothing, just a one off. You know me, I've never had a day's illness in my life, I'm as fit as a fiddle.' It was then that his daughter pulled the curtains open.

'Hello, Dad.'

As soon as she saw Deborah, Evelyn Fraser jumped off the bed as quickly as if she'd sat down on a bed of nettles, and Wilfred's eyes opened wide. But he couldn't make any sudden moves because his bed was littered with bags of fried fish and chips, all covered in thick, greasy batter.

'Don't mind me, dear, I was just passing, and ...'

Wilfred's pseudo-cousin was blushing a deep shade of crimson, and her father made a half-hearted attempt to push the bags away.

'Well, his family's here now, so you can go,' said Deborah.

'Yes, probably best.'

The woman looked more flustered than Deborah had ever seen her look before. It gave her a great deal of pleasure to witness one of her mother's main rivals in such a state, but she couldn't look at her father.

'Oh, and on your way out, please tell my brother to come in.'

Realising that she now had two Steinberg women to cope with, the expression on Evelyn's face was priceless. Humiliating the woman was nice, but doing the same to her father was making her feel sick.

He was discharged from hospital ten days later. The doctors insisted on keeping him in, although Wilfred asserted there was nothing wrong with him, even though his test results disputed that. His side of the family had a long family history of heart disease, and Wilfred was subsequently to lose two of his brothers to heart attacks within the next few years.

---

[12]*good deed*

The day before his release, the specialist tried suggesting some changes to his way of life.

'Take life easier, Rabbi – for at least six months – and to try to avoid stress.'

'Avoid stress, doctor, you must be kidding!'

'Rabbi Steinberg, you've been very lucky. That was a warning, and if you'll take my advice, you won't rush back to work, you'll eat sensibly and as I said, you'll try to avoid stressful situations.'

The congregation had been sending Wilfred gifts to the hospital and to his home. They included many boxes of chocolates, which he set upon devouring as soon as he got home. Also Frances had baked cakes to offer to people when they visited him, but Wilfred scoffed the lion's share himself.

The morning after his release from hospital, Jake stood uneasily in the doorway of his bedroom. Frances had finally stopped blaming him for his father's illness, but he still felt responsible for it.

'Can I get you anything, Dad?'

'Maybe a cup of tea son. Jake, I ...'

'Yes Dad?'

'Oh, nothing. A cup of tea would be much appreciated.'

'Dad?'

'Yes Jake?'

His son lingered shifting his weight from one foot to the other.

'No, it's ...'

'Did you say something?'

'I ... I'll get the tea.'

The tragedy for Jake was that he loved his father very much, probably more than his brother and sister did. Wilfred's tragedy was that he loved his last born a great deal, but never knew how to show it. Jake asked for little from his parents, and as a result got little in response.

CHAPTER 9

Three years later

'We've got to do something about Jake,' Deborah insisted to Michael.

These days their brother always seemed moody and distracted, and whenever his siblings tried to get through to him, he made it clear he wasn't interested in anything either of them had to say.

Jake appeared to have sailed through his early teenage years without too many problems. His command of Hebrew was excellent, and when he became thirteen, he not only recited all that a barmitzvah boy needed to, but also did the rest of the service single-handedly, causing many to mutter appreciatively 'like father like son'. Without putting much effort in, he was always top of his class at school, but none of this seemed to fulfil him or make him happy.

Jake only seemed content when he was locked inside his bedroom with his collection of classical music. Meanwhile the rest of the family listened to Beethoven, Bach and Brahms outside his locked bedroom door. Had they been able to see through the keyhole, they might have even seen him fast asleep while the concertos played. Unlike every other member of the family, classical music lulled his soul, and was his companion of choice.

'You know what's wrong with him? He needs to get laid,' was Michael's considered opinion.

'He's not old enough.'

'I did it when I was sixteen.'

'Who with?'

'A girl who worked on the sweet counter in Woolworths.'

'How old was she?'

'Bit younger.'

'I haven't done it yet.' Deborah said it with a sigh of regret.

'Well you shouldn't. Nice Jewish girls don't, that's why Jewish boys have to practise on the Christians.'

Because it had been drummed into her so often in the past, Deborah accepted the logic of this without question. Moreover, most of her female friends tended to agree with those sentiments.

'I've got an idea,' Michael continued with the same train of thought. 'You know it's his birthday soon?'

'So?'

'So why don't you and I give him the ideal birthday present?'

'Which is?'

'A trip to Amsterdam.'

'He went there last year with the school.'

'The school took them to art galleries and on the canals, but not to the working girls.'

'Working girls?'

'God, you're so ignorant, the ones who sit in the windows.'

Although exasperated by her lack of worldliness, Michael went on to describe what the girls in the windows did to make a living, and how he thought it would be the best birthday present they could ever give their brother.

'You and me could pay for the ferry ticket, which shouldn't knock us back too much.'

'But Mum and Dad would notice he was missing.'

'Not if we told them it was a school field trip to … France or somewhere. Then we could tell them we'd offered to pay for it as his present to save them the money. That way, it's a win-win situation for all.'

It didn't take much persuasion to get Jake to agree to the suggested present, but his brother and sister decided it would be more fitting if Michael made all the necessary arrangements.

'It's not really the sort of thing that our Deborah should get involved with,' he explained.

What they didn't bargain for was that Jake confided in his friend Nigel, who immediately decided to go with him. Jake advised Nigel to use the same excuse with his parents as Jake had done, but Nigel went one better and even managed to get his parents to pay for the so-called field trip.

The weekend arrived, and the two boys boarded a train from Manchester to Hull, from where they would catch the North Sea ferry to Amsterdam. Before he left, Peggy insisted on packing Jake some sandwiches.

'I've put some Kit Kats in as well, just in case you get peckish in the evenings, and you can share them with your school mates.' She then kissed him goodbye, and he winced as he took the parcel of food from her.

'Should we ask him to ring us when he's done it?' Deborah suggested to her elder brother.

'No, some things should remain private.'

The boys had booked to stay in a youth hostel on the outskirts of Amsterdam, and in their excitement at what promised to lie ahead, they devoured the parcel of sandwiches and Kit Kats before the train had even pulled out of the station.

The ferry crossing was rough, with high waves crashing against the side of the boat. It was a blustery November day, and neither boy had ever been on a boat before. Jake was the first one to be sick, but he managed to reach the lavatory before depositing the contents of the packed lunch and most of the Kit Kats down the bowl. Nigel was not so fortunate, and his offering went over the boat rail onto the deck below, with a good proportion of it landing on his shoes.

'God, you stink,' Jake said when they were walking the length of the Haarlemmerstraat in the red light district, that evening.

'It's my shoes, I tried cleaning them with the bathroom towel, but couldn't get it out from between the laces.'

'Whose towel did you use?'

'Mine, of course.'

'Well for your sake, I hope your bird isn't too fussy.'

They had quickened their pace, and were now walking through a narrow street where scantily dressed women were either sitting or standing in almost every window. Both boys' eyes were almost popping out of their sockets.

'Have a look at those Bristols.' An enormous breasted woman in a see-through top grinned at them from her window, and Jake started salivating.

'Ask her how much.'

'Excuse me … er, Miss.'

'Fifteen dollar for you.' She didn't have time to waste on niceties. 'And I make it ten dollar each if your friend also come.'

'At the same time?'

'Whatever you want.' The two boys had a hasty conversation, and decided they would prefer to go one at a time.

'Fifteen dollars is about ten quid,' Nigel said. 'You can go first.'

'I don't mind if you want to go first.'

'No, it was your idea to come, you go first.'

As they walked inside the building where she had her booth, both were trembling, and Jake could hear Nigel's teeth chattering as well.

'You OK?'

'Yeah, it's just a bit cold here.'

When they reached the outside of her booth, they knocked politely and she yelled out unceremoniously.

'You got Johnnies?' Jake looked anxiously at his friend, who dug into his rucksack.

'I got a packet for each of us,' Nigel whispered, sweat gathering on his forehead. 'Have you ever used one?'

'No, but I'm sure she'll show us how.'

Her booth was tiny, but there was a nylon curtain, which she pulled across when Jake went in. Nigel waited his turn on the other side of the curtain, growing more anxious with every second that passed. The woman, who was now clad only in a tiny G-string that barely covered her sagging pudenda, indicated that Jake should come onto her bed, but he didn't know what to do with his clothing.

'First put money on table, then take trousers off.'

'Only trousers?'

'Keep coat on if you like, it's cold tonight.'

Nigel listened intently to everything that was being said behind the curtain, and to his shame he found himself growing hard. He tried to concentrate on anything other than his tumescence, and even tried whispering the words of the French national anthem to distract himself.

Inside her cubicle, Jake had more important things on his mind.

As she had instructed, he let his pants fall to the floor, then watched her slowly lower her G-string. He tried to take off his Y-fronts, but his straining erection made that a more complicated business than it normally was. Except for girlie magazines, he'd never seen a woman fully naked before, especially one with such enormous breasts. Her huge areolas reminded him of well-baked bagels, and his eyes were rooted to them.

Unable to contain himself any longer, he lurched awkwardly towards the bed, but remembered the condom just in time. He turned round to look for it in his pile of discarded clothing, but unfortunately her breasts were jiggling impatiently, and completely distracted, he decided to ignore her instructions.

Then he hurled himself towards her bed, but before he could manage to get within inches of her, he came copiously over the dirty sheet, not having touched even one of her huge appendages. He felt the blood rise to his face in shame.

'First time?'

'Please can I try it again?'

'No, cost you another ten dollar.'

She had already pulled her G-string back on, so he quickly calculated his financial situation. To his dismay he realised that at this rate he would have gone through most of his money before he had even slept the night in the youth hostel.

He looked down at his limp penis disconsolately, then picked up his underwear and trousers. He felt like crying, but when he opened the curtain for Nigel to take his turn, his friend was nowhere to be seen.

'Tell your friend come in now.'

'He's gone.'

'Where gone?'

'How the hell do I know?'

'Then you give another five dollar.'

'Don't be crazy ...'

'Or I call police.'

Having walked the length and breadth of the red light district, he eventually found Nigel at the youth hostel, and although his friend insisted he had decided to try another girl, Jake was unconvinced.

'And you owe me five dollars, so pay up.'

'Less two and sixpence for the condoms.' Jake didn't like to admit that his was still in its packet. 'So d'you reckon she was worth it?'

'Course, how about yours?'

'Smashing.'

In spite of his apparent bravado, Nigel looked very disappointed, and the two of them spent the remainder of the evening watching a Dutch football match on the television in the youth hostel lounge, neither understanding a word of what was said.

The following morning Michael got an unexpected phone call from Jake who sounded very anxious.

'It's bloody freezing here, and when we got to the bloody docks they said there's no bloody ferries today because of bloody gale force winds, and they don't bloody expect to leave till tomorrow.'

'All right, keep your hair on.'

'But Mum and Dad will be furious if I don't arrive home.'

'So I'll tell them what you've told me.'

'But I'm supposed to be in France, and that's not on the bloody North Sea.'

'Mum won't know the difference.'

'But he bloody well will.'

'Don't worry, I'll think of something. Anyway, how was it?'

'What's he saying, did he enjoy it?' Deborah was tugging at her brother's sleeve.

'He can't get back, wants to know what we should tell them?'

'That's easy, say the ferries are on strike, they'll never know.'

'She's a genius, your sister.'

'I'm running out of money.' Michael could hear the beeps, so shouted into the phone:

'The ferry company's on strike and the whole school is stranded. We'll sort it out but you've got to tell us everything when you get back.'

That night a desultory pair of boys walked the streets of Amsterdam to pass the time. Between them they had barely enough money to buy a sandwich to share, then spend another night at the youth hostel.

When Jake finally made it home the following day, he assured his brother and sister that losing his virginity had been a mind-blowing experience, but Michael pressed him for more details.

'So what was she like, was she blond all over, if you know what I mean?'

'Don't be so disgusting.' Deborah wrinkled her nose in distaste.

'You never told me anything about your first time, so why should I tell you?'

'Because we paid for yours.'

'Don't worry, I'll pay you back.' With that he picked up his rucksack and made his way up the stairs to his bedroom.

'At least it proves he's not a homo,' Michael assured his sister when Jake was well out of earshot.

*

Deborah had never considered herself a sporty type, but that term, against all the odds, she'd been picked to be on her form's cricket team. Although it was an all-girls' school, they were encouraged to take part in all sports regardless of the gender they were usually associated with. Hockey and lacrosse were played in winter, and cricket and tennis in the summer. The girls were also made to do gym classes twice a week.

'Deborah Steinberg?'

'Yes, Miss Corfe.'

'Over here one moment.' Deborah looked across at her friends as the Games mistress beckoned her over.

Millicent Corfe was a powerfully built woman who had short, steely grey hair, and when she called out, her voice was as strident as a man's. Every day of the school week she wore sturdy grey shorts and a man's jumper, and the girls guessed that she probably wore the same thing at the weekend also.

'Don't dawdle, Steinberg!' the woman barked, running her hand impatiently through her crew-cut hair. 'You'll be pleased to know that I've decided to pick you for the first eleven cricket team this term.'

Deborah wasn't sure whether she was pleased or not. When she had been chosen to be on the lacrosse team the previous winter, 'Corfie' as the girls called her, had told her to play in goal. Throughout the season, the thought of getting hit in the face by a hard lacrosse ball had terrified her. Her mother had always made it abundantly clear that her face would ultimately be her fortune, and the protective padding the team were given to wear didn't stretch to any body parts above the shoulders.

Many of her team-mates were strapping six footers, even though they were still only teenagers. Most were the daughters of farmers from Derbyshire and the Peak District, and Deborah reckoned that they must have been reared like intensively farmed cows. Because of this, they were veritable amazons, and when they hurled a lacrosse ball at another player, the recipient needed to have all their wits about them to dodge the incoming missile.

Deborah was never one hundred per cent sure whether selecting her to be the goal keeper on the lacrosse team, wasn't just another subtle form of anti-Semitism on the part of the gym mistress. But thankfully for her the lacrosse season had now come to an end, and the cricket one had just begun.

Rumours had been circulating round the school for several weeks that there was to be an inter-school cricket tournament that would take place soon. It would feature all the schools that played cricket in the area, whether they were specifically girls' or boys' schools.

'At least we'll get to play at some boys' schools,' she told her friend Laura, who had also been chosen for the team.

In the first round of the competition, her school was due to play against an all-boys' grammar school, and because of that opportune fixture, the girls couldn't wait for the tournament to get started.

In those days, there was very little contact between different sexed schools, so a match like this was just the sort of opportunity the pubescent girls had been waiting for. For Deborah, there was also an added bonus. At last she would get to meet some of those exotic creatures who so far had played no part in her life at all, Christian boys.

In the event, the boys of the William Hulme Grammar school beat the girls of Withington High School, fairly and squarely. Maybe they deserved their victory, or maybe the girls on the opposing team were playing an entirely different game to the one they usually played when there were no boys around. At their own school the girls didn't keep stopping to reapply their lipstick, in fact they didn't dare wear any make-up at all.

In Deborah's case, when the tall blond boy bowled the ball to her while she was batting, she couldn't see him clearly enough through the thick layers of mascara she'd applied just before the match, and which were now threatening to restrict her vision. However, she did see enough of him to know that he was gorgeous.

After the match had been played, the boys served their visitors afternoon tea in the school canteen, and for the first time in her teenage life, Deborah got to talk to non-Jewish boys. Of course they had the subject of cricket in common, so there was no awkward segregation of the sexes or lining the walls, like in her synagogue youth club.

However, the main advantage for her during that day, was that she was the only naturally olive skinned girl amongst a sea of weather beaten English complexions. As a result, she stood out from the rest and had no shortage of admirers hovering round during tea.

The girls had arrived on a specially chartered coach, and they were expected to return to their school on the same coach. After tea, when Deborah was reluctantly dawdling back towards it, the blond Adonis who had bowled her out, rushed over to talk to her.

'Hi, my name's Ian, Ian Christianson.'

He couldn't have chosen a worse surname if he'd tried. But he smiled as he said it, and from then onwards it felt to Deborah that the sun was shining more brilliantly, the birds were singing more sweetly, and God was truly in his heaven.

'I'm Deborah … Steinberg.' She added her surname a tad reluctantly just in case he didn't like Jews. But he grabbed hold of her hand to shake it, and then even the angels in their firmament began to smile.

'Pleased to meet you, Deborah.'

From that day onwards, Deborah and Ian met most days after school. He engineered it so that he got on the same school bus as her, then he would walk her home. It was called walking, but in reality they dragged their feet as slowly as they could, and often stopped in bus shelters to hold hands while gazing into each other's eyes. Just to be on the safe side, she always made sure he never actually came too close to her road in case they were seen by anybody in her family.

'I'm going to play tennis with some school friends in the park,' Deborah announced one day. Peggy was somewhat surprised because Deborah had just spilled out a lot of information that she'd never actually asked for.

No sooner had she said it, then she flew out of the front door, and as soon as she rounded the corner, ran to the bus shelter where Ian was waiting for her. He had taken the precaution of bringing his racket, but they had no intention of playing tennis that day.

*

The differences between Deborah and Ian were immense, but the pleasure they got from discovering all of them was intense. The two of them came to the conclusion that there wasn't one thing they had in common, except each other. She was dark, he was fair. She was Jewish, he was Christian. She was warm-blooded, he was cool, but when they kissed each other, all the differences magically seemed to disappear.

He told her he thought about her so often that he couldn't study. Perhaps she did or perhaps she forgot to tell him that when she was supposed to be paying attention at school, she wrote his name over and over again in the margins of her notebook. Ian and Deborah Christianson, or Mr and Mrs Ian Christianson, just to see how it looked.

Her first real love affair nearly came to a sticky end because of the interference of the one person in the house that Deborah trusted the most.

'You do understand why you can't collect me from my house?' she asked Ian at least once a day.

'Because I'm not Jewish.'

'And it's much worse for me because my father's a rabbi.'

'I suppose so.' He appeared to understand her predicament, indeed it made their relationship seem even more poignant than ever, his Montagu to her Capulet, so to speak.

However, one day when they were dawdling near her road, she turned to give him a goodbye kiss, when she spotted Peggy rushing towards them, but burdened down by several bags full of shopping.

'I must go.'

'Let's go to the pictures on Saturday.'

'Can't.'

She saw Peggy getting closer, then ran from him and rounded the corner of their road. As soon as she reached her house, she let herself in then ran upstairs to her room with her heart thumping.

She heard Peggy come in and go straight to the kitchen. She also imagined her putting the groceries away, then finally heard her coming up the stairs. By that time she had surrounded herself with all her schoolbooks, and was pretending to be studying hard, so barely looked up when Peggy walked into her bedroom without knocking.

'Who was that boy?'

'What boy?'

'The one you were kissing.'

'Wasn't me, must have been someone else.'

'Oh really, she looked just like you.' Peggy watched her with a grim look on her face, and her feet planted firmly on the carpeted floor.

'Oh, that one – no, he's just someone we played cricket with. He was on the other team.'

She was doing her level best to sound nonchalant, but sweat had started gathering in her armpits, and she could almost feel new acne spots breaking out on her guilty face.

'And what do you think your parents would say?'

'About what?'

'A tall, blond boy, who if I didn't know better, I could have sworn wasn't Jewish.'

'Please, Peggy, you won't tell, will you?'

'That depends.'

'I'll do anything you want.'

'What is he, Catholic, Protestant?'

'I don't know.'

'Now, you listen to me, young lady, boys like him are only after one thing. And after they've got it, you'll never hear from them again.' Peggy's face looked pained, as if she was talking from experience.

'He's not like that, Pegs, honestly.'

But the maid didn't appear to be convinced, so from then

onwards Deborah did everything she could to stay in her good books. Every night, she helped her with the washing up, even though Frances scowled as if to say it wasn't her daughter's job. She offered to paint Peggy's nails before her next date with Eric, and one day she presented her with a new lipstick that she'd bought with her pocket money.

'I saw this, and I thought it would look super on you.'

Eventually Peggy appeared to be placated, and the threat of imminent exposure seemed to have died down. But just to be on the safe side, the young lovers continued to meet, but now more discreetly.

*

Wilfred was now fully recovered from his stay in hospital, and one morning he received a letter that bought a huge smile to his face.

'Why are you grinning like a Cheshire cat?'

'Because, my dear, the Hebrew Union College of America are planning to give me an honorary doctorate of philosophy.'

'Why you?'

'In recognition of my achievements in inter-faith relations, they say. So from now onwards, I can call myself Rabbi Doctor Steinberg instead of plain Rabbi Steinberg,'

'And can you see patients as well?' Jake asked.

'No, unfortunately I wont be that kind of a doctor.'

'If he was a doctor, he'd like to be a gynaecologist,' Michael whispered to his sister when their father was out of earshot.

The degree ceremony was due to take place the following month, and the university proposed sending him a ticket to fly to New York to receive his degree. Flying across the Atlantic in a Comet aeroplane would take the better part of a day, as they had to touch down and refuel in Newfoundland, after which passengers had to re-board the aircraft for several more hours to reach New York.

'Are you going with Dad?' Deborah asked her mother.

'He says it's too expensive for me to go with him, but I'm not really that bothered, it'll be nice having the house to myself.'

Four weeks later, the entire family stood at the BOAC check-in desk in Ringway airport whilst Wilfred completed the travel formalities.

'And don't forget to buy me one of those plastic see-through handbags,' Deborah reminded her father. They were all the rage among her contemporaries.

'What about you?' he asked Frances.

'Some new pearls would be nice.'

His sons had already put in their orders for baseball sets, so he pecked each of them on their cheeks before walking off towards the departure gates. Once he had gone through, Frances sighed contentedly.

'A few weeks of peace.'

After her father's departure, Deborah and Ian met more openly in the park. They ate at their usual bench, and she decided to share a Jewish joke with him.

'She was only a rabbi's daughter, but she enjoyed a good bench in the park.'

'What, like this?'

'I explained it to you, when we say 'bench', it means to say grace.'

'So she said grace in the park.'

'Give me strength!'

It suddenly occurred to her, and she felt bad even acknowledging it, that had it been one of her brothers who was missing the point, she would have yelled at them in frustration.

'It's not much of a joke,' he sniffed. 'Anyway, tell me why your father's gone to America?'

'To get an honorary degree.'

'He must be very clever.'

'That's what people say, but I've never noticed.'

'My parents are out tonight.' He let the statement dangle in the air while Deborah slowly digested this information. 'They should be gone for hours.'

'You mean we could go to your house?'

'If that's all right with you?'

This was the first time he had suggested being alone together, and the thought excited her. She felt she was on the brink of the next stage of her life, and was desperately considering the pros and cons of the situation. While he waited expectantly, she reasoned it wouldn't hurt to go with him and maybe just watch the television.

'All right, as long as I'm not home too late.'

Ian jumped up from the bench, then wasted no time in getting to his house, pulling her along besides him. Deborah noticed the determined look on his face as they were nearing his street.

'You've never told me what your father does,' she said in an effort to slow the pace down.

'Tax inspector.'

'And your mother?'

'School dinner lady.' Running along beside him, the thought occurred to her that her parents wouldn't have much in common with his.

In comparison to the Steinberg house, the Christiansons' home was starkly simple. It was a neat, semi-detached in a road of similar houses, but the main difference between their two houses, was that here most had small, lovingly tended front gardens. Whereas in her road they had all been covered in tarmac to save the owners the bother of cutting their lawns.

'Let's go to my room,' he said as soon as he'd put his key in the lock.

'Let me look round first.' Uncomfortable echoes of Peggy's warnings had started reverberating in her brain.

Walking into what he called the parlour – which she called the lounge – she couldn't help but notice that there wasn't one superfluous ornament, silver knick-knack, or family wedding photo anywhere. The only decoration, which was on a wall at the side of the television, was three porcelain ducks in mid flight. Otherwise the walls and sideboard were bare.

She insisted on taking a quick peek into their dining room. In comparison to most Jewish houses she'd been in, theirs looked almost nude. There wasn't even the slightest hint of velvet drapes or flock wallpaper. There were no communicating glass doors separating the lounge from the dining room like in most Jewish homes, and not a single picture on any of the walls.

Chez Steinberg, there were several Canaletto prints depicting the Grand Canal and other views of Venice, all chosen by Frances. It was her mother's dearest wish to go there one day, and although her children referred to them as the cannelloni, when Deborah looked around Ian's house for some hint that they were interested in anything other than their garden, she couldn't find a thing.

Ian waited for her at the foot of the stairs, and she could see the anticipation in his eyes. As soon as she'd completed her tour of the two downstairs rooms and the modest kitchen, he indicated impatiently that she should follow him upstairs. On reaching his room, he threw himself down on his bed, and beckoned her over.

'It's comfortable here.'

She looked around and saw that the walls of his room were filled with posters of his football and cricket heroes. A Manchester United scarf was draped over his dressing table, and he had left a pile of worn clothes in a heap on the floor.

As soon as she lay tentatively besides him on his pillow, his hands were all over her. She tried to relax but responded nervously, and after a few minutes, his hands started straying below her waistline, and his breathing became more laboured.

'They're all the same, only after one thing.' Peggy's words of warning were ringing like church bells in her ears.

'No, don't.'

'Please?'

'I mustn't.'

'Why not?'

Down went his hands again, and up went her defences. From deep within her came the implacable knowledge that she was now playing with fire. From as far back as she could remember, it had been relentlessly drummed into her that she had to remain a virgin until her wedding night.

'Because.'

'Because what?'

'Just because, that's all.'

Amongst her friends, it was commonly agreed that nice girls didn't go all the way. Certain areas of the body above the waist were fine for experimentation, but anywhere below the waist was strictly off limits. These inexperienced teenagers knew nothing about contraception, and more or less the same about how to create a baby.

Their only sex education had been taught in biology lessons, by studying the amoeba and common earthworm. If her memory served her right, the former multiplied by splitting their cells, and the latter were hermaphrodite, so no problem for them. As a result, neither species had done anything to increase her rudimentary knowledge of mating.

That didn't come to her until some time later when she became friendly with a girl whose parents were refugees to Britain. By the age of fifteen, this sexually precocious girl knew more about the art of lovemaking than most adults do in a lifetime, and eventually she became Deborah's tutor on the subject.

Her only other informant was Wendy, a painfully shy girl whose mother knew Frances from a sewing circle. Shy Wendy might have been, but sexually advanced she certainly was, and by a similar age to Deborah's other mentor, this girl had amassed enough knowledge to edit a pornographic magazine. But unfortunately for Deborah, all that knowledge was to come later in her life.

'Ian, I'd better be going home now.'

'But you can't leave me like this.'

'I'll be in trouble if I'm late.'

She was totally ignorant about the raging hormones of teenage boys producing erections. Even though he tried his hardest to persuade her to stay, she refused. The thought of her mother's and Peggy's combined anger made her even more determined to leave. She had strayed into territory she wasn't yet ready for, and a quick getaway seemed like the best solution.

'When will I see you again?' he asked.

'Soon, I promise.'

Something told her that this relationship could go no further at the moment, but she wasn't ready to abandon it just yet. Ian was her first love, but it had been drilled into her from as long as she could remember that if she did anything wrong she would bring shame on her parents, and that was a hard burden to carry at that age.

He walked her back towards her own home, both deep in their own thoughts. It never occurred to either of them that evening, that in time her maidenhead would be bartered to the man most willing to fork out the highest possible price for it. It took Deborah several more boyfriends to understand just how callous a person she'd been brought up to be.

*

Since Renee Mintoff had left the scene, Michael had become increasingly restless. He had one close friend from school; Graeme Sidebotham, a young man who had decided to become an artist when he finished his education. Not wishing to be left out, Michael saw himself as becoming a great author, and both he and Graeme made a decision that they would need to travel the world in order to gain inspiration for their chosen paths.

Michael was loath to confide his plans to anyone in the family, but increasingly spent more and more time plotting his future.

'You can't tell him anything,' Frances complained to Peggy. 'From what I can gather he intends to be a writer and travel the world, but as far as I know he hasn't written a thing yet. I blame that friend of his, he keeps filling our Michael's head with stupid ideas.'

'It's just itchy feet at his age, he'll grow out of it in time.'

In spite of her unease over her eldest, whilst Wilfred was away in America, his entire family seemed to be changing, and even Frances seemed happier. She laughed more, and had even started to make plans of her own for the future.

'How about you and I going on a holiday together, somewhere nice?' she asked Ruby one day. 'I'd love to go to Venice.'

'What about Capri, I've heard it's wonderful there?'

Ruby confessed that she'd fancied the island ever since she'd read that the popular singer Gracie Fields had gone to live there.

'I've seen pictures of her and that Italian husband in *Picture Post*. It looks so nice and sunny there, so what do you think?'

'Perhaps I should ask our Michael, he reads a lot about these sort of places.'

When she got round to discussing the idea with her eldest son, to her astonishment, he dropped his own bombshell.

'I'm going travelling too.'

'Where?'

'Around the world.' He said it as simply as if he'd just announced he was going to Blackpool, or maybe further afield like Cornwall.

'But what about school?'

'I'll do it after I've taken my highers.'

'And who do you think is going to support you on this jaunt?'

Shaken out of her reverie about sunny Italian islands, she now sounded more like Wilfred; even her voice had taken on his tone.

'I'll find jobs.'

She quickly realised that this new information went way beyond her ability to cope, so for the first time since he'd left, she started to look forward to Wilfred's return, when she was certain he'd put a stop to all this nonsense.

But Michael wasn't the only one planning change. Since his father's heart scare, Jake's state of mind had been one of perpetual unease, but because he kept his head down and got on with his schoolwork, nobody bothered to pay him much attention. Each individual member of the household had become so deeply entrenched in their own worlds that nobody could have had any forewarning of what happened next.

It was late on a Thursday evening, and Peggy and Deborah were watching television. Frances was knitting a cardigan by the fireside, and was totally engrossed in following the pattern. She had two coloured balls of wool in her lap, but because it was such an intricate design, hadn't looked up for at least an hour. When the television programme came to an end, Deborah stretched and yawned.

'Time for bed.'

It was then that Frances looked up for the first time. She closed the knitting pattern and tidied up her balls of wool, and asked casually:

'What time did Jake go to bed?'

'I don't know, I never saw him go up.'

'Hasn't he got an exam tomorrow? Deborah, be a love, and on your way up just check that he's not still studying.'

Deborah said goodnight, then headed up the stairs towards her brother's room. She noticed that the light was still on in Michael's room, so she put her head round his door.

'Night.'

He grunted by way of response, and she continued towards Jake's bedroom. The door was ajar, so she pushed it fully open. Once she stepped inside, the only light in the room was a reflection from the street lamp outside their house. She presumed Jake had forgotten to draw his curtains, so tiptoed into the room, intending to draw them for him. It was then that she spotted his bed was empty.

'He's not here!' she shouted out in surprise.

'Don't be daft.'

She heard Peggy running up the stairs, then the two of them searched everywhere, but he was nowhere to be seen.

'Ring Nigel, he's probably there.'

Deborah ran to the phone in her mother's bedroom and dialled the number. Nigel's parents were irritated to have been disturbed so late at night, and snapped at her in response.

'He isn't here, in fact Nigel hasn't seen him for weeks.'

Then they took it in turns to telephone all his friends, but none of them knew where he was. By now Frances was convinced that her son was missing, and the rest of them were becoming very anxious.

'This is ridiculous, it's nearly midnight!' Frances screamed in a voice bordering on hysteria, while pacing up and down and getting more agitated by the minute.

'Have you tried all his friends?'

'Of course, what do you take me for?'

'Then perhaps we should call the police?' Peggy suggested.

'That boy does everything he can to embarrass me, he'll be the death of me.'

'I'll speak to Eric, he'll tell us what to do.'

Peggy dialled his home number, and he told her to report it to the station. They only had to wait another half an hour before a police car screeched to a halt outside. Eric had gone straight to the station, and was one of the two policemen who arrived at the house.

'Mrs Steinberg, can you give us a description of what the boy was wearing?'

'How do I know, maybe his school uniform or even his pyjamas?'

'Was there anybody you know of that he intended to meet this evening?'

'Why are you asking me these silly questions, why aren't you out there looking for him?'

Eric and his colleague exchanged looks, and collectively decided to keep calm and not rise to the provocation.

'Do you have a recent photograph of the lad that we could use?'

'There's that one from his barmitzvah,' Michael suggested.

'Don't be stupid, he's grown since then.'

'Well if it's the best you've got ...'

'Wait, I've got one.'

Peggy rushed upstairs and came back down with her purse. She took out a much-thumbed photograph of herself and Jake, taken in a photo booth. Frances looked horrified because she'd never seen it before; the snap showed the two of them laughing together happily.

'You can have this one.'

Throughout that night, Deborah could hear her mother's footsteps pacing up and down her bedroom. The only one of the household who managed to sleep was Michael, because she could hear him snoring. Eventually, to while away the hours, Deborah took out her diary and started to write.

Wednesday, October the fourteenth, Jake is missing, and I'm really worried.

In spite of herself, she couldn't manage to get beyond that first line, and eventually dropped off to sleep with the pen still clutched in her hand and the diary open on the bed cover.

Early morning light was peeping through the curtains when Michael shuffled into her room. He sat down on the edge of her bed, rubbing the sleep out of his eyes. She woke with a start when his weight descended onto the bed.

'D'you think he's gone for good?'

She sat up, groggily trying to make sense of Michael's question.

'Who knows? I don't think he's been happy for ages.'

'That makes two of us. I'm going as soon as I can.'

'Where to?'

'China?' That jolted her upright. 'Anywhere, as long as it's as far away from here as possible.'

'Why China?'

'Well, it's very interesting,' he started as if he were delivering a lecture to a group of students, and she fought to suppress a yawn. 'There's a people there called the Moso. They live in villages, and it's a matriarchal society ...'

'A what?' She was too tired for this sort of conversation after such a sleepless night.

'Women make all the decisions, and they don't marry like we do. I've read a lot about them, apparently the Moso men don't know who their children are, and the kids don't need to know who their fathers are either.'

'Sounds ideal,' she murmured, then lay down again on her pillow and closed her eyes.

'That's why I'm going.'

CHAPTER 10

After he got his wife's phone call, Wilfred took the first flight back that he could get on. Unbeknown to them, as soon as he'd received his degree, he'd taken the opportunity to do some travelling. First he'd visited Washington, then gone to stay with the dean of the university, who lived in New England. He'd taken the precaution of leaving a forwarding address with the hotel in New York, so it didn't take them long to trace him when Frances phoned in a state of near hysteria.

At the time, Peggy also had to be restrained from tearing her hair out, and Michael and Deborah didn't know how to cope with the two women who were supposed to be in charge of them. Secretly they too were very anxious because Jake had been missing for three days now.

The police still had nothing concrete to report, and when Wilfred arrived back at Manchester airport, he looked unshaven and red eyed. He got out of the taxi at his house, and nobody in the family could ever remember seeing him looking so unkempt.

'Your wife's in her room, she hasn't had much sleep,' Peggy said, opening the door to him. 'Can I get you something to eat?'

'Can't you think of anything besides food?'

'I was only trying to help.'

'I'm sorry,' he muttered. 'He'll be the death of me, that boy.' How often had she heard that before?

'Not just you,' she said. 'I'll make us all a cup of tea.' Then, as if on cue, Michael came into the kitchen and asked:

'Anything to eat, Peggy?'

'Is that all you can think about right now?' she snapped.

'Oh, hi Dad,' he muttered as an afterthought.

Whilst they were drinking their tea, each one staring miserably into their teacups, there was the sound of another car drawing up outside the house. The four of them rushed to the front door, and Wilfred almost pulled it off its hinges to open it. A bedraggled Jake was struggling up the front path, half dragged and half supported by Eric and his colleague.

Hearing the noise downstairs, Frances got out of bed and was on the upstairs landing, dressed only in her night-gown. She was supporting herself against the banister rail, looking pale and drawn. When she caught sight of the policemen, her legs buckled under her, and she fainted in a dead heap. Wilfred ran upstairs to help her.

'Here's your boy, safe and sound,' Eric said, handing him over to Peggy.

Before anyone could stop her, she flew at Jake and punched him several times. She was reigning fierce blows on his head and body, and Eric tried to pull her away from him.

'Get off me!' she screamed, then hit him as well. 'And don't you dare do anything to me like that again!'

She continued thrashing out at the hapless boy, until both policemen managed to pull her off him. Wilfred abandoned his wife on the landing floor, and bounded down the stairs two at a time.

'It's most kind of you to bring him back, officers,' he said, trying to catch his breath. 'May I offer you something to drink – a whisky or a brandy, perhaps?'

'Just doing our job, Rabbi, but we mustn't partake while on duty,' Eric answered formally, although he was now looking anxiously at Peggy out of the corner of his eyes.

'A cup of tea, then?'

'Best be on our way. I think this young man could do with something though, says he hasn't eaten for two days.'

When the policemen had left, they crowded round Jake, waiting for some sort of explanation, but all he could say was,

'I need the toilet.'

They parted to let him through, but as soon as he got to the bottom of the stairs and caught sight of his mother struggling to lift herself to a sitting position, he sat down where he was, and wept.

They found out later that he had spent his time wandering round the park by day, and sleeping in the shelters at night. Because the park was situated in a leafy suburb, he hadn't been too disturbed by tramps, drunks or dogs.

He'd originally taken enough food to last for a day, but by the third day he was desperate. He'd started begging at a hot dog stand for something to eat, and when they refused him he tried at an ice cream stall. It was they who alerted the police that there was a teenage boy being a nuisance.

Back home, nobody in the house knew exactly what to do with him, and that included his parents. Even though everyone wanted to know why he'd done it, they instinctively sensed that a softly-softly approach was necessary or he might just decide to take off again.

Finally, it was Peggy who broached the subject. Wilfred and Frances were itching to tell him exactly what they thought of his escapade and the heartache it had caused, but hadn't dared do so yet. Wilfred was also smarting at his enforced departure from America, and his brother and sister were equally annoyed at the consequent absence of any presents.

Eric tactfully suggested that they should let him sleep it off, then bring up the subject when he was feeling in a better frame of mind. However, Peggy had other ideas, and as soon as Jake was in bed and his parents were outside in the garden blaming each other, she took a tray of food up to his room. Then she sat down on his bed.

'Now, Jake, you've got to tell me why you did it.'

He turned away, but Peggy had time and patience on her side, and she wasn't going to move until she got an answer, so eventually he whispered:

'Because I was so fed up.'

'With me?'

'No, this place … nobody understands.'

'Understands what?'

'I'm different, I know I am.' Then he started to cry.

'No pet you're not, you're just like me, we enjoy the same things.'

He glared at her.

'But I'm a boy.'

She tried to put her arm round his shoulder, but he pushed her away roughly. Then suddenly all her patience was exhausted, and she barked at him like a Liverpool stevedore on the dockside.

'Now you listen to me, Jake Steinberg.' He winced as if it was his father who was hectoring him. 'You're different, of course you are, we can all see that. You're too clever, that's your problem, and you're trying to fit in with people you have nothing in common with. Most boys of your age are stupid in comparison to you.'

He stared at her in amazement while she paused for breath. When he tried to interrupt her, she silenced him with an imperious wave of her hand.

'Do you know, since you were about eight or nine, I've stood outside your room on many a night and heard you listening to that Beethoven fellow on the record player. Now, you tell me what your friends listen to, eh – Bill Haley, Herman's Hermits? Of course you're different, Jakie, you're streets ahead of all of us, except it's your brother who thinks he's the clever one, but don't tell him. So I never want to hear any more of this daft talk, and just you remember, no matter what you'll always be my boy.'

Jake later confided in Deborah that for the first time in many months, he felt a lot better about himself, even though Michael still continued to regard himself as the superior sibling of the Steinberg household.

*

Wilfred made a decision to introduce a new ceremony into the congregation, after he'd seen it in America and been impressed by it. Now, he would no longer let just the boys have a barmitzvah or coming of age ceremony, he decided to give the girls an equal chance to have their own celebration or confirmation, as he decided to call it.

So after his return, he asked for volunteers amongst the teenage girls of the congregation, and sixteen of them put their names forward. He also decided that his own daughter Deborah had to be amongst this first group to be confirmed, even though she would be the youngest of the group.

In due time he met with the girls and their parents to talk about the form of the service, and everyone including his daughter seemed to be excited about the prospect. He informed the parents that the confirmation service would take place on a Sunday, so as not to confuse it with the ceremony the boys undertook, which was always on a Sabbath morning.

They also made the decision that on the day of the ceremony all the girls would be dressed in white, and would wear small white skullcaps on their heads.

'You'll look like bloody vestal virgins,' Michael scoffed when Deborah told him.

'What does vestal mean?' Peggy asked when he continued to poke fun at the proposed service.

'That doesn't matter, so long as she knows what virgin means.' He then retreated to his room still smirking.

'Take no notice of him, love.'

It was also decided that at the conclusion of the service there would be a tea party for the girls and their families. Later that same evening, they would be allowed to invite ten friends apiece to a joint party that would take place in the synagogue hall.

'Can I ask girls from my class?'

'Only if they're Jewish,' her mother insisted, which ruled out inviting Ian. So Deborah thought it would be best not to mention the confirmation to him at all. Although they still continued to see each other, Deborah tried to limit their meetings to the park or other open spaces, so as not to put either of them in temptation's way, for the time being.

Frances, Peggy and Deborah then spent hours poring over fashion magazines, trying to decide what sort of a dress Deborah should wear on the day. Her mother was determined that her daughter would be the best dressed of all the girls, and Deborah was duly sworn to secrecy so as not to let any detail of the dress become common knowledge beforehand.

'Broderie anglaise, that's what it's going to be,' Frances announced one evening, thumbing through a fashion magazine, 'and I've seen just the ideal material in Affleck and Brown's.'

'But it's my decision,' Deborah said, knowing full well that it wouldn't be. The other two women smiled conspiratorially.

'I'll speak to Madame Pauline tomorrow.'

'But I'm going to decide the shape, and don't you dare let her put any beads or shiny things on it.'

'A little bolero over the dress would be nice, and maybe it could have a full skirt, with shoestring straps?' her mother added as if her daughter hadn't spoken, then she smiled dreamily, 'After all, you'll be a young woman soon.'

Wilfred was also determined that his daughter would shine on the day. After he had constructed the format of the service, he decided that the choicest part, that of reading from the scroll of the law, would be undertaken by Deborah. The only problem was that the Hebrew text had to be chanted or sung in the traditional manner, and Deborah's voice, like her father's, left a lot to be desired.

'Rabbi, there's another girl amongst the group who sings like an angel,' the choirmaster suggested.

'But our Deborah looks better, and I can practise with her every day,' Wilfred insisted.

A tussle then ensued as to which girl would do justice to the reading more, and Deborah patently was not the one. So Wilfred reluctantly had to bow to the choirmaster's superior musical expertise, but as a compromise they decided that the other girl would do the singing, then Deborah would do an English translation immediately afterwards.

The long awaited day of the confirmation arrived, and when the sixteen girls walked into the synagogue at the beginning of the service, even Peggy had tears in her eyes. She was sitting in a place of honour next to Frances, and the participants looked the very pictures of purity and in only seven cases, innocence.

Deborah walked at the head of one of two lines of girls, with her head up but her eyes downcast. She knew she looked lovely because even her brothers had said so. But she was anxious that people shouldn't think she was flaunting herself because she was the rabbi's daughter, or that he'd put her at the front of the line, not to mention given her the second choicest part of the service.

The day passed smoothly, and in the evening, Eddie Flax was in charge of the party. Parents, except Wilfred, were not invited to the evening party, and on this occasion Deborah's feet barely touched the ground. She never had to wait more then a few seconds before the best-looking boys sought her out to dance, and that evening she finally felt the heady surge of power that comes with being one of the most popular in the room.

Later, eating refreshments with a boy stationed at either elbow, she smiled at them both coquettishly.

'Fiddle de Dee.'

'What?'

'Haven't you seen *Gone with the Wind*?'

'No.'

'You should, it's very good,' she trilled. 'Now, which one of you two's going to get me some lemonade?'

Being on such a high, Deborah and the other guests failed to notice that Jeanette, the oldest of the confirmation girls was deep in conversation with Wilfred, who had a concerned look on his face. She appeared to be sniffling and blowing her nose a lot, then shortly afterwards he ushered her out of the room and they went upstairs to his office.

She was the tallest and most developed of the sixteen confirmees, and no sooner had she followed Wilfred into his office and pushed the door shut behind her, than she threw herself bodily at him. He looked horrified as she then attempted to force him up against his desk.

'Jeanette, what do you think you are doing?'

'You're the only one who understands me Rabbi,' she breathed heavily, as she tore at the buttons on the front of her dress. 'The only man who's ever listened to me.'

'That's my job, ' he said in horror, 'now be a good girl and put those things away.'

She continued to tug furiously at the front of her impressive 38C bra, trying to pull out one of her bosoms as a sort of offering to him, but Wilfred looked around frantically for an escape route.

'My family hates me, even my sister's jealous of me ...'

'Yes, but ...'

'But you said you understood when we were downstairs.'

Luckily for him she was having great difficulty with her efforts on the bra front, and he managed to push her away.

'My dear child, I only asked you to come up here because you were crying so much.'

'But I thought you wanted me as much as I wanted you.'

He quickly edged behind his desk, desperately trying to decide the best way to deal with the situation.

' Now look Jeanette, you're a lovely girl and I'm very fond of you and all the confirmation class, you've been a credit to the synagogue and me. But that's as far as it goes. Now dry your eyes and ...' he waved his hands manically towards the front of her dress, 'and go downstairs and have a good time with the others.'

As she redid her buttons, Jeanette smouldered resentfully, but Wilfred kept his eyes firmly locked on the door.

'Now off you go and shut the door behind you, that's a good girl.'

Only after she'd slammed the door till it rocked on its hinges, did Wilfred's breathing return to a semblance of normality. He desperately replayed in his mind the conversation they'd had in the hall, in case he'd inadvertently led her on, but he couldn't remember saying anything that might have misled her.

When he finally dared to return to the hall where the party was still in full swing, he sidled anxiously over to Eddie Flax.

'These kids grow up so fast, it's terrifying.'

'One of them's left already, the big girl, she told me the party's too tame.' He tsked to himself. 'Tame, I ask you!'

Six months after Jeanette's confirmation, her weight ballooned at an alarming rate. Some of the other girls gossiped unkindly that she was probably pregnant, although no-one knew who the father was. Others alleged that she had several boyfriends at the time, and even she wasn't sure who it was.

However when her parents challenged her about the obvious swelling underneath her gymslip, her reply made her father turn white and quake in his shoes.

'The Rabbi did it.'

'What?'

'Right after my confirmation.' At least she had the decency to blush while she said it.

'Rabbi Steinberg?' His face had taken on a purple hue.

'But Dad ...'

'Wilfred Steinberg's the saintliest man I know,' he finally managed to splutter, 'he's as pure as the driven snow, now go and wash your mouth out, you slut.'

Shortly afterwards Jeanette's father moved the entire family to Australia. Amongst their circle of friends it caused quite a scandal but once they had left, none of the other confirmation girls ever heard from Jeanette again.

*

Peggy's romance with Eric had taken a turn for the worse. She clung on desperately, but in her heart of hearts she knew that their relationship was on its last legs.

Life for Michael, on the other hand, was looking up. As soon as he finished his higher school certificates, he made good his threat and told his parents that he now intended to travel the world for a year.

'And afterwards, what are you going to do?' Wilfred demanded, rather predictably.

'Go to university if I still feel like it.'

His flippancy caused his parents a great deal of consternation, even though they'd been forewarned of his plans, but oddly enough it was his Uncle Sam who spoke the most sense on the subject.

'Let the boy get it out of his system,' he advised them. 'It's good to see more of the world than just Manchester, and it should make a man of him.'

A compromise was reached whereby Michael agreed to stay long enough in each country to find some sort of work to support himself, and Uncle Sam generously offered to pay for his ticket for the first leg of the journey, which Michael insisted was to Casablanca.

Of course everyone wondered, why Casablanca? But in a rare confidence, Michael told Peggy that he saw himself as the Humphrey Bogart type, which in some ways was true because he always wore his raincoat collar up behind his neck.

'If he thinks he's going to find an Ingrid Bergman look-alike waiting for him when he gets there, he's going to be very disappointed,' Peggy told Jake.

As it turned out there was no Ingrid, but he did manage to get his first job washing dishes in a small café in Marrakech. He wrote home regularly, but failed to mention that because he'd not managed to find his Ingrid in North Africa, he'd decided to move on.

He explained that he was going to get a passage on a small cargo boat sailing to Sardinia. It was due to dock in the port of Ajaccio, where he had arranged to meet up with his artist friend Graeme.

He's also been travelling like me, he wrote, *and he should be arriving any day now. PS, the weather's lovely.*

But once he reached Ajaccio, whilst he waited for his friend he was forced to scrounge food and lodgings off some fellow travellers. Their standard of hygiene left a lot to be desired, and Michael ended up in the local hospital suffering badly from gastro-enteritis.

Worse was to follow, because when he returned to their lodgings, he had lost a stone in weight and all his possessions had mysteriously disappeared. So too had his new traveller friends.

If Graeme arrived at all, Michael never got to find out. By now, not only had he used up all his funds, but was also clearly losing the will to carry on travelling. Late one night, Wilfred and Frances received a reverse charged telephone call from their son, and he sounded pitiful.

'Dad, I'm not well, and I haven't got any money to pay for medicines.'

'But last time we spoke you told me you had enough to last for a few months.'

'I sort of got robbed.'

'You *sort of* got robbed?' Wilfred fought hard to keep his patience. 'Did you or didn't you?'

'I did. They took everything except my sunglasses.'

'Hold on, let me have a word with your mother.'

There followed a hastily convened parental discussion, after which his parents said they would pay for another boat ticket for him on the condition that he went to Israel.

'I'm not interested in going there.'

'But it's the right sort of place for a Jewish boy.' He could hear his mother's shrill voice shouting in the background.

'You mean it's all right to get robbed in Israel, but not here?'

'Take it or leave it.' Wilfred had lost the last remnants of his patience, and he shouted down the phone: 'And we're only doing it on condition you stay there for the rest of the year!'

Back then, the term 'gap year' hadn't yet been coined. So Michael's year away was just a nuisance to be stoically endured, as far as his parents were concerned. In the event, and realising he had no other options, he agreed to go to Israel if they would fund his present financial crisis as well as the ticket there. However, in the deepest recesses of his mind, he said he'd go but never agreed to stay there.

*

While all this was happening, his brother and sister were both trying to decide what to do with their own futures. Deborah had been toying with the idea of going to art school for some time now, but when she mentioned it to Frances, her mother reacted as if she'd just announced she wanted to be a prostitute.

'Everyone knows art schools are full of hippies living in communes, and that's no place for a daughter of mine.'

'But my art teacher says I'm very good, and that's where you have to go if you want to be a dress designer.'

'Since when did we send you to Withington High to become a dressmaker?'

'I said designer, and you didn't send me there, I passed the scholarship, not that either of you ever noticed.'

Having just lived through the experience of dealing with her eldest son and his financial problems, Frances was in no mood to be swayed. As far as she was concerned, art school, bordello; there was no difference between them.

'Besides,' she added as an afterthought, 'there isn't enough money to pay for you and the boys. They'll have to go to university and get a proper education because one day they'll be the providers. You, on the other hand, will find a husband to look after you.'

She explained all this to her resentful daughter, and added that in her opinion further education would be an unwelcome distraction from her real aim in life, which was to find the said husband.

Bizarrely, that was how she and others of her class thought in those days, and even more bizarrely, her daughter accepted it without putting up much of a fight.

'The best thing for you when you leave school would be a secretarial course.' For a woman like Frances, female emancipation meant mastering the twin skills of shorthand and typing. 'If you can do those, you'll be able to go anywhere you want.'

'You mean until I find a husband who'll keep me for the rest of his life?'

'Oh Deborah, why do you always have to be so difficult?'

Her daughter had spent so much of her childhood listening to her parents fighting, that at this point in time couldn't stand the idea of even more arguments if she insisted on going her own way. They, like so many others in those days, had a much stronger hold over their children, because it was they who held the purse strings.

*

Peggy's romance with Eric had reached a dead end, and she and Deborah now gave a lot of thought to the subject of love, and consequently spent hours discussing what had gone wrong in Peggy's relationship.

'Do you think he couldn't cope after he saw you attacking Jake that day?'

'That's possible, I've never been in such a state as I was that day.'

If Peggy did mind about the break, she tried hard not to show it, and pretended that life would go on much the same way as it had before.

'Sometimes, when I compared Eric to you lot, I realised he was a bit too staid for me.'

'You mean you need a more dysfunctional sort, like the men in our house?' Peggy nodded her head sadly.

One of the few advantages that had arisen as a result of Michael's absence from the household, was that Frances's health seemed to have reached a plateau where it neither got any better, nor got any worse.

'So how are you today?' her sister Ruby would regularly ask. 'I must say you don't look so down in the mouth.'

'So-so.'

Frances invariably gave a non-committal reply. What she declined to tell her sister was that she was feeling better because Wilfred was seeing less of Evelyn Fraser, who according to Frances, was beginning to show her age badly. However, unbeknown to her, he was in fact seeing more of a wider selection of women.

Also she was becoming very involved with her latest project, which was to introduce her daughter to the twenty three-year-old son of a wealthy family in the congregation. The young man's name was Gordon, and he worked in the family jewellery business. Whenever Frances spotted his parents in the synagogue, she would make a beeline for them as if they were her most favourite people in the whole of Manchester.

She had a dual purpose in this endeavour. The first was to get her own engagement ring restyled at the cheapest possible price, but by far the more important one was to encourage Gordon to pay closer attention to Deborah.

Gordon's mother Christine had converted to Judaism after her boss Cyril Helfgot, who later became her husband, made her pregnant. Christine had worked behind the counter at one of the family's jewellery shops, and Cyril, the prodigal son, had been unable resist her blonde hair, blue eyes and enormous breasts, which nestled temptingly on the counter in front of the customers and himself every day.

To the chagrin of his elderly, religious parents, they started going out together, and when she fell pregnant with young Gordon, it was to Wilfred that they turned for help. The Orthodox synagogues in the town wouldn't countenance a religious conversion for Christine, but Wilfred Steinberg did.

Gordon was born in the early days of Wilfred's ministry, and duly had his barmitzvah under Wilfred's tutelage. According to his mother, when Gordon was born he was pink and plump. While he was growing up, the pink skin disappeared but the plumpness remained, and once he became an adult, he was pink and plump again but now with a fine covering of five o'clock shadow.

Frances started paying court to young Gordon when she saw him drive to the synagogue in the latest model E-type Jaguar, a present for his twenty first birthday. From then onwards, as far as Frances Steinberg was concerned, Gordon was a marked man. That is, she had marked him out for her daughter, and she finally got to put her plan into action when he accepted an invitation to lunch after a Sabbath morning service.

The family minus Michael was sitting round the dining room table, which was as usual laden with food, except on this occasion there seemed to be even more of it.

'Deborah, pour Gordon another drink.'

'I'm fine thanks, Mrs Steinberg.'

He lifted his glass to take a drink, but did it a fraction too quickly, and some of the lemonade inside the glass dribbled down his chin. Jake and Deborah had to look away from each other so as not to giggle.

'So, Gordon, how's business?'

'It's good, Rabbi, we're opening another branch in September, and I'm going to be managing it all by myself.'

'Did you hear that, Deborah?' her mother asked, as if she was deaf. 'Gordon's going to manage it himself.'

'Wish my old man had a business for me to go into,' Jake commented.

'You could sell bibles,' his sister suggested.

'Not as good as diamonds.'

'You're too idle to sell anything,' Wilfred grinned good naturedly, 'bit like your brother.'

'Talking of which, where is your Michael now, Rabbi?'

'Bumming around some godforsaken country or another.'

Both parents were still feeling the disappointment of knowing that after only staying in Israel for three months, Michael had once again decided to move on.

'He says he's going to Nepal to live in a Buddhist monastery,' Deborah explained.

'Bit of a dreamer is our Michael. He says he'd like to help the people of Africa next,' Frances added wistfully.

'Work shy is more the expression I'd have used.'

'Just because he's idealistic doesn't mean he won't work eventually,' Jake said to his father, but Frances decided to change the subject.

'Do you know, Deborah, Gordon's been very kind and said I could come into the shop and he'd reset my ring for me?'

'Would you like to come too?' he suddenly blurted out to Deborah.

'No thanks, I don't wear jewellery.'

'Gordon dear, your mother was wearing such a beautiful ring last time I saw her.' Although Frances addressed the remark to Gordon, she looked knowingly in her daughter's direction.

'Oh, that one, it was for her anniversary. Dad's taking her on a cruise as well.'

Frances sat back in her chair, basking in the glory of how well the Helfgots lived.

'You should have seen it, Deborah, square cut, it was beautiful.'

'A perfect blue-white stone,' Gordon added, enjoying his hostess's enthusiasm, but Deborah pushed her chair back from the table. All this talk of jewellery was beginning to get on her nerves, and she gathered up some dirty plates.

'I'll help Peggy in the kitchen.'

'I'll help too.' Jake followed his sister out, then once they were in the kitchen, he pushed her into a corner and started to mimic their mother.

'And if you play your cards right, Deborah, you too could have a ring as big as Gordon's arse.'

'Shut up, you two, they'll hear,' Peggy warned.

'Only trouble is, if you take the ring you've got to take him too,' and this time the three of them dissolved into laughter.

'He seems nice enough,' Peggy said, wiping her eyes with the corner of her apron.

'Then you go out with him.'

After lunch, Frances took Gordon into the lounge to interrogate him some more, while force-feeding him from a box of chocolates.

'Try this one, Gordon, it's got real liqueur inside.'

'I'm absolutely stuffed, Mrs Steinberg, couldn't manage another thing.'

Wilfred came in and sat down in his favourite armchair. He yawned ostentatiously, and Deborah got the distinct impression that her father was feeling sorry for her and wanted no more of Gordon for today.

'Perhaps it's time I was going?' he said, picking up the vibes.

'Deborah dear, why don't you show Gordon to the door?' Frances's two offspring winced at the unfamiliarly affectionate language.

Gordon went across to shake Wilfred's hand, but he was already engrossed in the all-in wrestling on the television. So Frances took him by the shoulders and planted a motherly kiss on one of his pink cheeks. Deborah half expected her to pinch his other cheek affectionately while she had hold of him, but luckily her mother managed to contain her enthusiasm. When he turned to leave, Frances called out after him.

'Don't be a stranger, you know you're always welcome.'

Deborah was desperate to get him out of the house so that she could phone Ian and complain about her mother's manipulations, but Gordon lingered by the doorway. When she opened the front door to steer him out, his gleaming sports car flashed tantalisingly, and he saw her looking.

'Nice, isn't it?'

'Very nice.'

'I'll let you drive it if you want.' He allowed the offer to dangle in the air whilst he lunged for her hand, grasping it awkwardly inside his own damp one. 'Maybe next week?'

'Maybe.'

She instantly felt thoroughly ashamed that she could be swayed so easily, and as a result didn't ring Ian that day because she felt far too guilty. The very next day, Gordon telephoned. His excuse was to thank her mother, but in reality it was to suggest that Deborah go out with him.

'You can drive, we could go to Prestbury, nice open roads there.'

She hesitated. Should she admit to him that she only passed her driving test a fortnight before, and hadn't been allowed the use of anyone's car since?

'That would be nice.'

It seemed like the Jaguar had won; the thought of driving a luxury car while others envied her was just too tempting. But try as she might, she couldn't rid herself of worry in case Ian found out. He was still very much a feature of her life, but he could never offer her a treat like this. So she promised herself that she would only go out with Gordon that one time, then never again.

He collected her in the middle of the afternoon, and she looked around carefully before getting into the car, just in case Ian could be lurking nearby. She had no reason to suspect he would because he had a holiday job stacking shelves in a local supermarket, but her guilty conscience was making her feel wary.

Gordon sat in the passenger seat and bit his lips to conceal his anxiety at the jerky nature of her driving. Once they were through Didsbury and feeling more confident, she picked up speed, then drove onto the newly built motorway towards Prestbury, a small village in Cheshire comprised of bijou shops, expensive restaurants, and huge houses.

She felt wonderful being behind the wheel of such a powerful, open topped machine, and hardly cared what Gordon thought of her driving. She wasn't bothered that her hairstyle had gone completely to pot, and knew that had it been Ian in the car, she would have tried to preserve it at all costs.

It was a bright, sunny day, and Gordon's pink cheeks were reddening by the minute as the sun shone down on them. Deborah never gave Gordon a second glance until one of his podgy hands landed on her knee. She swerved carelessly as she looked down at it, and her stomach churned. Then, oblivious to the hooting from the car behind, she lifted it off her knee like it was a piece of putrefying fish, and placed it back firmly on his side of the car.

Not another word was exchanged, but he appeared to have got the message. He kept his hands firmly by his sides until they arrived in Prestbury, and he suggested she stop in front of a restaurant in the village. The tiny, cottage-like exterior of the restaurant was festooned with geranium filled window boxes and tubs.

'I've booked a table for dinner. It's a bit early, but the food's really good here.'

This was an unexpected turn of events. It had never occurred to her until that moment that she'd have to eat with him as well as drive his car. Ian had asked her to go to the cinema that evening, and they'd arranged to meet in front of the Odeon. She quickly glanced down at her watch, and knew there was no way she was going to get back on time if they had to stay and eat a meal first.

'Gordon, I'm not very hungry.'

'I'm ravenous,' he said, patting his stomach, 'I promise, you'll love it here. You can drive back afterwards, if you want.'

'That's all right, you can.' She reckoned he'd be able to drive a lot faster.

CHAPTER 11

The thorny issue of whether she should spend more time with Ian and his bicycle, or Gordon and his E-type, was praying on Deborah's mind. She discussed it in snatched whispers with Laura in front of their bunsen burners. As far as Miss Naylor, the physics teacher, was concerned, the two of them were busily getting on with their experiment.

'That's easy, which one of them do you like best?'

'Ian of course.'

'So why ask me?'

Physics was Deborah's least favourite subject and she did the minimum work necessary. But the one saving grace of the lessons was that she had plenty of time for gossip during the experiments.

Increasingly these days, she found herself wondering whether the luxury of the Jaguar compensated sufficiently for the amount of time she was forced to spend with its owner. She was even prepared to put up with the occasional grope if it meant speeding through town with her hair tied in a gingham scarf in the style of Brigitte Bardot, and sporting large sunglasses even if the weather was poor. She relished the envious looks she got from passers by, and duly pouted her lips in the most Bardotesque manner for her public.

By contrast, going out with Ian meant staying hidden from the eyes of the community, and there hadn't been many opportunities for intimacy since the abortive afternoon in his parents' house. But in private it was Ian she fantasised about, and was loath to admit even to herself, that she recoiled whenever Gordon came too close.

Unfortunately, he could offer her the sort of lifestyle she could never have aspired to otherwise, and the temptation was hard to resist.

'But Deborah, I just wanted to hug you, that's all.'

'Don't, it distracts me when I'm driving.'

'But you never let me get near you.'

'You have to understand, Gordon, I'm not one of those type of girls. I'm saving myself for when the time comes.'

That usually sufficed temporarily. For Gordon, as for many other young men in those days, the thought of being the one who would one day deflower the fragrant creature who was making full use of his car and wallet, was enough to keep him at bay for the time being.

*

Since Gordon came into their lives, cars were starting to play an increasingly important role in their household. Even Peggy fawned over Gordon's run-around, and Wilfred too began to look at his own car more critically.

'It needs changing.'

'Why?'

'I should get something a bit sportier,' he told Frances.

'At your age?'

'I'm not that old.'

'But you've only had this one for two years.'

Behind their backs, Jake laughed with his sister that their father must be looking for a better 'bird pulling' model. However, this gave the boy the ideal opportunity to press for some advantages of his own.

'Dad, can I have driving lessons?'

'You're still too young.'

'I meant just up and down the street.'

'I'm too busy to teach you.'

'Someone else then?'

'I don't mind as long as it's not in my car.'

Jake was feeling deeply resentful because Evelyn Fraser's son was about to take his driving test, and the boy had inadvertently let slip that Wilfred offered to take him out for some practice in his own car.

'That's nice of your dad, isn't it?'

'He's like that, my dad,' Jake replied ironically, 'generous to a fault.' Once again, the seeds of even more resentment had been sown.

Shortly after that, and to everyone's surprise, Wilfred drove home one evening in a brand new Humber Hawk. This was a much sportier model than his Ford Consul, and he parked it on the street outside their house, bursting with pride. His family duly went outside to admire it.

'Don't know where he gets the money from.'

But once Frances had slid into the front passenger seat, sniffed the leather interior and stroked the walnut dashboard, she appeared to be placated for the time being.

On either side of the driveway of their house were two sets of neo-classical stone pillars, and each pillar was topped with a large stone ball. On that first evening after his family had murmured suitable words of approval, they all went indoors for supper and Wilfred left his new car at the kerbside where he had parked it.

'Don't you think you should put it in the driveway?' Frances suggested. 'You never know what could happen to it out there.'

So when Wilfred finished eating, he went out onto the street, intending to re-park his pride and joy in their driveway. He got behind the wheel, turned on the ignition, and then swung the car round in the road in preparation.

But he wasn't as familiar with its contours as he had been with his old one, and turning the wheel sharply, he misjudged his proximity to one of the pillars. This was the pillar with the loose stone ball that Frances had been nagging him to get fixed.

Jake and Deborah had followed him out of the house to take another look at the car, and when they realised what was about to happen, their eyes opened like saucers and hands flew to their mouths in horror.

'Bloody hell fire!'

'Oh God.'

Their father hit the pillar on the passenger side of the car with a loud, gut churning thud. They held their breath, but when a white-faced Wilfred got out of the driver's side to see what damage he'd done, he trembled as the stone ball wobbled precariously.

'He's about to go mental.'

Then they stared in disbelief as the heavy stone ball rocked towards the edge of the pillar, then pivoted over, crashing onto the bonnet of the new car.

'I think he's crying.'

'Don't be daft.'

Tears were indeed rolling down Wilfred's cheeks in his vain attempt to lift the ball off the battered car bonnet. Finally the three of them managed to get it to the ground. Nobody said a word, but once the ball was firmly on the ground and out of harm's way, their father attacked it with such ferocity that they saw the toe cap of his shoe cave in, and heard him wince with pain.

In time the garage made good the damage, and a stonemason replaced the ball back where it belonged. Only then was Wilfred's equilibrium restored, although he never again drove that car with the same pride that he'd had on that first day.

*

Jake waited several more months before he asked Wilfred if he could drive up and down the road in the car, with his father in the passenger seat. Gordon had been giving him some driving lessons in the meantime, using his own mother's car, but Jake needed even more practice for his forthcoming driving test.

'Perhaps we could do it when you come home in the evening?'

'I told you before, you can't use my car until you've passed your test.'

'How do you expect me to pass if I don't get enough practice?'

'This car's been through plenty without having you crunching its gears as well.'

'You let Edward Fraser drive it, and he's thick as two planks.'

'Edward's a very steady boy.'

Deborah could see her brother's cheeks flushing with anger. She felt his resentment keenly, but a strange thing happened later that same week. Deep scratches mysteriously appeared around the entire circumference of the new Humber.

'Who did it?' Wilfred was apoplectic, but everyone in the family shook their heads.

'Must have happened whilst you were at the synagogue?' Jake's face was the very picture of innocence.

'It's bloody jinxed!' his father ranted. 'The damn thing's jinxed!'

'I'm sure the garage can make it right.'

'It's cost me a bloody fortune already.' And for a moment it looked like he was going to kick the car as well.

'Mind your shoes,' his younger son warned in what Deborah could have sworn was a mixture of delight and scorn.

*

Rosh Hashanah and Yom Kippur, the holiest days of the Jewish calendar, were looming, and it was at this time of the year that Wilfred went into overdrive. Sermons were written weeks in advance, and guests were invited to join the family for the New Year Rosh Hashanah, and the breaking of the fast at the conclusion of Yom Kippur, the Day of Atonement.

'I've invited that Indian fellow for lunch on Rosh Hashanah,' he announced to his wife during the week preceding the festivities.

'What fellow?'

'You know, the one who comes to synagogue every week. He's from Cochin and works at one of the hospitals. I don't expect he's got any family in town.'

Frances sighed in exasperation. She understood the reasons for inviting a stranger to join them at their table, but she would have preferred that stranger to be Gordon rather than an unknown Indian.

She'd already asked her sister and brother-in-law for the New Year, and in her mind's eye was plotting to add another chair for Gordon. But she realised that because of this new addition, her dining table wasn't large enough to take them all.

'I suppose we can invite him some other time.'

'What did you say?'

'Nothing.'

Whenever she tried to quiz Deborah about their friendship, her daughter was stubbornly non-committal. So Frances decided that when the time was right, she herself would have to do a bit more pushing to force the two of them together.

Rosh Hashanah was always a special time in their lives, and that year the festival occurred at the beginning of October. Although the weather was still dry and clear, there was a distinct nip in the air and signs that winter was not far away. So with Peggy's help Frances prepared all the traditional dishes, and when everyone sat down to lunch she beamed at the lavishness of the spread she'd laid out for them.

Their Indian guest was a quiet man, and referred to himself merely as Mister Singh. At the table Ruby, who was sitting next to him, tried to engage him in conversation.

'And what is your first name, what can I call you?'

He looked at her through his dark, lugubrious eyes.

'Mister.'

'No, what I meant, Mr Singh, is what is your Christian name?'

'I am from oldest Jewish community in India.' He was clearly affronted. 'My father Jew, my mother Jew, so I Jew too.'

'Eat your soup, Ruby, it'll get cold.'

Sam gave her the sort of look that indicated that in his opinion she shouldn't get involved. Deborah and Jake smirked behind their starched table napkins.

When Peggy brought a platter of roast chicken to the table, Frances indicated she should serve Mr Singh first. But as she leaned towards him and carefully slid a portion of chicken on to his plate, she shot up again swiftly, her eyes wide with shock. Then she glared at him and moved to serve the next person as fast as she could.

'Your cooking quite good.' Singh inclined his head towards his hostess. 'In my country we use many spices, make food taste better. My wife very good cook.'

'In our country we don't comment,' Ruby muttered.

Back in the kitchen Peggy was fuming. Nobody had ever groped her bottom like that before, and she was determined to tell her employers as soon as she got the chance. But Mr Singh had other ideas.

'Kindly tell me, where is toilet?'

He stood up abruptly, and the others looked surprised that he was leaving the table before he'd finished his course.

'Second door on the left after the kitchen.'

'Thank you, rabbi.'

He scraped his chair back noisily then left the room, and as soon as he reached the open kitchen door, he scurried inside. He tiptoed up behind Peggy, who was carefully washing some crystal glasses at the sink, then put his arms around her chest and squeezed. She shot round in horror then hit out at him with her soapy, rubber gloves.

'Get off!'

'I just want tell you that you very lovely woman,' he said, lurching forwards towards her bosoms again.

'Dirty pig!' She kicked him in the shins, but that only seemed to encourage him, and he lunged for her again. 'If you don't leave me alone, I'll scream for the rabbi.'

He shrugged nonchalantly, then sauntered out of the kitchen and returned to the dining table with soapsuds all over his jacket. Wilfred was busy regaling his brother-in-law about his favourite viewing sport, and the latest craze in the wrestling world.

'They're called tag teams, there's two of them in the ring and two of them waiting on the ropes …'

'Oh, very wonderful sport,' Singh joined in, sitting down in his place.

Everyone had finished eating, and Frances was poised to gather up the dirty plates, when Singh resumed eating. So she sat down again, and she and Ruby lifted their eyebrows in perfect unison.

'You know, rabbi, I have once seen naked mud wrestling.'

'Ugh.' Deborah shot their visitor a distasteful look.

'Naked men?'

'No, rabbi, naked women.'

'Have you finished, Mr Singh? I'd like to clear the plates away now.'

Frances didn't like where this conversation was leading, particularly on such an august day as the New Year.

'Interesting,' Wilfred murmured in Singh's direction. 'Actually, Sam, there's tag wrestling on television this afternoon.'

'With clothes on I hope?' Ruby asked.

'Of course. It's the BBC.'

When the last courses had been served, and lunch was over, Wilfred, Sam and Singh retired to the lounge to watch the wrestling on the television. Three hours later they were still there, but each one of them was fast asleep and snoring.

'Sam?' Ruby screeched from the dining room. 'Time we were going.'

'What's she say?' He roused himself slowly, and Wilfred opened his eyes, but Singh continued snoring. 'Been a wonderful day. Family, that's what it's all about, but looks like your Indian's here for the duration.'

'Let him sleep.'

Singh was slumped horizontally, occupying the whole of the three-seater couch, with his arms clasping a cushion to his chest. Every now and again he smiled in his sleep, squeezed the cushion, then turned over contentedly and resumed snoring. Later that evening, when the remaining members of the family tried to find somewhere to sit in front of the television, Singh was still fast asleep, occupying their usual seats.

'This is ridiculous, I'm going for a walk,' Jake announced.

'I'll come with you,' Deborah said.

It was now dark, but they walked through the park till the cold night air became uncomfortable and Deborah was shivering.

'Do you think he'll be gone by now?'

'I reckon he's put himself into a Yogic trance, but even he should have woken up by now. Dad and his bloody good deeds!'

At exactly the same moment as her son spoke these words, Frances looked across at her husband and mouthed similar words, but her husband was still suffused with the New Year milk of human kindness.

'Leave the poor devil alone, when he wakes, he wakes.'

'Well you can let him out then, I'm going to bed.'

Singh slept through until Wilfred shook him at eleven thirty. The rest of the family were in their beds, and Wilfred was also desperate to get to his.

'Er, old chap.' Singh shuddered but kept his eyes firmly shut, so Wilfred had to shake him hard. 'It's after eleven, you'll miss the last bus.'

'Oh dear me.' He sat up and rubbed his eyes. 'My last bus leaves eleven on the dot.'

'What about the night bus?'

'Oh my goodness, that doesn't go to Chorlton cum Hardy.'

'Maybe you can stay the night here on the couch? I'll get you a blanket and some pyjamas.'

'Rabbi, you truly a holy man. You are best person I have met in England, and the good Lord will reward you in heaven. By the way, I forgot to tell you, they have wrestling tomorrow on other side also. Maybe then I explain about finer moves of naked Punjabi mud wrestlers?'

'I'm afraid not, I'll be doing a service at the prison tomorrow. Just let yourself out when you're ready in the morning.'

Everyone except Peggy slept soundly that night. As dawn was breaking, she became aware that someone was in her room, and that same person was touching her inappropriately. When she screamed, a dark skinned man wearing the rabbi's pyjamas, rushed swiftly out of her room and into the nearby toilet.

The following morning she was determined to tell her employers about their guest. But coming down the stairs, she could hear steady, rhythmic snoring coming from the lounge. She opened the door gingerly, and saw his hand, which was underneath the blanket, resting suspiciously on his crotch area.

'Filthy foreigners.'

In the late afternoon, Wilfred returned home. He had finished his prison visiting, and was now looking forward to reading the papers with a quiet cup of tea. However as soon as he opened the front door, Frances came running to meet him.

'That Indian, he's still here.'

'Then tell him to leave.'

'He said you'd invited him to stay and watch more wrestling, and Peggy says he keeps molesting her.'

'I'll deal with it.'

He was tired, but he walked as purposefully as he could into the lounge to find Singh fully reclined on the couch, and watching the television contentedly.

'Now look here, Mr Singh, don't you have a home to go to?'

The Indian sat up at the sharp tone of Wilfred's voice then arranged the most pitiful look on his face.

'Rabbi, truly you are my guardian angel. You are holy man, and your wife and children are blessed. The Lord himself showed me way to you and said, Singh, he say, stay with this son of God until Yom Kippur when you can repent for your sins in the presence of my greatest disciple.'

'I'm afraid that won't be possible ...'

Singh let out a howl of pain then lowered his head into his hands. His shoulders started to heave violently, then he prostrated himself at Wilfred's feet and sobbed inconsolably. He tugged at Wilfred's trouser turn-ups, and Wilfred felt a shiver of fear running through his body.

'Now look, old chap, let's be sensible now ...' But the Indian didn't move. 'Just tell me where you live, and I'll take you home.' He could see that Singh's copious tears and the secretions from his nose were already staining the carpet.

'I have no home to go to.'

'You said you lived in Chorlton cum Hardy.'

'I have room in hospital there.' Wilfred could feel the sweat beginning to prickle his underarms. The only hospital he knew in that area was a mental hospital, and now sobbing uncontrollably on the floor, Singh did not look like he was one of the doctors.

Hearing the commotion in the lounge, Frances and her children appeared in the doorway and the three of them stared at the spectacle. Deborah didn't know whether to giggle or call for help.

'Phone the ...'

Wilfred tried to mouth the word *police*, but Singh looked up at him suspiciously. Deborah quickly summed up what was happening and rushed upstairs to the telephone in her parents' bedroom. She was panting when she dialled 999.

After what seemed like an eternity of trying to placate their unwelcome guest, a police car accompanied by an ambulance arrived outside the house, and after a brief explanation they took Singh away. Only then did Wilfred and his wife sink down into their armchairs, totally exhausted.

'I blame you, if you hadn't—'

'Oh shut up.' Even though his bones ached from nervous tension, Wilfred heaved himself out of the chair, leaving his wife staring at him resentfully. 'I'm going to bed.'

*

According to Frances, not only was Wilfred careless with the type of guests he invited, but also his choice of women left much to be desired. He seemed to have forgotten the lessons he should have learnt from meeting his sister Gwen in London, and ever true to form, his wife and children guessed that a new woman had taken his fancy.

He always followed the same patterns of behaviour when this was happening. This invariably meant him inviting the woman and her husband, if she had one, to share the hospitality of the Steinberg household. To further confuse matters, in a curious sort of way, Frances partly colluded with this behaviour because that way she got to know whom she was up against, even though she hated his disloyalty.

The next time he did this was at a tea party, which Frances had been planning for some time now. She badly wanted to entertain Gordon's parents, Christine and Cyril, for the obvious reason of forcing their two offspring together. Even though Deborah had managed to avoid Gordon recently, Frances had no intention of letting her get away with this any longer.

'My mother's impossible,' Deborah whispered to Ian one evening on the back row of the cinema. 'She keeps trying to push me into going out with this weedy boy she knows, just because he's Jewish.'

She felt it prudent not to mention that he was also very rich, and that she had perfected her driving skills in his E-type Jaguar. Obviously this had necessitated spending some evenings and afternoons with him, but she omitted to mention that as well.

'Then tell her you've already got a boyfriend.'

'But it's not as simple as that ...'

'Would you mind,' the man in front turned round to her, 'I'm trying to watch this film.'

They had chosen the back row because it afforded the most privacy and was one of the few places they could be intimate with each other, if necking and groping could be classified as intimacy. The cinema was warmer and comfier than the park bench, so they decided to stay put.

Frances had deliberately chosen to hold her tea party on a Sunday afternoon, Peggy's day off, which was a way of forcing Deborah to stay home and help her.

'What do you think, Deborah, should I make that chocolate cake your Gordon likes?'

'He's not my Gordon, so make what you want.'

'You're so snappy these days, I can't talk to you anymore.'

Her daughter knew from long experience that she wasn't going to win this argument, and that the tea party itself was going to be something of an endurance test.

Without consulting his wife until the last minute, by which time it was too late to cancel them, Wilfred had also decided to invite the latest object of his affection. She called herself Nicky, and her husband was Barney Segleman, a kosher butcher. Frances had never met either of them before because they lived in the other side of town, but as soon as the two came through the front door, everybody else in the family knew why they were there.

'Just look at those Bristols,' Jake whispered to his sister.

Deborah suppressed a giggle while Wilfred helped Nicky Segleman off with her coat, at which point an overpoweringly heady smell of perfume hit the room.

'Those two beauts defy the laws of gravity.'

Unfortunately Frances overheard this remark, and with a resigned sigh raised her eyebrows heavenwards as if supplicating God yet again. Brother and sister exchanged glances before Jake beat a hasty retreat to the safety of his room. Deborah knew she didn't have that luxury.

Barney turned out to be a taciturn man who said little, but was content to let his peroxide-blonde wife do the talking for both of them. She had a pert but buxom figure, and the tight dress she wore exaggerated her breasts, which thrust out in front of her and rested on Frances's pristine damask tablecloth. Wilfred used every opportunity to brush the crumbs off the table that had gathered in front of them.

Frances was fully occupied trying to impress her other guests, so she barely had time to monitor the glances going from her husband to the butcher's wife. The latter was explaining to the hapless Cyril that she was born plain Norma, but she preferred Nicky because it suited her personality more. Wilfred nodded as if this was the most erudite thing he'd ever heard, and when Cyril asked her what sort of a personality she had, she replied:

'Bubbly and giving.'

Meanwhile, Gordon ate steadily and quietly. With Frances's

encouragement, he finished off most of the sandwiches that the others had left, and he seemed perfectly happy eating and gazing at Deborah while she helped her mother serve.

'Bless him,' Frances remarked as she poured a second cup of tea for his mother, 'he's got a good appetite.'

'Don't you think you've had enough of those, Gordon?'

Deborah didn't wait for his answer before snatching his plate away from under his nose, and stacking it with the other used ones. However, when she and her mother went into the kitchen to collect the array of cakes made for the occasion, Frances sniffed as if she'd discovered a bad smell under her nose.

'Calls herself bubbly, who's she kidding?' Deborah picked up a cake stand filled with scones. 'Oh and by the way, try to be a bit more civil to our guests.'

'I take it you mean Gordon?'

'Yes, if you must know.'

'Then don't encourage him to eat like a pig, he's fat enough already.'

Once back in the dining room, everybody paid suitable homage to Frances's mastery of cake making. Christine had daintily finished a piece of cake when she remarked apropos of nothing:

'I think it's very important for a girl to be able to cook a nice meal for her husband when he gets home in an evening.' Deborah's ears pricked up.

'And lay a nice table too,' Cyril added solemnly. Frances nodded in agreement and her daughter didn't know whether to laugh out loud or cry.

'I've always said a well laid table makes all the difference, haven't I, Wilfred?'

In spite of addressing her husband, Frances looked straight at her daughter, who wondered if they had all taken leave of their senses. Unfortunately for her, the trio wasn't finished yet.

'Not many girls nowadays understand how important that is,' Christine added, to which Frances blurted out:

'Your Gordon's such a nice boy.'

Gordon thankfully had the good grace to blush, but Deborah began to feel the food regurgitating in her stomach, and she prayed fervently that God would make them all disappear.

'Yes, he's a good boy is our Gordon.' Christine regarded her son with a beatific smile.

'And a real asset in the business,' his father added.

'What business is that?' Nicky, alias Norma asked.

'We have a chain of jewellery shops.'

Then Frances shot a malevolent look towards Nicky as if to warn her to keep off. But the butcher's wife had already started twisting a big ring off her finger, and she passed it to Cyril.

'What d'you think of this?'

Cyril took out a jeweller's eyeglass from his top pocket, and lifted it and the ring to his eye.

'We bought it in Rimini, go every year to the Grand, it's one of the best hotels there.'

Then for the first time that afternoon, Barney spoke.

'Cost me a bob or two, I can tell you.'

'These are popular in that part of the world,' Cyril replied without expressing any opinion on the ring or its value, and Deborah was sure she saw him exchange a knowing look with Christine. 'Tell me, how's your Michael doing?'

'We're expecting a letter any day now. More cheesecake anyone?'

*

To Deborah's consternation, Ian had been offered a place at Bristol University, and with his supermarket earnings, he had recently bought an old jalopy, which he was lovingly restoring. On the evening of the abortive tea party, they parked it in a quiet lane by a disused railway line, and made as passionate love as was possible in a small, two-door car. The windows quickly steamed up, and Ian had to open them; not so much for fresh air, but more to dangle his legs through while they attempted their first act of union.

'Do you think I'm cheap because I let you do it?'

'I think you're wonderful.'

'Promise you won't tell anybody.'

'Why should I? We're going to be together for ever, aren't we?'

'Ian, what are you doing?'

'I can't get it in unless you lift your legs up.'

'But it's so uncomfortable.'

In the event, Deborah was convinced that the only penetration she experienced was from the gear lever, which was just as well because Ian's condom was eventually found resting on top of it. The next day he left for university.

*

Deborah had done well enough in her O-level exams, and her parents intended her to enrol at a secretarial college. Frances had convinced her that this was the only way she would find a good job, which in her opinion was just filling in time until she found a good husband. But before she acquiesced, Deborah made one last attempt to try to dissuade her.

'I got the top marks in art out of all the whole class, so why won't you let me go to art school?'

'Since when is scribbling a career?'

'Since when is typing?'

Deborah then tried appealing to her father, hoping he would intervene on her behalf, but he seemed content to leave this particular argument to his wife.

'Do you think your father has money to burn while you play with paints and crayons?'

'That's not what you do in art college.'

'So why do all the beatniks go to art college? Layabouts in their dirty clothes, with their long, matted hair.'

'They're not all like that.'

'I've seen pictures of those places in the newspapers, and I can tell you this for nothing, they're no place for a daughter of mine, thank you very much.'

She thought she caught a glimpse of pity cross her father's face, but Frances had spoken her last words on the subject, and against that sort of joint pressure, Deborah had little option but to cave in.

CHAPTER 12

From the very first moment that she stepped inside the Manchester College of Commerce, housed in an old Victorian building in the city centre, Deborah hated every second she spent there, and instantly knew that she wasn't cut out for becoming someone's secretary.

During the first introductory lesson, when the duties expected of a secretary were explained, her mind wandered to all the people she knew who employed them. Thinking about each of them in turn, and the list included Gordon, she instinctively felt that she was sharper than most of them and could run circles round the majority of them. Then, to think that her future would involve kow-towing to people like Gordon, she mentally switched off completely.

When it came to the curriculum, learning shorthand was easy enough, but touch-typing proved to be a nightmare. If she cheated and looked down at the keys the teacher told her off, but if she looked at the woman when she was dictating as she was supposed to, she pressed all the wrong keys and produced a page of gobbledegook.

However, the main bane of her life concerning typewriters, proved to be the filmy sheets of black carbon paper which they were instructed to use to make file copies. More often than not, in her anxiety to do it properly, she inserted the carbons the wrong way round. This meant that her copies were non-existent, but her typewriter and her fingers were subsequently covered in dirty black marks.

The students were subjected to regular typing tests, but because she had now become so nervous about getting it right, as soon as she sat down in front of her typewriter, she either felt sick, pre-menstrual or both, depending on what that time of the month it was. Because Ian was in Bristol, he could neither listen to her moans nor alleviate her stress. She missed him terribly, which was why she turned to Gordon for some light relief.

'Gordon, did you know that a new Italian film has just started at the Odeon?'

'*La Dolce Vita*?'

'Yes, that one.'

'Would you like me to take you?'

'What a good idea.'

She decided that he was just a good friend, so if there was a particular film she wanted to see, or a club she wanted to go to, she knew he was always willing to take her.

He seemed happy enough to play by her rules, and didn't demand much in return. If she gave him an occasional chaste kiss on his cheek or pretended in front of others that he really was her date for the evening, that made him feel better about his given role as her chauffeur or minder-in-chief. Added to which, her mother beamed with expectant joy every time she caught sight of the two of them together.

However, one evening to her horror, he tried to take the relationship a step further. They were sitting side by side in the cinema, and Deborah was not enjoying the film at all. Gordon had been systematically munching his way through a large box of chocolates, which he kept pushing in her direction, and could sense her boredom.

'I quite like it, but if you don't like it, we could leave. It's about the last war you know.'

'I'm not stupid, it's just so tedious.'

She resigned herself to staying until the end, so sat back in her seat and closed her eyes. It wasn't long before she became aware that the hand he wasn't using to delve into the chocolates had made its way round the back of her seat. As first she ignored it, then it slowly began making its way onto her shoulder, and his podgy fingers began stroking her neck.

'Gordon!'

He jumped, and several people turned round to look at her. She then took hold of the offending hand and pushed it back firmly onto his lap. From the corner of her eye, she could see that he was sweating with embarrassment.

Even though it gave her more than the occasional stab of guilt knowing she was using him mercilessly, she nonetheless decided that she could put up with Gordon and his E-type Jaguar, but not Gordon and his roving fingers.

*

The College was situated near several office blocks, which were occupied by the cotton and textile merchants who traded in the city. Many had been trading since the turn of the century, but with the decline of the cotton industry due to cheap Egyptian imports, several of the buildings now looked old and run down.

Deborah regularly walked away from the area during her lunch breaks, and felt she could breathe easier when she was as far away from the college as possible. She would usually head towards the city centre stores, and one day on her way back, she was waiting to cross the busy main road outside the town's central library.

'Hello there.' She looked around and realised she was being spoken to by a good-looking man in his late thirties. 'I know you, don't I?'

'I'm sorry, but I don't know who you are.'

'I'd recognise those big, brown eyes anywhere.'

'Maybe you've seen me with my father, Rabbi Steinberg?'

To her surprise, he then held her at arms' length, and before she had sufficient time to react, he'd taken hold of her elbow and was guiding her across the road. When they reached the opposite pavement, he let go of her arm and she turned to take her leave.

'What's the rush?'

'Got to get back to college.'

'You won't believe this, but when I saw you a minute ago, I thought, that girl's got such class she must be French.'

'Well I'm not,' she smiled, enjoying his compliments.

'Fancy a coffee?'

Something told her it was wrong to accept compliments and more from a total stranger – albeit one who knew her father – but the other part of her brain kept telling her, it's only a coffee after all.

Eventually, realising she would be late back at college if she took up the offer, common sense prevailed.

'I'm sorry, but I've got to get back.'

'How about dinner then?'

'Look, I don't know you.'

'We can easily rectify that.'

She was well on the way to being seduced by his easy charm, but the thought of Ian suddenly intruded into her mind, and she shook her head.

'Look, I really do have to go.'

'Pity, some other time perhaps? I'll keep my eye out for you. Oh, and give my regards to your dad; great man, you know.'

'Who should I say sent them?'

'Tell him the Russian.'

She gave him a tiny wave of her hand, then jauntily resumed her journey back to the college. That afternoon's typing test put all thoughts of the encounter out of her mind until later that evening when she told her father.

'He sent his regards to you and when I asked him his name, he just said the Russian.' At that, her father appeared to freeze in his chair.

'Now look here, Deborah, don't ever have anything to do with that creature, and if you see him again, just walk away in the opposite direction as fast as you can.'

'But he talked very highly of you.'

'So he should, I looked after him.'

'Looked after him, where?'

'Strangeways prison, he's just been released.'

'Oops.'

'Got eight years for grand larceny, living off immoral earnings and setting fire to a neighbour's business.' Deborah felt herself getting hot. 'So what did he want with you?'

'Nothing much.'

*

When Ian was due home for Christmas, Deborah anticipated that they would spend most of the time together. Current chatter amongst her friends was all about who was going out with whom, and what they were getting up to. It was rumoured that one of her acquaintances thought she was pregnant, and all the girl's friends collectively held their breath until her period arrived, three weeks late.

This potential mishap forced Deborah to think more carefully about the difficult subject of contraception. She was well aware that if anything like that happened to her, it would be the death of her socially, and more particularly within her own household. So she decided to ask some pertinent questions of her more knowledgeable friends.

'You have to get it from a doctor.'

'What?'

'It's called a Dutch cap.'

'But I've read about a pill that can stop you getting pregnant.'

'I heard about that too, but they said it's still being tested on guinea pigs. Anyway, you don't have a boyfriend, so why are you asking all these questions?'

She quickly realised it would be impossible to see her family doctor because all the Steinbergs used his practice, and she was certain he'd tell her mother if she went for advice. So she decided to try another doctor's practice, one that she'd noticed on her way to college. As Ian was due home shortly, she reckoned she didn't have much time to waste.

'Can I have an appointment to see the doctor please?'

The officious looking woman behind the desk scrutinised her carefully.

'Do you belong to this practice?'

'No, I'm just visiting the area.'

The woman then passed her a form and told her to fill it in. When she took a seat, Deborah could have sworn that all the people seated in the waiting area were looking at her as if they knew why she was there.

'Put in your temporary address,' the receptionist shouted out and Deborah flinched, 'and when you've done it, I'll see which doctor's available.'

Filling out the form with a false name made her very uneasy, but when it came to giving her address, she nearly freaked out. In desperation she put Ian's address then added a false telephone number underneath it. When she took it back to the receptionist, her clothes were sticking to her all over her body.

'Take a seat.'

The only magazines that were scattered around were dog-eared copies of *Reader's Digest* and *Woman's Own*. Deborah pretended to be reading one of them, but in fact she was seriously considering the possibility of bolting from the waiting room.

'Miss Berg?' She didn't move. 'Miss Berg?' This time the receptionist's voice was louder, and she looked up to see the woman's eyes boring into her.

'Oh yes, that's me.'

'Room three down the corridor.'

By the time she had walked the few yards to room three, her heart was pounding like a drumbeat. To steady herself down, she told herself this was all in a good cause, so she breathed in deeply several times, then tapped on the door.

'Come.' She pushed the door open. 'Take a seat Miss ...?'

'Berg, Susan Berg.'

'So what can I do for you, Miss Berg?'

Deborah's throat felt parched and constricted, and when she tried to speak, her voice came out like a sparrow's cheeping.

'I ... I ...' The middle aged doctor had a patient look on her face, and Deborah said a silent prayer of thanks that she was a female. 'I need advice.'

When she left the surgery a while later, she had in her possession a Dutch cap and all the paraphernalia to go with it, hidden inside her handbag. But her mind was in turmoil, not so much about the mechanics of using it, but more about where to hide her contraceptive until she needed it. Home wasn't safe enough; Peggy or her mother could easily find it.

'I can hardly bury it in the garden till I need it.'

'I beg your pardon?' The man in the next seat looked towards her. She was on the bus on her way to college and hadn't realised till that moment that she'd spoken her thoughts out loud.

'I'm sorry, didn't realise.'

She was now so embarrassed that even though it was still two stops before the college one, she stood up quickly, rang the bell, then alighted at the first possible moment. It took her another ten minutes to reach the college, but in that time she came up with the only sensible conclusion as to where to hide the cap. She would put it in her college locker, to be retrieved when needed.

*

During the Christmas holidays, whenever Deborah and Ian could snatch a moment to be together, they would. One afternoon his parents were out, and the two of them had the house to themselves. So they used the opportunity for their first attempt at lovemaking using the Dutch cap.

'I'll only be a minute.'

Deborah went into the bathroom to go through the routine that the doctor had shown her. She took the cap carefully out of its case, which resembled a large powder compact, and stared at it. On her only visit to that surgery, the doctor had shown her precisely where to put the accompanying barrier jelly, but now she couldn't remember whether the doctor had said on the inside or the outside.

Realising that time was passing and his parents were due home at six, she started to panic, and in desperation rubbed a large dollop of jelly all over the cap, both inside and outside of it.

She remembered that the doctor had told her to squeeze it into as narrow a shape as possible, lift her leg up against the bath, and then insert it inside herself. But because it was smeared all over in jelly, it had become so slippery that when she tried to do that, the cap flew out of her hand and landed like a flying discus near the bathroom door.

'Bugger!'

'Debs, what are you doing in there?'

'Trying to do the impossible.'

'Should I help you?'

'No, don't you dare!'

On the third attempt, she got the cap in place, but by this time she was almost crying with frustration. Not only that, but she was still unsure whether she'd inserted it into the right place, and whether it would be the preventative she needed.

The following ten minutes of lovemaking was so nerve racking for her, that eventually she begged Ian to use a condom as well.

'I thought you said you'd taken care of it.'

'I have, but ... I'm not sure.'

When they finally came together in unison, Ian said it was like being trapped inside a rubber dinghy wearing an inflatable life jacket, and Deborah had little to say on the subject. The whole experience had killed whatever passion she felt before they started, and she couldn't wait till the two hours were up, when she could take it out of her and have a nice, soothing bath.

*

Try as she might to avoid Gordon during the Christmas holidays, he kept reappearing. One Sabbath morning, the family was about to go home after the service, when they heard footsteps running behind them. Deborah didn't need to turn round to know who it was.

'Oh look, it's Gordon – poor thing, he's quite red from all that running,' Frances beamed.

By the time he caught up with them, the man was so out of breath that he could hardly speak, but he finally managed to splutter out:

'I was looking for you in there, Deborah.'

'Strange, I saw you.'

Her mother frowned; she knew her daughter's penchant for going to the ladies toilet when she wanted to avoid people. She turned to him with her most concerned expression.

'Gordon dear, we haven't seen you for ages.'

'Because I took my parents to Southampton – they were off on a cruise.'

'Oh, they have such a wonderful life. And where are they off to this time?'

'Just round the world, the usual.'

She clapped her hands in delight.

'Did you hear yourself, you said it like it was just round Manchester? Tell you what, dear, why don't you join us for lunch, but you'll have to take us as you find us?'

Gordon would have had to be blind not to notice the malevolent looks Deborah was shooting at her mother.

'Are you sure it won't be any trouble?'

'Of course not, dear, you're almost family.'

Then, as if to add insult to injury, her father put his arm round Gordon's shoulder and said: 'Actually, my boy, I've been meaning to have a word with you about a new watch.'

Behind his father's back, Jake was grinning maliciously. He pulled his sister aside and whispered: 'And what is our Deborah going to have to give Gordon in payment for the new watch, hey?'

'Shut up, moron.'

At lunch, Frances insisted her daughter sat next to Gordon, but Deborah tried to spend most of the time helping Peggy in the kitchen. Whenever she managed to escape briefly, her mother invariably called her back to the table.

However, during the main course, Deborah noticed that Gordon wasn't looking very well. He kept rubbing his stomach, and she figured out it was probably because he'd eaten too much. Suddenly he stood up. His face had gone a pasty white colour and he was trembling.

'What's the matter?'

'I need the toilet.' He rushed towards the door, but seemed to be unsure which direction to head in.

'Here, I'll show you,' Jake said, and led him out of the room. Then even Deborah felt somewhat concerned, because this was not like Gordon at all.

'Probably overexcited about seeing you again,' Wilfred grinned, then Jake came back into the dining room pulling a face.

'I think he's being sick.'

'Well, it's not because of anything he's eaten here.'

Frances seemed quite offended, but Wilfred pushed his chair back from the table and went towards the door.

'I'd better see if he's all right.'

When he left the dining room, the three of them put down their knives and forks and waited. It seemed rather callous to carry on eating until they knew what was happening, but suddenly they heard Wilfred shout out: 'Frances, Peggy! Come quickly!'

The two women ran out as fast as they could, and Deborah and

Jake hurried after them, in time to hear Peggy say: 'Oh my God, what a mess.'

'Deborah!' her father shouted. 'Call the doctor, tell him it's urgent!'

They laid Gordon out on Jake's bed while they waited for the to doctor arrive. That didn't bother Jake too much until he heard Gordon start retching and throwing up again.

'Hope none of that went on my sheets.'

'Don't be callous.'

'That's a first, my sister thinks I'm the callous one.'

Finally, when the doctor arrived, he went straight into the bedroom. No sooner had he started examining Gordon, than they heard him retching and vomiting again.

'Hope your mother's got a bucket handy!' Peggy exclaimed.

'Hope she caught it in time,' Jake replied.

The three of them waited in the dining room, and eventually heard the doctor and Wilfred talking to each other on the landing.

'But surely, Doctor, he'd be better off in hospital?'

'I'm sure it's a perforated ulcer, Rabbi, and it's far too dangerous to move him at the moment.'

'I'd better call his parents.'

'He told me they're on a cruise, and it would be almost impossible to reach them on the high seas. Best not to worry them yet; I'm sure he'll get all the attention he needs right here.'

Hearing their muffled conversation, Frances left the bedroom to join the doctor and her husband on the landing, while Peggy did her best to clean up in the toilet.

'His mother ought to be doing this,' she said, holding her nose. 'Always muggins who gets the dirty work.'

Frances led the doctor downstairs, and although she seemed very concerned about Gordon, Deborah suspected that her mother was quite pleased to have secured her prospective son-in-law into her clutches, and on her own premises as well.

'But how can we look after him, doctor?'

'What he needs right now is bed rest and quiet. I've given him something to settle him down and help him sleep, but if you need me during the night, you've got my number.'

'How long do you think he'll be like this?'

'Could take weeks.'

When she heard that, Deborah's mind went into free fall and she felt she too was going to be sick. She had so little time left before Ian went back to university, and now even that looked to be in jeopardy.

'Who knows how long these things take to heal?' the doctor murmured.

'Quite so,' Frances replied, already relishing her new role as Gordon's protector.

In the event, Gordon stayed with the Steinbergs for the longest six weeks of Deborah's life, and after the first few days, even her mother stopped pretending to be Florence Nightingale, and handed the hard work over to Peggy. But when Jake complained that he was fed up of sleeping on the couch, Peggy admonished him.

'Be fair, love, he's still peeing blood.'

Every day Deborah felt like she was spitting blood while he was in the house, because it was nigh on impossible for her to get to see Ian.

'Maybe if you were nicer to him he might get better quicker,' Jake suggested one day.

'Don't even go there.' His sister's look was warning enough.

'Well, the least you can do is take him up a cup of tea,' Peggy said, handing her the tray.

'I wish his parents would come home,' Deborah muttered to herself whilst she took the tea to Jake's bedroom.

When she pushed the door open, Gordon was propped up on several pillows in bed. He was wearing a pair of striped pyjamas that revealed the sparse hairs on his chest, and in spite of the fact that he hadn't been allowed to leave his bed for the past two weeks, he still looked as plump as ever.

'How are you feeling, Gordon?'

'Much better, thanks.'

'Do you think you'll be well enough to go home soon?'

'The doctor says it could take weeks before it heals.'

She tried putting a sympathetic smile on her face.

'Must go, enjoy your tea.'

'Deborah, sit down, please, you haven't been in to see me for ages.'

She perched reluctantly on the end of his bed so he that couldn't see her foot tapping the floor impatiently.

'Well, you know what the doctor said. You had to have peace and quiet, so that's why I didn't come in. Besides which I've had loads of typing exams, which I can't seem to get the hang of, and then there's French. Do you know, we have to be able to write business letters in French and German, and what with that and ...'

'I miss not seeing you.'

She panicked and wondered where this was leading. It nearly choked her to mumble an insincere 'Me too'.

'I've been thinking a lot about us.'

'Me and you?' She stood up sharply and started edging towards the door. She had no wish to hear what she suspected was coming next.

'About how well we get on, and how our families get on, so why don't we get engaged?'

'Engaged?'

'My parents think the world of you, and ...'

'But I don't ...'

'What?'

'No, I can't.'

'I'm crazy about you, Deborah.'

Then she ran out of the bedroom shouting desperately: 'No, it's impossible! I'm sorry.'

*

From that moment onwards, Deborah stayed away from Gordon's room as much as she could, and Gordon kept his humiliation to himself. But deep down he was seething at the summary way she had dismissed his proposal, and also her refusal to discuss it any more.

Meanwhile, everything else in the household that could go wrong did go wrong. It started when a letter arrived from Michael with a postmark that nobody could identify, but the date stamp showed that it was several weeks old. They all gathered round the kitchen table to hear his news, and her mother took upon herself the role of narrator.

'*And in Swaziland they have the most unusual people.*'

She nodded at her listeners, smiled and laughed as she related various anecdotes he'd written about the people there and then she came to a new paragraph that appeared to wipe the smile off her face completely.

'*Now for the good part, I've met a wonderful girl ...*' Frances had gone very pale, and was now reading through gritted teeth. '*And it was love at first sight for both of us.*'

'What did he say?'

'Here, you read it.'

She almost threw the letter at Wilfred who carried on reading silently with an ever-deepening frown on his forehead, and his nose and cheeks taking on that familiar purplish red colour that his family recognised as trouble.

'Tell us,' Jake insisted.

'*And as long as you have no objections, we are going to have a Swazi marriage ceremony within the next couple of weeks.*'

Wilfred picked up the envelope in desperation and re-examined the date stamp before letting out a howl of anguish.

'The fool, the stupid fool!'

Jake then pulled the letter out of his hands, scanned for the place and continued to read it aloud.

'It's not too bad – he says he'd be happy to go through a Jewish type ceremony when he gets back to Manchester. Her name's Mdinga, and she's sixteen, which should make for a colourful ceremony!'

'Don't joke, it's not funny,' Deborah hissed.

Everyone else seemed to be in shock, and nobody knew what to say next. Michael had finished his letter by saying that Mdinga's father was going to give her a dowry of two cows and a mud hut, and he was sure that in time his parents would grow to love her as much as he did.

'And he says that she cooks and cleans very well,' Jake added, 'but I expect they only eat maize out there.'

'Oh, that will be a great addition to the Friday night meal,' Frances snapped.

When Deborah looked across the table, she noticed that her father had tears in his eyes, and it was the first time she'd ever seen him crying. Then Frances started shrieking.

'Wilfred, we've got to stop him!' But her husband shook his head sadly and pointed to the date stamp on the envelope.

'Maybe it's too late?'

While the full impact was dawning on the family, and in spite of the shock, they were careful not to shout too loudly in case Gordon overheard. Frances had already taken great pains to concoct an elaborate façade of perfect family life in front of him. In spite of her suffering, she couldn't let the pretence drop just because her eldest son had taken up with the most unsuitable mate he could have found.

'I never thought the day would come when I'd have *shwartze*[13] grandchildren.'

'If I could get my hands on him, I'd wring his neck.'

'I blame you, you always gave in to him.'

He was about to retort in kind when Deborah mouthed the word *Gordon*, and put her finger to her mouth in a warning gesture.

*

As if on cue, within twenty-four hours of receiving the letter, Frances started having pains in her kidney region. This time the only thing that gave her comfort was when she and Gordon sat together and compared their symptoms. She would take him his breakfast in the morning, then install herself in a bedside chair.

'So how do you feel today, Gordon, did you sleep well?'

'Not too bad, Mrs Steinberg, and it's kind of you to ask.' Frances knew this was a dig at Deborah, who never asked how he was, but thought it best not to enquire about that any further. 'Anyway, how about you, you're still looking a bit peaky?'

After these daily chats together, they would both face the day more positively, but Wilfred on the other hand was having bouts of heart palpitations, and confided in no one. He put it down to the shock of Michael's news, and in spite of becoming breathless whenever he did anything more strenuous than drive his car, he carried on with his daily routine and said nothing about it.

'Kindly put me through to Basil Leveridge.'

Wilfred gripped the phone to his ear, and when his secretary

---

[13]*black*

put her head round the door to offer him a coffee, he waved her away impatiently.

'Who should I say's calling?'

'Wilfred Steinberg, and please tell him it's most urgent.'

He tapped his fingers anxiously on his desktop while he waited for the Member of Parliament for Gatley South, and a former lawyer, to come to the phone.

'Now then, old boy, what can I do for you?'

'Basil, I need to see you urgently.'

'No problem, can do, your office or mine?'

Leveridge was the only person in whom Wilfred decided to confide. He told him all the details he knew about Michael's Swazi marriage, which had either already taken place or was imminently due. After hearing him out, Leveridge assured him that he would look into the legality of such a marriage in British law, and would report back to him as soon as possible.

'I'm sure you've got nothing to worry about, old chap, sounds like some primitive tribal ceremony that we can get annulled as soon as the foolish boy gets back.'

'That's a great weight off my mind, Basil.'

'Why do these youngsters get into this sort of scrape? If you ask me, they should just sow their wild oats then come home and settle down with the right sort of girl.'

True to his word, within two days Leveridge telephoned Wilfred to tell him that, as he suspected, the marriage wouldn't stand up in a British court. For the first time in many days Wilfred breathed more easily, but Leveridge had some more advice to offer.

'Look, old boy, if you want rid of the girl, this is going to cost you. I suggest that as soon as she arrives, you pay her off.'

'What sort of sum do you have in mind?'

'Well, you're going to have to reimburse her father for the cows and whatever else he gave your son, then I would suggest a sum of five hundred pounds as well as her fare money home. That should take care of the rest of it.'

'Thank you, you've taken a great weight off my mind. You must come round for dinner once this is over.'

'The wife would enjoy that. Oh, and by the way, once you send her back you're going to have to do something with that prodigal son of yours. If he were mine, I'd pack him straight back to Israel until he starts university.'

'But he wasn't too keen on it the first time.'

'That's as maybe, but they have a fine army training programme out there, and it's probably just the thing he needs to keep him out of further trouble.'

Wilfred understood the common sense of this suggestion, and after discussing it with Frances, they both realised that they were going to have to deal with a very angry son before this could be achieved.

But before anything else, he had to make an appointment to see his bank manager to secure the loan with which to pay the girl off. Now, waiting in a bank anteroom, the palpitations were coming stronger than ever, but he told himself it was nothing serious, just his nerves playing up.

The manager received him courteously, and even offered him a cup of tea, which Wilfred immediately gulped down. After he made his request for the loan, he waited anxiously.

'I'll certainly lend you the money, Rabbi, but you know you're already quite overdrawn as it is.'

'I know, but it's just a temporary setback, I assure you.'

Once he'd completed the formalities and reached the security of his car, Wilfred found himself trembling. He knew there was no way he could reduce his overdraft in the foreseeable future, and as he drove off the palpitations began again.

*

The doctor who was looking after Gordon decided that he was now well enough to continue his convalescence in a nursing home. Sorry though she was to let him out of her clutches, Frances knew it would mean fewer awkward explanations on her part as to Michael's current whereabouts.

The family had just received another letter from him, giving a joyous description of his Swazi marriage ceremony, and telling them that he and his bride were due in Manchester shortly. So Frances asked Peggy to go with Gordon to the nursing home, to make sure that he settled in. She knew better than to ask her daughter.

*

Before boarding his overnight flight to Heathrow, Michael made a reverse charge call to his parents, to inform them that he and Mdinga would take the first available train to Manchester after landing.

'I certainly am not going to the station to meet them,' Frances asserted.

'Don't you think it would be better if we presented a united front?'

'What will I say to her? She probably doesn't even speak English.'

They finally agreed that Wilfred, Deborah and Jake would go to the station to meet their son and his bride, while Frances stayed at home to prepare lunch.

'He probably hasn't eaten a decent meal since he left.'

The following morning, Deborah and Jake realised that their main priority that day was to try to keep their father calm. Since refusing to eat breakfast, he had been pacing up and down in the lounge, and Jake even thought he heard him muttering to himself.

Once they left the house, he drove erratically through the traffic to the station, and to their consternation, continued his monologue to himself.

'Only nineteen, and the fool saddles himself with a wife, and he has to pick a *shwartze* on top of everything else.'

'She might not be very dark,' Jake suggested.

'What's the difference between light black and dark black?' His voice rose alarmingly, and he had to swerve to miss a cyclist.

'Please calm down, Dad, we don't want to kill anybody on the way there.'

'You sound just like your mother.' That was one insult too many, and Deborah sulked for the rest of the journey.

Piccadilly Station, a Victorian edifice blackened with soot, was just the sort of place to depress anyone coming to Manchester for the first time, especially those from sunnier climes. The three Steinbergs found the platform that the London train was due to arrive at, but by this time Wilfred was grey in the face. Jake suggested his father sat down while they waited by the ticket barrier, in case they missed them.

'I don't know how you'd manage to miss that pair.'

It was a cold, damp day, and Jake and Deborah huddled close to each other while they waited. Finally, the train drew in and the first passengers alighted, but they couldn't see any familiar faces coming towards the barrier.

'Are you sure this is the right train?'

'It's the one he said.'

Suddenly they spotted a bearded, scruffy man in full African dress walking down the platform, followed by a fully veiled woman who was carrying their entire luggage. Deborah and Jake dismissed them summarily, and Wilfred left the bench where he'd been sitting, to join them.

'He said he'd be on the eleven twenty,' Deborah said, but Wilfred seemed relieved that his son wasn't on the train at all.

'The next one's due in at two thirty, perhaps we should go home?'

Just as they were about to leave the station, the bearded man ran towards them with his arms open wide and smiling from ear to ear.

'Dad, it's me, don't you recognise me?'

'Michael?'

'Oh my God!' his siblings exclaimed in unison.

He stood in front of them expectantly, but looked so grubby and smelt so bad that not one of them wanted to touch him.

'And this is Mdinga.' He beckoned the woman over, and she lowered her eyes. 'Mdinga, this is my father, and my brother and sister.'

Deborah was unsure what to do, so she stuck her hand out in front of her and tried to find Mdinga's to shake it, but it was well and truly hidden. She took a quick look at her father, and thought he was going to pass out.

'Welcome home, Mick,' Jake said as heartily as he could manage. His eyes kept flitting from Michael to Mdinga and back, but nobody dared look at Wilfred.

The journey home was one of the most awkward the family had ever endured. Jake sat in the front with his father, and Deborah found herself wedged between Michael and his bride.

'Sorry about the pong, everyone, we've been travelling for three days without so much as a wash.'

Deborah had to open the window to stop her from heaving. Added to which, not one word had been spoken by their father throughout the whole journey, except when they reached their house.

'I can't bear to think what she'll make of this,' he muttered darkly.

In the event, Frances turned out to be the calmest of them all. She ushered them in with a steely look in her eyes; then, sniffing ostentatiously, suggested that they might like to freshen up before they had lunch.

'Good idea.'

'Take your time, Michael, no rush.'

As soon as the newlyweds were safely out of earshot, her face appeared to crumble, and she turned to her husband.

'Pour me a large whisky.'

'But you don't drink.'

'I do now.'

When Michael came downstairs alone, and looking more like his old self, the inquisition started.

'Who is she?'

'Didn't you get my letter? I told you all about my marriage.'

Wilfred sat down heavily in the nearest chair, and sensing trouble, his wife quickly handed him her tumbler of whisky. He gulped it down in one go, then got up and poured himself another.

'I know it was all a bit of a rush, Dad, but that's the way they do it out there.'

'And what made you think she was right for you in the first place?'

'You'll really like her when you get to know her.'

'Wilfred, I need another drink too.'

Once Wilfred had poured the whisky, he had to loosen his tie to breathe easier, and the bluish red tinge reappeared on his face.

'We'll get married again in synagogue if you like?' Michael waited expectantly, but there was no response from anyone because his family was still trying to absorb everything they'd heard so far. 'It was like, when I first saw her tending the cows,' he started to explain, 'I like, couldn't take my eyes off her, I thought she was absolutely gorgeous.'

Wilfred was now fanning himself with the *Manchester Guardian*. Even though it had begun to snow outside, the temperature inside the room was going off the scale.

'Anyway,' Michael continued, 'as soon as like her parents got word that she and I were friendly, they like sort of welcomed me to their hut ...' Wilfred spluttered into his drink. 'And after that like, what with one thing and another, I could hardly abandon her, could I?'

'What thing?'

'Urm ... her father sent her to my hut.'

'And you think she'll be able to settle down in the heart of Manchester?'

'With goodwill on both sides, why not?'

'My son the Messiah. Frances, I need to lie down, start lunch without me.'

As he spoke, Mdinga came shyly down the stairs. She had taken off her veil, and it was immediately obvious why Michael had been attracted to her, but Wilfred wouldn't even look in her direction.

'Michael, kindly come to my room after you've eaten, there are things we need to discuss.'

Later that afternoon, when Wilfred told his son that he was planning to send Mdinga straight back home, as they had expected, Michael ranted and swore every obscenity at his father that he knew.

'You're a dung-eating fucking racist, that's what you are! You're no better than Hitler, and just what makes you think I'm going to do as you say?'

'You're only nineteen, you still live under my roof, and there will be no further discussion about it. Besides, your marriage isn't even legal in this country.'

'So what? I'll marry her in a registry office if I have to, and just see what you can fucking well do about that.' He stood back sneering, confident that he had scored a victory.

'You want to see what I'll do, you fool, I'll cut you off without a penny, that's what I'll do.'

'But there's my university ...'

'Get a job if you want her, but don't expect me to support you.'

Throughout that afternoon, Michael banged doors so that their hinges shook, sulked and moaned and even shouted at Mdinga. But he soon realised that no one in the family wanted to get involved, and it was clear that his father and mother were of the same opinion and not going to budge.

It took two full days before Michael capitulated, then he locked himself in his bedroom, leaving Mdinga to fend for herself.

'It's not your fault at all,' Wilfred said, taking pity on the girl. He then explained, as gently as he could, that he was giving her an airline ticket to go back home to her own people. 'And I'll give you some money for your father to pay for your dowry.'

He handed her five hundred pounds in crisp fifty pound notes, and was completely taken aback at the speed with which she grabbed the money then shoved it down the front of her dress.

'Where ticket?' she demanded.

'Here, in my pocket.'

She grabbed it off him so forcefully that it almost tore in his hand. That also went swiftly down the front of her dress, and Wilfred wondered what else from the household she had secreted inside her bosom.

The following day he drove her to the airport, but Michael refused to accompany them. In fact, had it not been for Peggy taking his meals to his room and listening while he moaned and cried about the unfairness of life, he could well have starved during the next two weeks that he incarcerated himself inside his room.

*

While all this mayhem was taking place, Deborah was quietly nursing her guilty secret that she had spurned Gordon's marriage proposal. She was terrified that if her parents found out, they would then turn their fury on her once they no longer had Mdinga to worry about, and she had no wish to pour even more oil on the troubled waters of the Steinberg household.

'Peggy, when you next visit Gordon in the nursing home, can I come with you?'

'I thought you couldn't stand him.'

'I don't mind being his friend, but as his parents' boat is due back in Southampton in a couple of days, I thought maybe I should try to be a bit nicer to him.'

'I know your mother wants them to think that we took good care of him whilst he was with us, so how about you visit him on your own? I could do with some time to myself.'

But Deborah's motives were not quite as altruistic as she presented them to Peggy. Ian had returned moodily to university because Deborah couldn't see him as often as he wanted during the holidays, and after the fiasco of Michael's return, she was more anxious than ever that their relationship didn't come to light. She reckoned that by paying Gordon more attention, it might throw her parents off the scent.

'Gordon, can I come in?'

'Deborah?'

She walked into his room in the nursing home carrying a bunch of snowdrops, and she arranged her face into the prettiest and most sympathetic of smiles. He was sitting in an armchair in his dressing gown, looking as podgy as ever.

'I brought you these.'

'I never expected you to come.'

'Why ever not?'

'I thought it was all over between us.'

At this point she decided it would be prudent to be a bit contrite, so set about arranging her flowers and moving whatever else he had on his bedside table into the most favourable positions.

'Gordon, you and me will always be friends.'

'So you mean I've still got a chance with you?'

'Never say never.'

Then to her shame, she bent down and pecked him on his cheek. He blushed furiously.

'Gosh, Deborah, it's lovely to see you. My folks are coming in later, they'll be really pleased you're here.'

Damn, she thought, that means I'll have to stay later than I intended. She arranged her face as pleasantly as she could.

'My mother wanted you to be sure to know that it was a pleasure looking after you.'

'I like your mother.'

'She wanted to make sure you tell your mother that.'

'You'll see her yourself, so you can tell her.'

'The problem is, Gordon, Dad asked me to visit a sick old lady after I'd seen you.' She blinked several times, furiously trying to think of a plausible story to go with the old lady. 'Her family is destitute, and he thinks a visit from me would be a real tonic for her. And anyway,' she continued recklessly, 'I've bought her a present and I really need to deliver it before it's too late.'

'She's not dying is she?'

'No, no, I meant before she goes to bed.'

'I never realised you had such a soft side to you, Deborah. Please, would you pass me my jacket, it's hanging in there.'

She reached inside the wardrobe, wondering why he'd asked for it, but when she handed it to him, he searched inside the breast pocket and took out his wallet. Then he handed her three ten pound notes.

'Give her this, say it's from a well wisher.'

'Oh Gordon, you're so kind.'

'No, Deborah, it's you who's the kind one.'

When she left his room ten minutes later, she was feeling very ashamed, but after walking for a few minutes, debating which charity to give his money to, she decided it made sense not to let it go to waste. She reasoned that as she'd bought him the flowers, she was entitled to think of this as a perk, so once she was well clear of the nursing home, she headed straight for her favourite dress shop.

*

Having battled through so many personal problems recently, Wilfred was in the perfect frame of mind to acquire a new guru. The bearer of the title certainly looked the part, but would have raised his hands in horror to hear himself described as such.

His name was Rabbi Schmuel Lichtenstein, and he was the spiritual head of an ultra-orthodox section of Manchester Jews. In fact, he was just the sort of man Wilfred would have crossed the road to avoid under any other circumstances.

At the time of Gordon's protracted stay in his house, Wilfred had tried to make himself as scarce as possible, so had taken to his prison-visiting tasks more energetically then ever. One afternoon, while he was visiting his usual crop of die-hards, Lichtenstein was also at the prison, visiting one of his own flock, who had been had been sentenced to two years imprisonment for illegal accounting and larceny.

Once visiting time was over, Wilfred got into his car intending to drive home, but as he turned the key in the ignition, he noticed the other rabbi walking ahead of him towards Cheetham Hill. Wilfred drove off, and when he passed Lichtenstein he saw that although the other man had only gone a few hundred yards, he already looked exhausted and was puffing and panting. Wearing a heavy black frock coat and fur trimmed hat, Wilfred could tell that he was struggling.

Although he was going in the opposite direction, Wilfred couldn't help but take pity on Lichtenstein, so he turned the car round and followed the older rabbi. Drawing alongside him, he wound down the passenger window.

'Let me give you a lift.'

'Thank you, but the walk will do me good.'

'Please, get in, I'm going your way anyhow.'

Thus was born an unlikely friendship, which would prove to be Wilfred's salvation in the months to come.

Driving towards Cheetham Hill, the area where the majority of the ultra-Orthodox Jews lived, Wilfred and Lichtenstein engaged in light conversation, and were careful to avoid discussing any contentious religious issues. But Wilfred was curious as to why Lichtenstein didn't travel by car.

'Tell me, Rabbi, why didn't you come by car today?'

'Because, my friend, your people are a lot more generous than mine are,' he explained. 'When I asked my congregation to provide me with a car, they said it wasn't necessary because I lived near a bus route.'

'But a man of your age shouldn't have to use public transport, you should insist on it.'

'Unfortunately my *chevra*[14] don't think like yours.'

'Then they should be ashamed of themselves.' Wilfred mulled this over as he drove into the narrow streets of Broughton Park. 'I'll tell you what, some of my congregation have still got family amongst your people. Why don't I get them to put pressure on your lot, and we'll see what we can do to get you a car?'

---

[14]*people*

When Wilfred drew up outside Lichtenstein's house in Broom Lane, the other man had tears in his eyes. Several young children were playing football on the street, the boys wearing skullcaps, knee length breeches, all with long, curling *payot*[15] hanging in front of their ears. Most of the girls hung back shyly, all modestly dressed like their mothers would be.

'Rabbi, I don't know how to thank you.'

'My friend, you are the first of your people to call me by my title Rabbi, and not "that apostate".' Lichtenstein hung his head. 'And I must tell you, I appreciate that. But don't thank me yet, let's get the deed done first.'

'Who'd have thought it, me and you?'

'I'll be in touch as soon as I've got something to tell you.'

When Lichtenstein opened the passenger door, several of the children ran towards him. But before he shut the door, he introduced them all to Wilfred.

'This is Peshele and Itzchele, and this one's Rochele and the little one's Hannele. My other five must be inside. Children, say hello to the Rabbi.'

They chanted hello, but the older two boys stared in amazement at this rabbi who was both hatless and beardless.

Within a week, Wilfred had pressurised enough people within his own community to speak to enough people within the Orthodox rabbi's community to help buy him a car. But still the elders in the other rabbi's congregation vacillated, so Wilfred didn't even bother trying to get the money from them.

He realised they were probably turning their backs on his request because of who he was. Most of them regarded him as a traitor to the religion because he didn't follow in the old traditions, and he also regarded them as backward thinking. Years ago he had said to his own children: 'Those *yarmulkes*[16] they wear on their heads are like mental contraceptives, they prevent the birth of new ideas.'

So he decided to get some of the wealthier members of his own congregation to find the money for the car, and when he rang to tell Lichtenstein the good news, the older man cried down the phone:

---

[15]*ringlets* – [16]*skull caps* – [17]*decent human being*

'Rabbi, you're a real *mensch*[17], and I'm proud to call you my friend.'

Even Wilfred felt choked when he heard those words, which meant a lot to him, and which he would come to rely on at a later date when he found himself in serious trouble.

*

Although Ian's letters came fast and furiously, Deborah still wanted a social life whilst he was away. So after Gordon's discharge from the nursing home, she once again allowed him to accompany her to places she wanted to go to, and justified this by regarding it not so much as a date, but more as a practicality. He had the car and she wanted to go places.

One evening, she asked him to take her to a fashion show that was being held in a nearby Cheshire town. The organisers, a Jewish charity, had asked her and some of her friends to act as models, and during the evening she enjoyed sashaying down the catwalk and swinging her hips, as she'd been instructed to do. As an added incentive, the clothes supplier had offered each girl an outfit by way of payment.

Gordon insisted on driving the longest way home, taking an almost deserted country road, famed for its spectacular vista of the Cheshire countryside. Deborah argued that she was tired and that they wouldn't see anything in the dark, but he had driven on steadily, ignoring her views.

When she looked out of the window, she realised that they were now in the middle of another even narrower country lane, which was densely lined with trees. He drew into the kerbside and stopped.

'Why have you stopped?'

Then, without warning, he leaned over and kissed her urgently, even daring to touch her breast at the same time. She managed to pull away from him.

'Gordon, what are you doing?'

'But I thought ...'

She moved as close to the passenger door as she could without falling out, trying to gather her thoughts. This could be a tricky situation, and although perfectly aware of how callously she was treating him, she didn't want to mess things up just yet.

'Gordon, dear, I'm very fond of you, but you know my feelings on the subject.'

'But you're driving me mad. All I ever hear is Gordon take me here, Gordon take me there. I don't mind because I want to be with you, but I'm going crazy. I'm only human, Deborah.'

'You know I'm determined to stay pure till my wedding night, so I'm sorry but you'll just have to wait a bit longer.'

Desperately hoping that would pacify him, in the deep recesses of her mind she was already making plans to ditch him. He was becoming troublesome, so the best thing would be to go out with other boys as well. She'd already turned down several out of loyalty to Ian, but she'd never thought of Gordon in the date category, having always regarded him as a sort of neuter.

So very soon after Gordon's abortive attempt at intimacy, she telephoned her friend Laura.

'There's a dance next Sunday at the country club, do you fancy going?'

'I thought you were saving yourself for Ian.'

'I am, but even I get bored of doing nothing.'

'What's happened to your trusted lap dog and chauffeur?'

'I'm fed up of dodging his wandering paws.'

'OK, let's try and find some new talent.'

The following Sunday night, as soon as the two of them entered the ballroom, which at other times served as a bridge club, they looked around at the female competition, and decided that they were easily the best-looking pair there. It wasn't long before a boy came up to Deborah and held out his hand.

'Would you like to dance?'

'OK.'

'My name's Anthony Wilson.'

He had curly brown hair and a wry smile, and she liked the look of him. He was a natural, easy dancer and steered her round the floor effortlessly.

'I live in Prestwich, where do you live?'

'Just down the road.'

'That's convenient.'

'For what?'

'For taking you home later,' he said confidently.

She laughed and made a mental note that if she was going to see him again, the fact that he didn't live locally was a huge plus in his favour.

'You still haven't told me your name,' he said, twirling her round, then pulling her in closer.

'Deborah.'

'Tell you what, Deborah, as soon as I saw you come through those doors I thought, now that one looks a bit of all right.'

From then onwards they danced exclusively with each other, and any reservations she had about either Ian or Gordon remained firmly in the back of her mind for the rest of the evening. After the last dance had been announced, he looked at her.

'So, can I take you home?'

'Why not?' She looked around for Laura, who was also busily dancing, and gave her friend the thumbs up.

When they reached the car park, Anthony opened the passenger door of his small car for her, then went around to the driver's side. He turned the key in the ignition and asked: 'What's your other name?'

'Steinberg.'

'Steinberg?' A certain tension had suddenly entered the small space in the car that separated them, and he seemed to nudge ever so slightly further away. 'Not *that* Steinberg?'

'If you mean Rabbi Steinberg, I'm afraid so.'

He stared at her closely, as if he was considering something very important, and it felt like an icy shard had suddenly cut into her. She reached for the door handle to get out of the car, but he immediately put out his hand to stop her.

'I didn't know you were the rabbi's daughter.'

'And do you know my father?' she asked coldly.

'No.'

'But you recognised his name.'

'Everyone knows his name.' Then she could have sworn she heard him sigh with resignation, but he swerved the car out of the car park and drove on to the main road.

He hardly spoke on the journey to her house, and when his car pulled up outside, she was about to open the passenger door when she decided to challenge him.

'Is something wrong with me?'

He hesitated, as if he was struggling to find the right words to say. 'Well, yes, and I'm sorry but I can't see you again.'

'I thought we were getting on so well.'

She was angry about this sudden change, because no one else had ever treated her this way, but no sooner had she uttered the words than she heard that sigh escape from his mouth again.

'We were.'

'So why not?'

'I can't go out with you because you're not religious enough.'

That was it, he'd finally managed to get the words out, but when he did it was like holding the proverbial red rag up to the bull, and brought to the fore all Deborah's combative spirit.

'That's ridiculous. You are telling me that you can't ask me out because I'm not religious enough! I bet I know more about religion than you do.'

'Maybe, but my father would never allow it.'

'Do you always do what your father wants?'

'Not always.'

She reached for the door handle and opened her door. Then she slid out of the car, making sure to give him the best possible view of her legs as she did so.

'So I'll just have to think of you as the one that got away.' But before she had even managed to shut the car door, he blurted out: 'What's your telephone number?'

After that the two of them saw each other at least twice a week, and with every week that passed, they became closer. In spite of his initial reluctance, he was fun to be with, and their relationship progressed without the same degree of angst as her relationship with Ian.

She did however notice that he was always careful to avoid any talk of religion, but she put that to the back of her mind because they were having such a good time together. Unfortunately, Ian was due back from university shortly.

Because of this new man in her life, for the first time since she'd first met Ian at the cricket match, Deborah was seriously questioning the wisdom of making him part of her future.

'He's got to realise that I'm too young to sit around shuffling my feet while he's away,' she justified it to Laura.

'But didn't you sort of promise yourself to him?'

'And I meant it at the time, but I'm just not sure I can do it to my parents. They've been through so much with our Michael recently, and I can see what problems he's caused them.'

'Don't tell me our Deborah Steinberg's finally developing a conscience?' Laura scoffed.

'Honestly, Laura, I don't want to cause even more upset.'

*

Four weeks later, Ian arrived home and telephoned her at the first opportunity. It felt quite odd that her heart didn't miss a beat like it used to when he called; now it made her feel quite agitated instead. She knew they had to meet and that the outcome was going to be unpleasant for both of them. But when she replaced the receiver in its cradle she found herself trembling.

'God, Deborah, you don't know how much I've missed you.'

They were not sitting on their usual park bench because it was pouring with rain. Instead they'd gone to sit in the shelter alongside an elderly lady who was knitting, and a young mother rocking her baby's pram. Both women were pretending not to listen in to their conversation, but were in fact taking a great interest in it. Eventually, Deborah got round to the subject she was dreading.

'Ian, I've got something to tell you that you are not going to like.' The two women craned their necks. 'I'm sorry, but it's over between us, I've met someone else.'

'What!'

His face had gone deathly pale, and the older lady put down her knitting. Now both the onlookers were fully engaged.

'You're a wonderful man,' she whispered, 'but it's over.'

Suddenly he stood up, and completely oblivious to his audience, started shouting at her as loud as he could: 'You've met someone else? Who?'

She looked around anxiously, and the two women pretended to go back to what they'd been doing before they arrived. The rain continued pelting down and seemed to be a fitting accompaniment to the drama that was taking place within the shelter.

'I'm so sorry, I never meant for this to happen, but it wouldn't have worked out between us. You see, when Michael brought his African wife home ...' That made both women look up with renewed interest, so Deborah turned her back firmly on them, and tried to whisper. 'And my parents threw her out, and now they've sent him to Israel to the army, and everything's such a mess. So you must see that I couldn't do the same thing to them all over again.'

'But she was African ...'

'It didn't matter what colour she was, she wasn't one of us, and they wouldn't accept you even if you had a hooked nose and *payot*.'

'What?'

'Sorry – ringlets.'

The old lady looked at the young mother who raised her eyebrows and mouthed 'Jewish.' Then the older one renewed her knitting and eavesdropping, nodding sagely.

'But I've waited for you all this time.'

'Haven't you been out with anybody?'

'Not even once, just to the pub with the boys.'

'And you never chatted up any girls in all that time?'

He hesitated slightly. 'Hardly ever.'

'Ian, I tried, I really did, but eventually I got fed up.'

She thought it best not to mention Gordon, as that would only confuse the issue even further. He slumped down on the bench again, and hid his head in his hands.

'I just can't believe you've done this to me.'

Then without warning, he stood up angrily and hurled himself rugby-style against one of the glass partitions of the shelter, and then all three women looked scared. One of the panes splintered and sent glass fragments onto the stone floor and a few landed on the baby's pram.

'Oy, what do you think you're playing at?' The mother rushed to inspect her baby then clear the glass off the pram.

'Oh shit, I'm sorry!'

Ian looked mortified, and tried to help the mother remove the glass from the pram.

'I don't care what the little bitch 'as done to you, it's no reason to take it out on other folk.'

226

Deborah bristled, and was about to reply when she spotted the park keeper rushing towards the shelter.

'Quick!' She pushed him out of the shelter, then without saying another word to each other, he ran off with the keeper chasing after him. Deborah and the two women watched till the men were out of sight. 'I think he got away.'

'Just as well, the way you've treated him.' Then both women stood up, staring accusingly at Deborah, who had tears streaming from her eyes. 'You should be ashamed of yourself.'

'Mind your own business.'

She pulled out a handkerchief and blew her nose hard. Then she too ran through the sheeting rain, back to her house and the comfort she needed from Peggy.

CHAPTER 13

Deborah firmly believed that her guilt over Ian would never completely go away, but Anthony Wilson more than compensated for it at the present time.

However, throughout the time they were seeing each other, Anthony had avoided taking Deborah to his house, but she had not been particularly curious to meet his parents anyway. He had already met hers, but under the most embarrassing of circumstances.

One evening, after the two of them had been to the cinema, when he drove her home they both realised that her house was completely in the dark. Not wanting to miss this fortuitous opportunity of having the house to themselves, she made a quick decision.

'Would you like to come in for a coffee?'

They both knew that this was a polite euphemism for a warm drink followed by heavy necking, and after she made the coffee – which neither of them bothered to drink – they settled down in the lounge. He dimmed the lights, and Deborah put on her favourite Nat King Cole long-playing record, ideal background music for what they were now intending to do.

'When I fall in love, it will be for ever, or I'll never fall in love …' Nat crooned in his velvety style, while Deborah and Anthony lay full length on the couch, exploring each other's bodies to the full. 'In a restless world like this is, love is ended before it's begun …' They were so engrossed in each other that neither of them heard Wilfred's car coming into the drive, nor the front door opening shortly afterwards.

'Deborah?'

The lounge lights went on in a blinding instant, and Deborah and Anthony cowered in shock. Deborah made a vain attempt to button her blouse, only too aware that behind her Anthony would be desperately trying to cover the telltale signs of what they'd been trying to do before Frances arrived. She could feel her mother's eyes boring through her in an effort to get a better view of the boy hiding behind her daughter.

'And this is …?'

'I'm Anthony Wilson.' He stuttered and shuffled out from behind Deborah, and at that precise moment Wilfred too came into the lounge, and the young couple's shame was complete.

'It's late.' Wilfred stared from his daughter to Anthony, then his eyes rested firmly on the lower half of Anthony's body, or more particularly his swollen crotch area.

'Yes, sir, I'd better be going.'

Two weeks later, Anthony suggested to Deborah that she should meet his parents. She could see that this was difficult for him, so she tried to help him out.

'Do we have to?'

'I suppose so, if we're going to have a future together.'

'Did you just say what I think you said?'

'I must have done.'

She felt so elated that she kissed him passionately. He hadn't exactly asked her to marry him, but it seemed almost as good as; but a niggling doubt remained in the back of her mind. Why hadn't he actually used the right words? She was about to find out.

When he'd asked his parents if he could bring a special friend to tea the following weekend, an inquisition had started.

'How special?' his father asked, puffing deeply on his pipe.

'A girl I've been going out with for a while.'

'You're bringing a girl here, for tea?' His mother's eyes lit up expectantly. 'You've never done that before.'

'This one's special.'

'Did you hear that, David? He said this one's special.'

'Someone I'm very fond of.'

'Did you hear that, David? It's someone he's very fond of.'

'Stop wittering on, Emily, he'll tell us all we need to know when he's good and ready.'

Emily Wilson was disappointed that her husband had put a stop to her questions, but she was used to being bossed about by him. She was a small, neat woman with tightly curled grey hair, and she took great pleasure in her only son, who was the apple of her eye.

'Should I get my hair done?'

'Don't go to any trouble, Mum, she's not the sort of girl to notice that sort of thing.'

'Just tell me one more thing. Is she from round here?'

'No, Didsbury.'

David Wilson looked up. 'I hope she's not a Sephardi[18].'

'She's not, but wait and see for yourself when I bring her.'

Without noticing it up till that moment, Anthony realised that he'd crossed the fingers on both hands tightly whilst he'd been speaking to them.

During the time that her romance with Anthony was in its first flush of excitement, Deborah had again overlooked Gordon completely. She couldn't be bothered to contact him, and in her naivety, imagined that he would be as easy going about it as she was.

Unfortunately, what she failed to notice was that Gordon still kept in touch with Peggy. Indeed, whilst he'd been staying at their house, Deborah had once overheard a snippet of conversation he was having with Peggy. The maid had just taken in a tray of food, and something Gordon said would come back to haunt them all later.

'Palm Springs is a lovely place. I've got some photographs – here, take a look. The house is beautiful, it's got its own swimming pool, and I'm sure they'd give you a car if you wanted it.'

'They'd do that for a maid?'

'No, a housekeeper. That's much better than being just a maid.'

At that moment the telephone had rung, and Deborah was forced to go and answer it. By the time she put the receiver down, Peggy had left his room, and when nothing more was said on the subject, Deborah put the conversation to the back of her mind, then completely forgot about it.

*

---

[18]*Spanish & Portuguese origin*

The day of the tea party with Anthony's parents arrived, and Deborah spent hours getting ready. She now had a discarded selection of clothing scattered over her bed, and she had pulled Jake into her room for his advice.

'What do you think of this one?' She held out yet another dress in front of him.

'Too much flesh.'

'Oh God!'

'How about the blue one?'

'I only wear that one for synagogue.'

'You said his parents were religious, so it'll be perfect.'

Knowing that the religious odds were stacked heavily against her, she was nevertheless determined to make as good an impression on Anthony's parents as she could. But when he came to pick her up, it was obvious from the look on his face that he was anxious about the visit.

'My Dad's not the easiest man in the world,' he started by way of a warning as they drove away from her house. 'Thought I should tell you that. Oh, and you look lovely by the way.'

'Is my lipstick too dark?'

'Very kissable.'

'What about this dress?'

'Take-off-able.' In spite of his attempts at humour, his hands were gripping the steering wheel and she could see the whites of his knuckles.

'It can't be as bad as when you met my parents?'

'That was pretty awful, I'll give you that, but now we've got today to get through.'

He drove through the centre of town towards the northern side of the city, and he eventually came to a stop outside a small, pebble-dashed house in a narrow road in Prestwich. Deborah got out of the car nervously, then saw that his mother was on the doorstep waiting to welcome her. As she walked up the garden path, she was grateful to see that Emily Wilson was smiling.

Tea had been laid out formally in the dining room, and Anthony's mother fussed over Deborah, making sure that she was sitting in a comfortable chair, and finding out what her favourite sandwiches were. All the while, the three of them waited for David

Wilson to make his appearance. Eventually there was the sound of a toilet flushing, then David came into the dining room.

Deborah immediately stood up, and Anthony's father held out his hand to shake hers. She noticed that he hadn't dried his hand thoroughly, and her own now felt damp.

'Dad, this is Deborah.'

'Deborah …?' David Wilson looked to her expectantly, waiting for her surname to be announced.

'Mum, should I pour the tea?'

'No, dear, you sit down next to Deborah and I'll do it.'

David picked up a plate of sandwiches and pushed it across the table to her.

'You were saying?'

'I didn't say anything.'

'Yes, I asked you your name.' He took a large bite of an egg and cress sandwich, and some egg dribbled out of the side of his mouth.

'Oh that,' she smiled, 'Steinberg.' She bit into her own sandwich, uncomfortably aware that Anthony had suddenly gone rigid by her side and hadn't moved a muscle.

'Which Steinbergs are those, the Steinbergs from Cheetham Hill?'

'No, I don't have any family round here.'

There followed a sharp intake of breath from Wilson senior, and a distinct wilting motion from Wilson junior.

'Not Steinberg the rabbi?' His face had darkened, and he pushed his chair back from the table.

'Yes, that's my father.'

Anthony's cheeks were flushing a deep red, and before any of them knew what was happening, David Wilson had stood up and abruptly left the room without saying another word.

'David?' his wife called out in embarrassment.

Deborah then looked from her to Anthony, and to her dismay saw that he had covered his face with his hands.

'I'm so sorry, I'll take you home.'

Emily Wilson stared vacantly, not knowing what to say. Deborah stood up and, as if in a trance, made her way towards the front door. When she got into Anthony's tiny Austin Seven, she was trembling violently.

She stared out of the passenger window for most of the silent journey home, and when he drew up outside her house, he looked at her with tired, bloodshot eyes.

'I knew this would happen.'

'Then why have you been taking me out?'

'I tried not to, remember?'

'What's wrong with him?'

'He hates everything your father stands for, and thinks he'll be responsible for the death of Judaism.'

'That's ridiculous.'

'Maybe, but that's how he thinks, and I'm afraid there are plenty like him in our part of town.'

'What are you going to do?'

'I don't know.'

'Stand up to him.'

He looked across at her sadly. 'But he's my Dad, and I agree with him.'

That was the day that Deborah learnt all about humiliation. It was the first time in her life that she had been made to feel second class, and it cut her deeply. The worst part was that she really wanted to be with Anthony, and had been fantasising about their future together for several weeks.

'It even made Gordon seem reasonable,' she later confided to her best friend Laura.

*

Michael was in Israel again, but this time he adapted to the country better than he had the first time he visited. At Basil Leveridge's suggestion, reinforced by his father's insistence, he tried to join Nahal, the volunteer army. Unfortunately for the two older men, they turned him down, saying they were too occupied with border skirmishes to train a nineteen-year-old youth from England, especially one who was only staying until his university term started. Determined to prove to both men that he could accomplish something worthwhile whilst he was there, Michael hitchhiked to a kibbutz on the Syrian border, and asked if he could work there. They were only too pleased to accept the offer of help, and the kibbutz committee agreed that if he worked in the fields harvesting the fruit and vegetables, they would give him free board and lodgings in return.

He liked being in the fields in the open air, and worked uncomplainingly for six weeks before boredom set in. Living amongst the Sabras, native-born Israelis, they regaled him with stories of wars fought, friends lost in combat, and the need for constant vigilance against their enemies. Michael lay awake at night in his tiny room, dreaming of becoming a hero like so many of the men on the kibbutz.

'Do you know, I could see myself settling here?' he told his new friend Avi.

Avi Heksch had been born and raised on the kibbutz, and was due to join the army any time now. His present job was tending to the sheep, and he was forced to carry a gun everywhere he went, to deter local Arabs from stealing from the herd at night.

'I could do your job when you leave for the army.'

'You say that now, but you're not like us, you've been raised like a softie in Britain.'

That remark hurt Michael's pride.

'I can do anything you can do, my friend.'

'Do you know how to use a gun?'

'Sure I do.'

'OK, Mister Englishman, tonight I'll let you do my watch, and let's see how you get on.'

'Fine by me.' But Michael was already shivering.

'Better not say a word to the others, they'd kick up a real stink if they knew, and I'll sleep in your bunk in case they think you've gone missing. Now, are you sure you're up for it?'

'What do you take me for?'

Avi gave him a look of grudging respect, then spent the rest of the afternoon instructing him on everything he had to do during his night watch.

'Oh, and just one more thing, you must keep the gun with you at all times.'

When he finally handed the Uzi over, Michael felt an immediate surge of excitement course through him.

Dusk came quickly in winter, and the evening air was chilled in comparison to the daytime temperature. Michael borrowed

Avi's flak jacket and promised to return everything to him before daylight.

Making his way to the sheep pens in the dark, Michael felt like a true pioneer, then settled down in the bunker that his friend had told him to spend the night in. Sitting there, listening to the sounds of crickets chirruping, and the occasional barking of a dog, he muttered lazily to himself.

'There's nothing to this, don't know what all the fuss is about.'

After a few hours, it became very cold on the damp ground, and even the sheep huddled together for warmth. In spite of his determination not to, Michael dozed off. All of a sudden there was sharp crackling sound.

'Who's there?'

Nobody answered, but while he trembled, terrified to move, a large sheep walked away from the herd, treading on brittle twigs as it did so. Eventually, when the fear had settled down, he yawned then admonished himself to stay awake. The noises of the night were now frightening him, and he knew he had to do something while he was there to stay alert till the morning.

He decided to take the gun out of its holster and inspect it. He'd never handled one before, even though he'd seen the local men polishing them to keep them in prime condition. It was so dark that he could barely see the outline of the gun, so he ran his fingers along the barrel and searched for the trigger mechanism just to locate it.

It was then that he realised he needed to pee, and decided to do it behind the bunker. He stood up clumsily, because one of his legs had cramp in it, but the leg gave way and he toppled over, dislodging the gun out of his hand. He made a lunge for it before it hit the ground, but grabbed the trigger instead of the barrel, and the gun discharged.

'Holy shit!'

At first he thought a stray stone had hit him, but when he bent down, he felt a sticky wetness gathering in his boot. Then the awful realisation hit his brain, that he had accidentally shot himself. A stream of urine started to ooze down his pants, and the sound of his own tortured screams rent the stillness of the night. After that, he lost consciousness.

'Man, you had us all worried, but me I'm in even bigger shit, and I'll tell you this, my friend, the kibbutz can't wait to see the back of you once you're better.'

Michael looked around the small hospital ward. He'd noticed it before on his way round the kibbutz, but never dreamt he'd end up in it.

'But this Arab sniper shot me,' he protested.

'Yeah, and I'm David Ben Gurion.'

'You've seen the bullet wound.'

'Man, if an armed Arab had taken a pot shot at you, he'd have found a better target than your fucking foot.'

One of the nurses came to his bedside with a thermometer. Michael recognised her from the communal dining room where everyone took their meals, and she hissed at his visitor:

'Avi, scram, you've done enough damage already.'

She spoke in Hebrew, and Avi tried arguing with her. But she was adamant he had to leave, so he gave a small wave to Michael and made for the door.

'Now, let's take a look at the damage,' she said in heavily accented English.

Michael watched as she began peeling off his blood-soaked bandages. When she got to his foot, he nearly fainted at the sight of it. The foot was blackened and charred, and looked as if he'd never be able to walk on it again.

'You were lucky, the bullet passed through the gap between your toes, so it's just a nasty flesh wound. We'll have you mended in no time.'

'Can I have some water?'

He tried not to think about what he'd just seen because he didn't want the ignominy of being sick in front of her.

'Sure, when I've changed the bandage.'

She carefully cleaned and dressed the wound, and Michael averted his eyes from his foot to watch her. She was pretty, with dark olive toned skin and large brown eyes.

'What's your name?'

'Miri, it's short for Miriam.'

'Miriam, Mdinga,' he murmured, then closed his eyes and drifted off into a troubled sleep.

The next day she was there again, and she brought a tiny dish to his bedside. When he looked into it, she smiled.

'It's the bullet that landed in your shoe, I thought you might want to have it as a souvenir of your stay in kibbutz.'

'Mdinga …'

'Miriam,' she corrected him.

'What's going to happen to me? Avi said they wanted to send me home.'

'Not till you are well enough.'

Then a shocking thought hit him.

'Has anyone told my parents?'

'I expect so.'

A shiver ran down his spine as he began mentally preparing what he would tell them when they caught up with him, but a plausible story had started forming in his brain, and it started something like this:

'There was this Arab sniper, nasty looking bugger with a Kalishnikov pointing straight at me, but he came off much worse than I did I can assure you …'

*

When he received the telegram, Wilfred wondered whether he should read it to his family or not; but finally, after making his decision, he trembled while he read the contents to them.

'Shot?'

'That's what it says here.'

'Oh my God, is he dead?'

'It says he's going to be all right.'

'You'll have to go there immediately and bring him back. He needs to be in a proper hospital.'

'I'll book a flight as soon as I can.'

'Should I come with you?' Jake enquired solicitously.

'We're not made of money you know!' his mother screeched, and with that he had his answer.

*

237

Everything was going so badly for the Steinbergs, that Deborah found herself racking her brains as to what she could do to bring some pleasure into their lives. Her mother had taken to wearing her hot water bottle again, only now she tied it in an apron around her waist, and only took it off was when she went shopping.

Frances was sighing a lot, and these days would answer most questions with a weary sigh. Her daughter knew she was in pain, both mental and physical, but whether that was because of the circumstances or because of her kidney condition, she wasn't sure.

Wilfred was on his way to Israel, and news of Michael's accident spread fast amongst the congregation. Gordon's parents were amongst the first to pick up the phone to enquire about him.

'When they're young they give you little problems, and when they're older they give you big problems,' Christine said sympathetically.

'You're telling me!'

'I know just what you're going through, I was so worried about our Gordon, but I have to say, Frances, I don't know what would have happened to the poor boy if you hadn't taken him in.'

'It's the least we could do.'

'So whilst Wilfred's in Israel, I want you to come to dinner. How about this Wednesday?'

'So kind,' Frances murmured.

'The family as well.'

'We'll all be delighted to come, especially Deborah.'

That Wednesday the hot water bottle came off, and Frances went to the hairdressers. While she was out, she bought a large bouquet of flowers for Christine and a bottle of cherry brandy for Cyril.

Christine despatched Gordon to collect the Steinbergs in Cyril's Rolls Royce, and when Deborah was about to get into the car, Frances nudged her as if to say, look how nice this is.

After dinner was over, Gordon pulled Deborah aside and whispered in her ear.

'Do you fancy going out this weekend?'

In the past she would have been desperately searching for an excuse to say no, but in her newly chastened and rather depressed state, she nodded resignedly.

'That would be nice.'

Thus did Deborah and Gordon's relationship take a giant leap forward. She still felt the same way towards him as she had in the past, but now she was more careful to hide her true feelings and not to hurt his.

Both mothers looked on approvingly as their dates became more frequent, and Frances positively bloomed. Away went the hot water bottle, and back came the pink complexion. Peace descended on the household, that is until Wilfred returned from Israel, without his son.

'Why didn't you bring Michael back?' Frances screeched by way of a welcome.

'He said he wanted to stay, and the kibbutz relented and told him he could stay till he was due back.'

'But he needs looking after.'

Wilfred thought about the pretty nurse who always appeared to make sure that his son was getting what he needed.

'Don't worry on that score, the boy seems happy enough.'

Gordon asked Deborah the same question about Michael from the remote tree lined avenue he'd stopped at in the past. He was fumbling on the outside of her blouse and rubbing her clumsily, but she didn't stop him. He couldn't believe his good luck or guess the reason for her new passivity, but he was well aware that this was as far into her personal space as she allowed him to go.

'Apparently he's fallen for some girl out there. She was his nurse, and he said he doesn't want to come back till he goes to university.'

In spite of the inevitability of being with Gordon, which she was now coming to see was her fate, she still found it very irritating that he was nuzzling her neck and licking it at the same time, but she said nothing. Because of recent events, particularly the abrupt ending of her relationship with Anthony, a force other than her own free will seemed to have taken her over, and she was allowing herself to be dragged mutely along with it.

Up till that point, Deborah had always been a resilient person, so she didn't recognise the deep-seated depression that now lurked within her. What she did notice was that her mother looked at her expectantly every day, desperately hoping that she had some important information to impart on the subject of Gordon. She tried to avoid her mother as much as she could, but the day arrived when Frances's wait was finally over.

'Deborah?'

'Yes, Gordon?'

'Will you marry me?'

A voice inside her head was screaming, don't be crazy, get out of the car and run for your life. But her mother's expectant face loomed in front of her, and she knew she couldn't avoid her fate any longer.

'All right, Gordon.'

Even though the tone of her acceptance was delivered in a businesslike, unemotional voice, Gordon's joy knew no bounds.

'Oh Deborah, I do love you.' He grabbed her and kissed her wetly.

'Um, me too.'

This was the first of many barefaced lies between her and her new fiancé, and it gave rise to such a feeling of despondency that she almost wept. From then onwards she knew she would gamely have to try to ignore these feelings; so, duty bound to respond, she gave him a quick peck on his cheek.

*

Frances was planning to make the largest engagement party that Manchester had ever seen. She decided that it would be a tea dance for one half of the congregation from three till six, and afterwards a cocktail party from seven till nine for the other half, but in the same location.

'That way we can invite the entire congregation, and Deborah will get double the amount of presents.'

Her husband shuddered when he thought of the inevitable visit he would now have to make to his bank manager, asking for yet another loan, but he knew his wife wouldn't change her mind, so it had to be done.

The day after the couple told their respective parents, Gordon arrived at her house with the largest diamond ring Deborah or indeed her mother had ever seen. Subsequently, this was to prove to be a source of much embarrassment for the girl, because whenever she wore it in college, most of the lecturers crowded round her to take a look.

'Good Lord, it's bigger than the Koh-i-nor, how many carats is that?' The French teacher's mouth fell open in awe.

'Plenty I should say,' the typing teacher, who happened to be passing, replied.

'Sell that and you could cure world poverty.'

'Would you like to try it on?'

Deborah was trying to placate them all, but when she looked down at the typing teacher's minuscule diamond ring, she winced in shame at the size of hers. Her mother, on the other hand, found a new aspect of the forthcoming engagement party to get excited over with every passing day.

'Apparently, there's this very good shop in Blackpool we can go to for your engagement dress, and maybe I can start looking for your trousseau at the same time.'

Frances was in seventh heaven making all the arrangements, which was just as well because her daughter had little interest in them. With every day that passed, she was increasing feeling like a lamb being led to the slaughter, but didn't know what to do to prevent it.

The engagement had already been announced in the *Manchester Guardian*, the *Evening News* and the weekly Jewish newspapers, and to Deborah's further distress, Christine Helfgot had also began taking more interest in her, especially her choice of clothes.

'Why do you wear so many dark colours, dear? They're really not suitable for young girls. Here, put my necklace on, it will brighten that dress up.'

She then thrust her own necklace, consisting of several rows of multicoloured pearls, round her future daughter-in-law's neck. Deborah had to bite her lip to stop herself from refusing it.

'Young girls should only wear pastel colours, so much more suitable.'

'She wants me to look like a ruddy two year old,' she later complained to Laura.

'Why complain? Look at all the goodies you're getting.'

Not wanting to be outdone by his wife, Cyril bought her a gold watch as an engagement present. She liked Cyril, but she was finding Christine increasingly irksome. What bothered her most about her future mother-in-law was the fact that when Gordon was with his mother, he did exactly what she told him to do.

'Gordon, show Deborah how well you wipe the sink and draining board after we've finished the washing up.'

'She's not interested in that.'

'Of course she is, she'll have a house of her own to run soon, and she should see how we like it done.'

'Surely there's only one way to do it?'

'No, Deborah, the secret is to wipe from the outside of the sink inwards – show her, Gordon, and when you've done that you move towards the plug hole in decreasing circles. That way, not a drop of water will be left in the sink.'

Deborah dug her nails into her clasped hands as she was duly made to watch Gordon's expertise at sink wiping. When the display was over, she wasn't sure whether to laugh or cry.

'See, I told you she was interested.'

Back in the comparative sanity of her own home, Jake was inspecting her collection of new gifts. The two of them were standing beside the window of her bedroom, and he insisted on taking Cyril's watch there to get a better look at it.

'Are you sure that's real gold?'

'Of course it is.'

'I don't think it is, because real gold shines more than that.'

'How would you know?'

'Everyone knows that.'

'Don't be stupid, he wouldn't have given me a fake.'

'Only one way to prove it.' She listened uneasily, with a frown on her forehead. 'We should take it to another jeweller's shop and ask their opinion.'

'I don't think so.'

'Well, that's the only way you're going to find out if they think enough of you to give you the real thing. I'll come with you if you like, and if I'm right you can buy me tea and cakes, and if I'm wrong, I'll buy them.'

'Oh, the last of the big spenders!'

'Do you want to know or don't you?'

They decided that if they were going to do this, it had to be done discreetly because Deborah didn't want the Helfgots knowing she had been querying the gift. So Jake made it his business to stake out other jewellers in the city centre, then select one whose shop was as far away from the Helfgot's premises as possible.

'I've found one that's miles away from theirs,' he told her within a few days, 'we can go tomorrow if you like?'

After Deborah had finished college and Jake had left school the next day, they arranged to meet at the shop he'd selected. So instead of taking his usual school bus home, Jake boarded one going into the city centre, but after she'd left college that day, Deborah was feeling out of sorts.

She'd just finished two tests in French and typing, and because the latter was the subject she hated the most, all she really wanted to do was go home and run a hot bath. To further complicate matters, she was aware that dressed as a student and not a jewellery shopper, she now looked untidy and unkempt.

When she ran to catch the bus, she was already late for Jake, and by the time she arrived at the shop, she was feeling hot and sticky as well. She ran into the designated shop, and found Jake inside, studying watches in the display cabinets.

'Look,' he pulled her aside quickly, 'I told you – these cheap ones look exactly the same as yours.'

Deborah twisted her engagement ring round her finger anxiously, a gesture she had started to do a lot of recently, and these days she was feeling more and more anxious as every day went by.

'Can I be of assistance, sir, madam?'

A stern-looking man with thinning grey hair approached them. He was dressed in an immaculate pinstriped suit, and looked the two of them up and down with a distasteful look on his face.

'My sister wants to know if this is real?'

'Why don't you have a seat, sir, and you, madam?' He ushered them towards two high backed leather chairs, which were placed in front of the counter. 'Now, let me have a look.'

Deborah handed her watch over the counter, and as she did so, the assistant caught sight of the big diamond ring on her finger. Then, before making another move, he scrutinised both brother and sister closely. He saw in front of him a young girl devoid of make up, looking like an average college student dressed in cheap clothes. The boy was in school uniform, and the assistant asked himself where these two could have acquired such expensive jewellery?

'That's a very nice ring, madam, could I ask you where you got it?'

Deborah was taken aback by his question, and her first thought was that it was none of his business, so she declined to give much of an answer.

'From a friend.'

'And the watch?'

'That too.'

'I wonder if sir and madam would like to come into my office? It's far more comfortable in there.'

Not understanding why he wanted them to move, they exchanged puzzled glances, but meekly stood up and followed him into an office in the rear of the building. He left the door ajar.

'Please take a seat, and if you'll excuse me for just a moment, I've got an urgent phone call I must make. Before I do, I'd be obliged, madam, if you could tell me which jewellers shop your ring came from?'

'Well no, you see it's a bit embarrassing …'

'How so?'

'Because it came from my fiancé's shop.'

'You look far too young to be engaged if I may say so, madam.' He tried to smile, but it came out as a grimace.

'She's nineteen.'

'So young.'

'She won't tell you, but I will, the shop's called Helfgot's. It's just that my sister doesn't really like flashy things.'

'I see. Please excuse me – I'll only be a few minutes, then we can attend to the matter in hand.'

This time he shut the office door fully, and there was the unmistakable sound of a key turning in the lock. As soon as he'd left the room, Deborah and Jake lifted their eyebrows simultaneously.

'Bit of a crackpot.'

'Trust you to find the only nutcase in the jewellery business.'

They tried the door, and sure enough it was locked from the outside, so Jake tried putting his ear to the door, but could barely make out the muffled sounds of conversation taking place outside. However, he was sure he heard the word Helfgot's.

'Oh my God, he's ringing them.' Deborah clapped her hand

over her mouth in distress.

'No, I think he said police.'

'He can't be …'

The blood had drained out of her face, but as soon as she tried to open the door, she heard a key turning in the lock and the salesman came in with the watch still in his hand. He looked even more surprised than they were to find them standing by the door.

'Everything seems to be in order,' he said, looking quite disappointed, 'and to answer your question, sir, yes it is gold, twenty two carats as a matter of fact.'

When the pair walked out of the shop, the bemused salesman's eyes never left them. He shook his head from side to side, trying to figure out why such an ordinary girl possessed such extraordinary jewellery. Deborah could still feel his eyes boring into her well after she'd left the shop.

'You'd better buy me that tea, and fast!'

'Who'd have thought it was real? Just goes to show.'

Over tea and buttered scones in the café, Deborah insisted on going through all the possible scenarios as to what could have happened while they'd been locked in the jeweller's back office.

'I bet he rang the Helfgots, and now they'll know.'

'He won't have said anything bad; after all, we were only asking about the watch.'

'I just hope you haven't got me into trouble.'

'If Gordon says anything about it, you can tell him it was my fault.'

*

Frances had finally completed the arrangements for the engagement party. The venue and caterers had been booked, and she had even gone to the trouble of engaging a trio of amateur musicians from the college of music. She told them she wanted tasteful background music whilst the guests ate their mushroom vol au vents, four types of miniature sandwiches, and a variety of fancy cakes.

'Deborah, guess what? Michael says he's coming home for the party.'

To have her first-born home at the 'do' was the icing on the cake for Frances, and she waved the letter excitedly in front of her daughter. But when she looked across the table, for the first time since she'd started making plans for the party, she noticed the bleak look on Deborah's face.

'What's the matter? You look so miserable.'

'Nothing.'

'Silly girl, you should be on top of the world, like I am.'

But Deborah was mired in her own thoughts, wondering how to break the news that she was having serious doubts about marrying Gordon. It terrified her even more to think about ruining their plans at this late stage, or confessing that her future mother-in-law always made her feel so angry.

It would also mean having to admit that she'd only got engaged to give her parents something to look forward to, and worst of all, how could she tell anyone that the thought of having sex with Gordon made her feel physically sick?

But the jarring noise of a telephone distracted her temporarily. It was Gordon to tell her that he was sorry but he'd have to cancel their arrangement for that evening. When she asked him why, he mumbled something about seeing houses.

'Did you say houses?'

'Yes.'

'What houses?'

'Erm ... for us?'

'You're going on your own to see houses for us?'

'Not exactly, I'm going with Mum.'

Suddenly she felt very cold. Why would he go to look at houses with his mother if it was for the two of them?

'Let me get this right, you're going to look at houses for you and me, but you're not taking me with you?'

'Mum said that when we've chosen something nice, we'll take you along too.'

'But Gordon, this should be our choice.'

'Yes, but you know what Mum's like.' Then he tried to placate her. 'I'll let you into a little secret, but don't let her know I've told you. She's planning on buying you a car as well.'

'What sort of car?'

'A Mini, and guess what, it's a pink one!'

'I've got to go, I feel sick.'

She couldn't sleep at all that night, and tossed and turned for hours. Then at three o'clock in the morning, she crept downstairs into the kitchen to make herself a cup of tea. Nursing her tea miserably at the kitchen table, she didn't hear the footsteps coming in behind her.

'Mind if I join you?' Wilfred sat down at the table, looking concerned.

'Do you want a cup?'

'That would be nice.' She went over to the kettle, not wanting her father to see her red rimmed eyes, but when she put his cup down in front of him, he put his hand on top of hers. 'What's the matter, Debs?'

Then the tears that she had been holding back for so long plopped copiously down her cheeks.

'Oh Dad, I've made a horrible mistake.'

'I know you have, darling, I know you have.'

'And I can't bear wearing this damn thing any more.' She twisted the ring roughly off her finger, then threw it on the table in front of him.

Words and tears spewed out of her while she told her father everything, even her disappointment at losing Anthony.

'I blame myself for that, you know.'

'You, why?'

'There are a lot of Jews who have got it in for me, and up to a point I can understand them, but I never wanted my children to suffer because of it.'

'It wasn't your fault, the more I thought about it the more I realised I could never have lived with him in that ghetto.'

'I'm glad you've told me that, because I thought the same.'

Daylight was breaking when Wilfred offered to speak to the Helfgots. He would do so after Deborah had broken the news to Gordon that she wanted to end their engagement. Both father and daughter decided that it would be prudent not to tell Frances anything until the deed had been done.

The following morning, it took Deborah all her reserves of courage to pick up the phone and ask to speak to Gordon.

'I need to see you as soon as possible.'

'Is anything wrong, are you still sick?'

'No, but this can't wait.'

'I'll be round after breakfast.'

Deborah could hear the uncertainty in his voice, and when Christine saw the puzzled look on her son's face, she immediately asked him, 'What did she want?'

'To meet me now.'

'But you promised to give me a lift to the hairdressers. Phone her back and tell her it's inconvenient.'

Gordon nodded meekly, then dialled the Steinberg household, and this time it was Wilfred who answered the phone.

'Rabbi, would you tell Deborah that I can't see her till later, I promised I'd take my mother somewhere.'

'Gordon my boy, I think you should come over right now. I'm sure your mother will be able to manage without you.'

His tone alerted Gordon that this might be serious, but when he put the phone down his mother was looking triumphant.

'The sooner that girl realises that she can't order you around willy nilly, the better it will be for your marriage, Gordon.'

'You'll have to call a cab, I'm going over there now.'

Frances suspected something was amiss when he rang their front doorbell, and Wilfred rushed him inside into the lounge, where Deborah was waiting for him. Her father immediately shut the door firmly behind them, and insisted that his wife left them alone.

'I was only going to offer the boy a coffee.'

'Frances, they need to talk, and it's none of your business.'

'But if it's about the wedding, I need to know.'

'She'll tell you everything in good time.'

Deborah thought her legs would give way when she faced Gordon. He noted with alarm that her engagement ring was sitting in its box on the coffee table, and next to it was the watchcase.

'Deborah, if it's to do with the jeweller's shop, look I don't care ...'

She looked at him remotely, wondering how could she ever have got herself into this position.

'Gordon, I'm sorry, but I don't want to get married.'

'That's not a problem, we can postpone it for a few more months.'

'No, you don't understand, I don't want to get married to you, ever. I'm so sorry, I never meant to cause so much trouble. I won't keep a thing, I'll send back all the presents, and here's the ring and everything.'

She had neatly parcelled up Christine's pearls alongside the watchcase and ring box. Gordon sat down heavily on the sofa, unable to digest what she had just said.

For Frances, waiting in the kitchen, the suspense was terrible, and Wilfred had to restrain her several times from listening through the lounge keyhole. But when she eventually saw Gordon open the lounge door then scurry angrily towards the front door holding the jewellery, she nearly fainted.

'Gordon dear ...'

He barely heard her. The next thing she saw was her front door slamming shut, then heard the sound of his car revving up, and he was gone. She flew into the lounge as if jet propelled.

'What have you done?'

'It's over, I've told him.'

'You stupid girl, how could you do that to me?'

'Leave her alone, Frances, she was only doing what she had to.'

Deborah had never loved her father as much as at that moment, and she tried to stand up to kiss him, but her legs refused to support her weight, and she collapsed down into an armchair looking terrified. Meanwhile, Frances was just getting into her stride.

'What am I going to say to people? We'll be a laughing stock in the town!'

But her daughter was beyond caring, and when she finally managed to stand up, she went straight out of the room without saying another word. Her father watched her sadly as she climbed the stairs. She went into her bedroom and fell fast asleep on her unmade bed.

*

Returning several hundred unwrapped presents was no easy task, but living with Frances was far more difficult. Wilfred kept his promise and went to the Helfgot's house later that afternoon. He was grim faced when he returned home, but was carrying the watchcase in his hand.

'Cyril would like you to keep this, Deborah. He was very fond of you, and I got the feeling that he knew Christine gave you a hard time.'

'He was nice, but I really don't want it.'

'You should be grateful,' Frances snarled, 'after all the upset you've caused.' Wilfred lifted his hand to silence her. 'I should have known you'd take her side, and who do you think will marry her now? She's soiled goods, that's what she is!'

'Funny, that's exactly what Christine Helfgot said; now I fully understand why my daughter wanted out.'

After parcelling up frying pans, alarm clocks, bon bon dishes, and even a silk night-dress and negligee set, Deborah regularly took batches of gifts to the post office to mail back to the senders. She painstakingly wrote an appropriate note of regret with each one, but was glad to see the back of them.

One afternoon, she was about to go into the post office when she suddenly spotted Ian's mother going into the chemist shop next door. Although she was heavily weighed down with parcels, she decided to follow her.

'Mrs Christianson?'

The woman turned around in surprise. 'Yes, dear.'

'Remember me, I'm an old friend of Ian's?'

'Of course dear, you're that Jewish girl. He was very fond of you, wasn't he?'

'How is he?'

'Oh he's doing splendidly, thank you. He's now been posted to Saudi Arabia, you know.'

'Saudi Arabia?'

'Yes dear, a big oil company took him on straight from university, and they're very pleased with him.'

'That's so far away, have you seen him recently?'

'Of course dear, at his wedding.'

'His wedding?' She bit down hard on her lip to stop herself from screaming.

'He married Daphne, a very nice girl from our church. It was all very quick because of the job offer. She's a few years older than he is, but my husband thinks she'll be good for him.'

'That's nice.'

At that moment, Deborah wanted the floor to open up and swallow her, but she knew she couldn't leave the other woman, who was warming to her conversation.

'We're planning a trip there for Christmas, but between you and me, my Arthur's worried that he won't be able to get his pint of beer out there.' She laughed. 'Men, hey? Anyway, it's been lovely talking to you, dear, but I must hurry, Arthur hates it when I'm late.' She giggled as if she'd just told Deborah the punch line of a joke. 'Would you like a hand with those, dear? They seem very heavy.'

'I can manage, thanks.'

When she left the chemist shop and walked towards the post office, Deborah's eyes were stinging, and she found it hard to avoid banging into people on the pavement.

*

Gordon and his mother now had time to digest the situation, and they wanted revenge. Had either of them taken a look at Deborah at this time, they would have seen that she was suffering even more than they were, and might even have pitied her.

Frances openly blamed her daughter for every headache, backache or internal ache that she suffered. She seemed to take renewed pleasure in her illnesses, and rarely missed an opportunity of accusing her daughter of bringing the family name into disrepute, while at the same time ruining her health.

But because of all the time he'd spent with the Steinbergs, Gordon knew their Achilles heel, their weak spot, and was now being as devious as he could about it. Unbeknown to them, he made it his business to stay in regular contact with Peggy, and one day invited her to their shop to give her a gift of a gold plated charm bracelet. To Peggy, who didn't know the difference between real gold and gold plate, this seemed overwhelming in its generosity.

'Peggy, this is just my way of saying thank you for all you did for me when I was ill.'

'It's absolutely smashing, Gordon, but I can't accept something like this.'

'Why ever not?'

'I'd have to hide it away, it's so valuable.'

'Wear it every day, and if anyone asks …' She knew exactly whom he was referring to, 'just say I gave it you as a special thank you. But that wasn't the only reason I invited you here.'

He then went on to tell her that his cousin in Palm Springs was still looking for a housekeeper. He described the family in glowing terms, the idyll of the surroundings they lived in, and the huge sums of money they were prepared to pay.

'And do you know, Frank Sinatra lives in Palm Springs?'

'Is that so?'

'Like I said, the pay would be far better than anything you get from them.'

'Two children you say?'

'Bradlee, that's spelt with two E's, and Jacquie, spelt with a Q. She's so cute, and they're really well brought up, better than some I could mention. And you'd get to go on holidays with them as well. All in all, you'd have a much better life than you have now.'

'When would they want me to start?'

'Oh, as soon as you can.'

But to his extreme disappointment and annoyance, he could see that she was frowning.

'I'm not sure about this, Gordon, you see I'm just a simple girl …'

'But it's a fantastic opportunity.' Her expression told him that he now had to bring in the big guns. 'Besides, the Steinbergs don't appreciate you, even Deborah used to say …'

'What?'

'Oh you know, things like nobody's bothered about Peggy, she's not important, she's just the maid.'

'She said that, did she?'

'Well, not exactly in those words,' he had the grace to feel his face reddening, 'but I know that's what she meant.'

Gordon couldn't stop himself; he was on a roll, a man with a mission, and would do everything necessary to achieve his goal and avenge his beloved mother. At that moment, his task felt almost Shakespearean to him.

'If I agree to it, you won't say anything to the family, will you?'

'Not a word, I promise. Once you've handed in your notice, you can leave all the other details to me.''

'I'll miss my Jake so much.'

'You're far too good for them, and this is the best chance you'll ever have to better yourself. I'll tell you something else, my cousin's the chairman of her Hadassah group, which is a very big thing in the States, so you'll get to meet lots of important people, far more than you ever did with them.'

*

Peggy left their employ three months later. It took that long for Gordon to obtain a passport and visa for her, and then to buy her the cheapest airline ticket he could find.

When she finally handed in her notice, the Steinbergs knew it was futile to try to persuade her to stay. The truth was that they had nothing better to offer her, but her imminent departure from their household proved to be a bigger shock than the loss of Gordon as a son-in-law.

'And to think how much we put ourselves out for that ingrate,' Frances railed, clutching the water bottle to her stomach. 'But what can you expect from a convert's son?'

'It feels like part of my childhood has been taken away,' Jake confided in his sister. 'How do you think Mum's going to manage without her?'

'I have absolutely no idea.'

On the day of her departure, Peggy went off in a taxi, carrying the same suitcase she had arrived with so many years before. Although it was a sad day for all of the family, Frances finally pulled herself together. It seemed to bring out the best in her, her own personal Dunkirk spirit, and in time she coped better than the rest of them.

For the first few days after she left, Frances ran around the house with a duster and mop permanently attached to her side. Eventually she relaxed into a routine and looked happier than she'd been for a long time. She was once again mistress of her own home, and she liked the feeling.

But Wilfred fared less well. He had always depended on Peggy for clean shirts and a well-polished pair of shoes.

'If you want clean shoes, you'll have to polish them yourself, I've got far too much to do.'

But after a week of polishing his own shoes, and although Frances knew better than to try to get him to iron his own shirts, Wilfred revolted.

'Get a charwoman in to help you, we can't carry on like this.'

'All because you've got to polish your own shoes?'

He put his foot down, but afterwards they endured a succession of Bridies, Coleens, and once even a Concepta. However, none of them could iron or polish to the standard that Peggy had done.

'I feel lost without her,' Wilfred complained one Friday night when he was forced to take his own dirty dishes to the sink.

'You'll get over it,' Frances replied tartly.

CHAPTER 14

Michael was due home from Israel, and his homecoming was providing one of the few sources of pleasure for Frances to look forward to at the moment. In his last letter he'd hinted at bringing a surprise for them, but didn't specify what exactly the surprise was.

For this homecoming there were no family reunions planned at either train stations or airports. He told them simply that he would make his own way to the house, and to expect him in time for tea on the following Sunday.

Frances baked a cheesecake, which she knew was his favourite, for the day of his arrival. The house shone, she'd been up early that morning and ordered each member of her family to complete some cleaning routine, then walk barefoot or in stockinged feet so as not to create any new dust.

'It's only Mick, not the flipping queen of Sheba.'

'Do you begrudge your brother a clean house?' she snapped at Jake. 'Deborah, look in the oven, and see if the cake's done.'

Luckily Wilfred had a tombstone consecration to attend that morning, and he reckoned he'd got off lightly. After the service, he went back to the house of the bereaved and lingered longer than he usually did on such occasions. It took him all his willpower not to take up their offer of lunch as well.

In the middle of the afternoon, a taxi drew up outside the house. Peering out of the lounge window, Jake saw his brother alight then put two heavy suitcases on the pavement. When Michael went to pay the driver, Jake also spotted an olive skinned girl getting out of the far side door of the taxi.

'Oh dear, oh dear.' Jake nudged his sister, who also went to look.

'He likes the dark ones, doesn't he?'

'Not another *schwartze*?' Frances gasped from behind them.

'She's just sun-tanned.'

Michael picked up their bags as the taxi drove off, then Wilfred went to open the front door and greet them.

'Everyone, this is Miriam Finkleman, she's the angel who nursed me back to health.'

When the girl grinned and lifted her eyebrows heavenwards, Frances relaxed, taking this as a good sign that she'd fit in with their family whilst she was here.

'We're very pleased to meet you, Miriam.' Frances shook her hand. 'And I hope you'll enjoy your holiday with us.'

'I'm not here on holiday, I'm going to do a nursing degree in Bristol with Mick.' Frances went rigid, and her silence was palpable.

'Mum, say something,' Deborah hissed, while Wilfred led the pair into the lounge.

'At least this one's a Jew.'

The first thing Frances looked for when Wilfred helped Miriam off with her coat, was a wedding ring on either of the girl's hands. When she was satisfied that both were devoid of rings, she announced graciously that tea would be ready soon in the dining room.

'Mick, your mother's cheesecake is even better than my mother's.' In spite of her unease as to what exactly the girl was doing here, Frances glowed at the compliment. 'You must give me the recipe.'

'She can talk the talk,' Jake whispered to Deborah.

'Amen to that.'

'Hope you don't mind, Mum, but I asked my pal Graeme to pop in, we haven't seen each other for ages.'

'Isn't he that artist friend of yours?'

'That's him.'

As if on cue, the front door bell rang and Deborah went answer it. Standing on the doorstep was the tall, lanky frame of Michael's friend.

'Well hello, little Deborah,' he said, walking into the hallway, 'you've grown a bit since I last saw you.'

256

'Could say the same about you.'

'Has the boy wonder arrived?'

'He has indeed, follow me.'

'Stinky bottom!' Michael exclaimed when his friend entered the room.

'Swine turd!' Graeme replied. Frances grimaced as the two clasped each other.

'Miriam, this ugly creature is one of my oldest friends. He calls himself an artist, and if you ask him nicely he might even paint your portrait.'

'Only if she'll pose in the nude.'

'OK you two, less of the filth.'

'It was a joke, Mrs Steinberg – anyway, how are you both?'

'Bearing up nicely, thank you. Deborah, bring in another cup for Graeme, oh and you must try my cheesecake.'

Graeme took a seat beside Miriam, and Frances put a thick slice of cake on his plate, which he immediately devoured.

'This is delicious, and may I say you haven't lost your touch, Mrs S. By the way, where's your Peggy, she's always good for a laugh?'

'God, I didn't realise, where is she?' Michael said.

'She's in Palm Springs,' Jake sniggered. 'She was maidnapped by our sister's rich ex-boyfriend.'

'It's a long story, I'll tell you later,' Deborah snapped.

'But Peggy was one of the fixtures and fittings here.'

'Don't we know it, Graeme, don't we know it,' Jake muttered.

*

In spite of Frances's early misgivings, Miriam proved to be a welcome addition to the household. Not only was she diplomatic with Frances, but also because of her kibbutz background, she was a deft hand at cooking and cleaning.

Regardless of her prowess around the house, the only thing Frances wouldn't countenance was Michael and Miriam sharing a bed.

'But we've been living together in Israel, and the kibbutz didn't mind.'

'This is my home and I won't be accused of keeping a house of ill repute.'

'Chance would be a fine thing.'

*

Deborah could now breathe easier, because the piercing spotlight her mother had trained on her for the past year had now been lifted, and she was even starting to look forward to having a normal life again.

Graeme, Michael and his girlfriend spent most of their free time together, and if Michael had things to do, Graeme offered to show Miriam the sights of Manchester. They became like an established threesome, and more often than not Graeme joined the Steinberg family for supper.

When the time came for the couple to leave for Bristol, Frances waved goodbye with a tear in her eye.

'Such a nice girl,' she said after they'd left, 'and I wouldn't mind if they ended up together eventually.'

'He needs to get a decent degree before he can think about supporting a wife,' Wilfred insisted.

'Well at least she knows how to look after him while he's away.'

*

The first six months at Bristol went more smoothly for Michael than for Miriam. She found the English weather cold and uncompromising, and the syllabus she was being taught on her course was what she had already learnt and practised back in Israel.

'Cheer up, it'll be spring soon.'

Michael was doing his best to encourage her, but she still hunched miserably besides the radiator. She was wearing her overcoat, gloves and scarf, and the two bar radiator was the only means of heating their tiny living room.

'I'm going to bed, it will be warmer in there.'

'How about if we invite Graeme to spend the Easter break with us?'

'OK, it would be nice to be together again.'

Graeme was starting to establish a reputation for himself in the art world, and had already received a few commissions. But they were still not enough for him to live on, so to try to help him in his career, Wilfred agreed to sit for a portrait on the condition that the synagogue executive paid for the finished work.

So when Michael called to invite him to join them for the Easter holidays, he decided to pack his paints and easel, hoping to finish the work whilst he was in Bristol.

The three of them duly met up at the station, and Miriam was in a better mood than she'd been for a while. That evening they trawled round several city pubs, and by the time they got back to their lodgings, they were once again the threesome of old.

That night Graeme bedded down in a sleeping bag in the lounge, and Michael and Miriam slept in the single bed they had been using in the one and only bedroom.

The following morning, when Graeme awoke and needed to go to the toilet, he inadvertently pushed the bathroom door open while Miriam was taking a bath.

'Oops, sorry.'

'It doesn't lock.'

When she made a half hearted attempt to conceal as much as she could with the flannel, he gulped in embarrassment, but when she saw him shuffling from one leg to the other, she indicated carelessly that he could use the toilet if he wanted to.

'No, that's fine, I'll wait.'

He made as if to leave, but to further compound his embarrassment and in spite of his best intentions, his eyes remained riveted on her naked body in the bathtub.

'I'm off, you two, see you this evening!' Michael called out from the front door.

'Miriam, make the dirty sod some breakfast before he goes out, he needs fattening up.'

'Bugger off.'

But to Graeme's mortification, his voice came out an octave higher and without any of its stridency. Then Miriam shouted from the bathtub:

'I'll do it when I'm dressed.' When she heard the front door slam she said, 'For heavens sake take a leak or you'll explode.'

By the time Miriam had finished in the bathroom, she was wearing Michael's towelling dressing gown and Graeme was fully dressed and sitting uncomfortably at the small kitchen table.

'Bathroom's all yours, just move my underwear from the side of the bath if you need to.'

While he washed and cleaned his teeth, the sight of her tights and knickers hanging over the bath were too much for him to bear, and he found himself nursing a painful tumescence. But the smell of fried eggs and coffee came wafting into the bathroom, and although he wanted to grab her and make passionate love to her, he realised he hadn't eaten for a long time and was starving.

Miriam was busying herself with his breakfast when he came into the kitchen, but she was still dressed only in the loosely tied bathrobe.

'How do you like them?'

'Served by a beautiful woman.'

She giggled then put two fried eggs on a plate alongside some toast, and signalled to him to sit down at the table.

'Aren't you eating?'

'I never eat in the morning.'

'So that you can stay slim and beautiful?' She pulled out the other chair, then sat down opposite him at the narrow table. 'Sorry about barging in on you, by the way.'

'I should have remembered to tell you about the door.'

'I'm glad you didn't, you're a sight for sore eyes as we say in Manchester.' She smiled. 'I'd really like to paint you one day.'

'Me, why?'

'Because I know from first hand experience how lovely you are.' She poured herself a coffee, and regarded him with her hazel eyes. 'I'm free all day, so we could make a start if you want?'

'OK, why not?'

In spite of the breakfast in front of him, and the welcome mug of coffee, Graeme again felt the hardening between his legs. He tried to cover his unease by taking several large gulps of coffee.

'Great.' His voice had come out as a falsetto.

'The best light is in the bedroom, I could pose on the bed if you like?' This was almost too much to bear, but he managed to nod his head in assent.

After she'd cleared away the dishes, Miriam went into the bedroom to get ready, and Graeme presumed she'd be putting some clothes on. He took out his paints, easel and a canvas, pleased to have something to distract him from the other thoughts that kept pervading his mind. Eventually she called out:

'I'm ready!'

He put the easel under one arm, and carried the box of paints in his other hand. The door was ajar, so he pushed it fully open using his backside. When he turned around, the sight that greeted him made him harden again instantly. She had draped herself over the pillows and was stark naked.

'This is how you do it, isn't it?'

His fingers were shaking uncontrollably, but hiding his legs behind the easel, he just about managed to set it up. Then, painful though it was to bend down, he got out the paints and brushes. He tried his level best to avoid looking at her until he'd squeezed some colours onto the palette.

'Be professional,' he admonished himself.

'Did you say something?'

'No.' He swallowed hard. 'Could you just move your right leg slightly away from the other one.'

She carefully followed his instructions, and when she moved one leg away from the other, he got a complete view of her pubic mound and beyond. This was too much and before either of them knew it, the palette was on the floor, the easel had landed on top of it, and Graeme was tearing off his clothes. He jumped on top of her with all the finesse of a rugby prop forward, and when it was over, they lay panting in each other's arms.

'Do you still want to paint me?'

'I'd rather do this.'

'Me too.'

Later on, and almost sated, he gasped from underneath her breasts while facing in the opposite direction.

'Where did you learn to do it this way?'

'On kibbutz, I worked with the horses.'

They stayed there for the rest of the day, stopping only to make a pot of tea in the afternoon, and fully occupied as they were with each other, neither heard Michael's key turning in the lock.

When he walked into the flat, he looked into the kitchen area and saw the unwashed teacups, then heard frantic cries coming from the bedroom. His first thought was that someone was ill or in pain, but he moved gingerly towards the bedroom in case there was an intruder inside. He pushed the door open as quietly as he could.

'Yes, oh yes my big Goy[19]!'

'Aaargh!'

Michael was paralysed with shock and bewilderment, because for an instant he didn't recognise either of them. Graeme's naked bottom was bouncing high in the air, and all he could see of his girlfriend were her feet moving up and down on his shoulders in synchronicity.

'Miriam?'

'Michael!'

'Holy shit! Look man, this isn't what you think …'

*

Miriam and Graeme left that afternoon, and Michael didn't want to know where they were going. The next time he heard anything of them was about six months later, after he'd decided to jack in his course at the university.

'I can't go back there,' he told his parents, 'I'm too traumatised.'

They were also traumatised by his announcement, but had the good grace not to nag him at this moment. They decided to give him a few more days before subjecting him to their usual rigorous cross-examination, and Frances even attempted to keep him occupied and not dwelling on his problems while he was under their roof.

'Michael dear, will you go to Tesco's, I need a few things?'

'If I must.'

'It will do you good to get out of the house, you've been moping around here for far too long. By the way, I've left the list by the front door.'

While he was wheeling a trolley round the supermarket, he unexpectedly bumped into Graeme Sidebotham, who was also wheeling a trolley in the same aisle. Michael stared malevolently at

---

[19]*non-Jew*

262

his former friend, and both of them circled each other like feral cats. Finally, Graeme blurted out:

'I feel just shit about it, man.'

'How do you think I feel?' Michael screamed back at him by way of response, and several other customers stopped wheeling their trolleys to listen to what was going on.

'She only stayed two nights, then when I was sleeping she rifled through my pockets and took all my money. She told me she was going out for a walk, but I never saw her again, so I guess she went back to Israel.'

'That's tough, man.'

'Didn't have a sou left, so my folks said they'd sub me but only if I took up a place at Central St Martins. I'm so sorry man, I just wish I could make it up to you.'

'You could buy me a pint for a start.'

Frances didn't get her groceries till the next day, because her son and his friend spent the remainder of the day going from pub to pub and afterwards neither could remember why they got on a bus to Bellevue circus. In the event, the ringmaster telephoned the police when he found two drunken but happy young men trying to get into the lions' cage. Later, when the police cautioned them, they insisted that they were just looking for work.

'You've got to believe me, Occifer, I can't lie, you see my Dad's a rabbi.'

'S'true, his Dad's a real one,' Graeme added helpfully.

After spending a night in the cells, snoring so loudly that the other drunks complained, the two were released into Wilfred's custody the following morning.

*

And just when the family thought things couldn't get any worse, another bombshell hit them. Barney the butcher from north Manchester filed for a divorce, and in the petition he threatened to cite Rabbi Wilfred Steinberg as a co-respondent.

This was possibly the worst thing that could have happened to the family, and Manchester was abuzz with rumours. Deborah's broken engagement, Michael's leaving university before he graduated, all faded into insignificance and were as nothing in comparison to this new scandal.

The family was under siege, and Wilfred slunk around the house looking like a broken man. But no one reckoned on his old flame Evelyn Fraser, who on hearing the rumours, rushed round to their house then rang on the front doorbell like a woman possessed. When the hapless Wilfred answered the door, without uttering a word, she slapped his face a stinging blow across his cheek.

'How could you do this to me?'

Hearing a commotion outside her house, Frances went to investigate. She saw her husband clutching his cheek and rendered speechless by the attack. Now it was her turn, and she screamed like a virago at the other woman.

'Get out of my house, you harlot! I never want to see you or any of your family again!'

It was obvious she'd waited years to say that, but when she tried to close the front door, Evelyn stood her ground with one foot inside the doorway. So amazed was she that Frances was coming to her husband's defence, she stared open mouthed at her.

'Are you going to put up with it?' she screeched.

'I put up with you long enough didn't I?'

'But he's cheated on you with some ... nobody.'

'And like you were such a somebody? Anyway, it's none of your business, so get off my premises.'

With that Frances managed to shut the door in the other woman's face. Wilfred stood in the hallway, blinking and rubbing his cheek.

'You, into the kitchen, now!' she barked, and he followed her meekly.

*

The family held a council of war. All past problems were put aside because this one impacted on all their lives. Wilfred of course denied everything, insisting he'd never seen Nicky Segleman since the day of the tea party. Furthermore, he claimed the only reason he'd ever come into contact with Barney was to find a kosher butcher to supply synagogue functions.

Finally, to convince his family of the truth of what he was saying, he made the biggest mistake of all. He vowed that he'd only ever had one true love in his life, and that was their mother. Up till that point, they had almost believed in his innocence, but after that statement the family knew they were in deep trouble.

To try and ease the tension in the room, Michael promised he'd now apply to Manchester University to do another course.

'I know I've left it late, but I'm going to have to buck up my ideas.'

'About time,' Frances muttered.

'And we're all going to have to work together on this one,' Jake stated.

'But what are we going to do about these terrible lies?'

Frances clutched Wilfred's hand. In spite of all the evidence to the contrary, his comment about her being his only true love had touched a chord within her, and she desperately wanted to believe it.

Nobody could think of any solution, until all of a sudden Jake stood up with deep furrows etched between his eyebrows. He started pacing up and down the kitchen, and for want of anything better to do, they all watched and waited. Several times he looked to be on the verge of speaking, then stopped, having just discounted whatever idea was in his head.

Finally, when he reached the sink for the fourth time, and just when it looked like he had come up with something to say, he turned on the tap and poured a glass of water.

'I've had an idea.' Then he drank the water, and they waited.

Jake's idea was nothing short of brilliant, as were his powers of reasoning, and even Wilfred looked at him with new respect. It was as if his youngest child had suddenly become the head of the family, and it was an awesome thing to behold.

'Your friend, what's his name ... lightning strike or something?

'Lichtenstein?'

'That's the one. He's a *Dayan*[20] isn't he?' Wilfred nodded, wondering where this was leading. 'And as such, he'd be in charge of all the kosher butchers in the community?'

'Well, they'd certainly have to get their Beth Din licenses from his office – in fact they couldn't operate without them.'

'So much the better.'

---

[20]*religious judge*

Then he started pacing again in a way that was reminiscent of the days when he used to bang his head rhythmically against the sides of his cot. As such he was spellbinding, like the actor Raymond Burr when he played Detective Ironside in the television series.

'He owes you a favour, doesn't he?'

'I got him a car if that's what you mean?'

To his shame, Wilfred realised that he had now lost all his paternal authority, and felt increasingly like a defendant in the dock.

'Right, so it's now time to call in that favour.'

The entire family watched his performance in admiration, and Frances shook her head from side to side to think that she had spawned such a genius, and never noticed it before.

'He ought to be a lawyer, he doesn't miss a trick.'

As it turned out, it wasn't just Lichtenstein who owed Wilfred a favour, but several other influential men in the community did too, because in his time he had helped them all out of awkward situations.

Jake told him to draw up a list of people whose testimonies could help him, and when the list was complete, it contained the names of two bankers, one gynaecologist, one university professor, the Chief Constable and the matron of a nursing home for unmarried mothers, amongst others.

Then Jake suggested his father fix a meeting with Lichtenstein and one of the bankers in the first instance. The others he decided might be used later if things were not looking good. Jake instructed him to organise the meeting on neutral territory, and suggested the banker's office.

'You'll be there with me, won't you?'

'But I'm only fifteen, Dad.'

'I'm relying on you, Jake.'

'Then I should be there too,' Michael asserted.

'No way,' Frances butted in, 'they'd take one look at you and throw you out.'

Her eldest son started sulking, but the truth was that with his long hair and second-hand clothing from charity shops, these days he resembled a hippy more than a university student.

In the event, his resourceful younger brother ended up chairing the meeting in the banker's office, in spite of being technically under age to do so. The other men looked on in admiration as the young man took control of the proceedings.

'My father categorically denies any improper behaviour towards this woman. His only contact with her was when she and her husband came to tea on one occasion, when my mother and the rest of the family were present. As to the other times the butcher alleges the two of them met, we have influential members of the community who can testify that my father was with them on these occasions – which, gentlemen, makes a nonsense of all Mr Segleman's claims.'

With that, Jake puffed out his under-developed chest, really pleased with himself that he'd paid attention to all those courtroom dramas he'd watched with Peggy on the television. Then he sat down in the enigmatic manner of Ironside, and Lichtenstein immediately got to his feet.

'Gentlemen, I personally am willing to speak to Segleman,' he announced gravely, 'and I will tell him that unless he drops these ridiculous allegations against my dear friend Wilfred, I will take it upon myself to inspect his carving knives, which my wife assures me are not fit for purpose. Because of that, we will have no option but to take away his licence and he'll never be able to practise as a kosher butcher again.'

He stopped for breath, then drank a large tumbler of water while everyone waited to see if he had finished. Wilfred relaxed visibly in his chair.

'If, on the other hand,' Lichtenstein recommenced, 'he is willing to drop these charges, we can promise him a great deal of future business supplying all the functions that come under my jurisdiction.'

Finally, he sat down with a flourish, and Wilfred nodded to him gratefully. Then the banker decided it was now his turn to turn the screw further into the hapless butcher.

'And if none of these things work, gentlemen, I'll lower the boom and call in his overdraft. Quite simple – do as we say or he can look forward to zero credit with any of the banks in future.'

Yet in spite of all these reassurances, Jake wasn't fully satisfied. Like the rest of the family, he felt intense shame that this had ever happened. In the past, the family had always managed to contain Wilfred's peccadilloes; the ladies concerned were always discreet because they had as much to lose as he did. But this situation was different, because unlike the other cuckolded husbands, Barney Segleman was now on the warpath.

So Jake in his role of family mentor decided to put some extra pressure on the butcher, and that required the help of his sister and brother. He confided his plan to them, which was to make a series of anonymous, threatening phone calls to Segleman.

'And I suppose you're going to put a horse's head on his pillow as well?'

Jake was already feeling as tense as he needed to be, and his brother's humour only annoyed him.

'I've done all right so far, so either shut up or help me.'

'What do you want me to do?' Deborah asked.

'I need you to find his home number, rifle through Dad's jacket if you have to.'

'And what do you want me to do?' Michael asked.

'You'll be making the calls.'

Finding her father's diary was not easy because he kept it in the jacket he was intending to wear that day. But one morning, following Jake's constant nagging, Deborah took the risk.

Her mother was in the kitchen, and she could hear her father shaving in the bathroom. He liked to hum liturgical choir numbers whilst he was shaving and showering, and when she heard his voice rising for the soprano parts, she decided this was her moment.

She saw a jacket hanging outside his wardrobe, and quickly rifled through the pockets. The diary was inside the breast pocket, so she quickly thumbed through it. She looked under S for Segleman, but found nothing. Then she tried B for butcher, but again nothing. Finally she tried N for Nicky, but that complete page had been torn out and was missing.

When she heard the bathroom door opening, she put the diary back and decided not to push her luck any further. She went downstairs and found her mother slumped at the kitchen table, aimlessly stirring a sugar lump round and round in her teacup. Frances barely looked up when her daughter entered, so Deborah went to the drawer where the family kept their book of personal telephone numbers, and again opened the pages at S, B and N. Nothing was listed under any of those sections.

'What are you looking for?'

'The phone number for that Segleman woman.'

'Why?'

'It's not for me, Jake needs it.'

Frances nodded, as if it was all right for him to have it, but not Deborah. 'It's under T.'

'T?'

'Yes, I put her under T, for the tart.'

What perfect logic, her daughter thought, and grinned at her mother. She was rewarded with a rare grin back, and sure enough, there was the Segleman's telephone number listed under T.

Jake had spent the previous few nights preparing Michael's script. It contained phrases like, 'we know where you are' and 'we can get you any time'. The *pièce de résistance* was, 'if you think you can avoid what's coming to you, you'd better think again mate.'

As it ultimately turned out, none of the threats were necessary, because as soon as Barney Segleman heard that he might lose his kosher license, he caved in immediately and the divorce petition was withdrawn. Then Barney and Nicky took a surprise trip to Rimini, and as far as the Steinbergs were concerned, the Segelmans were peacefully reunited. But peace was far from evident within their own household.

Wilfred was suffering from constant bouts of indigestion; due, he claimed, to his wife's habit of cooking with garlic. It was a fact that she used the plant more and more, as a sort of retribution for all he'd put her through recently. But even though he called it indigestion, it would ultimately prove to be something worse.

*

However, Jake's star was still rising, and all the aggravation they'd been through had given him the impetus to study hard so that he could pass the Oxbridge exam.

He knew where his future lay, and he told his sister that his ambition was to be a High Court Judge by the time he was forty.

'Then I'll marry a rich girl, preferably a blonde with big tits, and I'll change my name by deed poll as soon as I can.'

'To what?'

'I like the sound of Jake Brown, or maybe Jake Benson.'

'Why not something with an S, like Jake Smythson or Jake Simons, at least people will recognise who you are?'

'Don't like either, far too Jewish.'

In the quiet of his own room he continued trawling through potential surnames. Jake Stratton, St John, even Jake Shelbourne. He rolled them round his tongue, but none quite fitted the bill, so he reluctantly decided that after he'd passed all his exams, he'd again look at the problem of the new surname.

Michael was accepted on a writing course at Manchester University. He told anyone who would listen, that he was sure he had a great novel inside him, and would be making a start on it well before the course started.

He and Graeme Sidebotham were buddies again. Michael had forgiven him for the affair with Miriam, and the two of them came to the conclusion that it wouldn't have happened if Miriam hadn't been so promiscuous. They decided that over several pints of beer, and during the same drinking session they also made plans to rent a cottage in the Yorkshire Dales so that Michael could get started on his novel, and Graeme could get a portfolio of work completed.

Deborah muddled along at the commercial college but still couldn't bear the thought of her future as someone's secretary. Because she had started dating boys again, she managed to put up with it. But all the while she promised herself that as soon as the course was over, she would try to find a job in fashion.

'Hey Debs, guess what I heard over the grapevine today? Only that Gordon and his family are moving abroad,' her friend Laura said.

'Why?'

But Laura looked equally puzzled, so Deborah decided to ask her father that evening if he knew anything about it.

'I did hear something about the taxman being after them.'

When she made further enquiries from friends they'd had in common, she learnt that there had been several irregularities in Helfgot's accounting systems, particularly with the new shop that Gordon was in charge of. According to her friends, Cyril Helfgot had thought it prudent to sell up and for all the family to leave the country, before the taxman completed his enquiries.

'So they left in Gordon's car, then they drove to the Continent,' Frances, who had been doing her own spying, reported over supper, 'and I have it on the highest authority that the boot of the Jaguar was stuffed with bags of diamonds.'

'Wonder if your engagement ring was amongst them?' Jake sniggered.

Soon afterwards it became common knowledge within the community that all three Helfgots were now ensconced in a mansion in Palm Springs, USA. Gordon now drove a Cadillac, and had apparently opened a delicatessen shop.

'I expect he only did that so he could sample all the food,' Deborah surmised.

'Think what a lucky escape you had, Debs. You could have been serving behind the counter by now,' her younger brother added.

CHAPTER 15

Out of the blue, a letter arrived from Peggy, the first communication the family had received from her. After all that had been going on in their lives recently, each one of them was interested to hear her news.

She wrote that she'd stayed with Gordon's cousin for only four months, then she'd run away in the middle of the night. She explained that she'd left because her new employer was a monster and the children were badly behaved brats.

'Just like us,' Michael grinned.

She continued that the woman had expected her to work seven days a week, with only one day off a month. This statement was followed by six exclamation marks. Then she explained that her employer had left her alone with the children day and night.

'*So I finally packed my bags and left when they couldn't stop me,*' Frances read out to her family. 'Poor Peggy.'

'But where did she go to afterwards?' everyone wanted to know, so Frances continued reading aloud.

'*I'm now with another family, they're called Wishnow, and they're much nicer people. And this is the best bit of news, I've found a boyfriend.*'

'Does she say who he is?'

'Be patient,' Frances admonished. '*He's called Judd, and he wants me to live with him in his mobile trailer home. He's a plumber by trade, and I think I can trust him.*'

'I'm so glad she's found someone.'

'Amen to that,' Wilfred said, and they all had nostalgic looks on their faces.

Deborah and Frances both wrote letters back, and they awaited her next letter eagerly. But nothing further arrived from her. However, one day several months later, Frances received a telephone call from a woman with an American accent.

'I'm so sorry to bother you,' the woman said, but to Frances's ears it sounded like *ahm so sorr te bother yuu*. 'My name's Barbie Wishnow and I'm Peggy's employer, and we're so worried because she's gone missing.'

'Missing!'

'And I rather hoped you could help me. She always talked so highly of your family, and I was hoping you might have some idea as to where you think she might have gone?'

'Oh dear, I'm sorry,' Frances told the other woman, 'all we know is what she wrote in her letter. But wait a minute – she did mention that she'd met a man called Judd, have you tried contacting him?'

'We did that immediately, but it seems his trailer has left the parking lot. The guy who runs the lot said that he thought Judd was heading New Mexico way, and you know what it's like out there.' Frances didn't actually know much about New Mexico, but she made the appropriate tutting noises in response. 'I'm afraid if she doesn't come back soon, I'm going to have to report her to the missing persons bureau.'

'Oh, I do hope she's all right, she means a lot to us does Peggy.'

Barbie Wishnow assured her that she would let her know if she heard anything, but neither she nor Peggy contacted Frances again.

*

After the spate of recent dramas in her life, Frances was not bearing up too well. So Deborah, who was her main confidante when it came to matters medical, was forced to sit down and listen to her.

'I feel so tired, Debs, and every time I pass water, it burns me down there.' She indicated her nether regions to her daughter.

'Then don't go near water … sorry, just joking.'

'I think I'll have to make an appointment to see the specialist.'

'Mum, you've already done that.' Deborah narrowed her eyes. 'You're due to go on Thursday.'

'Oh dear, I'd forgotten. Will you come with me?'

'I said yes when you asked me last week.'

Everyone could see that Frances was becoming more forgetful, and when she'd originally asked her daughter to accompany her to the specialist, Deborah feared being saddled with this role forever. But the pitiful look that Frances invariably wore these days made her daughter feel guilty, so she gave in.

Deborah left college early on the day of the appointment, and met her mother outside the hospital. Frances was smartly dressed for the occasion in a dark wool suit, and on her head she wore a cerise velvet pillbox hat.

Ten minutes later, Frances was called in for her appointment, but Deborah was deeply engrossed in a magazine.

'Put that down, Deborah, he's waiting.'

This was one filial duty too many, and Deborah decided to stay put. 'I'm not going in there with you, I'll wait here till you've seen him.'

She settled back to reading the magazine, when suddenly everyone in the waiting room was jolted by the sound of hysterical laughter coming from the doctor's surgery. They heard him cough several times in embarrassment, before he managed to stop giggling. Then the level of noise returned to its normal staid quietness, and everyone resumed reading their magazines.

After Frances's consultation was over, when they were leaving the building together, Deborah asked her mother why the doctor had been laughing.

'Oh that,' she snapped. 'A man like him should have known better. When I went in the silly man told me to get undressed behind the screen and call him when I was on the bed. So I got undressed like he said, then said I'm ready.'

'But why was he laughing?'

'Just because I'd forgotten to take my hat off.'

'So there you were, lying on the bed stark naked, except for your pink pillbox?'

That was when Deborah started to laugh until tears fell from her eyes. After that, her mother refused to speak to her for two days. However, before she'd left his office, the specialist had told her that he wanted her back in hospital for another series of tests.

The aftermath of this visit was another hospital stay where they put her on new medication. However, once she had been stabilised, when Wilfred went to the hospital to bring her home, the nurses insisted he wheel her out of the ward in a wheelchair.

'What do you think I am, a cripple?' she demanded to know.

'But a woman of your age ...'

'Get me the matron.'

'Just get in the damn thing till we get to the car,' Wilfred snarled, losing his last vestiges of patience.

'Very well, take me home.'

Those were the only words she spoke to him that day; and once home, to his extreme annoyance, she refused to get out of the wheelchair unless she needed to go to the toilet or to bed. Frances was now in the process of exacting her revenge.

*

More than ever, when Deborah saw former school friends who were now enrolled at art college, it made her feel increasingly envious. Her artistic ability was every bit as good as theirs, yet in spite of knowing she was in the wrong place, she still tried her hardest to learn all they were trying to teach her at the secretarial college. She still harboured the hope that one day, when she was earning money, she could plan a life independent of her parents, to do what she wanted to do.

She'd made a new friend at college, Jane Barber. Unlike Deborah, Jane was a natural born secretary, and particularly proficient at typing. Typing was the stuff of nightmares for Deborah, and Jane could never understand her friend's fear and loathing of it.

'Do you really get stomach ache as soon as you sit in front of the typewriter?' she queried in amazement.

'It's weird, but every time she starts dictating, my stomach begins to hurt and I feel sick.'

'I reckon it's constipation.'

'I don't, I'm quite regular.'

'My mother's good on these sort of things, I'll ask her, see what she thinks.'

The following day when Jane arrived in the college, she'd brought a huge bar of chocolate with her, and during their break time she encouraged Deborah to eat it.

'My Mum says it'll help.'

'Aren't you going to have any?'

'No, it's just for you.'

Deborah liked chocolate, so she munched away at it until she'd nearly finished the whole bar. When she got to the last few squares, she asked Jane what sort of chocolate it was.

'It's called Ex Lax, my mother thought it would help you through this afternoon's test.'

Deborah was blissfully unaware that the chocolate was a strong laxative, and that the normal dose for constipation was a few squares only of it, and certainly not the whole bar that she'd happily consumed. So when the bell for the lesson rang at three, and all the students filed into the typing room, Deborah managed only one step into the room, before she was doubled up in pain. But this pain was worse than anything she'd ever experienced before, and in desperation she pushed fellow pupils aside to rush to the toilets. It was there that she spent the next half an hour, sweating, crying and expelling everything she'd eaten during the past month.

When she tried to stand up, she collapsed onto the floor, then everything went blank until she woke up in hospital several hours later, minus her appendix.

'I must say, that was a close shave.'

Deborah's eyes fluttered half open, but all she could make out was a blurred white image, and it was leaning in towards her. She tried to say something, but the insides of her mouth felt like sandpaper, and the words refused to come out. The white form moved closer.

'Drink,' she just about managed to say, although it came out sounding more like 'dir'.

'Not until the anaesthetic wears off.'

'Mus ...'

The blurred image had started to become a bit clearer, and she could now make out a face above the white overall. Also there was something hanging from its neck.

'Plis ...'

'Well, only just a sip to wet your tongue.' The white being put a glass towards her mouth. 'Only a tiny sip, or you'll be ...' She gulped a few mouthfuls down, then within seconds vomited over the white coat. '… sick,' he said in a dismayed voice.

He made a valiant attempt to wipe the vomit off his stethoscope, then looked down his white coat and wanted to retch himself at the smell. He started to unbutton his coat, then tried to keep it at arm's length.

'Nurse, could you clear this up? I'll see to the patient later.'

The man in the white coat came on his rounds every day, and sometimes even twice a day, but usually with a pretty nurse hovering behind him. He explained to Deborah that he had been the registrar on duty when they brought her in, and apparently she had only been one step away from peritonitis when he operated.

By the end of the week, not only could Deborah make out all his features very clearly, but she had also started to look forward to seeing them, and ward rounds became the highlight of her day. She begged a nurse to help her wash her hair, which was not an easy task as she was still attached to drips, and from that day onwards she made sure she was always wearing a fresh night-dress when he came.

Jane was the first to visit her other than her family, and when the girl arrived, Deborah had prepared a list of things she wanted her friend to do.

'First get me a nice, pink lipstick as soon as possible. Also, can you buy me a lower cut nightie? My mother chose these and they're only fit for a convent. Oh, and I'd love some perfume, just to freshen up.'

'It will cost a bit.'

'I'll pay you back, I promise.'

One morning, when he was at her bedside holding her wrist in his warm hand and taking her pulse – even though the nurse insisted that she'd just done it – Deborah plucked up the courage to speak.

'Doctor?'

'Yes?'

'I was never very good at biology, can you tell me what the appendix is for, and where exactly is it situated?'

He sat down on her bed, and lowered the bed covers. When he put his hand gently on the wound where the appendix had been, both she and the doctor blushed scarlet, but when she looked up, she could see the nurse pursing her lips in disapproval.

'More or less there.'

But he didn't remove his hand, and Deborah couldn't have been happier. The nurse coughed none too discreetly behind him.

'Doctor Cohen, other patients are waiting.'

'I'll tell you more about it when I do the rounds this evening.'

As if by magic, the sun seemed to burst through the clouds outside the hospital windows. She was convinced that the birds were singing sweeter melodies than they had before, and Deborah now knew there was a God, and he was watching over her with approval.

Doctor Benjamin Cohen was tall, dark and rather shy. He wore his hair a little too long and his trousers a little too short. His shirts were a little frayed at the cuffs, and more often than not, one of his shirttails protruded out of his trousers. On his horn-rimmed glasses, which he kept taking on and off, one of the sides was attached by a piece of sticking plaster, and Deborah fought the urge to tidy him up every time he was by her bedside.

'Doctor, your shoelace is undone.'

'Oh thank you, I hadn't noticed.'

'And um ...'

'What?'

'Oh it's nothing.' She had to keep reminding herself that she was beginning to sound more and more like her mother.

'Well, Deborah, I think we can probably discharge you tomorrow.'

'What a shame.' She blushed in embarrassment when the words tumbled out of her mouth. 'It's just that I've got quite used to this place.'

'I must admit, ward rounds won't seem the same without you.'

That was when the nurse coughed again. 'Doctor Cohen, you're operating in ten minutes.'

'I'll be there, nurse.'

Then he surreptitiously did the most wonderful thing, which took Deborah completely by surprise.

'Can I have your telephone number? We're not supposed to do this, but you'll be leaving anyway ...'

'262 0384.' She could hardly get the numbers out fast enough, and even offered him her biro. He quickly wrote them on the inside of his white coat.

'My name's Ben by the way,' he grinned.

'I'm Deb—'

'Yes I know, Deborah Steinberg. Must go.'

For the rest of that day, Deborah wrote the name Ben Cohen over every spare space on her newspaper, and before she lay down to sleep, she even wrote Mrs Ben Cohen, then crossed it out immediately.

*

Deborah and Benjamin Cohen started dating barely a week after she was discharged. Their first dates were rather sedate, because he insisted she didn't rush around so soon after the operation. Even so, their relationship was by any standards whirlwind, and within six weeks they were talking about a future together.

'Deborah?'

'What?'

They were lying on a grassy knoll in the grounds of a stately home. It was a Sunday afternoon, and Ben had spread a plaid rug on the ground in the warm sunshine.

'You're getting a tan.'

'So are you.' She traced the outline of the skin on his face, then bent down to kiss him.

'You taste of strawberries and cream.'

'I bet you say that to all your patients.'

'Only the pretty ones.' They sighed then kissed again.

'Ben?'

'Yes?'

'Nothing.'

'The answer's yes.' She propped herself up on her elbow.

'How did you know what I was thinking?'

'I was thinking the same.'

'Now I'm embarrassed.'

'Don't be, I want to make love to you too.'

'I was going to ask you to come to the Beatles concert with me.'

'Oh, bloody hell.' He blushed scarlet, then pounded the ground. 'But can we make love afterwards?'

'Only if you pay for the tickets,' Deborah giggled, then kissed him again.

As soon as he was sure he wouldn't do damage to her stitches, they made love on his tiny hospital bed with his bleeper on the bedside table, because he was still on call.

Then a miracle happened, and when Deborah went back to college, she no longer feared the typewriter, but no longer ate chocolate either. Ben now wore a new pair of tortoiseshell spectacles handpicked by her, and a smart leather belt put paid to the problem of shirt overhang.

Trendy slip-on shoes replaced his old lace-up brogues, and worsted trousers gave way to jeans and corduroys. It didn't take him long to realise that not only did he need her to choose his clothes, but also needed her with him because he was crazy about her.

'Will you marry me?' he whispered one night while they were lying on his bed.

'Pardon, doctor?' She'd heard him all right, but wanted to make this moment last as long as possible.

'I said ...'

Then his bleeper went off. He reluctantly started to pull on his clothes, then headed for the door. Before he opened it, she called out:

'Yes.'

'Really?'

'Yes, really, now go and cure someone else.'

'I love you,' he hissed from the door.

'I love you too.'

She lay back on his pillow, grinning from ear to ear. Ben didn't return until three hours later, by which time she'd got dressed and gone back home. A week later he presented her with a blue ring box, and when she opened it, she found an engagement ring inside.

'Wow, that's ...'

She tried desperately to search for the right words to express maximum pleasure, but to her shame she realised that she had compared this ring to Gordon's, and in comparison this one came off rather badly.

'Don't you like it? I can change it if you don't like it.'

'It's beautiful.'

'Put it on.' She slipped it on her finger, and it twinkled prettily in the light. 'It's all I could afford, but when I'm a consultant I'll buy you one as big as an orange, and that's a promise.'

'I don't care about that, this is from you and that's all that matters.' She had her fingers crossed behind her back, and wondered if her nose had just grown a little longer.

*

Ben was different to most of the other men she'd been out with. Born, bred and educated in Sheffield, he was a man who was confident in his own skin, and never had to throw his weight around to get noticed.

When he'd first arrived at Manchester University, he'd gained a reputation as being one of the hard drinking sets of students. In his hometown he'd never dated Jewish girls, in spite of the fact that his father was the President of their local synagogue.

'Ben, you must meet Milly Felstein's daughter.' His mother constantly entreated him to try going out with Jewish girls. 'Milly says she's very clever.'

'I'm too busy studying, Ma.'

Invariably this was his reply, but what he omitted to tell his mother was that he was also busy pursuing a Quaker steel manufacturer's daughter who had a penchant for circumcised men.

At his father's behest, the rabbi from their synagogue also tried to fix him up with daughters of members of his congregation.

'Her father's one of the De Keysers, the family's worth a fortune, and apart from the acne, she's a lovely girl.'

'Thank you, rabbi, but you know how it is when you're busy studying.'

All attempts at matchmaking were in vain, and as soon as he arrived in Manchester to study medicine, he quickly established himself as a favourite amongst the non-Jewish students. After graduating, he went on to become a junior doctor at the Royal Infirmary. Here, nurses replaced the female students who had made his life sweet in university, and not one of his new girlfriends was of the faith.

In his wildest dreams, Ben never expected to fall so heavily – and with a patient of all people. Meeting Deborah was like a *coup de foudre*, and the same bolt of lightning hit her as soon as she could focus properly after the anaesthetic had worn off.

Every time he did his ward round, he sat on Deborah's bedside far longer than any other patient, and she in turn had spent the previous two hours making herself look as delectable as possible for the doctor. It quickly became a source of irritation amongst the single nurses when they realised that their favourite had suddenly found his own particular favourite.

'I expect it's all that time I spent hanging round hospitals as a child,' she decided, 'I probably smelt of ancient ether, and that's what he liked.'

'Or vomit?' Laura suggested.

*

Deborah threatened her mother that she wouldn't introduce her to Ben unless she got out of the wheelchair and started acting normally.

'So who is he, this young man of yours?'

'His name's Ben Cohen and he's a doctor ...'

'A doctor!' A beatific smile descended on her mother's face, and her eyes lit up. 'And what does he specialise in, this Ben?'

'General surgery.'

'Oh.' Some of the gloss had just worn off.

'But I'm sure he'll have an expert opinion on your case.'

Wilfred winked at his daughter behind his wife's back. Deborah had decided not to tell them that she'd accepted Ben's proposal until after he had met her parents.

'Why don't you invite your young man for Friday night supper, I'll make something nice?'

'He's a vegetarian.'

There followed a stunned silence in which it was obvious that Frances was already questioning the wisdom of this relationship.

'We'll soon cure him of that.'

'But Mum, he doesn't like meat.'

'I don't like garlic, but has that ever stopped her cooking with it?'

Wilfred and Frances took an immediate liking to Ben as soon as he stepped into their home, and Deborah had warned him beforehand about the portion of chicken that might find its way onto his plate. Thus forewarned, when Frances served him his dinner with the chicken hidden under a mound of roast potatoes, Ben politely moved the offending item to one side. He and Deborah bided their time until Frances was distracted, then Ben slipped the offending chicken into a paper napkin that Deborah passed him. She then dropped the chicken portion into her handbag, and that was where it stayed until the next day.

When he'd finished eating the pile of vegetables that surrounded it, he inclined his head towards Frances and complemented her profusely on the meal.

'Mrs Steinberg ...'

'Do call me Frances.'

'Frances, that was delicious.'

She turned to the others. 'See, I told you he'd eat what I made.'

A week later, Deborah told her family that she and Ben were planning to get engaged, and that was just the impetus her mother needed to set her on the path to recovery. As a result, Frances started making copious plans again with a renewed spring in her step and a permanent smile on her face.

*

There were times when Ben seemed to be somewhat overwhelmed by the fuss and hullabaloo connected with getting engaged.

'Do I really have to wear a suit to the engagement party?'

'Only if you want to keep both your balls,' his brother-in-law to be advised. 'You've met my mother, you decide.'

In spite of that, Ben quite liked being the centre of all the attention that was being lavished on him at the moment. It was a novelty he'd never experienced before, and compared favourably to the cool receptions he'd received in the past from Christian girls' families. Equally promising, the more Deborah got to know his family, the more delighted she was to realise that they were everything the Steinbergs were not.

She noticed with relief that the typical types of disagreement in the Cohen household were whether Lily Cohen had bought the kind of cheese Alec Cohen liked or not. She also noted that whenever disagreements occurred between the pair, they were dealt with politely and quietly; in fact the total opposite of how they were handled in her home.

Alec Cohen was a retired family doctor, and Lily his wife, an avid collector of antiques that she trawled around country fairs to collect. Also pleasing to her future daughter-in-law, the pair had enough interests of their own, not to need to pry into other people's lives, all of which was a bonus.

Ben's married sister Grace, a heavily overweight woman, was as different to her name as was possible. A good-natured sort, her two children, Max and Emma, unfortunately took after her and not their stick-thin father Eric.

'Emma would love to be a bridesmaid, and Max would make a perfect pageboy,' Grace told her brother.

When he delicately broached the subject with his fiancée, who having just met the children, told him kindly but resolutely that she didn't want to have any attendants at all on her big day.

The engagement party took place at the Steinbergs' house, and on Deborah's explicit instructions, was restricted to immediate members of their two families. She remembered only too clearly the fiasco over her brief engagement to Gordon, and was determined that everything connected to her and Ben should be as different as it could from the last time.

'Morning Mrs S, you're looking well today,' Frances's latest cleaning lady remarked the day after the engagement party, 'shall I make us a brew?'

'Thank you, Anunciata, but I'm far too busy.'

With the engagement safely under her belt, Frances was now entirely taken up with her daughter's future nuptials, and set about organising their wedding with probably more attention to detail than the allies drew up when they were planning the Normandy landings.

Occasionally she remembered that there was another family to be considered, but once their opinion had been received, such was her determination to choreograph Manchester's wedding of the century, that she barely took any notice of their wishes.

Luckily, the Cohens presented her with no major challenges, but her daughter soon discovered that Ben wasn't quite the pushover that other members of his family were, particularly when it came to decisions concerning their future.

'I've been offered a senior position at the Halifax Royal Infirmary after I've finished here,' he told her, 'so I'm afraid that's where we're going to set up home, my sweet.'

'But isn't Halifax that dirty little place with lots of mill chimneys?'

'It won't be that bad, as long as we've got each other,' he assured her.

However, when she met up with her girlfriends and they wanted to know the details of her wedding plans and where she and Ben would be settling after the honeymoon, she was reluctant to admit where they would be living.

'Er ... Halifax.'

'In Yorkshire?'

'My God, Deborah, what will you do with yourself in that hell hole?'

'It won't be that bad, Laura.'

'Don't they still wear clogs out there?' Jane wanted to know.

'And knitted shawls,' Laura answered, sipping her cappuccino, 'and I'm sure they haven't heard of coffee bars yet.'

'Oh shut up you two, you're just jealous that I've bagged the tastiest man and you haven't.'

'I'm really going to miss you when you've gone.'

'But Jane, I won't be going that far away.'

'But who knows where the hell Halifax is?' Laura said, lighting up a Balkan Sobranie and taking a long drag on it. Deborah looked across at her sophisticated friend, reluctant to admit that she didn't know either.

Frances then decided to take up the cudgels on her daughter's behalf, hinting to Deborah that perhaps Ben should reconsider the offer and try for a fellowship in Manchester instead.

'She's only saying that because she wants me as her personal consultant,' Ben insisted after Deborah told him what her mother had suggested. 'Don't worry, we're going to have a wonderful life there, you and me.'

For Ben's sake Deborah tried to summon up as much enthusiasm as she could, but deep down the thought of the dour mill town that was going to be her future home, was not exciting her as much as he insisted it would.

'Besides, Halifax will be an ideal place for me to gain experience.'

'But what will I do all day there?'

'Same as every other housewife.' He gave her a kiss to soften the blow.

However, he underestimated his mother-in-law to be. Frances was not yet finished on the subject, and still had plenty to say to her future son-in-law.

'How can you live there? There are no Jews in that loch.'

'So much the better.'

'But what if you have children?'

'I'm sure Wilfred would see to their Jewish education.'

Realising that her influence over Ben amounted to very little, from then onwards whenever people asked Frances where the young couple would be settling, she made out as if Halifax was on an equal footing with all the major medical centres of the world.

'Besides, it's only short term, before he moves on to greater things.'

Ben, who had quickly got the measure of Frances, now even took a sadistic pleasure in kidding her along.

'You see, Frances, it's just that I've achieved all I originally set out to do in medicine, so Halifax will suit me fine for the rest of my life.'

And there were even times when Deborah began to wonder if her family's dysfunction had already started to rub off on him too.

*

Before the wedding there was still a major source of friction to be resolved between Deborah and her mother. Deborah had resolutely refused to wear any of the dresses that Frances had earmarked in the bridal department of Kendal Milne's.

Apart from taste considerations, Frances favoured the meringue look and Deborah favoured simplicity. Also, Deborah was well aware that her parents simply couldn't afford one of those overpriced creations.

'Now that one looks lovely.' Frances's eyes misted over as the assistant at Kendal's brought in yet another bridal dress comprised of acres of tulle.

'Sorry, don't like it.'

'Just try it on,' her mother pleaded, all the while trying to keep her composure in front of the assistant.

'How about I bring you a veil to get the full effect?'

As soon as the young woman had left the cubicle, Deborah turned to her mother and snarled.

'It's grotesque, and have you seen the price?'

'We're not going to buy it, stupid, I'll get it copied by the Finklestones.'

'Who?'

'Neil Finklestone, you know the *faigele*[21], he's just wonderful with his hands.'

Neil Finklestone, a fifty-something tailor from Cheetham Hill, worked with an assistant and sometime boyfriend, Charles d'Ath. It didn't take long before Ben and Deborah took to calling him the Kiss of De'ath. To complete the team in his bridal emporium, which was otherwise used as his dining room, was his elderly, hunch-backed sister Shaneleh, whose equally nimble fingers did the embroidery for Neil's creations.

Deborah took an immediate liking to Neil, and between them they designed a simple but elegant silk dress, which was as far away from her mother's taste as was possible. Neil appreciated Deborah's artistic bent, and she appreciated his fey one. Charles, his partner of eleven years, was like an old mother hen fussing around, and Neil's crippled sister did indeed do magnificent embroidery.

With the females of his family being so involved in the wedding plans, Wilfred had been almost completely sidelined.

'Do you realise this wedding is going to cost a fortune, the way it's going?' he complained to Frances one night. 'And I haven't got that sort of money.'

'Then you'll have to speak to the president, and tell him you need a salary increase.'

'But they gave me one only last year, and I can hardly see them agreeing to another one.'

'Then you'll just have to borrow the money from the bank.'

Frances stood her ground, in no mood to be challenged. Because Wilfred still feared she might rake up former grievances about the

---

[21]*fairy*

butcher's wife, he realised he had no option but to speak to the bank manager yet again, and not wanting to spoil his daughter's happiness at this time, decided to keep his uneasiness to himself.

As a result, nobody took much notice of the signs of stress he was showing. However, Ben did remark on the greyish tinge to his complexion, but Frances dismissed it as being normal for Wilfred. For the first time in her married life, she was firmly in charge, and she had no time for anyone or anything that might get in her way.

Jake prudently kept well out of the way, studying for his A-level exams. He was expected to do well and had already been offered a place at Oxford University pending his results.

Michael was also trying to keep a low profile. He had recently decided to jack in his English course, although he refused to discuss it with his parents.

'Why should I listen to them? They're the ones who've been responsible for all the problems in my life,' he told his brother Jake.

He also declined to confide in his sister either because as he explained to Jake, she had now joined the ranks of the bourgeoisie that his parents belonged to.

'We writers don't need university, we just need to write.'

'So where will you go?'

'Somewhere in the country, anywhere but Manchester.'

'And what will you live on while you're writing it?'

'I'll manage, other great writers have done you know.'

Without realising it, Jake was sounding more like his mother than his usual self.

'But what about our Deborah's wedding?'

'They won't notice my absence, nobody in this house has noticed me for ages.'

'I don't understand you, Mum will shit a brick.'

'Well if I have to, I'll come back for that one day only.'

'But she wants you to wear all the gear, so you'll have to get fitted at Moss Bros with Dad and I.'

'God, what a fuss over nothing. You know my size, hire one for me at the same time, we'll all look like bloody penguins anyway.'

In spite of Michael's announcement, his mother had never looked better. The wheelchair was now firmly tucked away in a cupboard, and the wedding planning was her major preoccupation. She would allow nothing to get in the way of that – neither insufficient funds, her eldest son's angst, nor least of all, her husband's health.

'Now I want only the best singers from the choir, and it's up to you to give the sermon of your lifetime.' Wilfred raised his eyebrows. 'After all, she's your only daughter. Also I've been thinking, in my opinion you should make fidelity within marriage your main theme.'

Occasionally, Deborah noticed her father looking distracted, and she often caught him rubbing his chest as if in some discomfort, and also refusing food because he said he had indigestion.

'Are you all right, Dad?'

But his answer to her question was an invariable shrug of his shoulders, and a reassuring smile.

'Don't you worry about me; after all, it's not every day that I get to officiate at my own daughter's wedding.'

What Deborah refused to tell him, especially when he was looking this way, was that she had a lot of reservations about being married by her own father. In particular, she hated the thought of being lectured by him under the *chuppah*[22] on the sanctity of marriage. Furthermore, she couldn't discuss her reservations with Ben, because nobody had yet enlightened him on the true state of Wilfred and Frances's marriage. Try as she might, she couldn't see any way of asking her father not to officiate on the day, without causing a major row.

So like everyone else in the household, she mutely agreed to all her mother's plans, and began counting the days until she became Mrs Benjamin Cohen, aged twenty and a half, and more than ready to move out of her childhood home for good.

---

[22]*marriage canopy*

CHAPTER 16

Ben wasn't the only one to have fallen in love with a Steinberg. In a bizarre twist of fate, his family had also fallen head over heels with her family.

Lily Cohen, not wishing to be outdone on the party scene, decided to make her own engagement party for the young couple in Sheffield, to give their friends a chance to meet the Steinbergs.

'They're so colourful,' she told all her friends at the badminton club, 'and her father's one of nature's gentlemen, an old-fashioned charmer. My Ben's so lucky to have found them.'

Her husband Alec was no less effusive. 'The girl's as pretty as a picture, a real little smasher,' he boasted to his golfing friends, 'and her father's a famous rabbi you know. I never thought he would, but finally he's done us proud has our Ben.'

The only Steinberg who wouldn't co-operate in this love fest was of course Michael. He refused point blank to leave his newly rented cottage in Derbyshire to attend the Sheffield celebration.

'I'm too busy with my writing,' was the only explanation he gave.

'I do hope you'll find the time to turn up for the wedding.'

'If I have to, I will.'

Frances had done her best to persuade her son away from his best seller for just one evening, but to no avail. However, Wilfred saw the situation from a different point of view.

'Better to leave him where he is, at least that way he can't embarrass us in front of them.'

A few days before the second engagement party, Frances loyally tried to explain Michael's absence to her hostess.

'I'm so sorry, but he's writing a book, you see, and you know how temperamental these artistic types are.'

When the day came, Frances and Wilfred travelled to Sheffield by car, but Jake begged Deborah to let him have a lift with her and Ben.

'If I have to listen to another word about bloody mushroom vol au vents, cheese blintzes or the best Klezmer musicians in Manchester, I'll emigrate, so help me I will.'

The Cohen family lived in Dore, on the outskirts of the city, and that evening Alec and Lily proudly introduced Deborah's family to their friends. Many of them knew of Wilfred by repute, such being the nature of the Jewish Mafia, or by extended family tentacles.

'I hear your husband's a famous rabbi.'

'Yes, I suppose he is.'

'And your son's a famous writer too.'

'Ah … look, it's been so nice to chat to you, but you must excuse me, nature calls as they say.'

A red faced, rotund man, standing barely five-foot in his built up shoes, rubbed his protruding belly against Deborah.

'By the 'eck, Alec was right when he said you were a little cracker.'

'Nice of him to say so.'

'Not nice at all love, it's truth.'

She tried to edge sideways out of his way, but when she did the fob watch he was wearing round his belly inadvertently got caught in the material of her dress, forcing the two of them to move even closer to each other. While she tried to release herself, the smell of beer and tobacco on his breath almost overpowered her, and she looked towards Ben in panic.

'I see you've met Uncle Silas.'

'Ben, you're a lucky bugger, I'd like to be in your shoes on't wedding night lad.'

He laughed so hysterically at his own comment, that Deborah was forced to jiggle up and down in unison with him. So she gave one frantic tug at the dress, and it immediately tore, but by now she couldn't have cared less, because she'd finally managed to release herself.

Meanwhile, Uncle Silas was still laughing so much that he started to choke. When he went blue in the face, Ben grabbed him from behind to do the Heimlich manoeuvre, and the old man finally caught his breath. Deborah looked on in horror, wondering whether all Ben's relatives were the same.

'Wilfred, let me get you some food from the buffet.'

'Thank you Lily, but I can manage.'

Then to his astonishment, Deborah's future mother-in-law came so close to him that barely a centimetre separated his body from hers.

'It's so nice that we're going to be family, don't you think?'

'Yes, wonderful that the young couple have found each other.'

'And we've found each other too.'

It usually took quite a lot to shock Wilfred, but as he looked down at Lily Cohen's grey hair now resting near the sleeve of his dark jacket, he shuddered involuntarily.

'You must be feeling chilly, let's move nearer to the fire.'

'Perhaps I'd better go and find my wife if you don't mind, Lily, she must be wondering where I've got to.'

Meanwhile Jake was having problems of his own. He'd watched in amusement when his sister got attached then unattached from the old man. He'd even spotted his father being accosted by Ben's mother, but when the nubile teenage cousin sidled up to him, he began to wonder if there was something in the Sheffield air that made them all so amorous.

'I take it you're Jake.'

Up till that moment he'd been sitting on a sofa devouring a plate of cold meats and assorted salads. The girl, who was wearing the shortest and tightest of mini skirts he'd ever seen, hovered above him.

'Mind if I sit next to you?'

'No.'

When she took a seat rather too close to him, he blushed because her skirt rode up even further.

'I'm Ben's cousin Gina. That's my Dad choking over there.'

'Will he be all right?'

'Yeah, it's his regular party piece.'

Then to his further astonishment, she put a cocktail sausage into her mouth, and sucked on it suggestively. Jake's eyes opened wider when she took a long swig from a pint of beer in her other hand.

'How old are you?'

'Fourteen, fancy a spliff?'

'Don't smoke.'

'What about a shag then?'

She watched for his reaction, which was entirely predictable, then bit into the sausage with as much force as she could, and Jake felt a sharp pain course through his genitals.

'Everybody says I'm well developed for my age.'

'And I thought my family were colourful.'

'You what?'

'Nothing.'

After Silas's choking fit died down, Alec Cohen heaved himself up onto a dining chair, then tapped the side of his glass for silence. He then informed the gathering that he wanted to make a toast to welcome the Steinbergs to Sheffield.

'We're just a small community here, not like you big city types …' Jake looked heavenwards when he heard that. 'But we Yorkshire folk know a good thing when we see one, and we can see that our Ben and your Deborah are perfect for each other.'

'Hear, hear,' Silas spluttered.

'We also can see that she's from a lovely, united family.' Wilfred then felt beads of perspiration running down his neck. 'The sort of people who understand the true meaning of marriage.' Jake and Deborah exchanged anxious glances, as he continued. 'I said to our Lily only this morning, "Lily," I said, "those Steinbergs are quality folk." And we couldn't be happier that our two families will be joining together. So I want you to raise your glasses …'

'We would, Alec, if you'd given us something to sup in 'em,' Silas barked, then had another laughing and coughing fit. Obviously well used to him, Alec continued with his toast.

'… and drink a toast to the happy couple.'

'The happy couple.'

Frances caught a sob in the back of her throat as she joined in. At the end of the evening, after most of the guests had gone home, Ben took Deborah aside.

'I imagine you've seen enough of my family now to change your mind about this marriage?'

'Not at all, but when we're married I just want to lock us away in our own little nest, and leave the rest of the world to do what they like.'

'If only life were that simple, Debs.'

*

The Finklestones and Charles d'Ath had been commissioned to create Frances's outfit as well as Deborah's wedding dress. Frances had selected an emerald green silk for the dress and jacket, and Neil's crippled sister embroidered both with matching sequins. Frances daydreamed about making her entrance into the synagogue on the day, with all the guests straining their necks to marvel at her outfit.

'Wouldn't it be a good idea to ask Ben's mother what colour she's going to wear?' Deborah suggested.

'Is it necessary?'

'You wouldn't want to find yourselves wearing the same dress, would you?'

So a few weeks before the date, Frances rang Lily, ostensibly to invite her and Alec for Friday night supper, but also to go over the final details of the big day.

'And you'll be able to see the presents at the same time. Do you know, Lily, they've already had twenty five stainless steel carving dishes?'

'Never?'

'And I can't tell you how many Pyrexes.'

'You can never have too many of those.'

'And my poor Deborah's already had to write over two hundred thank you letters.'

'Poor love.'

'She's getting tetchy about it, I can tell you. She said to me only this morning, if I have to write another blooming letter, I'll scream. Oh, and while we're on the subject, what colour have you chosen to wear, Lily?'

'Well, me and Alec went down to London to Madame Rojas, that's where my friends told me to go.' Frances took a sharp intake of breath, wondering why she'd never thought of that. 'And I saw this lovely chiffon dress with floaty sleeves, quite long in the back and ...'

'What colour?'

'I'll just finish the description, well like I said the sleeves are long and see-through, and in the front the material's sort of gathered into rosettes, oh and Frances it's lovely.'

'Yes, but what colour is it?'

'And on my head, they're going to find me some matching feathers to make a little hat.' Frances was now getting quite edgy. 'Oh yes, the colour. Well it's not exactly yellow, and it's not exactly green ...' Frances went cold. 'I'd say it's a sort of mossy, yellowy, greeny colour.'

'Then it's green?' She steadied herself on the edge of the table, and gripped the phone tightly.

'Not exactly.'

Now Frances began to pray. 'And you've already bought it?'

'Yes, it's ordered.'

'Did they do it in any other colours?'

'I just loved that one, why?'

'No reason.' Her throat was dry, and her daydream was disappearing fast. 'Anyway, see you Friday.'

'We're so looking forward to being with you again.'

'Umm, us too.'

When she had put the phone back in its cradle, she sat down on the nearest chair and fought back the urge to scream out loud.

On the afternoon of the dinner, while Frances was preparing the meal she was giving to the Cohen family, Michael burst through the back door. She looked up in astonishment, and before she could say anything, he plunged his hand into the bowl of chopped liver she had just finished making, and stuffed it into his mouth.

'That's not for you.' She grabbed the bowl off him and placed it firmly behind her back.

'What happened to hello, nice to see you Michael, how are you keeping son?'

'Why didn't you say you were coming home? I've only laid for seven.'

'One more won't make any difference.'

'I'll have to water down the soup, anyway you weren't due home till next week, so why are you here?'

'And it's nice to see you too, mother.'

'Look, I haven't got time for your funnies, just answer the question.'

'Who's coming anyway?'

'Ben's family, and you still haven't told me why you've come home early.'

'Can I have a cup of tea at least?'

'If you make it yourself.'

She was still holding the chopped liver out of his reach when he filled the kettle with water. Only then did she reckon it was safe to put the bowl back down on the kitchen table.

'And don't touch that liver,' she ordered.

After a thorough interrogation, Michael admitted he was home because he didn't have enough money to pay the rent on the cottage.

'Then the bastard changed the locks while I was out … bloody little Hitler.'

'It's not so terrible, at least now you can go for a try of your morning dress.'

'Not so terrible? He's only got all my stuff still locked away inside!'

'Well, it's only a few old clothes.'

'But my writing, mother, he's got all my writing.'

'Ask for it back.'

'I did and he said only if I pay the back rent.'

'Go and pay him what you owe him then.' He looked at her with woebegone eyes. 'Don't tell me you've used all the money? Michael, it was six hundred pounds, I can't afford to give you any more.'

'If it was for our Deborah you'd find the money.'

'Don't be ridiculous, she's getting married.'

'And I'm going to be a great writer, so which is more important? If I never make anything of my life, it will be your fault, yours and Dad's.'

With that he kicked the kitchen chair out of the way, then made his way angrily upstairs to his bedroom.

'You'll have to move all the wedding presents off your bed!' she shouted up after him. 'And make sure you don't touch any of them!'

*

Ben had chosen their honeymoon destination, which was to be a fortnight in Crete, but insisted on keeping all the details a secret from Deborah.

'Just give me one little clue.'

'OK, it's somewhere hot.'

'That could be dozens of places.'

'Precisely.'

'This is so unfair, I won't even know what to pack.'

'Hopefully we'll spend most of the time in bed, so all you'll need is a bikini.'

He was due to take up his new posting in Halifax after their return from honeymoon. Neither of them had much spare time before the actual wedding date, but they did manage to drive to Halifax one Sunday a few weeks before the day.

On the advice of Ben's new colleagues, they decided to drive around the outskirts of the town, but having grown up amongst the red brick of Manchester, Deborah was unprepared for her first view of the area. Most of the formerly splendid old homes overlooking the Calder valley were now old and grimy, and what had once been their pristine Yorkshire stone-clad exteriors, were now mostly blackened with soot.

'Aren't the views wonderful?' Ben enthused.

'But they're all of factory chimneys.'

'That's because these houses were built for mill owners and their workers.'

She had to admit that the suburbs of Shibden and Ovendon were leafy and well maintained, but the views from their gardens were mostly of mill chimneys belching out the noxious smoke that kept them operating.

She tried as hard as she could to disguise her first, negative impressions because Ben was so obviously fired with enthusiasm. She still yearned to see just one street of cement rendered or red brick houses, but didn't dare confide that to him.

After trawling round fruitlessly for the best part of the day, they decided that as soon as they were back from their honeymoon, Deborah's main task would be to find them a suitable new home.

'Look Ben, over there.'

He was about to drive back towards the main Pennine road that linked Yorkshire to Manchester, when she suddenly spotted a brand new housing development being built in the grounds of a former mansion.

'Stop the car, they look nice over there.'

He drove to the entrance of the building site, and they got out to take a better look. All the houses were being built to the exact same specification, and all in mock Georgian style. But the best feature of all for the bride to be, was that each of the new houses was white cement rendered, with only small slabs of clean Yorkshire stone as decorative features.

'Ben, they're perfect.'

'But they're all identical.'

'So what?'

'But what if we come home drunk one evening and go into the wrong one?'

'Oh ye of little faith, I'll make sure ours looks different to the rest of them.'

'How?'

'Well we'll have a mezuzah on the front door for a start.'

'I bet it will be the only one round here.'

'Oh Ben, I can't believe we've found the perfect little Georgian house.'

'Mock Georgian, my sweet, alas very mocking.'

'You're such a cynic, but don't you just love it? I'm going to contact them tomorrow.'

Because she'd finished her college course a few weeks earlier, she now had enough time to pursue the house hunting issue. The very next day, she borrowed Ben's car to drive back to the housing estate outside Halifax, and went straight to the site office.

'We can only afford one with three bedrooms,' she told Ben from a telephone box, 'but it's got a garage and a nice little garden, and I'm sure we can make it so pretty.'

'I'll have to see about getting a mortgage, but if you like it then so do I.'

'Oh Ben, I do love you.'

'Show me just how much tonight.'

'Is that all you ever think about?'

'Shush, my patient might hear you.'

When she told her parents excitedly about the house, her father seemed pleased for her but Frances began another of her customary interrogations.

'Where's Shibden? I've never heard of it.'

'Maybe you haven't, but it's very nice.'

'Do they at least have a synagogue there?'

'Maybe there's one in Halifax.'

'What about shops, a cinema?'

'Look, I was far too busy on the building site to go looking for the local cinema.'

'In my day, girls took their parents along with them when they were looking for their first home.'

'Things have changed.'

'And more's the pity.'

*

The house was due for completion within the next few weeks, and after the mortgage agreement had been drawn up and contracts had been signed, Deborah and Ben reluctantly decided to leave the remaining details to their two mothers to complete whilst they were away on honeymoon. However, they made both women swear a solemn oath that neither would change a thing that had already been agreed upon, and delay any major decisions until Deborah and Ben were home.

'Between these four walls, Frances, surely they won't mind if we put some fresh flowers in for their return?' Lily suggested during a clandestine telephone conversation.

'Or some food in their fridge?'

'And Alec and I could plant out the garden for them while they're away.'

'Wilfred's not very good at that sort of thing, but I'm sure I could find something useful for him to do there.'

'Perhaps you could start unwrapping the presents and putting them away.'

'And maybe we could both arrange the furniture so that they won't have to do it when they get back?'

'But not a word about it before the wedding, Frances.'

'Lily, do you think I'm mad?'

*

On the eve of her wedding, Deborah found it hard to sleep. For most of the previous week, she'd been having the same recurring nightmare where she was running through the centre of Manchester in her wedding dress trying to find the synagogue. When she eventually found it, her dress was tattered and dirty, and once she made it inside the only person sitting in the pews was her mother, sobbing.

On this particular night, after tossing and turning for several hours, she got out of bed and went into the bathroom at three in the morning to get a glass of water. But when she opened the bathroom door, she found her father already in there, swallowing some pills. Father and daughter looked at each other ruefully.

'I suppose I should be imparting some gem of wisdom to you right now,' he said sadly.

'Do you have to? It will be bad enough listening to your sermon tomorrow.'

He looked stung, as if that came as a surprise to him.

'Never knew you felt like that.'

'Let's face it, Dad, your marriage has hardly been one of the greatest examples to follow.'

'Yes, you're right.'

Now that she was leaving his care within a matter of hours, she felt at liberty to be honest. He mulled over her words, and didn't say anything for a while, then when he did, Deborah was shocked to see how old and tired her father looked.

'You know, it hasn't been easy for me either.' She instinctively took hold of his hand. 'But I did the best I could.' Then a tear plopped onto his pyjama sleeve, and she took the hand she was holding and kissed it.

'Don't lay it on with a shovel tomorrow, that's all I ask.'

He took her face in his hands and kissed her forehead, then shuffled towards the bathroom door.

'Be happy.'

The sound of the front doorbell woke Deborah the following morning. She opened her eyes and caught sight of her wedding dress and veil hanging from the wardrobe, and felt a flutter of nervousness. She put on her dressing gown, and could hear her mother downstairs taking delivery of the wedding flowers.

'It's smaller than the one I ordered.'

'No madam, this is exactly the same as the one you saw in the picture.'

'Then tell your boss that his pictures are misleading, anyway you can put them over there.'

'I hope the bride enjoys her day.'

'And I hope she's not disappointed with that bouquet.'

When Deborah heard the delivery man being ushered out, she decided to make her way downstairs to the kitchen.

'What are you doing?' Frances asked as she poured herself a cup of tea.

'I'm going to have breakfast.'

'Oh no you're not, Jewish brides are supposed to fast on their wedding day, I did.'

'This is the first I've heard about it. Anyway, you can't expect me to last until two o'clock without anything inside me.'

'That's as may be, but it's the *din*[23]. Anyway, the hairdresser will be here soon, so you'd better have your bath so that you're ready for her.'

When Wilfred came into the kitchen a moment later, Deborah appealed to her father to challenge Frances, but he grimaced and shrugged.

'Better not get her started today of all days, hey?'

The hairdresser arrived, and as soon as she came through the front door, Michael waylaid her and demanded that she do his hair as well.

'It needs doing and I haven't had time, so if they expect me to look like a tailor's dummy, I'll need a haircut.'

The girl looked at the mane of hair he was thrusting in her face, and quickly consulted her watch.

'There's Deborah and your mother to do first, then if I've got any time left over, I'll see what I can do.'

---

[23]*rabbinical law*

'But what about me?' Jake came down the stairs looking dishevelled from sleep, but this time the girl just grinned.

'You look lovely as you are.'

As soon as the hairdresser reached Deborah's bedroom, the bride turned her round and told her to go straight back into the kitchen to ask Frances for a plate of sandwiches.

'It's all right, Deborah, I've had my breakfast.'

'You might have, but I haven't. Please, just say you're hungry, and tell her to make you a pot of tea as well.'

Three hours later, each of the Steinbergs was dressed, coiffed and awaiting the photographer, who was busy putting up spotlights and rearranging the furniture in the lounge. While they were waiting for him to finish, Ruby and Sam breezed in, looked the family over approvingly, and then went to kiss the bride.

'Only one thing, darling, your veil needs ironing.'

With those prophetic words, Ruby sailed into the kitchen her fox furs flying, to make her and Sam yet another cup of tea.

*

The synagogue was awash with flowers as Michael solemnly escorted his mother up the aisle. There was a steady buzz of murmured conversation, and Frances graciously acknowledged familiar faces on her way to her place under the chuppah. She smiled and nodded to the Cohens, who had entered before her and were already standing there.

The best man, a friend of Ben's from university days, twiddled nervously with the ring in his pocket. Meanwhile, Frances glanced around to check on the floral arrangements stacked on plinths around the canopy, whilst taking immense pride at their beauty and her choices.

Suddenly she caught sight of a pool of water that had obviously leaked from one of the arrangements onto the carpet. She was about to go and wipe the mess when she remembered why she was there, and admonished herself not to move. However, throughout the whole service, her eyes kept straying to the damp patch on the carpet, which she endured like an indelible stain on her character.

The organist began another hymn in preparation for the arrival of the bride, and the congregation went silent. Frances glanced towards her sister in the front row, and Ruby immediately pointed to the puddle on the carpet. Frances quickly looked away so as not to be further dismayed at this hitch in her meticulous planning. Outside in the hallway, Deborah allowed herself to be ministered to by Neil Finklestone, before entering the synagogue on her father's arm.

'Now don't forget, sweetie, head up high. You look lovely, so smile, smile, and smile,' Neil lisped.

Charles d'Ath held onto her flowers while Neil's little sister was busy smoothing down the wild silk of the skirt so that it fell into perfect columns. As she stood nearer to the floor than most, she was in an ideal position for this task.

'Break a leg, kid.'

'Darling,' Neil chided Charles, 'she's about to get wed not star in the Follies.'

When Deborah finally entered the synagogue, the choir broke out into a rousing anthem, and everything in front of her became an instant blur. Walking up the aisle, or in her case being encouraged up it by her father's steadying hand, she vaguely heard the music and vaguely noticed the flowers. Even the faces of the guests whose eyes were upon her, had all merged into one.

Try as she might to smile like Neil Finklestone had told her to, she was barely able to compose her mouth into a weak grin. Then, when they had almost made it to the top, she saw Ben turn and look at her from under the canopy, and for the first time that day, her muscles relaxed. They grinned at each other, but when she spotted her mother, the muscles tensed again.

At Ben's side under the chuppah, Deborah knew that the worst was not yet over, and steeled herself to blot from her mind whatever her father was going to say in his sermon. In spite or their chat the night before, she dreaded having to listen to platitudes about the sanctity of marriage that she had so often heard him say to other newlyweds, advice that he never quite managed to adhere to himself.

However when it came to the time of his sermon, her father spoke without a note and gave the most sensitive sermon of his life, which reduced most of the congregation, including Ben and Deborah, to tears.

'And all I say is, be true to yourselves, my dear daughter and Benjamin. That's all we will ever ask of you both.'

*

At the reception, Michael was balancing a glass of champagne in either hand, sipping from each one alternately, while he looked for his father to congratulate him on his sermon.

'That was so moving, Dad, especially the bit about being true to yourself.'

'Nice of you to say so, Mick.'

'I'll tell you what, it got me thinking.'

'About what?'

'My future.'

At those words, his father let out a sigh of relief, and patted his son affectionately on the shoulder.

'I never thought I'd hear you say those words.'

Michael grinned, pleased with himself that he'd finally said the right thing to satisfy his father.

'So after I've finished my book, perhaps I'll become a rabbi like you?'

Wilfred leaned against a table to support himself as the colour drained out of his face. A waitress passed by with a tray of drinks, and Wilfred managed to grab a whisky off her.

'A rabbi, you said?'

'Well I'm good at managing people, and what with my writing skills as well, it struck me as being just the job for me.'

'Perhaps we'd better talk about this at a more suitable time?'

Up till that moment, Wilfred had looked the happiest he'd been for a long time. He'd greeted his congregation and old friends alike, spoken proudly of his family, even complimented Frances effusively on how lovely she looked and how well she'd arranged the wedding. But this new bombshell wiped the smile off his face completely.

When the time came for Deborah and Ben to leave the reception to set off on their honeymoon, Wilfred took his daughter to one side.

'I'm so sorry for letting you down,' he whispered.

Hearing this, she became so choked up with emotion that she couldn't reply, and realised with a start that she had felt closer to him in the last twenty-four hours than she had for most of her adult life. He kissed her gently on her forehead, then pushed her towards Ben.

CHAPTER 17

After the pressures of the last few weeks, Crete was an idyll for the newlyweds. True to his promise, during the first few days there they made love so often that she hardly got to wear her bikini.

'Ben, I'm now walking with bandy legs because of all that retsina you keep drinking.'

'It's a very nice drink and remarkably cheap.'

'But you're insatiable afterwards.'

'Don't complain, woman, I'm going to order several crates to take home as well.'

As soon as Christos, the owner of the local taverna, found out that the young English couple were on honeymoon, he made sure to have a bottle of his home brew waiting for them every time they visited.

'This drink make very good babies, is why my mother have thirteen of them.'

'Did he mean bottles or babies?'

'Probably both.'

Christos wasn't exaggerating because every night there was a different brother or sister helping him in the bar. When he insisted on giving Ben a couple of bottles for the hotel bedroom, Deborah used them mainly to kill the myriad of crawling creatures that roamed freely round their room.

'You're wasting it.'

'You've already had enough in his café.'

'You know I'm only drinking it because the water isn't safe.'

'And if I have thirteen babies, God help you.'

After the first week, they decided to explore the island by hiring bicycles, which only added to Deborah's leg problems.

'Do you know, I'm convinced I lost my virginity on the cross bar of Michael's bike?' she called back to Ben.

'But you told me I was the first.'

They had been cycling for half an hour up a mountain path. It was late afternoon and the sun was low in the sky. They stopped when they reached the crest of the hill, then stared down, marvelling at the view and the azure sea below. She dismounted then laid her bike down and massaged her sore thighs. Ben came up behind her.

'Isn't this beautiful.'

He nuzzled into the nape of her neck and caressed her through her half open blouse. 'No, you're beautiful.'

'Don't, Ben, someone might see us.'

'I've not seen a soul except for a few sheep. How about we try for one of those thirteen babies right now?'

They lay down on the nearby gorse, and he slowly started to undress her, but when he was about to take off his own shorts, she screeched.

'What's that smell?'

'What smell?'

'Must be on your shoes.'

'It will go away.'

'No Ben, it's horrible.'

He picked up one of his discarded shoes and looked underneath, then threw it away in disgust.

'Bloody sheep droppings.'

Laughing hysterically, they pulled their clothes back on, then remounted their bicycles and cycled back towards the town. After returning the bikes, Ben jettisoned the offending shoes in a dustbin.

'Don't you need them?'

'I've had them since university, better to give them a decent burial here.'

'I bet some needy peasant finds them and takes them home.'

'He'll probably enjoy the smell, remind him of home comforts.'

After showering at their hotel, they decided to round off their evening at Christos's bar.

'Tonight you eat my mama's cooking, she make the speciality just for you. First I bring you some meze, we have dolmades, taramasalata ...'

'Whatever you bring me, my friend, I know it will be good.'

'But first Englishman and lady, a toast ...'

*

While they were walking back rather unsteadily to their hotel, Deborah began to feel nostalgia for this island that they would shortly be leaving.

'Only one more week before reality sets in.'

'Don't worry, my sweet, they say the Costa del Halifax is particularly beautiful at this time of the year.'

They dawdled back towards the hotel, in no particular hurry to let the evening end. When they finally went through the hotel door, and asked at the reception for their room key, the receptionist handed them a telegram along with the key.

'This night you had many telephone calls,' the woman said, 'and is most from same peoples.'

'Calls for us?'

'Yes, he say is your brother, must to call him immediately, is very urgent.'

A cold band of steel seemed to clutch at her throat, and Deborah grabbed Ben's hand, nearly crushing his fingers.

'It must be Mum.'

'I'll call them now if you like?'

'No, I'll do it, she's probably just in hospital again.'

Hospital for Frances was such a regular occurrence that it had no special significance for her family, and as Deborah uttered the words she desperately wanted to believe them. But for some inexplicable reason, she couldn't be certain this evening, and the effects of the alcohol were draining from her body by the second.

It took a further two hours to get through to the house on account of delays on the flimsy island telephone line, but when she finally did, Jake answered the phone after the first ring.

'Deborah, thank God.' He sounded distraught. 'I've got some very bad news.'

'Mum, is she ill?'

'It's Dad … he died last night.'

'Oh my God.'

She dropped the phone, and when Ben saw the colour drain out of her face, he grabbed hold of it and continued talking to Jake. 'What happened?'

'Massive cerebral haemorrhage. The doctor said he wouldn't have suffered too much.'

When he put the phone down, Deborah's face was creased in pain, and he hugged her tightly to his body.

'I should have let him say whatever he wanted at the wedding. It's my fault.' Then she collapsed sobbing against her new husband.

*

Word spread like wildfire around the small Cretan village. The operator, who had listened in on the conversation, then relayed the news to everyone that she knew. Within hours, most of the regulars from the bar and all Christos's family, were waiting in the small hotel reception to see if they could be of help to the English couple.

'My cousin, she work at Olympic Airways desk, and I already speak with her and she arrange to get you on first flight tomorrow,' Christos told Ben when he came downstairs to thank them for coming.

'That's very kind of you Christos.'

'Is not kind, is what I must to do for my good friend. How your lovely wife feeling?'

'She's very upset.'

'Is her papa, of course she cry.'

'He was a good man, Christos, and very famous in his city.'

'You know what we say in Greece? When old person die, a new baby will soon come into life.'

Then he beckoned to some of the other people to come nearer. Although the majority spoke no English, many of them were carrying parcels, which they heaped on Ben. He looked quickly inside the first bag, laid in his arms by an old lady dressed only in black. It was full of freshly picked lemons. He tried remonstrating with her, but she smiled sadly at him, kissed her hands then offered them to him in a gesture.

'This is so kind.'

'She say is nothing,' Christos interpreted.

Next, one of the regular drinkers at the bar thrust an enormous bottle of retsina at him, then kissed him on both cheeks. After that Christos's sister pushed her way to the front, with a huge jar of olives, which she also pushed on him.

By now he was feeling somewhat desperate, fervently praying there were no more gifts, as he doubted they would fit inside their suitcases. Finally Christos himself reached inside his shirt, then took out an enormous salami with such a flourish, that it looked to Ben as if he was producing a rabbit out of a hat.

'How can I thank you all?' Christos solemnly translated for the others who beamed in delight. 'You have all been so generous and kind.'

'Then you come back next year with baby, and we all celebrate together again.' He then translated that sentence for the others, and they cheered.

'I promise, we'll be back.'

*

Deborah wept quietly against Ben's chest until their plane touched down at Manchester Airport. Then feeling totally drained of emotion, she straightened herself up and prepared to face the rest of her family.

Michael had driven Wilfred's car to the airport to meet them, then the three of them hugged each other in a desultory manner, and drove back to the house in silence.

Drawing up outside the house, Deborah thought back to the last time she had been there, on the day of her wedding. That day, the sun had shone brightly, and a few neighbours had gathered on the pavement to wave goodbye to her in her wedding regalia, and shout messages of good luck. Today there was no sunshine or neighbours, and no feelings of excitement and expectancy.

In the car Michael had told them that Frances had been on her own the night he died. Wilfred had gone to bed early, telling her that he had a bad headache.

'Do you want an aspirin?' she had asked.

'I've already taken some, if I get a good night's sleep it should help.'

'Very well, I'll sleep in Deborah's room so as not to disturb you.'

'Thank you.'

The main reason for this unusual spurt of generosity on her part was that 'Double Your Money', compered by Hughie Green, was on the television that night and she didn't want to miss it.

Earlier that evening they'd gone through the proofs of the photographs taken at the wedding, sitting together in companionable silence at the kitchen table. Frances had noticed that he looked pale, but he seemed so happy reliving the highlights of that day, that she thought little more about it.

'Tell your father to come down for his breakfast, it's getting cold,' she said to Michael the next morning.

Michael went up the stairs muttering something about never getting any peace in this house, and when he opened the bedroom door and looked inside, he saw his father lying quite still in bed.

'He's still asleep.'

'Better wake him up, it's not like him to sleep so long.'

'Time to get up, sleepy head.'

Michael shook his father's icy shoulder, and everyone who heard his screams felt chilled to the bone. Jake rushed out of his bedroom in his pyjama bottoms, and Frances bounded up the stairs with a speed and alacrity no one in the family knew she was capable of.

'Oh my God, Wilfred, speak to me.'

'Doctor Fenton, this is Jake Steinberg, you've got to come immediately ...'

Shortly afterwards, when the doctor pronounced him dead, Frances started to wail so loudly that it alerted the next door neighbour, who rang the front doorbell to see if everything was all right.

'It's ... my Dad.'

'The rabbi?'

'He's dead.' Then Jake fell against Cosmo's shoulder and howled.

CHAPTER 18

The day of Wilfred's funeral was one of the worst of the autumn. A torrential downpour had fallen steadily all morning, and the pavements looked damp and greasy.

'Tears of the Gods,' Evelyn Fraser murmured, looking out of her bedroom window.

She was having great difficulty choosing an outfit for the funeral. It had to be one which showed the proper amount of grief and respect, but at the same time accentuated her better features, just to remind anyone who was still interested, that she had been one of his favourites in her time.

Even though they hadn't been close for many years, she felt a huge sorrow sitting like a pile of bricks on her shoulders. Its weight had descended the moment she'd heard of his death, and now seemed to be living with her like a tombstone.

'Hurry up or we'll be late!' Hershel shouted up.

'I don't know what to wear.'

'It's a funeral, not a job interview.'

When they arrived at the cemetery, rivulets of mud were running amongst the gravestones, forcing the mourners to walk carefully. Most of them were sheltering under umbrellas, but some pragmatists, unwilling to ruin their shoes, stayed close to the chapel walls. Those who managed to get inside huddled together in silence, awaiting the arrival of the Steinberg family and the hearse.

'Stand back please, let the family through.'

One of the undertakers tried to make a pathway, but the crowd shuffled, having nowhere else to go, then regrouped again but in a slightly different formation. It was crowded to capacity, and many mourners were still standing outside sheltering under their umbrellas.

Deborah, Jake and Ben walked in first, and each kept their eyes downcast. They made their way to the front of the chapel and waited. Then a sight greeted the crowd, which caused a few to gasp. Michael, helped by one of the undertakers, was manoeuvring a wheelchair inside the small building. Sitting huddled in it was Frances, looking very frail and wizened. Her black coat enveloped her as she was pushed to the front of the room alongside her children.

The last time the family had been assembled in front of so many people had been at Deborah and Ben's wedding, and today none of them wanted to make eye contact with the crowd of people watching them.

When the hearse was lifted into the chapel, a collective sob gathered in many throats as the undertakers placed the coffin gently on a bier. It was covered by a plain black cloth, and seemed so insignificant in comparison to the memory of the man whose body lay inside.

The congregation had brought in a colleague of Wilfred's to take the service. He had come especially from London, and seemed to be as moved as the others in the chapel.

'Wilfred, you were a friend, a loving husband and father, and a mentor to so many of us. You will stay forever in our hearts, and be sorely missed. Rest in peace my friend amongst our heavenly fathers, and I know that when you stand in front of our maker, he will surely say welcome home my son, all is forgiven.'

*

After the service was over, the mourners followed the cortege in silence towards the burial plot. The tyre tracks of Frances's wheelchair were imprinted in the mud all the way to the graveside. Two sets of parallel lines, like slithering lizards. Michael had appointed himself her wheeler in chief. That way he could concentrate on the wheelchair's route rather than on his own feelings.

When Frances had taken to her wheelchair the day after he died, her children had tried to dissuade her.

'But you don't need it, Mum,' Deborah had argued.

'Leave me alone, if I want to sit in it, I will.'

'It's become like her security blanket,' Deborah told Ben, 'but she can't stay in it for the rest of her life.'

'Leave her till after the funeral, then I'll have a word with her.'

Rabbi Elphinstone started the graveside prayers to the accompaniment of the rain ricocheting off his hat then trickling down the back of his neck. His wife saw the bottom of her husband's black gown flapping even more mud against his trouser legs. The turn-ups were badly splattered, and she wondered how to remove the stains after they returned to their beige carpeted hotel room.

When he got to the end, Jake and Michael recited the *kaddish*[24], then they dug the first shovels of earth and threw them over the coffin. Ben was next, then all the male mourners stepped forward to complete the task.

Deborah shivered, and had to bite her lip to stop herself from crying out. She moved nearer to her mother, but Frances huddled even deeper into the chair, refusing to look up. The casket was still only half covered with clumps of earth. Most of the men had shovelled as much as they could, but the final covering would have to be completed by cemetery employees when the rain stopped. When Deborah looked towards her younger brother, she noticed a streak of mud down one of his cheeks.

The rabbi asked the crowd to regroup in the chapel, but Deborah and Jake were in no hurry to leave the graveside. Ben stood aside whilst his wife and her brother lingered by the half-filled plot, reluctant to leave their father to this waterlogged, final resting-place. The two of them stared bleakly at his coffin, sighing in unison.

Deborah felt leaden walking back down the aisles of graves to rejoin the others. Ben held onto her arm as they passed headstones that belonged to familiar names from their past. She nudged Jake who was walking alongside them.

'Remember her?'

'Wasn't she the one sang in the choir and fluttered her eyelashes whenever he was around?'

Ben was taken aback when they both sniggered suggestively, then Jake pointed to the stone.

---

[24]*mourners' prayer*

314

'Look at the wording, says her devoted husband sadly misses her, little did he know.'

They passed an impressive headstone that seemed to tower over its companions. It was made from a rough-hewn slab of granite, and the inscription read, *In loving memory of Alex Jacobi, beloved husband, father and grandfather*.

'That granite looks as hard as he was,' Jake muttered.

'Look Jake, that's the Aarons kid over there, the one who died of meningitis.' Then they fell silent; lost in their own thoughts, and when they reached the Chapel, the crowd again parted to let them through. Before Deborah stepped inside the prayer house, she looked back at the graves, thinking about how much of her past was steadily decomposing there.

It was now hot and stuffy inside, but Frances steadfastly refused to leave the security of the wheelchair. She felt safe within it, and her identity as a sick woman was once again re-established. Her face remained immobile, she had cried all the tears she needed to cry, but for her the tears were for what might have been rather than for what was.

The rest of the family stood beside the rabbi as he announced that prayers would take place at eight o'clock at the family home. This was the signal for them to sit down on a hard wooden bench, while the crowd started filing past them in an orderly queue. The rabbi wheeled their mother's wheelchair next to the bench so that she too could receive the mourners' condolences.

'I wish you long life,' was the customary greeting from most people.

'Thank you so much.'

'He was a great man, you know.'

'Yes, thank you.'

'It's so nice that he was there for your wedding.' At this, Deborah could only sigh.

'If it hadn't have been for your husband, I'd have left the religion years ago,' someone said to Frances, who inclined her head in acknowledgement.

'If only I'd had a father like yours,' Deborah overheard a young girl say to Michael, who nodded his head sagely. Casting a quick glance at her brother, for one horrible moment Deborah thought he was going to giggle.

'Yes, we realised he was very special.'

*

That evening, most who came for prayers were unable to park in the street. Although the rain had finally stopped, the pavements were still damp and greasy, and several of the women in high-heeled shoes must have come perilously close to slipping as they teetered towards the house. But they were not going to miss this final opportunity of saying goodbye to the man who had made many of their lives more tolerable for a quarter of a century.

Some of their husbands slouched behind them, with their coat collars turned up against the weather.

'United are at home tonight,' one of the men muttered to another.

'I'd rather be there than here.'

'Least we could do, after all he was a good bloke.'

'My missus thought the sun shone out of his arse.'

'Get a move on, Percy, we're late,' the woman in question snarled.

They crowded into the house as best they could, but several were forced to stand in the hallway, as the lounge was already overflowing with people. The wheelchair was propped against the hall table, and there were small pieces of mud on the carpet. Someone had placed a fresh tea towel over the mirror in the lounge, and for some inexplicable reason, this annoyed Deborah so she took it off. The rabbi raised his eyebrows, but said nothing.

Frances sat with the other members of her family on low mourner's chairs that had been brought in from the synagogue. Although she had abandoned her wheelchair for the occasion, propped up at the side of her was a walking stick.

'Where did she get that from?'

'Cosmo, next door,' Jake whispered to Deborah, 'he broke his ankle months ago, so she got me to borrow it from him.'

'I can't bear it, she wants to be an invalid.'

'If it makes her happy, leave her.'

After the rabbi had finished the prayers, he launched into another homily about his friend and mentor Wilfred.

'One of the finest men it was my privilege to have known ...'

'Dad never spoke of him,' Jake whispered to Deborah.

'And his guidance and inspiration will endure with this splendid congregation, which was his legacy.'

Frances listened stony faced. She resented this man, whom she saw as a pale imitation of Wilfred. He was eulogising him too insincerely for her liking, and she wanted to tell him to stop. But if she were to retain her dignity, she would have to keep her own counsel.

Finally it was over, and the last remnants of the crowd were leaving. An elderly gentleman, still wearing his skullcap, clutched at Frances's hand. He had been telling her about his family's escape from Nazi-held Vienna during the war. He was so engrossed in his story of how Wilfred had persuaded him to stay within the faith and not become a Quaker after finding refuge in Britain, that he hadn't noticed she'd long since nodded off in her chair, her hand still clasped within his.

'I'm going to make some tea,' Deborah said to Ben.

'I'll do it.'

'No, I need a break from this lot.'

They went into the kitchen, and while Deborah filled the kettle and turned on the gas, she hadn't noticed Michael sitting at the table chewing on sandwiches that someone had brought in earlier. Jake followed them shortly afterwards.

Waiting for the kettle to boil, Ben started rifling amongst a pile of long playing records, which were stacked on the sideboard.

'Who do these belong to?'

'I'd forgotten about those.' Jake's eyes lit up.

The kettle whistled, and Michael finally looked up with a lugubrious expression in his eyes.

'The real you will forget the misery ...' he intoned. The others stopped what they were doing and stared at him. 'Remembering it only as flood waters long gone. Job eleven, chapter fourteen.' He tilted back on his chair.

'Belt up,' Jake said.

'What's he on about?'

Ben's eyebrows had risen in the style suspiciously reminiscent of the genuine members of the Steinberg clan, but Deborah said nothing.

'I've been studying the holy book.'

'He thinks he's going to step into our father's shoes,' Jake sniffed.

'I'll go and see if Mum needs anything,' Deborah said.

She thought it was time to rescue her mother from the loquacious Viennese; however, when she went into the lounge, it was quite empty apart from her mother, who had transferred herself onto the sofa and was fast asleep. Deborah decided to leave her be.

Drinking tea in the kitchen, Ben inspected what was left of the sandwiches, trying to find one that still looked edible. But Michael had consumed the best of them, as if he hadn't eaten any food for the past week.

'I reckon the only one missing today was Peggy,' he said, offering the remainder to Jake.

Jake rejected the offer and pushed the plate back to Michael a bit too forcefully, and it looked as if it was going to slide over the table edge.

'Howzat.' Michael caught the plate, hoisting it into the air triumphantly before doing a quick impersonation of batting at the wicket.

'I don't suppose they'll have heard the news in Palm Springs or wherever it is she lives.'

'Suppose not – hey Debs, did I ever tell you that she came to us from the nuns? Another of his good causes, I suppose.'

Jake stood up from the table abruptly and went back to inspecting the records, except this time seemingly without much pleasure.

'Ever wonder what would have happened to her if the parents hadn't taken her in?' Michael continued.

'Or us?' Jake muttered.

Deborah collected the used teacups, and Ben began washing them while she dried. They smiled reassuringly at one another throughout their routine, and her brothers felt at a disadvantage because of their obvious togetherness.

'Why are you raking all this up now?'

'Uh oh, little brother Jake's getting touchy.' Deborah shot round and fired a warning look at Michael, but he was now on a roll and wouldn't be silenced. 'She had very nice tits, I remember.

'Can't we talk about something else?'

'Touched a raw nerve, have we?' he persisted. 'She was like a mother to you, wasn't she?'

'Look, if I wanted to talk about Peggy Purnell, I'd rather do it with a psychiatrist.'

With that, he slammed the sleeve of the Beethoven Violin Concerto that he was holding back down on the sideboard, then rushed out of the room, slamming the kitchen door as well.

*

Ben was due to take up his post in Halifax four days after they should have returned from honeymoon. While they'd been in Crete, they'd decided to name their new house Retsina, and Ben promised to get a sign made for it as soon as he had the time.

'I think you should stay with your Mum a bit longer till you get her settled.'

They decided on this as soon as the weeklong mourning period was over. However, Frances was still receiving visitors daily, and had become accustomed to using her daughter as waitress, refreshments provider and also nursemaid. Propped up on either side by cushions, she would position herself comfortably in her wheelchair, then receive her visitors in a queenly manner.

'Deborah, make a cup of tea for Mrs Pfeffer.'

'Just milk, dear, no sugar.'

'You're sweet enough already, Sadie.'

'I'm glad to see you haven't lost your sense of humour, Frances.'

'What can I do? My beloved Wilfred's gone, but no-one wants to see an old woman without a smile on her face.' At this Deborah's mouth fell open. 'Close your mouth, dear, it looks so unattractive, and don't forget some biscuits.'

Deborah reluctantly agreed to stay on, even though she'd have preferred to be starting her married life with Ben in Retsina. However, she knew certain things still had to be sorted out in Manchester before she could leave.

'So do you think you'll stay on in this house?' she asked her mother when her guest had left.

'As long as I can manage.'

'But you won't if you're in a wheelchair.'

'The boys will help me.'

'Jake's due to go to university, and Mick's doing … whatever Mick's doing, so you can't rely on either of them.'

'Don't you worry about me, I'll be fine.'

'But I do. Look Mum, I haven't discussed this yet with Ben, but do you think you'd like to come and live near us in Halifax?'

'That god-forsaken loch? Do me a favour, I'd rather be put in an old age home. I'll be fine here on my own, thank you very much.'

Deborah had lain awake in her old bedroom wondering what would become of her mother now. Her brothers made it clear each in their own way that they didn't consider themselves responsible for their mother's wellbeing, and Deborah could hardly blame them. Frances was in her late fifties, an age when other women were getting on with their lives, and the more Deborah lay awake, the more angry she became.

The following day, after another sleepless night, she got out of bed determined to tackle the subject again. Her mother had slept downstairs on a couch since the funeral, insisting that it was too difficult to get upstairs in the wheelchair. Deborah took a cup of tea to her in the lounge.

'Thank you, dear, now be an angel,' she pointed to the wheelchair, 'and pass me the chair.'

'No I won't.'

'Pardon?'

'I said no, if you want it, stand up and get it yourself.'

'Mick!' she screeched. 'Come down here immediately!'

'They're both out.'

'But I'll be stuck here all day.'

To further emphasise her point, Deborah then pushed the wheelchair into the hallway, and returned triumphantly.

'If you want to stay there all day, do so.'

'But what about the toilet?' Her mother's voice was turning into a semi-hysterical scream and had risen several octaves.

'Wet your pants, see if I care.'

With that she ran upstairs and got dressed as fast as she could. Then she flew back down the stairs and opened the front door.

'Don't bother waiting for me, I'll be out all day.'

When she returned in the early evening with carrier bags full of things for Retsina, her mother refused to look at her. In spite of that, Deborah was gratified to see that she was at the kitchen table eating a sandwich and drinking tea. She made no comment, but on her way to her room with her parcels, she noticed that the wheelchair had once again been put away in the cupboard under the stairs.

It was while she was making plans to return to her own home and Ben, that Deborah missed her period. She took no notice because it wasn't unusual for her to be late. At the same time, and as he always planned to do, Jake left Manchester to take up his place at Oxford University.

Michael, not wishing to be outdone, announced that with his late father's blessing, although they had never actually spoken of the subject in any depth after the wedding, he intended to study to become a rabbi.

'I know it's what he would have wanted, and I know I can do just as good a job at it as he did.'

Furthermore, he told his mother that after speaking with Rabbi Lichtenstein, the rabbi had agreed to get Michael enrolled at a religious seminary in Jerusalem. What Lichtenstein failed to mention to him was that this was a strictly Orthodox seminary, just about as far away from his father's values as was possible to find.

'So maybe next year you'll all be able to come and visit me in Jerusalem, and who knows, I might be married too?'

'Have you met someone?' Frances enquired anxiously.

'Not yet, but the rabbi told me that they like to find suitable wives for all their students.'

'Orthodox wives, who wear a *sheitel*[25]?' His mother and sister looked horrified.

'A wife is a wife.'

'I hope you know what you are doing?'

'Trust me, mother.'

Then Frances lowered her head to her hands, and brushed her fingers roughly through her hair. 'Not one of my children will be nearby.'

---

[25]*wig*

'We'll come and visit,' Deborah insisted, but was interrupted by the noise of the telephone ringing. 'I'll answer it.'

She went to pick up the receiver, and after saying hello, her eyes opened wide in disbelief, and an enormous smile spread over her mouth.

'No, I can't believe it.'

'Who is it Deborah?'

'It's Peggy, she's back.'